CONSUMED

THE VAMPIRE AWAKENINGS, BOOK 8

BRENDA K DAVIES

Copyright © 2018 Brenda K. Davies
All rights reserved.

This ebook is licensed for your personal enjoyment only. This ebook may not be re-sold or given away to other people. If you would like to share this book with another person, please purchase an additional copy for each recipient. If you're reading this book and did not purchase it, or it was not purchased for your use only, then please return and purchase your own copy. Thank you for respecting the hard work of this author. Thank you for downloading this ebook. This ebook is the copyrighted property of the author, and may not be reproduced, copied and distributed for commercial or non-commercial purposes. If you enjoyed this book, please encourage your friends to download their own copy.

ALSO FROM THE AUTHOR

Books written under the pen name Brenda K. Davies

The Vampire Awakenings Series

Awakened (Book 1)

Destined (Book 2)

Untamed (Book 3)

Enraptured (Book 4)

Undone (Book 5)

Fractured (Book 6)

Ravaged (Book 7)

Consumed (Book 8)

Unforeseen (Book 9)

Coming 2019

The Alliance Series

Eternally Bound (Book 1)

Bound by Vengeance (Book 2)

Bound by Darkness (Book 3)

Coming September 2018

The Road to Hell Series

Good Intentions (Book 1)

Carved (Book 2)

The Road (Book 3)

Into Hell (Book 4)

Hell on Earth Series

Hell on Earth (Book 1)

Into the Abyss (Book 2)

Kiss of Death (Book 3)

Coming Late 2018/2019

Historical Romance

A Stolen Heart

Books written under the pen name Erica Stevens

The Captive Series

Captured (Book 1)

Renegade (Book 2)

Refugee (Book 3)

Salvation (Book 4)

Redemption (Book 5)

Broken (The Captive Series Prequel)

Vengeance (Book 6)

Unbound (Book 7)

The Kindred Series

Kindred (Book 1)

Ashes (Book 2)
Kindled (Book 3)
Inferno (Book 4)
Phoenix Rising (Book 5)

The Fire & Ice Series
Frost Burn (Book 1)
Arctic Fire (Book 2)
Scorched Ice (Book 3)

The Ravening Series
The Ravening (Book 1)
Taken Over (Book 2)
Reclamation (Book 3)

The Survivor Chronicles
The Upheaval (Book 1)
The Divide (Book 2)
The Forsaken (Book 3)
The Risen (Book 4)

Mollie Jean Schaller.
I hope you enjoy Mollie!

CHAPTER ONE

MIKE PUSHED OPEN the door to the small, smoky, dimly lit bar and stepped inside with Doug and Jack following him. The scents of stale alcohol and cigarettes choked the air, but beneath it he scented the nearby ocean and lemon polish. The door closed on the howling wind. It might be early June, but this far north in Canada, the storm rolling off the sea brought colder air with it.

Stomping his feet, Mike clasped his hands and blew into them as he surveyed the vampire bar they'd entered. The small town on the coast of Labrador had a population of only a couple thousand, but it had attracted a fair number of vampires.

Whether that was due to the shorter daylight hours, which attracted Savages, or the fact vampires were fleeing the growing Savage problem in the States, Mike didn't know. Unfortunately, the three of them couldn't detect a Savage by their scent like a pureblood vamp could, so he didn't know if they'd just walked into a room full of killers or not.

He did know most of the patrons were vampires, as like knew like.

"Guess we won't be settling into this area," Jack muttered.

"I don't think they're killers," Doug murmured.

"What makes you say that?" Jack asked.

"The humans are still alive," Mike answered as he surveyed the fifteen vampires and the handful of humans seated amongst the scarred wood tables.

Jack's hazel eyes narrowed on him in annoyance; strands of his light brown hair had fallen into one of his eyes, but he didn't push it away before he huffed out a breath and stalked over to the bar. Doug chuckled while he ran a hand through his short, dark blond hair. His ocean-blue eyes twinkled with amusement as he watched Jack slide onto a barstool and order a beer.

"I take it we're staying for a drink," Doug said.

"I guess we are," Mike replied.

Their boots thudded on the wood floor, and the planks bowed beneath Mike's weight as they strolled over to join Jack. Like Jack, they settled onto stools where they could watch the patrons behind them in the mirror lining the wall behind the bar. Liquor bottles filled the shelves and reflected in the glass, but Mike still had a clear view of the patrons.

The bartender placed a beer in front of Jack before turning wary eyes on them. Mike nodded to her, but her blue eyes revealed no warmth and a smile didn't curve her mouth. Glancing around the bar again, Mike realized most of the occupants had stopped talking and focused on them. He didn't sense hostility from them, but more distrust. Mike didn't blame them for being uneasy; he didn't trust them either.

"What can I get you?" the bartender asked. Her clipped New York accent was out of place in this northern land.

"I'll take a Crown and ginger and an ashtray," Mike said.

"Scotch on the rocks," Doug said.

"You got it." The woman pushed an ashtray toward Mike and turned to fill their order.

Mike pulled out the pack of cigarettes he'd tucked into the inner pocket of his coat. He undid the packaging and tapped one free. It had been a few months since he last smoked, but he'd purchased the pack at the border last week.

Now seemed as good a time as any to light one as most of the patrons held a cigarette or had a pack before them, and he knew well how smokers congregated to talk. *When in Rome.* He removed his silver Zippo from the pocket of his jeans, flipped the top open, and lit the cigarette. He inhaled a drag as the bartender returned with their drinks.

"What brings you to these parts?" she asked, her gaze on Mike.

"We're doing some traveling," he replied, "and exploring the area."

"Planning to move north?"

"Maybe, if we find something we like."

Mike didn't want to move, but with the growing Savage problem, he and his friends weren't taking any chances. After some careful consideration, they'd all decided it would be best if they had a safe place to retreat to if it became necessary.

The past two times they'd moved, they had to search out a property before leaving, but this time they would have one ready and waiting. There were too many children to protect now for them not to have a backup place.

And they sought a property more remote than their compound in Maine. They could have searched online or hired a realtor to help them, but they wanted to keep their trail as small as possible should something go wrong and they were forced to flee. Mike also preferred to see the land, surrounding towns, and the residents instead of relying on Internet searches and real estate agent phone calls.

So far, the three of them had found numerous tracts of land for sale, but they were hoping to find something with houses, or at the very least one home, already on it. Building new houses would take more time than they were willing to spend to get their emergency retreat ready.

Unfortunately, they hadn't found anything that would work yet.

Mike wasn't ready to give up. They'd all prefer to stay near the coast, but they might have to forego that or perhaps find a lake or pond. David wouldn't be happy about boating around a pond, but he would have to suck it up.

The bartender leaned closer in such a way that she revealed more of her breasts in her low-cut, black top. He didn't know if she was trying to distract him with her cleavage or if her interest in him had taken a turn toward the sexual.

Either way, he wasn't interested.

Maybe, if it was thirty years ago and he was still in college, or twenty years ago when he'd only been looking for a good time, or ten years ago when boredom propelled him from woman to woman and new thrill to new thrill. But over the past few years, apathy had taken its toll and extended into every area of his life.

At fifty-two, he was too young to be bored with immortality. No, not bored with immortality—bored with the way he'd been living his life. The only problem was, he didn't know how to change it. But this bartender sure wasn't the change he was looking for, he decided as he flicked his ashes and inhaled another drag of his cigarette.

"I might not be able to help you find a place, but I could help you find something else you might like," she purred.

From the corner of his eye, Mike saw Jack roll his eyes, and Doug smirked before sipping his drink.

Unwilling to offend the woman—they might be able to get some useful information out of her about this place and the area—Mike smiled back at her. "What's your name?" he inquired.

He didn't want to lead her on either and felt asking her name was a neutral question.

"LeNae," she replied, and smiled to reveal her white teeth. With her dirty-blonde hair and pale blue eyes, she was pretty and had an alluring figure, but he felt no interest in her.

"Nice to meet you, LeNae. I'm Mike, this is Doug, and that's Jack."

Doug's wholesome face broke into the grin that had disarmed

more people over the years than any military truce. LeNae smiled back at him. Jack remained stone-faced before turning his full attention to his beer, finishing it off, and pushing the bottle across the bar toward her.

"Would you like another?" LeNae asked.

"Yes," Jack replied, and leaning back on his stool, he turned to survey the occupants of the bar.

Most of the customers had gone back to drinking, but a few still watched them. Mike braced himself as he waited for Jack to say something to annoy someone, it was what he did after all, but he turned back around.

LeNae returned with his beer and set it before him.

"How long have you lived here?" Jack asked her.

"A few months," she replied.

"Why did you come here?"

"The same reason most everyone else in this place did."

"Which is?"

"Things are getting a little ugly down south, and we all know it." Her gaze traveled over them. "Isn't that what brought you here too?"

"It is," Doug said, "but it's a little strange to see so many vamps in such a remote location."

The bracelets on LeNae's wrist jangled when she set her hand on the bar. "Remote might be the only thing keeping us all alive and out of harm's way... until that doesn't work anymore."

Mike hoped she was wrong and the problem with the Savages would soon be handled, but he wasn't willing to take any chances either, and neither was the rest of his family.

"Everyone in this bar is okay?" he asked her.

"Depends on your definition of okay, but no one is a killer, and we don't tolerate them here either." LeNae gave each of them a pointed look.

Mike stubbed out his cigarette before raising his hands; Doug gave her his winning smile again, and Jack drank his beer.

"I wouldn't either," Mike assured her.

"None of us would," Doug said.

LeNae's attention shifted to Doug. Mike didn't mind; he'd met his fair share of fickle women over the years, and she'd have better luck with Doug anyway. Doug wasn't burned-out like he was or as cynical as Jack.

His burn-out wasn't helped by the fact two of his best friends, and an increasing number of what he considered his nieces and nephews, had met their mates, fallen in love, and settled down. Watching how happy they all were with each other, Mike sometimes found himself longing for someone he could spend an eternity with too.

He cursed himself for being an idiot. He would either find his mate one day or he wouldn't, but getting bogged down by his desire for it to happen wouldn't help anyone, especially not him. Besides, he could always discover his mate only to have her reject him and ruin his life. In that case, single was the far better option.

CHAPTER TWO

Mike took another cigarette from his pack and lit it. He rarely smoked two cigarettes in a day, but he found himself eyeing the box and wondering if he might have to buy another. Today felt like a smoking day. Sliding the Zippo back into his pocket, he set the pack on the bar for later.

He surveyed the crowd in the mirror as Doug and LeNae leaned close to talk. All the customers had stopped paying attention to them and were either focused on their drinks or their companions. Jack lifted his beer, rose from his stool, and walked over to sit on Mike's other side.

"I'm not in the mood to listen to Casanova over there," Jack grumbled.

Mike smiled and rested his elbows on the bar. "Were you into her?"

"Hardly," Jack snorted. "I'm not here for women."

"This place seem legit to you?" Mike asked, pitching his voice so only Jack could hear him.

"Yeah. I think they would have jumped us by now if it wasn't."

"I agree."

"But, I think we should move on before morning. Vampires are sure to tell other vampires about this place."

"I agree."

"They may have already alerted all their friends and family about their new safe haven."

"It's a possibility," Mike said. "We'll finish these drinks and go."

"We might have to pry lady killer over there away."

Mike glanced over at Doug as he examined LeNae's bracelets and asked what each of the charms represented. Mike almost rolled his eyes, but not so long ago, it might have been him. A part of him wished to be as happy as Doug still was, but the larger part of him wanted more from life than random hookups. He stubbed out his cigarette, pulled out his lighter, and lit another one.

"Easy there, Smokey," Jack said. "Maybe you won't get cancer or wrinkles, but yellow fangs are sure to be a turnoff for most women."

Mike's lips quirked in a smile. "I'll keep that in mind."

In the mirror, Mike watched a vampire extend his hand to a human who blushed prettily before taking it and rising to her feet. The vamp draped his arm around the woman's shoulders and was leading her toward the front door when it opened.

Mike couldn't see who stood in the doorway, but something metal clattered as it bounced across the wood floor. A plume of smoke burst into the air, and then something else bounced off the floor. Mike put out his cigarette and rose from his stool as the front door closed without anyone having entered. The cloud of smoke floated toward the patrons at the tables.

What is going on? Did someone knock over an ashtray and start a fire? But that didn't make sense, as there were no flames.

The couple closest to the door stumbled back; tears streamed down their faces as they coughed. The woman clasped her throat before falling to her knees. Her coughing spasms abruptly ended when she slumped to the floor. The vamp with her stumbled back a few more feet and collapsed to his knees. When he tried to rise again, his knees wobbled and his legs gave out; he face-planted onto the floor.

"Holy shit," Jack said as he rose to stand beside Mike.

The remaining patrons filling the tables leapt to their feet as the smoke twisted insidiously through the air until it covered the entire front half of the bar. If he hadn't been a vampire, he never would have seen the vamps and humans falling to the ground within the thick mass. Then the front door, tables, chairs, and customers overtaken by the smoke were swallowed by the cloud.

The rest of the crowd continued to stumble away from the smoke, but it was only a matter of time before it consumed them all.

Mike tasted something bitter on the air as the cloying smoke clogged his nostrils. LeNae, her face pale and her eyes wide with horror, backed into the shelves of booze lining the wall. Two bottles rocked precariously before toppling off and shattering at her feet. LeNae jumped and bit back a scream when liquid splashed over her sneakers.

More patrons collapsed while the rest backed into the bar as the smoke neared.

"What is going on?" Jack demanded.

Grasping his beer bottle by the neck, Jack bashed it against the bar. He held the jagged remains before him as he prepared for something to charge out of the smoke at them.

"Is there a back way out of here?" Mike shouted at LeNae and slapped his hand on the bar to get her attention.

Her eyes rolled toward him; her fingers reflexively gripped the shelf, but she didn't respond. Reaching into his coat, he removed one of the stakes tucked into a pocket there. He suspected there were vampires out there, waiting for them to succumb. Only a vamp would have a gas strong enough to knock out or kill another vampire.

Placing his hands on the bar, Doug leapt over it and strode toward LeNae while speaking to her in a soothing tone. "Is there another way out of here, gorgeous?"

Adjusting his grip on the weapon, Jack jumped onto the bar and slid over it. Mike kept his eyes on the smoke and the few vampires and humans still standing as he lifted himself onto the bar and over the top.

Doug had taken LeNae's hand, and she calmed as she spoke with him. "This way," LeNae said when Mike stepped next to her.

LeNae kept her hand in Doug's as she led them down the back of the bar toward the opening at the end. She paused to remove a key ring from under the cash register. To the left of the bar was a set of silver, swinging doors. Two of the customers slipped through the doors, but they quickly reemerged.

"There's no way out through there!" one of the men shouted at LeNae.

"I didn't say there was," LeNae retorted as she shouldered her way past him.

Mike's nostrils burned, and tears pricked his eyes as the smoke spread to their area of the bar. Then another rattling ting bounced off the floor, and Mike realized someone had thrown another smoke canister into the building. They only had a minute or two to escape before the smoke overtook them too.

His hands fisted as he resisted the impulse to charge through the smoke and destroy whoever was doing this, but even if he held his breath, he doubted he would make it out the front door before the smoke overwhelmed him.

He exchanged troubled glances with Doug and Jack as the canister settled into place and everyone froze. The distinct thud of boots hitting wood broke the ensuing silence. Someone had entered the bar—multiple someones judging by the vibration of the floor beneath his feet. The smoke muffled the approaching footsteps, but Mike spotted shadows slipping through the haze toward them.

We're being hunted.

He didn't know where the thought came from, but once it hit him, he knew it was true. But by who and *why*?

Some of the patrons balked when LeNae led them into the smoke, but Mike held his breath and followed the woman. They had no other choice but to trust her, and he didn't think she could fake her earlier terror. LeNae traveled only ten feet through the smoke before splitting off into another hallway and breaking into a run.

The air here in the hall was less choked with smoke than the rest of the building, but it was spreading through here too. Mike released his breath on a harsh exhale as he ran behind LeNae to another set of swinging doors.

LeNae pushed through the doors to reveal a shadowed room full of dust-covered, stainless-steel appliances. The appliances were of little use to most of the new customers of this establishment, but they'd been of some use to the previous owners.

"There's no exit this way either!" one of the customers protested, apparently knowing the restaurant well.

Mike's lips skimmed back as he focused on LeNae. If she'd led them into a trap, he didn't care if it was the last thing he ever did, he'd kill her.

LeNae held up her arm, and the keys in her hand jangled. "One of these will open the door."

"It better," Jack growled, and Mike agreed.

At the end of the room, a thick, steel door blocked the way out. LeNae's hands shook, and the keys clicked together as she sorted through them in search of the one she sought.

"Hurry," one of the women urged. "They're coming."

Mike retreated and turned so he could see anything coming through the swinging doors. He didn't hear any more footsteps, but another canister bounced off the walls and floor. Before the noise stopped, smoke started seeping through the cracks around the doors.

He glanced back at Jack and Doug before slipping his hand inside his coat. Being an ex-Boy Scout, and surviving this many years amid vampires and humans, had taught him always to be prepared. The weapons stashed inside his coat wouldn't do much against smoke, but if any of the fuckers who had done this came near him, he'd fight them to the death.

He returned the stake to his pocket and slid his crossbow free. He checked to make sure it was loaded before tying the string at the end of it to a belt loop on his jeans and releasing it to hang at his side. Reaching into his pocket, he retrieved the stake.

Jack came to stand beside him with his broken bottle top in one hand and a stake in the other. Doug remained with LeNae, talking calmly with her as she chewed on her bottom lip and tried to fit another key into the lock.

"I can't… I can't remember!" she cried.

"Can we break through the door?" Mike demanded. There were two other vampires and a human with them; they might be able to tear the steel down.

"No, the owner designed it so no one could get in or out this way without a key. The front door looks like wood, but it's also steel. He was concerned about vamps ripping him off. I… I can't find the key!" LeNae wailed.

"It's okay," Doug assured her. "Let me see the keys, and I'll try them."

Doug took the keys from her and tried another one in the lock.

"He's the vampire equivalent of Mother Teresa," Jack muttered. "What do you think is going on here?"

"I don't know, but it's not good."

"Oh, it's not? I assumed they were coming to take us to Disneyland," Jack quipped.

Mike glared at him but held his tongue. He knew his friend well enough to know that when Jack was stressed, he became more sarcastic. Under normal conditions, Jack could be as friendly as a yellowjacket, but when he was tense, Jack was as friendly as a hornet's nest someone bashed with a baseball bat.

"I hope Mickey eats you," Mike muttered.

"We have no idea what's coming through those doors, so he might," Jack replied.

"I've got the key," Doug said, drawing Mike and Jack's attention to him.

The lock clicked seconds before the door swung open. A flash lit the night beyond the door before Doug started jerking like he'd stepped on a live wire. LeNae reached for him but pulled her hands back.

"Doug!" Mike yelled as a familiar clatter sounded seconds before smoke started filling the kitchen.

With their hope of getting away dwindling, the remaining patrons panicked. Two of them turned and fled toward the swinging doors while another raced toward the steel door Doug had opened while Doug continued his odd dance. LeNae remained frozen with her hand over her mouth, but the woman running toward the door darted past Doug and plunged outside. Her scream pierced the air before abruptly cutting off.

Adrenaline flooded Mike's system; his fangs elongated as he searched for an enemy he could fight, but he saw no one through the smoke and confusion. When Doug groaned, Mike spun away from the doors and ran for his friend. He was only feet away when two, simultaneous blows pounded his back and chest.

Pain raced through him as sharp points pierced his skin and lodged inside him. His body made the same awkward, jerking motion as Doug's when electricity flooded it. The scent of burnt hair and flesh filled his nostrils, and he realized it was coming from him. A hand curled around the edge of the door Doug had opened; against the steel, the long red fingernails, honed into lethal points, were a vibrant splash of color before they retreated.

The color of death.

The next spasm caused him to chomp on his tongue, and blood flooded his mouth. Mike couldn't see Jack anymore as his vision dwindled to a pinpoint on Doug. He tried to take another step toward Doug when his friend hit his knees. Mike fought against going down, but his knees wobbled with his next step.

Jack shouted behind him, but the blackness creeping in around the edges of his vision made it impossible to see more than a foot or two in front of him anymore. When his chin drooped against his chest, blackness swelled and took him under.

CHAPTER THREE

Mollie shifted uncomfortably in the steel cage she'd called home since yesterday. She eyed the bars in front of her with hatred. The dim light of the moon crept through the cracks in the boards of the barn, but Mollie couldn't see much beyond the bars surrounding her. If she ever got out of this mess, she'd kill *every single person* involved in whatever this was.

Never before had she contemplated murder, but she gleefully did so now. Because if she didn't contemplate murder, then the terror would sink back in, and the last time the terror sank in, she'd become a raving lunatic who yanked uselessly on her bars and screamed her throat raw. She'd uttered the most animalistic sounds she'd ever heard—sounds she *never* expected to hear coming from *her*.

But that was because her captors had come inside, opened Aida's cage, and taken a struggling Aida away. Mollie tried not to look at where her sister had been locked in her cage only hours ago, but her gaze was irresistibly drawn back to it.

Where had they taken her little sister? What were they *doing* to her?

Images of sex trafficking, forced prostitution, rape, and every other appalling thing she'd ever heard happening to kidnapped people flooded her mind. Closing her eyes, she rubbed at her eyelids as she resisted another meltdown.

Not Aida, please not Aida.

Mollie would give anything to be the one they'd taken from here instead of her beautiful, vibrant, eighteen-year-old sister. Aida had endured so much bad over the years, to have her experiencing whatever she was now…

When madness started creeping around the edges of her mind, Mollie shut down the possibilities. As tempting as it was to give in to the screaming again, she'd never get out of this mess if she went bonkers.

Deep breaths, relax, in and out. Her years of yoga and counseling were not helping, not when facing so many unknown possibilities. She didn't care what became of her, but she wanted her sister back, *now*.

Shifting, she tried to find a more comfortable position to sit, but the five-by-five steel cage wasn't built to accommodate someone of her five-ten height and the bars under her dug into her ass. After being in it for at least a day, her legs and back were screaming in protest.

She'd explored the cell for hours and examined every bar for weakness after first waking. She'd tried picking the lock with two of the bobby pins tucked into her hair, but working from behind the lock in the dark had rendered her attempts useless. Afterward, she tucked the ruined bobby pins into her bra.

Escape seemed impossible, but she wouldn't give up on getting out of here.

She glanced at the small, silver pan tucked into the corner of her cage and almost kicked it against the bars. The only problem was, she'd broken down a few hours ago and used it to relieve herself. If she kicked it, she'd only wind up covered in her urine. She could pour it outside her bars and onto the dirt floor of the cavernous barn, but she was hoping her jailers would come back to remove it and she would have a chance to attack them.

The chances of that happening were probably slim, considering they hadn't opened her cage since she was tossed into it, but she'd bet on slim over nothing any day. They kept her cage locked the one time they bothered to bring her food, and her captors hadn't opened it the two times they slid a small cup of water through the bars.

At first, Mollie refused to drink the water and eat. She had no idea what these bastards had done to it, but when she saw some of the other people in the cages surrounding her eating and drinking, she conceded to the water but refused the food. She didn't trust it would be okay, and there were others who weren't eating.

Granted, those others were only given cups of water and no food, but there had to be a reason for that. Mollie wondered if it was because they refused food before or were already drugged, had experiments or whatever done to them, and were now being starved to death because they were considered useless.

Shifting again, Mollie winced when her tailbone dug into the bars beneath her, making it impossible to get comfortable or sleep. Exhaustion succeeded in pulling her under a few hours ago, and she'd dozed for a bit, but like food, sleep was scarce.

Her stomach rumbled as her thoughts returned to food; she tuned out the noise and the pangs following it. She'd gone without food for longer than this, so if these pricks thought she would cave and eat, they had another think coming.

No one could starve her any more than she'd starved herself for more years than she cared to recall.

When her stomach gave another loud rumble, she dug in to her pocket and fished out her crushed pack of gum. They'd taken her wallet and coat, but left her with the gum. Pulling out a piece, she unwrapped it and slid it into her mouth. It didn't ease her hunger, but the act of chewing made her feel better.

Plus, the smell of spearmint filling her nose was much better than the human waste and body odor scent of the barn. She'd been in a few barns before, at a fair. She'd examined the animals and held her mom's hand as they walked through the cows, sheep, horses, and chickens on display. The scent of their shit and animal aroma had been overwhelming, but she'd also smelled hay and feed. In this place, she detected only the faint hint of hay or straw and no animals.

The two-story-tall doors at the far end of the barn suddenly slid open, each of them going in opposite directions. The small influx of light entering through the doors, nearly two hundred feet away from her, caused Mollie to blink even as she strained to see more.

She sat up and gripped her bars. She wished she could kneel, but the last time she tried, her knees dug into the bars beneath her.

Aida! Are they bringing Aida back?

She held her breath as anticipation warred within her. *Please, please, let them be bringing her back!*

From the numerous cages surrounding her, some of the other people sat up to see what was happening. The last time the doors opened, they'd come in and removed Aida.

In the faint glow of the headlights, dust motes danced on the air as the man who opened the door turned away. When the doors opened for their first feeding, Mollie tried counting the cages within the massive barn, but there were so many around her that she lost track after fifty. Most of those fifty were full of men and women.

If this was a sex trafficking ring, then the operators weren't picky about age, as some of the men and women looked to be in their fifties or sixties, and others appeared to be in their teens or early twenties.

She believed they were still somewhere in Canada, but she couldn't be sure. The last town she remembered before her car broke down had a population not much bigger than this barn, yet somehow these sicko perverts managed to gather quite the collection here.

But then, for all she knew, they weren't in Canada anymore. They could be somewhere in the United States, and she'd have no idea. The last thing she remembered was trying to change her flat tire, someone stopping to offer help, and then blackness.

She'd woken here afterward. Judging by the time on her grandpop's Rolex wristwatch when she awoke, Mollie assumed she was only unconscious for a couple of hours. But for all she knew, it could have been more than fifteen hours or a day later.

That meant she could be beyond the U.S. as she could have been on a freaking plane without knowing it. They could be in Europe or Mexico right now. Her head started pounding, and she decided not to think about it. She'd never be able to puzzle out where she was while caged.

When she first woke, with cottonmouth and a headache, Aida was sleeping in the cage next to hers, but that was twelve hours ago. They'd taken Aida from her two hours ago. She'd kept careful track of time since waking; it was the only thing she could control in this place.

The man reemerged, and the headlights pulled away as the truck turned around. Standing in the doorway, silhouetted by the lights on the back of the vehicle, the man waved his hands in the air to direct the driver into the barn. The backup alarm sounded until the box truck came a few feet inside the barn doors.

When the alarm stopped, the man gripped the back doors and flung them open. An interior light turned on to reveal the bodies piled inside. From both sides of the truck, men and women appeared and climbed inside. Like an assembly line from Hell, they started removing the bodies and tossing them out to their waiting cohorts.

Mollie gulped and edged away from her bars as some of those in the cages closest to her growled low in their throats. The noises they released made the ones she issued earlier sound human as they crept closer to their bars and wrapped their hands around them.

A shiver of unease ran down her spine. She'd vowed to examine the locks on some of the other cages more closely the next time she had some light, but with those noises, she'd prefer not to be anywhere near some of the other prisoners. Mollie edged further away from the bars when she saw a flash of red in some of their eyes, and that red had nothing to do with the backup lights on the truck.

That can't be possible; it just can't.

But no matter how impossible it was, Mollie suspected she'd been tossed into something she couldn't begin to fathom. Out of all the horrific possibilities for her current situation, she had a feeling she hadn't hit on the truth yet.

Mollie didn't dare look at the occupants of those cages again; she'd lose her mind if she did, and she couldn't risk doing that. Some of the others wept as they cowered in the corners of their cages and pleaded to be left alone. They'd already given up.

She would *not* be one of them.

Mollie pressed against the bars at the back of her cage. Behind her was nothing but the wood wall of the barn, but she still felt as if eyes were boring into her nape from the shadows. Shivering, Mollie wrapped her arms around her knees, but she didn't give in to the impulse to look behind her—mainly because she feared coming face-to-face with two vibrant red eyes blazing out at her from the dark.

She ignored the prickling sensation on her neck as she watched the offloaded bodies being tossed into cages. One of her captors stalked toward her with a large male draped over his shoulder. He opened the door on the cage next to her—the one Aida had resided in—tossed the body inside and slammed the door.

She glimpsed the golden patch on her captor's black coat when he turned away. Earlier, she'd seen it well enough to know the patch read "Security," but she couldn't make out the word on it now. All the others who freely entered the barn wore the same patch on their coats, but what they were the security of, or if they were the security of anything, Mollie didn't know.

She glanced at the new, unmoving occupant in her sister's cage and tried not to think about what his presence there meant for Aida. Her sister was all Mollie had left in this world. Aida couldn't be dead.

Mollie had worked relentlessly to give Aida as normal a life as possible and to let her sister live her dreams after their mom died. Those dreams could *not* be lost now.

Aida was going to college in the fall—something Mollie had

happily sacrificed doing to take care of their mom after she got sick, and then to finish raising Aida after their mom passed. They'd done the college tours together and chosen the classes Aida would take after she finally settled on a small college in Rhode Island. The school was close to home and reasonably priced. They'd still see each other often, and financial aid would cover most of her tuition. Aida enjoyed the idea of small campus life, and she'd loved the dorms.

They'd both been happier than they'd been in years, but now it could all be gone.

What were any of her dreams, or even her *life*, worth if she lost Aida?

Unable to think about the possibility, she studied her new neighbor. The only sign of life he showed was the subtle rise and fall of his shoulders. Judging by the amount of him curled up in the cell, she guessed him to be around six three, and with his broad shoulders, he had a much tougher time fitting into the cage than she did. He was going to be really uncomfortable when he woke.

With his face turned away from her, all she saw was the back of his sandy-blond hair. She was unreasonably disappointed by this fact since she wanted to see more of him.

Her attention returned to the front of the barn when a door shut and the truck pulled forward. The barn doors closed, and darkness descended again.

CHAPTER FOUR

"You're awake," a gentle voice said from beside Mike as he tugged uselessly at the bars surrounding him. He'd heard of bars that could withstand a vampire before, but he'd never encountered them.

Mike released the bars and turned toward the voice. In the dim moonlight filtering around the edges of the large double doors at the far end of the building, and through the cracks in the boards surrounding him, he detected movement in the cage next to his. Then the sweet scent of apples and the crisp scent of spearmint drifted to him. From the voice, he'd known it was a female; from the smell, he knew she was human and enticing.

"Who are you?" he demanded, unable to make out much of her features, but she probably couldn't see him at all and only knew he was awake because of the noise he'd made while yanking at the bars.

Mollie opened her mouth to say her full name but decided against it. This guy appeared as screwed as she was, but she didn't know anything about him, and it was better to play it safe.

"Mollie. Who are you?"

"Mike. Where am I? What's going on?"

"I don't know."

"What do you mean, you don't know?"

"I mean that I know nothing about this place and the people who put us here. Yesterday, or at least I think it was yesterday, I was taking an extended road trip with my sister, and today I'm in a cage."

Mike contemplated her words as he turned his attention to the numerous cages inside what he was beginning to realize was a barn. Glancing at the loft over his head, he picked out bits of hay sticking through the slats. He hated haylofts.

As a child, he'd spent a couple of weeks at his grandparent's farm in western Massachusetts every summer. When he turned ten, they sold the farm to move to Florida, and he started staying home with his friends. When he was really young, he'd been forbidden to enter the hayloft on their farm. Which, of course, meant it was the one place he wanted to go. At five, he gathered the courage to climb the rickety ladder into the loft.

He'd strode out to the middle of the hay stacked within it before realizing the bodies of a couple dead barn sparrows lay scattered amid the bales. He loved to watch the birds, and his grandfather would often lift him to peer into the nests when the baby barn swallows were born. Seeing them this way stole his breath and his courage.

Suddenly, he was no longer on the adventure to explore the unknown that he'd started out on. He became convinced monsters were up here, slaughtering the birds, and now they were all focused on *him*, the far larger, more meaty prey. Those monsters hid behind the bales, and every creak of the old barn was the sound of their approaching footsteps.

Frozen in the middle of the loft, he hadn't known which way to go to evade the monsters, as he was certain they would head him off before he returned to the ladder. An hour later, his grandfather found him there, still frozen in place and with urine sticking his pants to his legs.

Lifting him, his grandfather carried him from the hayloft and down the ladder. Mike was sure he'd be sent home afterward or spanked for disobeying. His grandparents agreed his imagination had been punishment enough, especially once he started blubbering on about monsters and never going into the loft again.

He learned a couple of years later that if he'd gone ten feet further, he would have stepped on some rotten boards his grandfather was planning to fix. He most likely would have fallen through the boards to the concrete floor below. And it wasn't until years after, when Beth changed him, he learned monsters were, indeed, real.

Mike tore his attention away from the loft and back to the present. "Who brought you here?"

"I don't know. I'm assuming the same people who brought you here," she whispered.

Lured in by the scent and sound of her, Mike found himself leaning closer to her. "Were you at the bar too?"

"The bar?"

"Yes, the bar," he said impatiently. "Did they take you from the bar too?"

"No, we weren't in any bar. My car got a flat tire; I was on the side of the road changing it when someone stopped to offer their help."

"Who?"

"I *don't know!*" Mollie cried. This guy did not know how to listen. "A man came up and asked if we needed help. I told him no, and that was the last thing I recall. I don't know what he did to me, what they did to my sister, or where she is now. Do you know who brought you here?"

"No."

"Then *stop* asking *me*. And no one else here has any idea either, though only a few of them will talk to me."

"Were others brought in with me?" Mike asked as he scented the air for Doug and Jack, but there were too many aromas for him to differentiate his friends from the numerous others. If they were here, they weren't close to him.

"Yes. They brought in about twenty with you. They're locked up too."

"Doug! Jack!" he called, but he got no response from his friends. If they were here, they must still be unconscious. He refused to believe they were dead.

"Shh," someone hissed from the shadows. "Sometimes they come back if someone makes too much noise."

"And then what do they do?" Mike demanded.

He was up for a fight against these bastards, and if they killed him, so be it. He suspected he'd prefer death to whatever these assholes planned for him.

He ran his hands over his body as he searched for any weapon his jailers might have left on him. They'd taken his coat and weapons, but as he felt the pockets of his jeans, he realized they'd left him with his Zippo. They probably didn't see any threat in letting him keep it, or they hadn't found it when they searched him.

"No one knows what they do," someone else whispered. "Everyone they take never comes back."

In the cage next to his, Mollie's breath sucked in and her heart rate skyrocketed. Mike froze in the act of pulling his Zippo from his pocket when her distress beat against him. His hand clenched around the lighter, and his teeth clamped together as he was seized by the irrational urge to destroy whatever upset her.

"Never?" she croaked.

"Not that I've seen," another murmured. "But I think I've only been here for a few days."

"But they took my sister!" Mollie lunged toward the front of the cage and gripped her bars. "Aida wasn't making any noise, and they took *her*!"

"Sometimes they take hum—ah… others, just because," a woman whispered.

Mike didn't miss the near slip from the woman he assumed was a vampire. "Sometimes they take *humans*," was what the woman had been about to say, and there was no, "*just because.*" They took humans to feed on them.

Mike hadn't gotten close enough to his captors to confirm what they were, but he had no doubt they were vampires, most likely Savages. And if they were imprisoning humans and vampires here, it meant one thing: they intended to starve the vamps until all they could think about was feeding and killing.

His blood ran cold when he realized they most likely planned to turn him and his friends into Savages.

Yes, he'd much prefer to be dead, because if these bastards succeeded in turning him, then all his nieces and nephews and all *their* children would be at risk.

CHAPTER FIVE

MOLLIE RELEASED the bars and shifted toward the back of her cell. A hush descended over the barn again, and her hand fell on the bobby pins tucked into her bra. Tomorrow, when the sun was up and there was more illumination in the barn, she'd try to get a look at the locks on the other cages and attempt picking hers again.

Rustling in the cage next to her drew her attention, but she couldn't see what Mike was doing. Then something clicked open, flicked, and light flared. Mollie scurried toward the flickering flame he held.

"Put that out!" someone spat.

Mike ignored the command as he moved the flame over the bars surrounding him before locating the lock on the front of his cage. Leaning closer, he examined the steel frame of the door, or whatever metal this cage was made of, as it was stronger than steel. He banged his fist against the back of the locking mechanism before throwing his full weight against it. The cage didn't have the decency to pretend he had any effect on it.

"Stop that. It's pointless, and they might come for you," someone else said.

"I hope they do," Mike muttered as he used the Zippo to examine the rest of his cage, but he didn't see any weaknesses in the welded seams of the bars.

"Can I have the lighter?" Mollie asked.

He turned the flame toward her and froze when it illuminated her face. Her black hair was pulled up on her head, but much of it had straggled free to hang around her shoulders and frame her narrow face. Enough of her hair remained up that he recognized the remnants of a French twist. He'd listened to his niece, Vicky, prattle on enough about hair over the years to have picked up on a few things.

The straight edge of Mollie's nose had a small upturn at the bottom. Her rosebud lips were compressed into a line as she stared at the dancing flame with a ravenous gleam in her eyes, and those exquisite eyes stole his breath from him. Not only did she smell of apples, but her eyes were the exact shade of a green apple.

He'd never seen anything like them or the woman herself before. She wasn't pretty or beautiful, but she was striking, and she fascinated him so much that for a minute he forgot all about their surroundings and circumstances as everything in him became focused on *her*.

"Mike."

Mollie frowned as he continued to gawk at her like she was something straight out of a spaceship from Mars. She had to look like shit, who wouldn't after being stuck in a cage for hours on end? But she wasn't a freak show, and he didn't have to look at her like she was.

Or at least Mollie didn't think she was a freak show, and if she was, she didn't care. She had far more important things to worry about than her appearance.

"Mike," she said again.

"What?" he asked, and his hand jerked.

Mollie bit back a cry when the flame sputtered before surging back to full strength. "Can I see your lighter?"

"Put it out!" someone hissed.

Those in the cages closest to them recoiled as far as they could from the two of them. Mollie ignored them as she remained focused on Mike's royal blue eyes as they sparkled in the flame. His broad face and square jaw gave him the look of a man who belonged in a shaving commercial, especially with the blond stubble lining his jaw and cheeks. The sandy-blond hair on his head stood on end as if he'd been running his hands through it.

Normally, a man as good looking as him would make her feel self-conscious, but now all she cared about was getting her hands on his lighter. If Mollie could see one of the locks, if she had a better idea what she was dealing with, she might be able to get this damn cage open.

Then she'd find Aida and get her somewhere safe no matter what it took.

"Can I see your lighter?" she asked again.

"What are you going to do with it?" Mike asked.

"Hopefully, it's going to help me get out of this cage," she said.

"You're both going to die," a voice promised.

"Fuck off," Mike replied before focusing on her again. He didn't bother to ask her how she planned to break out; he suspected they didn't have much time before their captors returned. "You can have the lighter if you agree to release me too."

"Deal," she said and thrust her hand through the bars toward him.

Mike hesitated before holding the Zippo out to her; he liked having it, but there was nothing he could do with it. He had to trust she would use it to her advantage and keep her word about freeing him.

Mollie snatched the lighter from him and scurried to the opposite corner of her cage. Ignoring the pain it caused her knees, she knelt on the bars and held the flame out toward the cage next to hers. She couldn't see the lock on Mike's cage, but this one was turned toward her. When Mollie snaked her arm through the bars, she was able to get a good look at the lock.

Mollie recoiled when the man inside hissed at her before scurrying into the opposite corner of his cage. Mollie's trembling hand caused the flame to sputter. She swore she'd seen a flash of red in the man's eyes before he retreated.

No! Not possible! But her hand still shook.

"It's okay, he can't harm you," Mike assured her as he glowered at the vampire. If the man tried anything with her, Mike would find a way to make him pay for it, and he wanted the vamp to know that.

Mollie bit her lip and gathered her flagging courage. Red eyes or not, she had to see one of the locks better if she had any chance of getting free. *Aida,* Mollie reminded herself. She crept closer to the bars and extended her arm through once more.

Cowering in the back of his cage, she saw no red in the man's eyes as he stared at her. Mollie examined the lock for a minute before returning to the one in the center of her cage. Setting the lighter down, she pulled the pins from her bra. She pictured the lock on the other cage as she bent and twisted the pins into a position she hoped would work.

Watching her, Mike couldn't help being a little skeptical about her intentions. However, the concentration on her face fascinated him. "Do you think that will work?" he inquired.

"I don't know." Mollie spoke around the bobby pin she'd placed between her teeth. "But I'd rather they came back and killed me for trying to escape than sit here and wait for them to rape me or sell me to the highest bidder."

He didn't tell her they had far worse plans for her; she didn't have to know that unless it became necessary. Besides, he agreed with her attitude.

When she assumed she had them about right, Mollie removed the pin from between her teeth and stretched her hand around the cage. The metal was cool and smooth beneath her fingers as she searched for the keyhole until she found it.

She couldn't see anything, but she closed her eyes while her fingers felt over the keyhole. Going on instinct, she slid the first pin into the top part of the hole and held it there while she used her free hand to maneuver the other pin into the bottom.

When she had them in place, she started moving them around. Mollie tried not to become frustrated with her inability to see what she was doing, but sweat beaded on her forehead and the ticking second hand of her watch sounded like drumbeats ticking away her life.

Each passing second was one second closer to those freaks returning for them.

She concentrated on her breathing and kept her hands steady while she worked. The slightest tremor might screw it all up.

Mike tore his gaze away from Mollie to inspect the barn again. He almost told her to hurry, but he bit the words back. Rushing her wouldn't do either of them any good, and there was no guarantee she'd succeed.

He searched for cameras amid the rafters and spotted one in the right corner of the barn. Their captors weren't too close, if they'd been next door, they would be here by now, but the Savages were monitoring their actions and had to know they were up to something.

A click sounded before the creak of hinges filled the air. His head shot back toward Mollie as her cage door swung open. She sat with her mouth half open and her hands on her knees as the door stopped a few inches away from her.

All around the barn, gasps filled the air, and the increased beat of hearts resonated. Mike stared at her in amazement as she snatched up the Zippo and scurried from her cage. When she tried to rise, she staggered and nearly went down. Lurching sideways, she fell against the bars of her cage.

"Are you okay?" he demanded. He reached for her through the bars but came up short of where she stood.

"My legs are cramped, and it's been a while since I ate, but I'm fine," she muttered before removing the pins from her lock.

She spat her gum into her cage and clutched the bars as, on wobbly legs, she made her way over to Mike's cage and handed him back his lighter. The pins and needles were working their way out of her legs, and the longer she stood, the stronger they felt. She shifted from side to side, stretching her muscles as she examined the lock on Mike's cage. It was the same as the others.

Maybe it wasn't the best idea to set Mike free when she had no idea who he was, but he'd helped her, and she'd promised to help him. She couldn't walk away and leave him to whatever fate awaited him here. No matter how desperate she was to find Aida, she'd hate herself for the rest of her life if she left him caged.

Besides, with as large as he was, his friendship might come in handy for whatever awaited them outside this barn. She certainly didn't want him as an enemy, and that's what he'd become if she left him here and he somehow got free.

"Hold the lighter here," Mollie instructed.

When she grabbed his hand to move it into position, a jolt went through her the second their skin came into contact. Gasping, she nearly released the pins when she jerked her hand away from his. Trying to get her galloping heart under control, she refused to meet his eyes when she bent her head to the task of picking his lock.

What was that? Never had she experienced anything like it, and her body remained electrified by the jolt he'd given her. *Had he felt it too? What does it matter if he did? You have far more important things to worry about.*

Which was very true. Mollie ignored the tingling in her hand as she remained focused on the lock. She didn't look up when she felt his eyes burning into her head as she wiggled the pins.

"How did you learn to pick locks?" he asked.

A faint smile curved her mouth while she remained focused on her task. Her mom had been dead for two years now, but out of habit, she always made sure she had a couple of bobby pins on her, as well as a lockpick kit, but her kit was wherever her car was now. Bobby pins had always been her go-to as they were easier to carry, and a nine-year-old toting around a lockpick set probably would have attracted the attention of child services.

"My mom was always locking herself out of places, or her keys *into* places," Mollie said. "I couldn't tell you the number of times she locked us out of our house, car, or rooms *in* our house. After a while, instead of calling a locksmith or breaking a window, I learned how to pick a lock. I saw it in a movie once and thought it looked like fun."

"Why didn't you just carry an extra key with you?"

When she glanced at him, her incredible eyes danced with mischief and stole Mike's breath. Without thinking, he reached through the bars and stroked the gentle curve of her cheek. Her skin was like silk beneath his fingers as the same thrill he'd gotten from touching her before ran up his arm. What he wouldn't give to be free of these bars and this place so he could explore more of her.

Mollie gulped and tore her attention away from him when one of the pins nearly tumbled from the lock. She struggled to recall what they'd been talking about as she focused on freeing him.

"Now what would be the fun in that?" she asked in a tone meant to be teasing, but she sounded more like Kermit the Frog.

A click silenced his answer.

Mike stared in amazement when his door swung open before his gaze shifted back to her. All her humor vanished as she backed uneasily away from him and toward her cage. He understood her sudden distrust; their situation didn't exactly scream faith in others.

"I'm not going to hurt you," he vowed.

Approaching headlights drew his attention as they illuminated the edges of the barn doors while he crawled out from his cage.

CHAPTER SIX

MIKE'S GAZE shot to Mollie when she stopped edging away from him and froze to gawk at the doors. Rising, he ignored the stiffness of his legs as he ran over and claimed her hand. A small jolt of electricity raced through him, and his hand instinctively tightened around hers. He'd get her out of this no matter what it took.

"This way," he said and tugged on her hand.

Pulling her with him, they ran toward the ladder leading to the hayloft. He despised the places, but he reached around her to grasp the rungs of the ladder and jerked on them. The old wood creaked but remained firm, and he believed it would hold their weight.

He nudged Mollie toward the ladder. "Climb."

Mollie balked. "We'll be trapped up there, and there's a side door over here." She pointed to the left side of the barn. "I saw it behind those cages before they took Aida."

"They'll have that door covered already," he said as the truck engine turned off. The headlights remained shining on the barn.

"But they'll know we never left the building!" she protested.

"We have no other choice. The longer we remain free, the better our chances of escaping. *Go!*"

She gazed uncertainly at him before reluctantly grasping the rungs and climbing the ladder. Mike watched her tall, supple body move with grace and speed. Her black, long-sleeved shirt emphasized pert breasts that would fit perfectly in his hand. His gaze fell to her round, firm ass in her form-fitting jeans.

He tore his attention away from her when he found himself growing aroused. Now was not the time or place. Grasping the rungs, he climbed swiftly as Mollie pulled herself into the hayloft. She glanced back at him before vanishing into the shadows above. Seconds later, Mike followed her into the cavernous space as the large barn doors opened.

He slid further into the shadows where he could stay out of view but still see what was happening below. Mollie crept forward and knelt at his side. The headlights spilling inside illuminated the dirt floor and the hundred or so cages tucked inside the barn; most of them were full. Many of the occupants threw their hands over their eyes and cringed away from the light.

Mike spotted Jack in his cell, sitting with his back against the bars and a knee drawn up against his chest. An insolent look of disdain was on his face as Jack tapped his fingers against his shin. Mike didn't see Doug anywhere, but he could be in one of the cages inside the stalls.

However, Mike couldn't get a good view of the dozen or so stalls in the barn. Judging by the size of the barn, Mike suspected there had once been more stalls, but they'd been ripped out to make room for more cages.

The first vamp who strolled into the barn held a rifle; he tapped the barrel of it against his palm while he surveyed the cages. Mike focused on the gold patch on the man's coat, but he was too far away to read what it said. Beside him, Mollie slid further into the shadows and crouched lower.

Mike searched for more cameras and found three of them tucked into the corners of the barn; he didn't spot any in the loft though—not that it mattered, whoever was watching them already knew where they were. He didn't know if they had some way to relay that information to these bastards, but he suspected they did.

Two more vampires entered and flanked the first. They wore identical coats, but they didn't have a rifle.

"Two piggies got out," the woman said.

The one holding the gun smirked. "Not very bright piggies."

"Not at all," the other man agreed.

Mollie tried to keep her breathing even as she watched the lunatics sauntering into the barn, but it was difficult when her heart was running faster than a racecar's engine, and a clammy sweat coated her body.

We never should have come up here. As she thought it, the barn's side door opened, and two more men entered.

If they had gone out the side door, they would have been caught or dead already. They were trapped in the loft, but at least they were still free for whatever short amount of time they had. Mollie jumped when Mike reclaimed her hand and jerked his head to the side.

She remained crouched low as they made their way across the loft. The brief realization the wood beneath them might be rotten and could give way at any second flitted across her mind, but she dismissed it. Rotten floorboards were the least of her problems, and there was no way for her to know if they were or not, so there was no point in worrying about it.

Mike led her around the old, molding bales of hay scattered throughout the loft. The vamps most likely knew they were up here, but the smell of the hay should cover their exact location, which might allow him to get the drop on some of them. But before he tried to go after them, he had to get Mollie somewhere as safe as he could considering what they faced.

Mollie shoved her finger under her nose when Mike led her around a pile of hay and the dust tickled her nose. *Do not sneeze! Do not sneeze!*

Over the years, she'd watched countless horror movies and screamed at the fleeing women to take off their heels, or not go that way, or to *stop* being so loud! She would not be one of the idiot horror victims who sneezed in the hayloft.

Mike gestured for her to kneel behind a stack of three bales before settling in front of her. Even in the dark recesses at the back of the loft, Mollie's startling eyes were vivid. His words died on his tongue as he found himself momentarily lost to those wide eyes with their thick fringe of black lashes.

He didn't know what it was about her, but he would *not* let anyone or anything hurt her.

Leaning close, he rested his lips against her ear. "Stay here."

When she started to shake her head and pull away from him, he tenderly clasped her neck and held her close. The soft strands of her hair caressed his face while the scent of her engulfed him. It took all he had not to turn his head and run his lips over her skin before pressing his lips to hers.

"I'm going to try something," he said, "and I'd prefer you stayed safe."

"I can help you," she whispered.

"Not yet."

Not ever, but if he told her that, she would argue with him. He sensed a well of strength and determination running through her; she would rebel against being relegated to a lesser role than what she believed she could handle. It was a trait he admired when it wasn't working against him.

However, judging by the fact she'd said "people" when they were discussing who had caught them, Mollie didn't know about vampires, and he'd prefer to keep it that way. He certainly didn't want her to witness what he planned to do to the bastards below, if they didn't kill him first.

She didn't know what she'd been plunged into, and if he could, he would keep the worst of his world from her.

You can make her do as you say. He could use his powers to make her stay here, but something inside him recoiled at the idea. It might be safer for her if he forced her to do his bidding, but he wouldn't mess with her mind in that way.

"Stay here," he said, "until I have a better idea what's going on."

Mollie hesitated before giving a small nod of agreement. Mike's hand squeezed hers, and she leaned closer to absorb his warmth and strength.

"Be careful," she whispered.

"I will."

For some inexplicable reason, tears pricked her eyes when he pulled away and crept back toward the center of the loft.

CHAPTER SEVEN

MIKE CAUTIOUSLY CIRCLED to the left. He stayed away from the ladder as he approached the edge of the hayloft and knelt there. Below, the vampires had split up and were ambling through the cluster of cages.

"Have you seen the piggies?" the man holding the gun asked, poking a woman in the ribs with it.

The woman cried out and pressed more firmly against the bars at the back of her cage. When she cowered in the corner and covered her head with her hands, the man laughed before strolling away. Mike realized the vamp wasn't looking for an answer; he was merely relishing the torment of his victims. He, and all the others in the black coats, had to be Savages.

When Mike got his hands on that Savage, he was going to enjoy killing the bastard, and killing was not something he relished.

"Have you seen the piggies?" the Savage asked, shoving the barrel of the rifle into the face of a gawking, rail-thin man.

How long have some of them been here? Mike wondered as he surveyed the cages.

Long enough that some of the vampires and humans bordered on starvation. More than a few of them wore baggy clothes he suspected fit when they'd arrived here, and their cheekbones stood out against their pale, dirty skin. Either the Savages didn't care about feeding the humans, or they didn't want them to put up any fight when they turned the starving vamps loose on them.

A creak from behind him drew his attention away from the others. He expected to find Mollie hovering nearby; instead, he met the golden eyes of a black cat. Startled, the cat turned and fled into the shadows of the barn.

"Here piggy, piggy, piggy!" the man with the rifle taunted.

Mike turned back to find him pulling the gun out of the man's face before continuing through the cages.

"Oh, piggy, where art thou?"

Mollie cringed when the man's voice rang through the rafters until it came from everywhere at once. She poked her head around the bales of hay and stifled another sneeze when more dust drifted to her. Closing her eyes, Mollie pinched her nostrils as her eyes watered. What a fantastic time to discover she was allergic to hay.

I will not sneeze!

The words became a mantra in her head until the urge finally faded and tears streaked her cheeks. Opening her eyes again, she searched the loft for anything she could use as a weapon but saw nothing.

Crawling to the other end of the bales, she poked her head around that side and spotted Mike kneeling at the edge of the loft, watching the proceedings below.

"Little pig, little pig, let me in!" the man called in a booming, baritone voice.

His words echoed throughout again, but this time, Mollie pinpointed his location. Her gaze fell to the hay and dust-covered boards beneath her. If she was correct, then he was *right* below her.

"Not by the hair on my chinny, chin, chin!" the man yelled in a higher-pitched falsetto.

Back in his deeper baritone, the man called, "Then, I'll huff, and I'll puff, and I'll *blow* your house in!"

Mollie didn't know what instinct caused her to move, but as Mike was coming at her, she was leaping to her feet and scrambling over the top of the bales. The thunderous explosion of a gunshot reverberated through the barn as the floor she'd been kneeling on blew upward. Shards of wood pelted her calves before she flung herself over the bales and crashed onto the other side of them.

Dust burst into the air around her, and the breath was knocked from her lungs, making it impossible for her to breathe as she stared at the wooden rafters over her head. If she'd been able to scream, she would have when she spotted a set of golden eyes peering down at her. But thankfully her inability to breathe kept her from shrieking over a cat.

Dust swirled around her as she attempted to get her arms and legs under her. Then solid arms were encircling her as the floor burst apart behind her again.

Mollie bit back a cry when Mike's arms tightened around her while he rolled until she was dizzy and had no idea where they were in the loft. When he came to a stop, he lowered one arm to her waist and kept the other locked across her back as he launched to his feet.

Dangling against his side, Mollie instinctively slipped her legs around his waist and cleaved to him as he released her to grasp an overhead beam. She'd nearly had her ass blown off and was being stalked by a madman with a Three Little Pigs obsession, but Mollie felt a rush of desire when his powerful body flexed against hers.

She held on as Mike lifted his legs off the ground and gripped the beam with them. She marveled at the strength he possessed while he scurried up the rafter and toward the center of the barn before swinging out to catch another beam. She finally managed to draw in her first deep breath as he made his way across the rafters with the ease of a monkey swinging through the trees. Except, he carried a hundred and forty pounds of *her* weight with him.

The strength he showed was impossible, wasn't it? And why was she questioning this when a lunatic was firing at them through the floorboards?

But the gunshots had ceased, and she heard only the frightened whimpers of those in the cages. Mike propelled them further up the rafter and nearly to the peak of the barn.

Coming to a stop, he swung out with his free hand and clasped the next beam only a foot away from them. Mollie kept her head tucked into the hollow of his shoulder and her arms around his neck as she flattened against him.

I will get you out of this, he vowed.

Gripping another rafter, he swung out with one leg and hooked around it before swinging over. He glided through more of the beams before coming to a stop close to the edge of the hayloft but a hundred feet away from where he'd knelt before. Feeling secure in the fact the vampires wouldn't know exactly where they were, he nudged Mollie a little.

When she lifted her head to look at him, he pointed to her and then the rafter. Understanding his meaning, she eased her grip on his shoulders and reached for the overhead beam. Mike pushed her up until she spun around to straddle the rafter while he hung underneath her.

Her eyes met his before he swung away from her and onto the next beam. Mollie watched as Mike spun himself around the rafter and perched on it. He'd carried her a good fifty feet across the loft, yet sweat didn't bead on his forehead, and his breathing was no faster than before.

Who is this guy? She wondered as he leaned over to peer down at the barn below.

"Little piiiiiiiiggies!" the asshole with the gun called. "Come out, come out, wherever you are!"

Mike remained still as the man stopped near the ladder to the loft and tapped the barrel of the gun against a rung. The man couldn't see Mollie from where he stood, but he could see Mike if Mike moved.

"This little piggy went to market," the man said as he slung the gun over his shoulder and grasped the rungs. "This little piggy stayed home; this little piggy had roast beef." The vamp climbed the ladder as he spoke. "This little piggy had none, and this little piggy cried all the way home because I gutted him and feasted on his blood!"

Mollie recoiled at the words and the vehemence with which they were declared, but more than that, she recoiled from the amusement in the man's voice. This monster would enjoy doing such a thing to someone—to *them*.

Mike tensed when the vamp's ascent briefly made it so he couldn't see him on the ladder. Mike used that moment to drop out of the rafters and place his feet silently on the ground.

"*Stay,*" he mouthed to Mollie, who frowned at him but didn't make a move to leave her spot.

Mike glided toward the ladder. He'd prefer Mollie didn't know what he was, but Mike doubted he'd be able to keep it from her if they succeeded in getting out of this alive. And her staying alive was far more important than keeping his secret.

He doubted metal bullets filled the vamp's gun, so he had to disarm him the first chance he got. Mike's heart thudded as he listened to the creaking ladder and the Savage growing closer with every passing second.

Then the vamp's head poked over the edge of the loft. While he'd been out of Mike's view, the Savage had unslung his gun, and the barrel of it was aimed directly at Mike's chest. The bastard had known where he was the whole time.

"Sooooooey!" the Savage shouted as he pulled the trigger.

When the muzzle flashed, Mike twisted to the side. The wooden bullet skimming across his chest tore his shirt and sliced his skin, but it didn't hit his heart. Mike charged the Savage as the man pulled the trigger again. The next bullet slammed into his shoulder but didn't deter him.

The Savage released the gun and fumbled for something as Mike leapt at him. Wrapping his arm around the Savage's neck, Mike yanked the monster backward. The vamp scrambled to keep his grip on the ladder, but Mike's heavy weight ripped him free.

The air rushing around him tore at his hair and clothes as they plunged toward the barn floor.

CHAPTER EIGHT

MOLLIE GASPED when Mike and the man vanished. Mike had been *shot*! She'd seen the blood on his shirt and his grimace, yet it hadn't deterred him from attacking the man. Frozen in disbelief, Mollie's fingers dug into the beam as a crash sounded below, and she realized they'd fallen on top of one of the cages.

She remained frozen for only a second more before sliding down the rafter and descending to the ground. Mollie fell to her knees at the edge of the hayloft as Mike and the man rolled across the top of a cage and tumbled off the side.

They punched and clawed at each other as they hit the ground. The occupant of the cage lunged forward and snatched the man's coat. He yanked their captor back and pinned him against the bars as the man was lifting the rifle to bash Mike in the face with it.

The gun fell from his hands as he reached behind him to claw at the hands of the prisoner holding him. The prisoner snarled as Mike pulled back his fist and smashed it into their captor's chest. Mollie slapped her hands over her mouth to stifle her scream as bone crunched and blood slid from the corner of the security officer's mouth.

Once, caught up in the clamoring excitement spreading around her school, she'd gone with a group of kids to the local park and listened to the chants of "Fight! Fight! Fight!" as two idiots pummeled each other.

The only difference was, when those kids hit each other, their fists hadn't gone *into* the chest of the other. She wanted to deny it because it could *not* be possible, but her eyes were telling her Mike's hand was now buried up to his wrist in the cruel bastard's chest.

What's going on? What have I gotten involved in? What are some of these things? What is Mike*?*

She had no idea what the answers to any of those questions were as her mind labored to process what she was seeing. She didn't want to look anymore, yet she couldn't turn away.

Mike dug deeper into the vamp's chest; he almost had his hand around the Savage's heart as the bastard lunged against the vampire holding him, but the vamp in the cage didn't let go.

"Mike, look out!" Jack shouted from another cage.

Plunging forward, Mike enclosed his hand on the Savage's heart as someone leapt onto his back. The fingers digging into his neck pulled back his flesh, and blood ran free. The animalistic sounds the Savage on his back issued became more excited when the scent of his blood hit the air.

Mike tore the heart from the Savage's chest and reeled backward. Throwing his weight back, he smashed the killer on his back into another cage before leaning away and doing it again, but the vampire only grunted and dug in deeper.

The occupant within the cage, a human, cowered in the corner. He had to find another vampire; they would tear into anyone who had imprisoned them in this place and pounce on their chance to feed. The vamp who had caught the Savage with the gun didn't care he was dead as he drank his blood.

"Mike! There's another one on your right!" Doug shouted.

Despite his increasing unease over this situation, relief filled him at the sound of Doug's voice; his friend was alive. The breath of the one on his back tickled his neck as fangs scratched his flesh. Mike's pulse skyrocketed when he realized it was going to bite him, and if that happened, he was as good as dead. The agony of having his blood drained unwillingly from his body would most likely render him almost useless.

He clasped the Savage's hair as its fangs started to pierce his flesh. He yanked its long hair forward so violently, he tore a handful of it from its skull. He realized the Savage on his back was a woman when she squealed; her fingers shredded his skin as she scrambled for purchase while Mike continued to drag her over his back.

"All three of the others are coming!" Jack yelled at the same time Doug shouted, "Move to your left!"

Mike succeeded in dragging the woman over his shoulder as he staggered to the left. Grasping hands stretched through the bars of the cage he crashed into. Inhuman, ravenous sounds issued from within as the vampire in the cage slammed the woman against the bars.

She screeched and tried to pull away, but the imprisoned vamp yanked her arm into the cage with enough force to break it before sinking his fangs into her wrist. The woman's squeals went on for a few seconds more before her legs gave out while the vamp greedily consumed her blood.

With his back against the cage, Mike rolled around to the side of it as two Savages pounced on top of it and a third stalked him from the other side. Turning, Mike ran behind the cage and into the maze of them. He had to figure out a way to kill off these last three before more Savages arrived, as he seriously doubted the five who had entered the barn were the only ones behind this operation.

Metal clattered behind him, and when he glanced back, he spotted the vamps running across the tops of the cages in pursuit of him while the other remained on the ground. Those on top of the cages stayed to the ones housing humans as vampires crouched in wait for them in the others.

Mike came around the side of one of the cages and ran back toward the ladder. As he sprinted through the maze of bars, he spotted Mollie kneeling next to the Savage he'd killed. She had her hands in his pockets. She pulled something free and shoved it into the pocket of her jeans; it was only then he realized she clutched the rifle.

Rising to her feet, she leveled the gun at his chest. For a second, Mike was sure she would shoot him, and he wouldn't blame her after what she'd witnessed, but then she shifted the rifle and fired at something over his head. A screech filled the air, and Mike turned to find one of the Savage's clutching its chest while it tumbled off a cage. The shot had struck its heart.

Mollie spun the rifle toward the other man chasing Mike and fired. The vamp had been poised to leap, and she caught it in mid-launch when she fired. Off the mark, this shot pierced the man's shin; he howled in response.

Is it a man? She pondered as he fell to the ground only feet away from her. Well, it was obviously male, but was it *hu*man? And that's where she would have to answer with a big old *no*. But what exactly was it, and what was Mike?

She refused to look at the creature still drinking the blood of the bastard who'd nearly killed her in the hayloft, but the disgusting slurping sounds were all she heard.

Are they vampires? I did remove wooden bullets from that guy's pockets, and they are loaded into the rifle...

No, that's insane. There is no such thing as vampires. This isn't a horror or romance novel; no one is going to sparkle, and no cross will deter these beasts. Then what are they?

She might be okay living the rest of her life never knowing the answer to that question. Unfortunately, she didn't think she'd have the option.

Mike stalked the man Mollie had shot in the shin and cornered him against one of the cages. With no time to waste, he seized the man's throat, lifted him, and twisted his head around. He tore his head from his shoulders and lobbed it aside as the nearby humans sobbed.

He ran back out of the maze of cages and found Mollie where he'd left her. She had the rifle against her shoulder as she surveyed the barn for the remaining Savage.

"Mollie, look out!" Mike bellowed when he spotted the monster slipping through the shadows toward her.

A sound from her left drew Mollie's attention as the remaining security thing lunged out of the shadows at her. Staggering back, she lifted the rifle and aimed at the man who not only wanted to kill her, but would do it in the vilest ways possible.

Fangs! The sight of them hanging over his bottom lip registered even as the guy advanced on her with inhuman speed.

Off balance, Mollie fired seconds before fingers curled around her wrists and the bullet dug into the ground at the man's feet. The thing's fangs and reddened eyes filled her vision when he lunged at her.

He's going to kill me. She didn't doubt it as the more she struggled, the deeper his fingers dug into her flesh.

Mike poured on the speed as the Savage dragged Mollie toward him. Lowering his shoulder, Mike barreled into the man's side and flung him back, as if he weighed no more than a child. The Savage tried to cling to her, but the force of Mike's blow knocked him free. Mollie staggered back and collapsed near one of the cages while the Savage scampered into the shadows.

Mike spun to make sure Mollie was okay before chasing after the Savage. The vamp hadn't made it far as the breath wheezing from it alerted Mike that he'd broken some of its ribs and those ribs had pierced its lung.

Keeping his back to Mollie so she couldn't see what he was doing, Mike knelt next to the vamp and placed his knee on the creature's back. Bearing down on it, he ignored the crunch of ribs and spine as he gripped its head and twisted it to the side. The creature squealed and kicked its feet while its fingers clawed at the barn floor. When Mike succeeded in rending its head from its shoulders, silence descended.

Mike watched the blood seeping from the headless Savage. Usually, the sight of death made him turn away, especially if he was the one who unleashed the brutality necessary to do such a thing. But for the first time, he didn't loath the ruthlessness residing in him if it helped to keep Mollie alive.

He didn't look at the head before lobbing it into the shadows and dragging the body behind some of the cages. Maybe he couldn't keep the truth from her, but he would hide as much death from her as he could.

When he reemerged, Mollie stood where he'd left her, looking dazed, but her eyes were resolute when she lifted the rifle and aimed it at his heart.

CHAPTER NINE

"What are you?" she demanded. "What are *they*?"

"Mollie." Mike raised his hands in a conciliatory gesture. "Lower the rifle. I won't hurt you."

Under normal conditions, she was far enough away that he'd be able to move in time to avoid taking a kill shot from her, but he still had the other bullet embedded in his shoulder, was losing blood, and had broken a rib when he crashed into the cage with the first Savage. If she fired that weapon, there was a chance she might kill him.

"Now is not the time for this," he said. "We have to get out of here before more of them arrive."

"Then answer my question. *What are you?*" Mollie bit out as she sensed the other occupants of the cages creeping closer to them. "And don't lie to me."

Mike debated how to answer her question; would the truth cause her to fire the gun anyway? But after what she'd witnessed, she had to suspect the truth, even if she didn't want to admit it to herself.

"Vampire," he said, and her finger twitched on the trigger. "I am a vampire, and those things we just killed, and the ones who *will* be coming for us, are monsters."

"Aren't they vampires too?"

"They are, but we're not all the same. If I wanted you dead, you would be."

Those words were more comforting to her than they should have been because they were true. She'd seen what Mike could do and the speed with which he could move. He could drain her dry before she could count to two. In the hayloft, he could have left her to fend for herself and allowed her ass to be blown off; instead, he ran toward the danger, used his body to protect her, and carried her into the rafters.

But he's a vampire! This whole mess had her wondering if she'd somehow ingested magic mushrooms and was hallucinating everything. Maybe she'd hallucinated her entire life. That seemed as plausible to her as the *actual* existence of vampires!

Blinking, Mollie stepped back as she realized mushrooms had nothing to do with this situation. This was real, Mike was real, the gun in her hands was real, and Aida was in the hands of the creatures Mike had just described as monsters.

"Mollie—"

"I'm going to find my sister; will you help me?" she demanded as she cut off Mike's words.

"Yes," Mike said without hesitation. "I will help you find her, and I *will* get you out of this."

Mollie wanted to believe him, but she didn't know what to think in this strange world she'd been forced into. "The wooden bullets in this gun, will they kill you?"

"Yes," Mike answered, knowing she needed the reassurance of her weapon. "Me and any other vampire you shoot through the heart."

"If you're lying about helping me or if you try to attack me, I'll kill you," she vowed.

"Understood, and you have nothing to fear from me."

"Okay." She didn't see what other choice she had. After what she witnessed here, she'd require his help to get Aida back, and he hadn't done wrong by her yet. Lowering the rifle, she slid it over her shoulder and secured it against her back with the strap connected to it. "Don't make me regret trusting you."

"I won't."

Mike didn't tell her he'd easily be able to take the weapon from her now that it wasn't aimed at him. He had no intention of taking it from her. Allowing her to keep it would help build her trust in him, and the rifle could kill any enemy who came after them.

"Please let us out of here," a woman pleaded from the shadows.

Mollie gulped as she examined the numerous cages. There were so many of them, but which ones contained humans, and which ones were vampires? She'd prefer not to have more of the bloodsuckers crawling around this place. Mike had agreed to help her, but that didn't mean the others wouldn't eat her the first chance they got.

She shuddered as Mike knelt next to the body of the bastard she'd taken the gun from. "What are you doing?" she asked.

"Looking for keys."

He would not leave here without Jack and Doug, and he'd like to get as many of the others free as possible. Some of the vampires had been here too long. They would have to remain caged as he couldn't trust them around Mollie and the other humans he intended to free, but the other vamps would provide an excellent distraction to the Savages who would pursue them. Some of the vamps would flee, but others would seek revenge.

The enemy of my enemy and all that.

Something jingled behind him, and he glanced over his shoulder to discover Mollie dangling a set of keys from her hooked index finger. "I already took them from the guy."

Rising, Mike walked over and held his hand out to her.

"Are they going to eat me if you let them out?" she demanded.

"I'll never let them touch you, and I'll kill anyone who tries it."

The fevered tone of his words eased some of her wariness, but she hesitated before handing the keys over to him.

"Thank you," Mike said. Clasping her elbow, he hurried her through the cages until they stood outside Jack's.

Jack's eyes burned with rage when he crawled toward the door of his cage. "You took your sweet-ass time killing them," he muttered.

"Glad you're alive too," Mike replied and slid the only silver key on the ring into the lock. He'd try the other keys if it didn't work, but he was hoping the silver key went with the silver cages.

"More of those fuckers are going to be coming for us."

"I know." Mike turned the key, the lock clicked, and the door swung open.

Jack crawled out and rose with a groan. His hand went to his back as he remained stooped over like an old man. Rising, Jack groaned again and cracked his back. "You okay?" he asked Mike when his eyes focused on the bullet hole in his shoulder.

"Fine."

"I thought she was going to shoot you." Jack gave Mollie an irritated look; she scowled back at him and gripped the strap of her rifle.

"Me too," Mike admitted. "Jack, this is Mollie; Mollie, this is one of my best friends, Jack."

"So, he's a vampire too?" she asked, eyeing Jack like he were about to eat her.

"Yes, but you're safe with him," Mike promised before focusing on Jack. "Check the other dead security guards for keys, and if you find a set, start turning vamps and humans loose."

"You can't let more vampires loose!" Mollie protested.

"We have to," Mike replied. "They're as innocent as you or me in all this. Plus, some of them could be helpful against the bastards trying to hold us here."

Mollie opened her mouth to argue further, but the words died in her throat. If these vamps were also innocent in this, she couldn't leave them here, even if they survived on blood. She ate things others thought were disgusting too.

Yeah, your obsession with pickles on pizza is totally the same thing as drinking someone's blood. But it didn't matter; she couldn't leave them caged.

Jack stepped closer and pitched his voice low. "You want all the vamps out?"

"Only the ones who don't look half-starved," Mike whispered back.

"Will do," Jack said.

"If there aren't any more keys, keep watch. We don't have much time before more Savages arrive."

"No, we don't," Jack agreed before jogging away.

"Doug!" Mike called into the cages.

"Back here!" a voice called from the other side of the barn.

Mike reclaimed Mollie's arm and led her toward the voice.

"Do you know everyone here?" Mollie demanded as she jogged to keep up with Mike's brisk pace.

"Jack and Doug are two of my best friends; I briefly met the bartender at the bar we were taken from, but everyone else here is a stranger."

"Hmm," Mollie grunted when they stopped outside another cage.

The blond-haired man inside, Doug she assumed, smiled at her. Mollie didn't smile back.

"Mollie, this is Doug; Doug, this is Mollie," Mike said.

"Hi," Doug greeted.

"Hey," Mollie muttered.

"It's a good thing you were able to get free."

"Yeah," Mollie said.

She shifted her stance as she studied the barn. She still couldn't wrap her head around the fact she was standing next to a vampire, while surrounded by cages full of vampires and humans. It was all surreal, yet Mike's warm body against hers, the jingle of the keys, and the hopeful faces gazing out at them were all *very* real.

If this was what their captors were doing to them, and if they were all monsters from some horror story, then what were they doing with Aida?

Mollie swallowed the lump in her throat and blinked away her tears. She *would* find Aida and get her free of this mess, and they would deal with the consequences of it all afterward. Together, the two of them could get through anything.

"I've got another set of keys!" Jack called from somewhere amid the cages.

"Good!" Mike called back as he swung open the door to Doug's cage. Doug climbed out and stretched his back as he rose to stand before Mike. "I need you to keep watch for more Savages. They've got to be on their way."

"I will. Should I take Mollie with me?" Doug asked.

Mike contemplated this as Mollie scowled at them. If Mollie were with Doug, she'd be away from the rest of the vampires who were set free. However, he hated the idea of having her out of his sight, and he didn't trust anyone to protect her as fiercely as he would.

That realization startled him as he trusted Jack and Doug with *his* life, just not *hers*.

"No, she'll stay with me," Mike finally said.

Doug looked surprised but hid it when he replied, "I'll be by the doors."

Mike watched as Doug weaved through the cages. Vampires and humans reached out to him as he passed while Doug mumbled apologies for no keys and dodged their hands.

Mike kept Mollie close by his side as he set to work freeing the humans and vampires closest to them. He didn't fully trust any vampire outside his close-knit family, but he had to hope some of them would prove to be allies. No matter what, *all* of them would be a distraction to the Savages who'd put them here.

He skipped over the vamps who were too thin and unable to control the red of their eyes. Mollie edged closer to him when the livid shouts of those he left behind filled the barn, but he didn't regret his choice. Getting out of this mess and keeping Mollie safe was what mattered most.

"Mike! Jack! There are lights on the horizon!" Doug called from the front of the barn.

Mike froze, and lifting his head, he examined the numerous cages filling the room. Between the two of them, he and Jack had managed to open almost half the cages, but there were still so many to go, and they were out of time.

"Shit," he hissed, and twisting the key in the lock, he set LeNae free.

"Getting closer!" Doug yelled.

Mike glanced at Mollie's round, frightened eyes. She'd taken the rifle from her shoulder and held it against her chest. If she weren't involved in this, he would set a few more of the prisoners free, but he couldn't risk her being caught again.

"We have to go." Taking her elbow, he tossed the keys to a whimpering human pleading to be set free and rushed Mollie toward where Doug stood in the middle of the double doors.

The headlights from the approaching vehicles were only a few hundred feet away.

"Jack, we have to go!" he bellowed into the shadows.

"Heading for the side door!" Jack yelled. "Meet you outside!"

Mike didn't look back at those who remained trapped, holding Mollie close against him, he plunged into the brisk night air.

CHAPTER TEN

ADRENALINE COURSED through Mollie as she slung the rifle over her shoulder and followed Mike out of the barn. Her heart sank when she got her first good look around and realized only a wide-open field stretched before them. A few hundred yards away from them, the field became woods, but they'd be open targets if they ran across the field. That hadn't stopped some escapees from sprinting across it.

Two of the vehicles broke off to give chase to the dozen or so men and women fleeing across the field. One of the vehicles was a pickup truck with two Savages standing in the back, holding rifles. The Savages shouted as they lifted their guns and aimed at the escapees. Shots rang out and shrieks resonated from the runners as two of them went down.

The other vehicle, a Jeep Wrangler, surged toward the front and skidded sideways in the field. Dirt flew up behind the Jeep as it raced to block the runners from the trees fifty yards ahead of them.

"Oh no," Mollie whimpered when the truck ran over a woman.

"Shit," Mike muttered.

He pulled Mollie toward the side of the massive barn where at least the building covered them from the approaching vehicles. Jack waited there as vampires and humans fled into the field on the other side of the barn. Except, this field was much smaller, and only a hundred yards separated them from the woods beyond.

"We'll never make it," Mollie whispered.

"We only have to be faster than the slowest ones, and we're faster than all the humans," Jack said.

Mollie paled, but Mike knew Jack's assessment was right.

"I need to carry you," he said to Mollie.

"What?" she demanded, stepping away from him.

"I'm a lot faster than you."

"You're injured; let me do it," Doug offered.

"No!" Mike snapped. The angry response not only astonished him but caused Doug's and Jack's eyebrows to rise. Doug had a point, but it didn't matter; the idea of anyone, including his best friends, touching her was not something he could tolerate. *He* had to get her out of here. "I will do it. Mollie?"

Mollie stared at the three of them. She hadn't missed the hard edge of Mike's voice or the surprise on his friends' faces, but she didn't have time to ask about it. She disliked the idea of anyone carrying her, but she hated the idea of dying more.

"Fine," she relented.

Before she could ask how this was going to work, Mike stepped before her, placed his hands on her hips, and lifted her off the ground as easily as she plucked a flower. Mollie gasped when she found her chest crushed against his.

"Shouldn't I go on your back or something?" she asked when the intimate contact caused a shiver of desire to run down her spine.

"If they start shooting at us, my body will protect yours."

His words caused a strange sensation to run through her as unexpected tears pricked her eyes. This man, this stranger, this *vampire* planned to use his body to shield her from bullets that could kill them both.

"Wrap your legs around me," he ordered.

Mollie did as he said and draped her arms around his neck.

"Let's go," he said to Jack and Doug.

Mike clasped Mollie's nape with one hand and placed the other in the small of her back before sprinting away from the barn and into the field with Jack and Doug at his side. Lowering her head, Mollie turned it on his shoulder to stare at the world whizzing past them.

The whipping wind made her feel like she was riding in a convertible with the top down. The sensation would have been freeing if it weren't for the screams and gunshots peppering the air. Mike's powerful body flowed beneath her as he zigzagged to avoid any bullets coming their way. When she shifted her hold on him, the blood from his bullet wound seeped onto her palm, and she yanked her hand away before she hurt him.

"Almost to the woods," he said.

Mollie tried to turn her head to see the woods, but the wind whipping her hair into her face stung her cheeks and eyes. When she turned back, the air blew her hair away from her eyes. More gunfire pierced the night, and behind Mike, the earth churned up as bullets riddled the ground.

Mollie suppressed a scream when two of the runners threw out their arms as they tumbled to the ground. One of them tried to crawl forward, but another round of bullets ended their movement. Mike's muscles bunched beneath her, and before she knew what was happening, he leapt into the air.

Mike's foot came down on top of the split rail fence, and he launched himself off it as a fresh round of gunfire pierced the air. Holding Mollie closer, he bent partially over her to keep her protected as he propelled himself off the fence and into the woods. Not expecting the embankment on the other side, his front foot came down awkwardly and twisted.

Mollie cried out when his leg gave out. From the corner of his eye, he saw Doug grab a tree branch, but Jack bounced off the ground as he tumbled ahead of them and out of view. Mike staggered and almost caught himself before his other knee gave out and he plunged forward.

Mollie bit her bottom lip to keep from screaming when they hit the ground. Her breath wheezed out when Mike's heavy weight came down on top of her before they rolled over. The rifle bounced against her back, dirt and rocks battered her, but Mike kept hold of her when they flipped head over heels down the embankment.

Mike grunted when his back crashed into a tree, but better his back than Mollie's. When they started to roll over again, he thrust his body to the side to ease their downward plummet. Mollie burrowed her head in his shoulder; her fingers clawed his back when the movement caused him to come down on top of her again while they skidded down the hill at an alarming speed.

Slipping his leg between hers to keep her trapped against him, he released his hold on her and smashed his hands into the ground over her head. Dirt and rocks tore up beneath his fingers as their momentum slowed but didn't stop.

Spotting a tree on his left, he lifted his hand from the ground and swung out to grasp it. His palm slammed against the trunk, and his fingers dug into the bark. One of his fingers broke from the impact, and his wounded shoulder screamed in protest, but he didn't release the tree. Jerked to a halt, a muscle in his shoulder tore, but it was the least of his concerns as he took a minute to catch his breath and survey their surroundings.

They'd come to a halt halfway down the steep embankment. Some humans and vampires were still tumbling past him while others were running down the hill at a sideways angle to keep their footing. One human was bent around a tree, their spine broken from the impact and their awful moans mingling with the gunfire above.

He searched for his friends in the chaos, but he didn't see Jack or Doug anywhere. Thankfully, their trackers were also nowhere in sight... yet.

Lowering his gaze, he stared at Mollie's bent head as she panted against his shoulder and clutched at him. A tenderness he hadn't known he possessed took over when he brushed the hair back from her forehead. He *had* to see her eyes and know she was okay.

She lifted her head from his shoulder, and their gazes met. Like the first time he saw her, the striking color of her eyes stole his breath from him. Without thinking, he bent and kissed her forehead. The action was entirely out of place but felt so natural it was as if he'd kissed her a thousand times before, and he wanted more. He inhaled her sweet apple scent as it mingled with the earthy aroma of the freshly turned up dirt surrounding them.

Mollie's breath froze when his warm lips caressed her skin. Vampires *kissed* others? Of course, they did in the books and shows, but in real life? It seemed impossible, but then maybe she was hallucinating this.

No, she was not hallucinating the weight of his body against hers or the firm press of his thigh between her legs. She was not imagining his enticing scent of cedar with the faint hint of cigarette smoke. She definitely was *not* hallucinating her body's utterly inappropriate response to him as her nipples hardened and the urge to rub herself against his thigh hit her.

When his lips moved from her forehead to her cheek, Mollie turned her head, so their mouths were only a few inches apart. She shouldn't want him to kiss her, yet she did. He was more enticing than a KitKat bar. Perhaps he was only doing this so he could drink her blood, but when his breath tickled her lips, she didn't care what his reasons were.

She found herself staring into his turbulent, royal blue eyes while he gazed at her with a look of awe that more than matched hers while their breath mingled, but their lips didn't touch. She wanted to end the torture of this near kiss by lifting her lips to his, but she couldn't break the moment as the rest of the world faded away until it was only the two of them.

A spatter of much closer gunfire drew their heads toward the top of the hill as more screams rent the air. Their captors were coming.

Mike suppressed the snarl seeking to tear free. He would destroy every one of these bastards for what they'd done, but first he had to find somewhere safe for Mollie. Releasing the tree, Mike braced his feet apart as he rose and extended his hand to Mollie.

Mollie clasped it, and he helped her to her feet. Their tumble had caused her shirt to pull down and expose the top of her simple black bra. The rifle had almost come off her back. She adjusted her shirt and the gun as headlights flashed over the top of the embankment and a truck rolled to a stop.

The glow of the headlights lit the tops of the trees and reflected off the ground. The shadows they created came alive as they slithered across the forest floor in such a way Mollie had the insane idea they were demons rising to drag them into the pits of Hell. *Too late.*

"They're coming," she breathed.

"This way." Keeping a firm hold on her hand, Mike led her at an angle toward the bottom of the hill.

CHAPTER ELEVEN

"We can stop to rest here for a bit," Mike said.

Mollie glanced at her watch to discover it was nearly two in the morning. They'd been running, walking, and running some more for the past five hours. And once her adrenaline started to wane, she felt like she'd crawled for the last hour, but onward they trudged.

Occasionally, they would hear or see someone else making their way through the woods, but Mike didn't approach any of them. He'd set the others free as a distraction and to possibly fight against their captors, but he didn't dare trust them enough to approach them. He hadn't seen Jack or Doug at all, and it had been an hour since he'd heard or seen anyone else.

Mike glanced at the woods surrounding the small stream he'd stopped beside. A grouping of thick tree branches from a red maple dangled in the water. Mike pulled back some of the branches and peered into the small space created beneath the limbs. The thick vines and brambles mixed in with the tree branches and leaves would further shield them from anyone passing by. The aromas of water and fish would mask their scents.

He'd prefer it if they didn't stop until sunrise when the Savages would be less likely to be out, but Mollie was barely lifting her feet anymore, and the grumbling of her stomach grew increasingly louder. He could carry her again, but he would be better able to defend her if his hands were free, and he didn't think they'd come across a much better hiding spot than this one.

"Hurry," he whispered, gesturing her inside.

Mollie scrambled past him and into the secluded space no more than seven feet deep and four feet wide. Careful to avoid the thorns that could take out an eye, Mollie shrugged the rifle over her shoulder before resting her back against the tree trunk. She held the weapon before her as Mike crawled into the tiny space; he moved the branches and vines back into place.

She couldn't see him, but she listened as he crept toward her. His body warmed hers when he settled against the tree next to her. Mollie remained rigid as she waited to see what he would do.

He'd saved her life; did he expect something from her in return? After he'd almost kissed her, would he expect sex? Could a vampire have sex; weren't they dead or undead or some such thing?

When she found herself hoping it was possible for him to have sex, she decided she'd officially lost her mind.

"What now?" she whispered.

"Now we wait until sunrise."

"What happens then?"

"Most of the Savages, the vampires who enjoy killing others, can't tolerate sunlight."

"But you can?"

"Yes."

"You said *most*, why just *most*?"

"Some of them haven't killed enough to completely lose their ability to walk in the day," Mike answered. "If these bastards have any Savages like that working for or with them, then they'll probably hunt us in the daytime too. Also, these woods are so thick, there won't be as much direct sun, so some of them will be able to move through here without an issue. Sometimes, humans also work for

Savages, and they can hunt us too. We're going to have to find a way out of this forest tomorrow, if we can."

"And find Aida," she stated.

"And find Aida," he agreed, though he planned to get Mollie somewhere safe before looking for her sister.

"Why would humans work with these Savages?" she asked, appalled by the idea of anyone agreeing to help these monsters.

"Some people will do anything for a chance at immortality."

"And vampires are immortal?"

"Yes."

The possibility of never dying boggled her mind. What must it be like not to fear any of the millions of ways humans could die every day? Probably empowering and more than a little overwhelming. She also suspected eternity might get a little boring after the first thousand years or so.

"So, will you ever age beyond what you look like now?" she asked.

"No."

Mollie blinked at him. He looked a little older than her, but only because there was a sad wisdom in his eyes that most twenty-something-year-olds didn't possess. However, he could be two thousand years old for all she knew.

"How old are you?" she asked.

"How old was I when I was turned, or how old am I now?" he inquired.

"Both."

"I was twenty-one when I became a vampire; I'm fifty-two now. I'll be fifty-three July eighth."

Mollie's breath sucked in; he wasn't two thousand, but he was over double her age!

Her grip tightened on her gun as she debated braining him with it and bolting out of here and away from this insanity, or staying here and letting it play out.

In the end, she had no choice; she wouldn't make it on her own out there. She had no idea what she was up against, but he did, and she would do anything to find Aida.

"And what about you, Mollie? How old are you?" he asked.

The deep baritone of his voice warmed her to the tips of her toes.

"I turned twenty-three on October thirteenth," she murmured before stifling a yawn.

"You should rest."

"I can't."

How could she possibly sleep next to someone who would drink her blood? But then, maybe he didn't drink blood. She'd seen the other vamp drinking the blood from the assmunch who shot at her, but maybe Mike was different. He hadn't tried to suck her dry yet, after all.

"Do you drink blood?" she blurted.

"Yes."

Mollie huddled closer to the tree and shifted her hold on the gun.

"I won't drink yours unless you offer it to me," he murmured when he detected the increased beat of her heart.

"Offer it to you?" Mollie croaked.

"Yes. If you offer me your blood, I will gladly accept."

Mollie jumped when his finger caressed the side of her neck. She should knock his hand away; instead, she found herself breathlessly questioning what he would do next.

Then his finger stilled on her throat. "I bet you taste better than you smell."

She hadn't realized he'd moved so close to her. Other than his finger, no other part of him touched her, but his breath caressed her neck when he spoke. What would it feel like if he did drink her blood? Or what if he kissed her as he almost had earlier? As disgusting as having him drinking from her sounded, her skin tingled at the possibility, and she found herself feeling more alive than she'd ever felt.

"And what do I smell like?" she managed to ask.

"Apples, but not just any apples, you smell like the apples that match your eyes. Granny Smith, I believed they're called."

His nearness was making her head spin, or maybe it was spinning because there was nothing in her stomach and she'd been through Hell these past two days. Either way, she needed distance from him. His finger fell away when she turned her head to the side.

Mike buried his disappointment when she shifted away from him. When her stomach grumbled again, he sat back from her. "I'll get you some food in the morning," he promised.

"It's okay; I'm used to going without eating."

"What do you mean you're *used* to going without eating? Why?" he demanded.

Mollie lowered her head into her hands and rubbed at her forehead. She must be more drained than she realized if she'd said those words aloud. "I didn't mean anything by it. I'm tired."

"You'll feel better with something to eat."

"Okay," she muttered in the hopes he'd drop the topic.

She rested her head against the tree and closed her eyes. Sitting still, the brisk air seeped through her clothes to caress her skin. Back home, it would have been warmer at night, but this far north in Canada the nights were still cool. Then she recalled she had no idea how far north they were or if they were even still *in* Canada. With a sigh, Mollie set the rifle beside her and hugged her knees to her chest.

"Will you let me hold you?" Mike inquired. "It will keep us both warmer."

Mollie almost said no; she both liked and feared the way he made her feel, but freezing to death wouldn't solve anything, and though she could be stubborn, she wasn't stupid.

"Yes," she said.

When his arms swept around her and he pulled her against his chest, Mollie realized she'd agreed to this for more reasons than to stay warm. She'd missed the feel of his arms around her. She was too tired to analyze her feelings as she cuddled closer and closed her eyes.

There was a chance he could kill her while she slept, but she couldn't bring herself to care as his warmth enveloped her. Though she'd been certain she wouldn't be able to fall asleep next to him, she was out almost instantly.

CHAPTER TWELVE

Mike found himself staring down the barrel of Mollie's rifle when he crawled back into their tiny alcove the next morning. She stared at him for a minute before lowering the gun. The circles shadowing her eyes before she fell asleep last night had eased, but she stifled a yawn as her shoulders slumped warily.

He'd brought something back with him that he hoped would revitalize her. Peering out of the alcove, he scanned the area and scented the air before dragging the two rabbits he'd caught and roasted inside.

"What is that?" Mollie inquired when the enticing scent of cooked meat wafted to her.

Mike turned and held out two tiny, blackened carcasses. Saliva rushed into her mouth, and for a second, her vision blurred. She had no idea what they were, but they smelled delicious.

"Rabbit," Mike said, holding them toward her.

Now that he'd said it, she could tell they were bunnies. "Thumper?" she murmured, uncertain how to feel about eating the cute creatures with their oversized ears and twitching noses.

"No, not Thumper," Mike replied with a smile. "Do you want them?"

Under normal circumstances, she would have turned down the meal—she didn't even like chicken on the bone—but this was far from normal. Besides, the rabbits were already dead; making the trip into her belly couldn't be any worse for them, and she couldn't let them go to waste.

"No," she said. "I mean, yes! Yes, I want them."

When Mike held the bodies out to her, she stared at the back legs dangling from his large hand. She reached for them, but she didn't know how to take them.

"Here," Mike said.

He handed her one, and she closed her fingers around it. The rabbit was still warm in her hands as she picked off a piece of meat. She would have given anything for something to wash down the meal as she was unbelievably thirsty, but she didn't dare drink from the stream. She didn't know what kind of bugs and parasites it might contain.

"How did you catch, skin, and cook them?" she asked then moaned when the meat hit her tongue. It was difficult to chew but delicious. *Sorry, Thumper.*

"I'm a hunter by nature, and it doesn't matter if the prey is human or animal," he replied.

Her fingers hesitated on the rabbit before she pulled off another piece of meat. "I see."

"I cooked them over a mile away, so the scent of fire and meat wouldn't bring any predators near you."

"But they could have found *you*," she said. The possibility of him going out there and not returning made her skin crawl. He'd left after daybreak to scout the area and hunt, but she hadn't expected him to take such a risk.

"I was counting on the sun driving most of the Savages away, and I found a small alcove, like this one, to cook in so the scent and smoke were kept to a minimum. Before I left, I set another fire outside and placed another rabbit over it to cook. If there are any

Savages still hunting for us, they'll be searching in an area we're heading away from."

"Smart."

The grin he flashed her did funny things to her insides and caused her to freeze in the middle of chewing.

"I'm more than an extremely handsome face," he said and winked at her.

Mollie gulped her rabbit down as she tried to think of some response, but his smile rattled her brain. "That's still up for debate," she finally said.

He laughed. "So that means you think I'm handsome."

Was he flirting with her? Vampires *flirted*? The idea was preposterous, but she couldn't deny that's what he seemed to be doing as his blue eyes twinkled in the light filtering through the branches and vines.

"It means I'll have to see if you're more brains or brawn," she muttered.

"I'm both," he assured her. "And just so you know, I'm okay with you finding me handsome as I find you quite intriguing."

"I bet you say that to all the girls," she snorted, but she couldn't stop a blush from scorching her cheeks.

He found *her* intriguing? She wasn't sure what he meant by it, but the idea pleased her more than she would have believed possible. She resisted tugging at the collar of her shirt as her blush spread to her body.

His amusement vanished as his eyes held hers. "I've never said that to anyone but you." Sensing her increasing discomfort, Mike decided to change the subject. "Where are you from?"

"Where are *you* from?" she retorted defensively. She was still trying to get her blush under control and had no idea what to make of him.

Mike hesitated as he contemplated how much to reveal to her, but he could give her enough of the truth to retain her trust in him while also keeping his loved ones protected. Messing with her mind and taking her memories from her was not an option for him. He didn't know what he would do when the time came for Mollie to return to her life; it wouldn't be safe for her to retain her knowledge of vampires, but that was a problem for another day.

He also had the problem of the memories of the other humans they freed. Some of them might not know who imprisoned them, and might not have seen much, but some of them had seen enough to be aware of what captured them. He would have to figure out a way to locate those people and change their memories; but first, he had to survive.

"Originally, I'm from Massachusetts. Then I moved to Oregon, and now I live in Maine with my friends and family," he said to Mollie.

"You have a family?" Mollie held her breath as she waited for his answer. *Please don't be married.*

"Yes; they're not blood relatives, but they're my family all the same. My parents both died in their fifties. My mom from a heart attack, and my dad had an aneurysm. Going by my genetics, it's probably a good thing I became a vamp, or I might be dead by now. I never had any siblings, but my friends are closer to me than any brother or sister could be. My friend Liam's children, and their children, are my nieces and nephews. We've all been together for many years, and we've been through a lot more than most families."

His strange life fascinated her, but so many questions tumbled through her mind that she couldn't settle on one.

Finally, she asked, "How did you become a vampire?"

Mike sighed and draped an arm over his knee. "When I was in college, a vampire named Beth fell in love with Liam, or at least she *claimed* to love him. After everything I've seen when it comes to vampires and their mates, she most definitely was *not* in love with him. Beth changed Liam, but when he rejected her, she hunted down his best friends and decided to change us too. She thought it would make Liam fall in line with her and we'd be one big, fucked-up family."

Mollie set the remains of the first rabbit aside and picked up the second. Her stomach still rumbled, but she was starting to feel a little fuller. "What a strange thing to do."

"Beth was more like the ones hunting us than like myself and my family."

"And you and your whole family are good vampires?"

"I'm not sure you could call us good. We've killed to protect those we love, but we don't kill humans or innocents, and that is what turns a vampire into a Savage."

"I see."

Mollie munched on the rabbit as she contemplated what he'd revealed to her. Outside, the song of the birds became increasingly louder as the morning crept onward. "Wait, you said Liam's children and their children, vampires can have sex?"

Mike snorted before flashing her a cocky grin. "Quite well, I assure you."

That damn blush was back again as she recalled how his body felt against hers and the way it had made her react. Despite what she knew him to be, she couldn't help speculating what sex with him would be like—mind-blowing.

"So you're not, like, dead or the living dead?" she asked.

"No, we have heartbeats, blood, and sperm. During the change, there is a second when our mortal heart ceases to beat and our immortal one takes over."

"Wow," she breathed. "And you can all have kids?"

"Yes."

"Are they vampires too?"

"Depends on the parents. If both parents are vampires, then they will have a purebred offspring. If one parent is human, then the offspring will be human but can be stronger than a normal person."

"I thought the only way to become a vampire was to die or exchange blood or something like that."

"An exchange of blood while dying is one way to become a

vamp, but purebred vampires are born, and they're stronger than a turned vampire, such as myself."

"What a strange, fascinating, creepy world."

Mike laughed. "You don't know the half of it."

"No one ever knows the half of anything."

"Very true. You can never tell anyone what I've revealed to you."

"Who would I tell? Who would believe me? The existence of vampires is safe with me until the day I die."

For some reason, her casual mention of her death caused his fangs to lengthen. He'd caught and fed from two deer earlier, it should have been enough blood to keep him sated for at least the next couple of days, but hunger scorched his veins as his gaze traveled to her neck.

I will not allow her to die! But he had no choice; as a mortal, her life would run its course until the inevitable end, unless he changed her.

Never before had Mike considered creating another vampire. It wasn't a fate he'd wish on anyone. Yes, he had a large, loving family he would die to protect, and Mike cherished every one of them, but he'd experienced far more death, violence, and uncertainty in his life as a vampire than if he'd remained human.

In some way, there was also more loneliness in his life as a vampire. He'd known a lot of women over the years, but he'd never gotten close to them, and none of them had been his mate. When he watched his friends, nieces, and nephews finding their mates and falling in love, he was happy for each of them, but a part of him was also jealous.

One day, he wanted to find someone to share his life with, and he wanted children. He didn't require a mate to have a child, but he wanted to be bound to someone before he shared kids with them.

"Your shoulder looks a lot better," Mollie said.

She licked the rabbit juice from her fingers as she tried to hide her unease over the fact he'd been shot yesterday, but no blood trickled from the injury anymore. What she could see of the bullet hole through his torn shirt appeared to be healed.

Mike rolled his shoulder back. It was still sore, as was the rest of him, but most of his injuries healed during the night, and the rest repaired themselves after he fed. "It is better," he said.

Mollie gulped. "Um, is accelerated healing a vampire thing?"

"It is."

Interesting and freaky. "Did you see anyone who escaped with us while you were out?" Mollie asked as she set aside the remains of the second rabbit.

She'd had enough of learning about vampires. It was great Mike was on her side, but there were plenty of inhuman beasts out there who would gladly see her dead, caged, or turned into a vampire snack. From what she'd seen, she didn't think she had much of a chance against them.

"No. I think everyone has gone into hiding and is waiting for the sun to rise." He'd hoped to find Jack and Doug, or at least some sign of them, but he'd discovered nothing about his friends. After he got Mollie to safety and found help, he would come back for them, if they hadn't already made it to civilization by then too.

"Like us."

"Yes, and if you're done, it's time we get moving."

"I'm ready. Are we going to find Aida?"

"Hopefully."

Mollie dug into her pocket and pulled out a pack of gum. She removed a piece and shoved it in her mouth to ease her dry throat and get rid of her morning/meat breath. She held the pack toward Mike. "Gum?"

Mike studied the pack before removing a piece. He couldn't remember the last time he'd chewed gum, and he would have preferred a cigarette, but they were probably still sitting on the bar where he set them. Unwrapping the gum, he stuck it in his mouth and, without thinking, reached out his hand to her; she took it.

CHAPTER THIRTEEN

WITH A FULL BELLY and a couple hours of sleep, Mollie felt better when they set out into the woods again. In the dim light filtering through the branches of the maples, oaks, and conifers surrounding them, the dense foliage wasn't as sinister as last night, but she constantly searched for a monster lurking to pounce on them.

The crisp, spring breeze would have chilled her if the exertion of their trek didn't keep her warm. Shadows shifted and played across the pine needles, and rotting leaves covered the ground while newly sprouted, fresh green leaves filled the trees. The pine trees here were some of the largest she'd ever seen, and it was easy to imagine they were in some magical land where time stood still. If a velociraptor or a giant suddenly materialized, she wouldn't have found it extraordinary.

Normally, she would love a brisk walk in the woods. She and Aida spent many weekends exploring the nature trails near their home, but now she would give anything to be free of the creaking trees and countless hiding places.

Not even the singing of the birds could ease her trepidation over this place. Some of the thick trunks of the pines, oaks, and maples could hide three men behind them, and she kept waiting for someone to jump out at them and shout, "Sooooooey!"

She edged closer to Mike as the possibility festered in her mind until she felt jumpier than a flea. Mike had brought the sharpened stick he'd used to cook the rabbits on back to their alcove and still clutched it in his hand.

"Do wooden stakes kill vampires?" she whispered.

"Yes, but it has to be to the heart. Fire and decapitation work too."

"I doubt I'll get close enough to decapitate or burn one without them killing me first."

"Very true," he agreed. "But the more you know."

Mollie gave a small snort of laughter as she recalled the public service commercials she'd seen on TV over the years; "the more you know" had been their tagline. "What are you, a PSA?"

"Just spreading wisdom to the youth of America."

It jolted her to recall she was the youth of America, compared to him, and that he was in his fifties and *not* her age. It was such a disconcerting realization considering the way he looked that for a second, she felt dizzy.

"Unless of course, you're a Canadian and not American," he said. "And then I'm spreading wisdom to the Great White North."

"I'm American," Mollie absently answered.

"Well, you finally shared some knowledge with me beside your name and the fact you have a sister. Instead of being the Unsinkable Molly Brown, you're the Tight-lipped Mollie."

She couldn't help but smile at his teasing tone. "I'm not exactly eager to spill too much about myself to a stranger and a vampire to boot."

"Are we strangers anymore? I think we crossed that line when we had neighboring cages."

"Perhaps."

"Besides, I've revealed more to you than I should have with a stranger and a human to boot. The truth of our existence isn't exactly public knowledge."

"But you couldn't have kept the truth from me after what happened in the barn."

"I could have taken the memory of what happened to you."

Mollie came to an abrupt stop. "You could *what*?"

Turning to face her, Mike scanned the forest and scented the air, but he detected no one close to them. "Vampires can assert control over the minds of others. If I didn't want you to remember the barn, you wouldn't. I shouldn't have left you with the memory; it would be safer for me if I took it from you, but I won't."

Mollie gawked at him before closing her mouth; it fell open again. "You're kidding, right?"

"No, I'm not." He clasped her elbow and nudged her forward. "We have to keep moving."

Mollie's feet felt like lead weights as she trudged along beside him. He could control her *mind*? "If it's safer for you, then why didn't you take the memory from me?"

"Because I'm not going to mess with your mind."

"Uh, thank you," she said uncertainly.

The confusion emanating from her made him stop and face her again. Resting his hands on her shoulders, he held her before him. "You have *nothing* to fear from me," he promised. "I'm going to get you out of this."

A part of her didn't think she should believe him, he was a vampire, and she'd seen what they could do in the barn, but Mike had protected her and been honest with her from the start. Maybe she'd put her trust in him and get burned for it, but so far he'd only earned it.

"Why are you so willing to help me?" she asked.

It was a question he didn't know the answer to either. "Because I like you."

"You barely know me."

True, but he still felt connected to her, and what he did know of her, he liked. "You're strong, capable, you don't complain, and you're loyal to your sister; what's not to like?"

Mollie had found plenty not to like about herself over the years, but she didn't say that. She'd moved on from those darker times, and she would not plunge herself back into that cycle of self-hatred and misery she'd been bogged down in for far too long.

"Plus, you saved me. You could have left me in the cage," Mike said when Mollie didn't speak.

"No, I couldn't have," she muttered, and he squeezed her shoulders. "Can all vampires do that mind control thing?"

"Yes, but some are better at it than others. The older a vamp gets, the stronger their powers get. I'm a child compared to some."

"Why didn't they keep us under their control when they had us in their cages?"

"It takes a lot of power to control someone's mind, and it can be draining for a vampire. There were a lot of humans and vampires in the barn. It would have been difficult to keep all of them manipulated. Plus, with what I think they planned for us, it would be far more fun for them to let everyone have control of their minds."

His words caused the hair on her arms to rise. "And what do you think they planned for us?"

"I think our captors intended to starve the vampires they captured until those vamps were mindless with hunger before turning them free, and I believe they were going to use the imprisoned humans as the food source for those vamps to kill."

Mollie's stomach plummeted. "What?"

"The vampires in there were all originally like me, just trying to go about their lives without harming anyone. The killing of humans is what leads to a vampire becoming Savage. Lately, there has been a growing movement to turn more vamps and humans Savage."

"Why?"

"I don't know, no one does. But one of the things the vampires behind the movement are doing is capturing vampires or taking humans and turning them; then they're starving those vampires until they're so mindless they'll destroy anything in their way. Each death pushes them more toward becoming a Savage while it strengthens and weakens them."

"How can they be strengthened *and* weakened?"

"Savages tend to be stronger and faster than the average turned vamp, though a vampire's power increases with age. However, after enough kills, a Savage can no longer tolerate sunlight or cross large bodies of water."

"I've heard of those things being weaknesses of vampires!" she blurted.

"And they *are* weaknesses for some vampires."

"Everything you've told me is both fascinating and terrifying."

Mike chuckled as he drew her a step closer to him. Unable to resist, he bent to kiss her forehead. "Welcome to my world."

Stunned by the gentle, almost natural, gesture, it took Mollie a minute to form her next question. "Have you ever killed anyone before?"

"Vampires, yes. Humans, no."

Phew. Mollie mentally wiped her brow. Perhaps he was lying, but she doubted it. Mike walked freely through the sun, and there was no reason for him to lie. If she attempted to run, he'd catch her. Plus, she had nowhere to go, and she doubted she'd succeed if she tried to kill him.

Reluctantly, Mike released her and stepped away. Now was not the time to get swept up in the warmth of her body and the allure of her scent.

The sad set of his shoulders when he turned away tugged at Mollie's heart. The heat of his kiss lingered on her forehead as he started through the woods again. Mollie shifted the rifle on her back before starting after him.

"So, Mollie, what are you doing in Canada?"

"Are we still *in* Canada?" she countered.

"Judging by the temperature and the fact most of the vegetation is fresh growth, I'd go with yes, but what do I know anymore?"

Mollie had to agree as she studied the leaves overhead and inhaled the brisk air. Back home, she'd be in a T-shirt, but she found herself missing her coat. However, the long-sleeved shirt was warm enough when she was moving.

"You know the same as me," she said.

"I know far less about you than you do about me. Are you an escaped convict? A thief on the run? On a treasure hunt? In witness protection?"

Mollie chuckled, and her hair bobbed against her shoulders when she shook her head. She'd tried to pin her hair back up while Mike was hunting this morning, but she'd lost most of her bobby pins during the events of the night. She'd finally given up and tucked the few remaining pins into her pocket.

"My life is far less exciting than any of those things would suggest," she said.

"Then you've come to Canada to study the birds or collect pinecones?"

"No." Mollie was reluctant to tell a vampire anything about her, but she found herself wanting to reveal more to him because she liked him, even if he thirsted for blood. "My mom was from Canada, and she still had family here. Her last living uncle, and the last of her family, recently passed away. After Aida and I attended his funeral, we decided to take a more scenic route back to Rhode Island rather than sticking to the highway. We figured we'd probably never come this far north again; we planned to see more of the land and maybe hike some trails. It was supposed to be an adventure, but this is *not* what I had in mind."

"What about your mom? Why didn't she come with you?"

"She died from breast cancer two years ago."

"I'm sorry."

"It's okay. She was diagnosed when I was eighteen, and she fought it for three years."

He sensed her grief in the set of her shoulders and the avoidance of her gaze. "And then she lost the battle."

"She didn't lose anything!" Mollie retorted. "I hate when people say that. She struggled through things no human should have to deal with, and by saying she lost, it sounds as if you're negating everything she went through before she passed. She battled cancer and beat it for years; that makes her a winner in every sense of the word."

The vehemence of her words astounded him, but he understood what she was saying. He almost told her sorry again but suspected that would only make her angrier.

Mollie ducked her head to wipe away the single tear sliding down her cheek. It had been two years since her mother's passing. For the last year of her life, Mollie knew her mother was dying, so she'd prepared herself for it, but it hadn't mattered. Her heart still broke the day her mother stopped breathing, and she continued to grieve the woman who'd been her rock.

Mike rested his hand comfortingly on her shoulder. She stiffened beneath his touch, but she didn't try to pull away.

"After she passed, I got custody of Aida, who was sixteen at the time. I was twenty-one. I swore I'd protect her and give her as normal a life as possible…"

Mollie's voice trailed off, and she shrugged away from his touch. She didn't feel like being comforted while her sister was in the hands of monsters. Not when Aida could already be dead too. For a second, she couldn't breathe through the lump clogging her throat.

She'd vowed to keep Aida safe, and she'd failed.

"I don't want to talk anymore," she said.

"Okay." Mike was beginning to realize part of the reason she didn't reveal much about herself was because some of it was too painful, and though he wanted to learn more about her, he wasn't going to push.

They didn't speak again as they made their way through the woods and toward a hill rising high on the horizon. They were halfway up the hill when Mike caught the first, faint whiff of the ocean.

CHAPTER FOURTEEN

"Stay here," Mike said when they arrived at the edge of the forest.

Before them, the hill rose another fifty feet before plateauing into something he couldn't see. No trees or any other cover dotted the open expanse of land.

Mollie grabbed his arm when he went to step out of the trees. "You can't just stroll out there."

"I have to get a better understanding of our surroundings and what we're dealing with."

"Dying isn't going to help you do that."

"I'll be out in the sun, and I'll be fine."

"But what if it isn't a Savage lying in wait, or what if it's a Savage who can still tolerate daylight? What if one of their human sidekicks with wooden bullets is out there? What if it's a freaking trap?"

Mike squeezed her hand on his arm. "I can take care of a human."

Mollie scowled at him. "Great, so you kill the human and end up being weakened by it too, or they put a bullet through your heart, and you don't have to worry about any of this anymore."

He had to see more of what they were dealing with here and try to learn if they were anywhere near civilization, but her terror weakened his resolve. "We'll continue running parallel through the trees until we find someplace better to see what's on the other side of the hill." Judging by the increased briny scent on the air, and the distant crash of waves, it was the ocean, but that didn't mean there was *only* water out there. "But the day is nearly half over, Mollie. We have to figure out where we are, formulate a plan, and find somewhere to bed down before the sun sets."

Mollie twisted her arm over to look at the man's wristwatch she wore. Mike's eyes narrowed on the watch as he wondered about its original owner, an ex-boyfriend perhaps? But if she still wore it, then it was most likely a current boyfriend. The idea of possible competition for her made his teeth grind together, but he could handle competition, and he would win.

Her forehead furrowed before she glanced at the sky. "I didn't realize it was so late already."

Taking her hand, Mike glanced left and right as he tried to decide which way to go before heading to the left. They hurried through the woods, running parallel to what he assumed were cliffs. They traveled nearly a mile before they encountered a sagging house on the edge of the woods.

The house had once been white, but years of neglect chipped away most of the paint. The front porch lay in pieces, and the rotting pile of wood from it covered half of the battered door. Glass remained in only a few of the windows; those panes were wavy and distorted by age. Holes marked the brown façade. On the far side of the house, the top half of a fallen pine leaning against the brick chimney partially blocked the view of the lighthouse at the end of the home.

The main section of the house was double story, but beyond that, the home turned into a single-story structure connecting to the easily hundred-foot-tall lighthouse. A front yard of about fifteen feet separated the building from the cliffs beyond as he could see the edge of the sudden drop-off now. No glass remained in the windows of the lighthouse, and it had probably been years since any light shone from it, but if he could get up there, he could see for miles.

"Stay here," he said to Mollie. "If you hear or see anything, yell for me."

Her mouth pursed. "You're not going in there."

"The lighthouse might be our only chance of learning anything more about where we are before nightfall."

"I don't think that building is going to support your weight."

"I'll be fine."

"Then I'm coming with you."

"You'll be safer out here."

"I'm capable of deciding where I'll be safer, and I'd like to see more too. Plus, I'm not going to stand out here while you fall through the floor and break a leg or stake yourself on a board on the way down."

His eyebrows shot up. "I'll survive a fall, but what if you go through and the floor breaks your neck?"

"I weigh less than you, and I'll follow you to make sure the wood will support me."

He couldn't argue with her reasoning, and he'd prefer not to have her out of his sight. He hated leaving her this morning, but it had been necessary for him to hunt. Throughout the day, he'd seen no sign of anyone else in the woods, yet they were out there. He would sense someone if they were close, but once he went inside, Mollie couldn't sense someone approaching.

If he could find Jack or Doug, he'd have some help. He'd hoped to find some trace of them over the course of the day but discovered nothing. By now, they could be fifty miles or more apart and all of them in different directions. Plus, Doug and Jack probably didn't have a human slowing them down. They would bring back help if they found it, but until then, he and Mollie were on their own.

"Okay, let's go," he said, and clasping her hand, he led her to the back of the battered house.

Over the years, the woods had crept in to reclaim their land and now crowded the back half of the house. He pulled pine branches out of the way and held them aside for Mollie to duck under before following her. Closer to the home, thick bramble bushes swarmed the bottom of the two steps leading toward the open doorway.

Settling his hands on Mollie's waist, he lifted her over the thick thorns and set her inside the doorway. Unable to lift himself over the bushes, they tore at his jeans and sliced his skin as he battered them beneath his feet and pulled them out of his way. The steps sagged and creaked beneath his weight but held firm until he stepped into the doorway.

Mollie had already made her way to the center of the old kitchen when Mike's shadow spilled over her feet. The layer of dirt and rotting leaves covering the floor was so thick she couldn't see what lay beneath. Mollie's nose wrinkled at the potent stench of mildew and rotting wood filling the air.

Spiders and other bugs didn't bother to skitter out of the way as they explored; the insects had claimed this house as theirs, and they weren't giving it up without a fight. It was a battle she was more than happy to let them win.

Two pots sat on the burners of the dust-covered, cast iron stove. When she peeked into the pots, she discovered one was filled with debris, but the other had a ladle leaning against the inside of it. Mollie turned away from the stove as Mike stalked across the kitchen to the doorway leading out. Her gaze fell on the table and the four, grime-covered plates sitting on it.

"Mollie," Mike said, but she ignored him as she approached the table.

Two of the chairs were turned over and lay a few feet away from the table. The wind, animals, or any number of things could have caused the chairs to have fallen over the years. However, Mollie couldn't shake the idea the prior residents of this home were sitting at the table when something caused them to flee.

The walls of this house held secrets, and she heard them whispering to her in every creak of the old wood, but she didn't know what they were trying to reveal. Mollie rested her hand on a tarnished spoon as she tried to picture the family who once resided here.

"Mollie," Mike said again. "We don't have a lot of time."

Reluctantly, Mollie stepped away from the table and followed him from the kitchen. Mike ducked through each of the doorways as they passed into the dining room and then beyond to the living room. They made their way swiftly through the rotting furniture that would have been considered new during World War II.

When they moved from the double-story house to the single-story section, they encountered a raccoon. The creature screeched its displeasure at them before darting into a hole. Mollie's hand tightened on the strap of her rifle; she didn't mind wild animals, but she'd read *Cujo,* and she was not about to take any chances. The raccoon was smaller than a Saint Bernard, but it could still do some damage with those claws. Plus, rabies was not on her bucket list of things to try.

"Do you think there are any bats in the lighthouse?" she asked Mike.

"It's probably too cold for them up there."

"Good."

Mike stopped outside the closed door of the next room and gripped the handle. The rotten knob broke off in his hand. He tossed it aside and slid his fingers into the hole the missing knob created. The old, swollen wood groaned before a crack zigzagged down the middle of the door and it splintered apart.

Gripping the edges, Mike tore the pieces away with an ease that left her gawking. When he succeeded in clearing the wood, he froze before turning toward her.

"Mollie, stay there."

His hand shot out to stop her from stepping forward, but she'd already seen what he was trying to keep from her. Resting her hand on his arm, she pushed it down as she gazed at the bodies within.

In the corner of the room, four corpses sat against the wall. Their eyes had rotted away, but their gray skin was strangely mummified as none of their bones showed through it. A knot formed in her stomach as something niggled at the back of her mind. There was something so *wrong* about this, but she couldn't quite put her finger on what.

The corpse wearing a necklace and a golden wedding band had its arms draped across the shoulders of two smaller bodies. While the other, larger corpse had its hand over the leg of one of the smaller bodies and resting on the thigh of the one with the necklace.

Mollie realized she was gazing at a family. She suspected they were the same family who fled their kitchen in the middle of a meal, but what had they attempted to run from?

She didn't know the answer, but the more she inspected them, the more they seemed entirely out of place. They'd fled here and, what, died sitting together like that? Why hadn't they left through one of the windows or continued on to the lighthouse to send out a distress signal?

She bit her lip as she shuddered. The furniture in this place was nearly a hundred years old, and *all* of it was rotting, yet these people appeared…

"Desiccated," she whispered.

Mike gazed at the corpses while Mollie's word reverberated in his mind. These people certainly hadn't progressed through the stages of decay normally, but only a vampire could have drained them so completely of blood.

"There were four plates at the table," Mollie said. "The chairs were turned over as if they were fleeing something, and they should be nothing but bones if they lived here in the thirties or forties, which is the time period everything in this home appears to be from."

"These might not be the corpses of the family who originally lived here. If the Savages have brought other humans and vampires here, this could be an entirely different family, and they might not have died all that long ago."

"Their clothing, or what little remains of it, looks pretty old to me."

"Isn't vintage a thing with humans now?"

"Maybe for some, but..." But none of the bodies had enough rotting clothing left on them to make much of a distinction about it. Maybe it was new vintage, but then wouldn't there be more of it left? All that remained were tatters except for the set of shoes on the other bigger corpse, which she assumed was a man because of those shoes. "Something's not right here."

Mike wanted to tell her it was fine, they had enough to deal with without adding the mystery of the desiccated corpses to it, but she was right. Something *was* wrong here. He stepped into the room with the family and knelt beside them.

Leaning forward, he inspected the woman's corpse. He guessed it was a woman only because of the oval-shaped, faded gold necklace she wore. Other than that, she barely looked different from the other, nearly naked, adult corpse.

Grasping the necklace, he pulled it toward him and examined the squiggly etching on the outside. Pushing the button on the side, he was surprised when the old lock clicked and the locket opened. Mike realized the engravings on the outside were ivy leaves only because of the inscription inside the locket: *To Ivy. With love, Harry. 5/1/38.*

"They're not recent corpses," Mike murmured as he looked at the woman's wedding ring.

"How do you know that?" Mollie asked.

Mike read the inscription to her before settling the necklace against the woman's chest.

"Did vampires do this?" she demanded.

Mike leaned closer to inspect the woman's neck but didn't see anything there. He did find marks on the man's neck and one of the children's wrists. The other two corpses were bitten in a place hidden by their decomposition, and he wasn't going to search for the marks.

"Yes," he said.

Mollie glanced nervously behind her. She had the unsettling feeling of eyes staring at her from the shadows, but these weren't the eyes of the living. No, these were the burning red eyes of the irate ghost family haunting this place. The hair on her arms stood on end as she cursed her overactive imagination, but once the image weaseled its way into her mind, it remained lodged there.

"You said, *'Lately, there has been a growing movement to turn more vamps and humans Savage.'* I realize you're immortal and your concept of time is probably different than mine, but I took lately to mean within the past few months, maybe a year. Hell, I'll give you *two* years. However, these people have been lying here for about eighty years. If there were vampires here then…" Mollie's voice trailed off as she looked helplessly toward the bodies. "They just killed them; they didn't try to turn them into something else."

Mike rested his hands on his knees before rising. "No, they didn't try to turn them."

"What is going on here?"

"I don't know. The vampires could have come in and killed this family so they could take over this piece of land. Those vamps could have been here all this time and only recently decided to start turning others into Savages, or they could be doing something else here."

"What?"

"I don't know."

"Have you ever read *The Island of Doctor Moreau*?"

"Many times. I'm not much of a reader, but H.G. Wells is one of the few authors I enjoy."

Mollie couldn't help but smile over this revelation; the man had taste. "What if this is something like that? What if these vamps are performing experiments on humans and vampires and have been for years? What if we weren't in those cages to be turned into Savages or used for food, but for something far worse?"

"It's possible, but I believe it is more likely they meant to turn us. These vamps may have been in the area for years, and these people paid the unfortunate price for that, but the Savages want blood and more vampires like them, not experiments."

"Hmm," Mollie grunted doubtfully.

"Come on; we should check out the lighthouse."

CHAPTER FIFTEEN

Mollie's knees were knocking together by the time she stepped off the last rickety stair and into the top of the lighthouse. She'd been convinced that with every step she took, the stairs would collapse and she would plummet to her death. A cold sweat coated her body, but entering the lighthouse didn't make her feel any safer. Instead, she just had farther to fall if the rotten floor gave way.

A three-foot-wide path separated the outer half walls of the lighthouse from the inner half walls protecting the area where the flame once warned ships away from the land. The glass from the broken outer and inner windows once encircling the lighthouse tower and its beacon littered the floor along with debris from nearby trees. Chips of white paint remained on the outer and inner walls of the structure.

She winced when a pinecone crunched beneath her feet, and Mike glanced back at her. The sound wasn't any louder than usual, but she felt as if she'd rung the dinner bell for every bloodthirsty vamp in the area.

Mollie crept carefully behind him to the front of the round structure and rested her hands on the wall. Beneath her palms, the wood was more mushy than solid; she pulled her hands away when dozens of pill bugs and centipedes spilled out to skitter across the wood.

Shuddering, Mollie wiped her hands on her jeans, but it did nothing to erase the feel of the wood and bugs from her flesh.

Mollie took a deep breath and looked away from the rotting wood to the sea beyond. From here she could see that the cliffs dropped a good hundred feet to the white-capped ocean below. In some spots, massive boulders jutting up from the sea broke the waves and sent white plumes of spray into the air. To her left and right, more waves crashed against the rock walls of the cliffs until the forest swallowed her view of them.

Seagulls cawed as they banked through the air before diving toward the rocks where hundreds of them had settled. Dozens of gray seals sunned themselves on the rocks while others leapt into the water to catch fish or play.

The spectacular vista was so out of place with the events of the past few days that, for a second, Mollie almost forgot where they were and what happened. Something this beautiful could *not* coexist with the horror they endured. But coexist it did, and though it was beautiful, it offered them no hope for help or finding Aida.

However, if she did end up dying here, she was glad she got to see this first. When the sea breeze brushed against something wet on her cheeks, Mollie realized tears were sliding down her face. She wiped them hastily away before spinning and striding to the other side of the tower. Mike went the opposite way around the structure and met her there.

Whereas the other side was beauty and the promise of the known, this side was beauty and the promise of the unknown. For as far as she could see, trees spread out in all directions. In the center of the seemingly endless trees, a large barn and acres of cleared land were visible.

Behind the barn, the burned-out remains of a crumbled building lay scattered across the ground. She suspected it was once the farmhouse that went with the barn, and that whoever had lived there didn't survive the fire.

Mike studied the terrain as he tried to formulate a plan for their next move. Beyond the barn, the woods stretched out for acres again, but he saw the hint of a brick chimney sticking up from the trees. His angle and the trees made it impossible to tell if another clearing surrounded the building, what the building was, or if there was more than one, but something was there.

It had to be where the Savages were staying, as the distance between it and the barn would explain the time it took for the Savages to reach them last night. He also didn't see anywhere else the Savages could be staying, but that didn't mean the forest wasn't hiding more buildings.

Mike glanced at the sea behind him before looking toward the land again; they had no choice but to head back toward the barn.

"All I see is the barn," Mollie muttered. "And I *know* Aida isn't in the barn, or at least she wasn't."

Mike realized her human eyes hadn't detected the chimney. "There's another building beyond the barn. It's a few miles away. I'm not sure if it's another home or something else, but I see part of the chimney."

"We'll go there," Mollie said. "That must be where Aida is."

"Maybe."

He didn't want to get her hopes up about finding her sister. Thousands of acres of woods surrounded them, and he had no idea how far the forest stretched beyond what he could see. They could pass within half a mile of where her sister was, or closer, and never know it. Plus, he doubted any Savage kept a human alive this long without changing them. And if the Savages had changed Aida, Mollie's sister might be beyond saving, but he couldn't bring himself to tell her that.

"We should get down before someone spots us," he said.

Clasping her elbow, he pulled her away from the rotted railing and led her down the rickety stairs to the ground floor. Mollie kept her head averted from the corpses as they made their way out of the room.

"We'll search the rest of the house for anything we can use before we leave," Mike said.

"We're not staying here tonight?" The idea of spending the night in a house with corpses made her skin crawl, but they had shelter here, something they might not have if they went out there again.

"No. There are too many ways someone could get inside to defend them all. Someone could enter without us knowing."

Mollie hid her disappointment; he was right after all, but she was less than thrilled about having to return to the woods. She would have loved the chance to give her aching feet and legs a break. She was used to hiking, physically fit, and thankfully she'd swapped her clothes and dress shoes for sneakers after the funeral, but she was not used to this terrain, walking for so many hours, and going without water. Adrenaline continued to be her primary source of fuel, but exhaustion was starting to win out. However, she would keep going no matter what it took, and she would not complain about it.

Together, they made their way back through the rooms on the first floor before climbing to the second. Three doors led off the shadowed hall there, and they were all open to reveal the bedrooms beyond.

Mollie was halfway through searching the second bedroom when she realized the house didn't have a bathroom in it. She paused for a moment as it hit her just how frozen in time this place was. Again, she had the feeling of being watched, but she refused to give in to the impulse to look behind her as she worked, because if she saw a ghost family, it might be the straw that broke the camel's back.

In the last bedroom, an old trunk sat at the foot of the bed. Mollie blew the coating of dust off the cover, then coughed and waved her hand in front of her face when the particles floated into the air around her. Opening the trunk, she bit back a delighted cry when she spotted the quilt inside.

She pulled the thin blanket from the cedar chest and shook it out. Age had yellowed the white patches on it, but the blue and green diamond pattern was still evident. The reek of mildew clung to it, but the quilt was in good shape. Refolding it, Mollie tucked it beneath her arm and closed the trunk. It would be annoying to carry, but she didn't care, she wasn't giving up the blanket.

"Did you find anything?" Mike asked when he appeared in the doorway. He'd gone back downstairs to raid the kitchen.

Mollie held up her quilt. "I did. How about you?"

He pointed to a tarnished silver cup and small pot; he'd slid his belt through the handles to secure his find to his waist. He'd been careful to keep them apart, so they wouldn't clink together when he moved. "For when we find water for you."

She would have drooled at the prospect, if her mouth wasn't so dry.

THE SUN WAS TOUCHING the edge of the horizon when Mike discovered the small alcove created by a pile of rocks. Years of erosion caused the stones to rise out of the earth and lean against each other in such a way they created a small cave.

Mike bent to peer inside the alcove. The space was about five feet deep and four feet high and would help keep them warm against the growing wind coming off the ocean only fifty yards away.

"We can stay here for the night," Mike said as he rose to survey the woods. "I'll gather some branches to cover the entrance and mask our scents."

"I'll help you."

Mollie tossed the quilt into the shelter and went to help Mike gather dead branches and rocks. When they had enough supplies, they crawled inside the small cave and used them to block the entrance. They worked until only a bit of fading sunlight filtered through the branches covering the opening. Mike used some of the smaller rocks, dirt, and forest debris to plug the larger holes while Mollie retreated to the back of the shelter.

Her breath sounded abnormally loud in the small space as she gathered the quilt and settled against the rocks at the back. Draping the blanket around her shoulders, she used it to block out the coldness of the stones. She propped the rifle against her knees while she watched the daylight fade completely.

"What if they find us?" she whispered.

"Then we'll kill them."

He said this as if taking a life was so simple, but then, if it came between her and one of those things, Mollie would gladly take them all down. Her fingers stroked the barrel of the gun as she strained to hear anything beyond the rocks.

Aida. Closing her eyes, she refused to shed the tears that thoughts of her sister brought to her eyes.

A strange, animalistic howl pierced the night. Mollie gripped the rifle closer as a shiver ran down her spine. "Are there wolves in Canada?"

"That wasn't a wolf," Mike said.

"Then what was it?"

"The Savages are hunting."

Mollie gulped. "They're not very stealthy about it."

Mike turned away from the barrier, and undoing his belt, he pulled the pot and cup free. Setting them on the ground, he crept toward her. When he settled in beside her, his shoulder brushed hers in the small space.

"They'll be stealthy when they're homing in on someone; now, they're trying to intimidate their prey," he said.

"So, when they go silent someone is in trouble?"

"Yes."

Mollie lifted the quilt from her shoulder and held a piece of it out to him. He took it from her and slid under it. His body warmed her far more than the quilt, and she found herself melting against him.

It made no sense, he could kill her as easily as any of those things, but she felt a thousand times safer with him by her side.

Draping his arm around Mollie's shoulders, he cradled her protectively against him.

"I'll keep you safe," he promised.

CHAPTER SIXTEEN

A BLOOD-CURDLING SCREAM jolted Mollie awake. She went to bolt upright, but a hand on her shoulder kept her restrained from leaping to her feet.

A hand! Why is someone touching me?

Panic flooded her, and a scream lodged in her throat as some instinct told her to remain silent. She searched desperately for the source of that hand, or to see *any*thing, but the darkness was absolute. She went to jerk away from the hand, but Mike's whispered words froze her in place.

"It's okay."

The memories of the past few days crashed over her, and Mollie relaxed beneath his grip. Another scream pierced the night and rose higher until it bounced off the walls. She clasped her hands over her ears as the person's agony dug into her until she was certain it became a part of her. Mike held her against his chest and rested one of his hands over her ear.

The scream abruptly cut off, leaving them in nerve-racking silence. Mollie slowly lowered her hands as she pressed closer against him. Mike's heart lumbered beneath her other ear while his chest rose steadily. She didn't have to witness what happened; she knew the screamer was dead.

Mike lowered his hand from Mollie's ear when she sat up beside him again. In the rays of the moon filtering through the cracks of their barrier, he could barely make out her extraordinary eyes. She looked helplessly at him before turning her attention to the front of their hiding place.

"That didn't come from too close by," Mike assured her.

"How do you know?" she whispered.

"By the sound quality."

Another howl pierced the night, and then the maniacal, hideous bastards out there hunting the escapees *laughed*. She loathed them all.

"Is that the first one they've caught?" she asked.

"No."

She'd slept through the death of at least one other then. Gripping the rifle, she drew it closer and held it against her chest as more howls answered the first. The final cry sounded far too close for her liking.

When she tensed against him, Mike ran his hand over her hair to soothe her, but she didn't curl up and relax against him as she had while sleeping. He'd enjoyed the warmth of her body, the feel of her fingers against his chest, and her steady breaths.

Then the Savages caught the scent of their prey and woke her.

And he was glad she was awake because he needed her to help ground him. He despised it, but a part of him was as enticed by the prospect of the hunt as it repulsed him. He hated those things out there, he'd rather die than become one of them, but he could not deny his vampire nature, and it was lethal.

His hands stilled on her hair before sliding around to clasp her head. He tugged her gently toward him and held her against his chest. She remained rigid before gradually relaxing and melting into his embrace.

He rested his lips against her ear as he spoke. "It will be okay."

Mollie didn't reply; she was too afraid something might hear her words. She cuddled closer to him as the excited sounds of the chase outside amped up before cutting off. In the ensuing quiet, the tick of Mollie's watch sounded abnormally loud.

She didn't know how much time passed before a woman screamed and excited shrieks pierced the night.

SHE DIDN'T THINK she'd ever sleep again, but somewhere near dawn, when the howls and screams died away, she drifted off again. When she woke, she discovered light filtering through their barrier and Mike's cheek resting on top of her head as he snored softly. He must have fallen asleep after her.

She should wake him; they had to get moving, but he'd slept less than her, and she didn't want to disturb him. Glancing at her watch, she saw it was only seven. She'd give him another hour.

Leaning into him, she ignored the aches in her tired legs as she inhaled his scent and savored the strength of his large body against hers. She'd dated a handful of guys over the years—nothing serious as she always had so much going on in her life, but all of them were about her height or shorter and barely weighed more than she did.

Aida claimed she went for the mousier guys because she didn't have anything to fear from them. She'd wanted to tell Aida that was ridiculous, but it wasn't. Mollie couldn't deny she *did* go for guys she wouldn't become attached to.

Over the years, she had enough counseling to know that when she was younger, her number one relationship was anorexia. As she grew older, she came to terms with her disorder and gained control over her eating in time for her mother's cancer diagnosis.

Her mother, having fought Mollie's battle with her, had spent many sleepless nights worrying Mollie would destroy herself. After the diagnosis, it became Mollie's turn to lie awake worrying cancer would destroy her mother.

Determined to make up for the terror she inadvertently put her mother through during the worst of her eating disorder, Mollie vowed to care for her mother until she was better. That day never came. Then she'd taken care of Aida.

She never resented any of it, but for many years, she'd put her life on hold and never really experienced what so many others did as a teen and twenty-something-year-old.

When she was younger, her anorexia kept her from doing many things. She'd avoided parties where there would be too much tempting food and shunned places where she might have to wear something revealing, like swimming pools. At her lowest weight, she was less than a hundred pounds and convinced she was fat. Far too often, she'd stood in front of a mirror, pinching her skin and hating herself for the supposed fat she saw on her hips and belly.

Not to mention, she'd been depressed, withdrawn, and too tired to embrace all the adventures her friends from high school were experiencing. In the beginning, her friends had called to get her to join them, but they gave up after she kept refusing, and she didn't blame them; by then, she'd given up too.

When her mother realized what was going on, Mollie was already well-engrossed in her disorder. Her mother put her in counseling, and at first, she resisted. Anorexia was the only friend Mollie had by that point, and she refused to lose it. However, after a while, some of what the counselor said started making sense, and she started seeing what others did—she was destroying herself, her mother, and Aida.

It was an uphill battle, but by the time she was seventeen, she'd gained enough confidence that she stopped locking herself away and her obsession with food eased. Mollie still struggled with her disorder, she probably always would, but she would *not* slip away again. Her mother would be so disappointed in her if she did, and she would not let Aida or herself down in that way.

During her senior year in high school, some of the friends she'd pushed away came back, she made new ones, and went on a couple of dates. She attended prom with her best friend who wanted more than she did, but he took it well when she turned him down.

Then, her mother got sick, and dating was the last thing on Mollie's mind. She gave up the idea of college, went to work, took her mom to her appointments, and made sure Aida's life remained as normal as possible.

After her mother died, she went on a few dates with a guy from work and tried a couple of online sites to meet men, but she never found one who excited her.

She'd never gone for the burlier guys, but she found herself extremely attracted to the one whose breath ruffled her hair with every one of his exhalations. Mollie felt more for this man in the short time she'd known him than any of the other men she'd dated for a couple of months.

With everything she knew about his life, getting involved with him would be the biggest mistake of her life, but she couldn't stop her fingers from running down the center of his chest and over the chiseled abs beneath. She bit her bottom lip as excitement pulsed to life in her.

Mike's fingers twitched on Mollie's shoulder before his head jerked up. Beneath her ear, his heart raced while he surveyed their small enclosure. When Mollie ran her hand over his chest in an instinctive effort to calm him, he eased against her before clasping her hand and flattening it against his chest.

Mollie didn't try to pull away when his thumb rubbed the back of her hand before rising to her wrist and then up her arm. Warmth pooled in her belly and spread through her limbs as her breath caught in her throat. When his fingers slid under her chin, she didn't resist him when he turned her head to his.

Mike stared into her turbulent eyes as she gazed at him with longing and trepidation. He should pull away, take down their barrier, and leave this place; they had to use every bit of daytime they could to their advantage, but he found himself unable to resist her. She inhaled sharply when he bent his head and brushed his lips against hers.

Mollie forgot all about the fact her morning breath would probably make a dragon tuck tail and run when his mouth settled over hers. If her breath didn't scare off the guy with the super senses, it couldn't be as bad as she believed, and then she stopped caring about it as his mouth burned into hers until she felt branded by his kiss.

Her toes curled, her hands gripped his forearms as his tongue flickered over her lips, and she opened her mouth to him. She'd expected him to plunge in and thrust his tongue against hers; instead, he leisurely explored her as he stroked her lips again before slipping in to caress her mouth.

Never had she been savored in such a way, but she felt as if he were memorizing every detail of her. Her head spun from the heady sensation, and she found herself slipping further away from reality as their small space, and all the danger of the last few days, slid away until it was only the two of them.

The taste of her reminded Mike of the apples he'd picked and eaten on his grandparent's farm. She was as sweet as those apples, and he wanted to gorge on her as he had them; except, she wouldn't give him the belly ache the apples had. No, she would give him the release he'd been seeking from his increasingly lonely, mundane life.

She was what he'd been seeking and missing.

Releasing her chin, he wrapped his hand around her head and drew her closer as he deepened the kiss. He settled his other hand on her hip beneath the quilt. Her palms slid up from his chest, over his shoulders, and around his neck. Her breasts pressed against his chest, and his cock stiffened when he felt the puckering of her nipples through her bra and shirt.

Mike growled and pulled her into his lap to nestle her there. The quilt tangled between them, but he jerked it aside before trailing his hand up her side to clasp her breast, which was a little smaller than his hand. With his thumb, he rubbed the puckered bud of her nipple and relished the arch of her body against his hand when she sought more of his touch.

Against her ass, Mollie felt his erection. Before, such a sensation with someone she barely knew would have frightened her, but now it aroused her further. She didn't know him, and he wasn't human, yet for some inexplicable reason, she felt more comfortable with him than she ever had with anyone else.

In such a short time, Mike had managed to get past the barriers she started constructing the day her father walked out of their lives when she was seven and Aida was two. For years, the image of her father standing in the doorway with his suitcase haunted her, but not so much as the moment he walked out the door. He hadn't so much as glanced back or waved behind him while Mollie sobbed in her mother's arms and pleaded for him to return.

The memory of her father's betrayal caused something within Mollie to recoil. The desire of seconds ago faded away as the pain of the past returned. No matter how stoically her mother forged ahead without her husband, Mollie had often woken to hear her crying in the middle of the night. And on those nights, Mollie vowed never to let a man break her heart in such a way.

Mike was not one of those mousy guys who could never own a piece of her. He would get inside her heart and tear it out before she could stop him, and she would *not* allow that.

Mike sensed a change in Mollie before she broke their kiss and turned her head away. His dick and fangs throbbed with their need to be inside her, but his hand stilled on her breast.

"Mollie—"

"We should go; we have to move while we can."

She scrambled from his lap when he eased his hands away from her. Mike battled his disappointment while she folded the quilt and gathered the rifle. She didn't look at him as she worked.

CHAPTER SEVENTEEN

When Mollie glanced at her watch, she saw it was almost one o'clock before Mike stopped walking and settled onto a group of boulders. Striding away from him, Mollie stopped at the edge of the cliff and gazed at the water a couple of hundred feet below.

In this area, the woods offered them shelter right up to the cliffs, and the cliffs were higher than they'd been by the lighthouse. She tasted the salty water on her lips as the wind whipped up the sea. Usually, she would have found it all soothing and beautiful, but she had no idea where they were, where her sister was, or where the monsters hunting them were, and nothing was comforting in that.

Despite her aching feet, trembling legs, grumbling stomach, severe thirst, and all-around misery, Mollie would have preferred to keep walking. Stopped again, she might have to look at Mike, and she couldn't do that without blushing.

Move away from the edge! Mike snarled the command in his head as Mollie stood far too close to the cliff for his liking. He bit back the harsh words in case they startled her into stepping over the edge.

"I'm going to find you something to eat," Mike said.

When Mollie turned, she discovered he'd risen from the rocks and stood only a few feet away. She'd never heard him move. "I'm good. I can go longer without eating."

"And how much longer can you go without water?"

That she couldn't continue much further without. The ache in her head was from dehydration, as was the cramping in her legs. It was a good thing it wasn't hot out, and Mike had done the running, or she would have dropped by now.

Mike's jaw clenched when Mollie glanced away from him. She was hungry, thirsty, exhausted, and weakening from it. She lagged more and more with every passing hour and mile they traversed. His fangs pricked and slid halfway free before he regained enough control of himself to retract them.

He studied the slouch of her shoulders and listened to the steady beat of her heart. She was so strong in some ways, yet so weak in her mortality. *She doesn't have to be.*

The impulse to change her following on the heels of the sudden thought rocked him back a step. His fangs slid free when his gaze fell on the delicate curve of her neck. He could change her, make her immortal, take away her mortal hunger and thirst, and replace it with an inhuman one far more incessant than the ones she dealt with now.

Struggling to get baser instincts he'd never possessed before under control, Mike turned away from her. Years ago, he'd learned how to deal with his thirst for blood, but he'd never dealt with this compulsion to change another. He'd never expected to have to deal with it unless he encountered his mate and she turned out to be mortal.

Mike's head swiveled toward where Mollie stood at the edge of the cliff as a new idea occurred to him.

Is she my mate? His fangs lengthened again as he contemplated the possibility while studying her. He'd never reacted to someone the way he did her, but they'd barely spent any time together. However, in the short time they'd been together, he'd come to know her better than most of the other women he'd encountered over the years, and unlike them, he planned to learn *more* about Mollie.

He had to get her out of this mess before something happened to her. He didn't know how he would react if that occurred.

But first, he had to take care of her.

"There's water nearby," he said.

"How do you know?"

"I can smell it," he said. "And where there is water, there will also be animals to hunt."

"I'm coming with you."

He didn't disagree with her; he wasn't ready to let her out of his sight. "Come on." He held his hand out to her.

After a hesitation, Mollie took it and ducked her head as a blush crept into her cheeks. She couldn't bring herself to look at him again while he led her through the woods. When they arrived at the small stream, Mike released her to hunt, while Mollie made her way to the edge of the shallow creek.

Around her, the birds sang and fluttered through the trees, but even they seemed more subdued than typical birds. It was as if they couldn't erase the horrors of the night from their minds either. Kneeling, she pushed up the sleeves of her shirt and washed away some of the grime on her hands. If her mouth weren't so dry, she would have drooled at the tantalizing water sliding through her fingers and over her skin.

Do not drink it. Do not drink it. She had to repeat this over and over again as she resisted cupping her hands and bringing the cold water to her lips.

Unable to take any more, she retreated from the creek and settled on a rock with her back to the water. Shrugging the rifle off, she held it before her as she studied the woods and listened for anything unusual while Mike stalked the forest animals.

MOLLIE CLIMBED out from between the branches of the pine tree Mike helped her climb into before he went to cook the squirrel and rabbit he captured. The scent of the pine and the thick needles kept her hidden from anyone who happened by—no one did.

Her mouth watered as the scent of the cooked creatures drifted to her, but more than that, she focused on the cup of water he handed to her like it was the lifeline it was. In his other hand, he held a pot full of more tempting water, and tied together by a strip of fur, the rabbit and squirrel dangled over his shoulder.

She restrained herself from snatching the water from him and gulping it down. She'd make herself sick if she did, especially on her empty stomach, and vomiting would not help her dehydration. Lifting the cup to her mouth, she took a couple of small sips of the hot water.

She swished it in her mouth before swallowing. Reluctantly setting the cup aside, she grasped the squirrel and rabbit he offered her. She was so hungry she didn't bother to think about how cute they were when they still had fur.

"Where did you learn to shoot a rifle?" Mike asked when she tossed the squirrel remains aside.

Mollie wiped her mouth with the back of her hand before replying. "My mom rarely came back to visit her family in Canada after she left because it was so far away, but she grew up around hunters, and though she didn't like hunting, she enjoyed shooting. She believed her daughters should know about guns too, and when each of us turned thirteen, she took us to a firing range and started teaching us."

"Can you use other guns too?"

"Yes. I'm no sharpshooter, but I hit my target more often than I miss it."

"That's good." She may be weak in her mortality, but at least she had this advantage over the Savages stalking them.

"Yeah," Mollie said before turning her attention to the rabbit.

"What about your dad?" he asked.

Mollie's fingers froze on the rabbit before she lifted her head to look at him. "What about him?"

She willingly spoke of her mother, but hostility shimmered in her eyes and her shoulders stiffened at the mention of her father. Mike was eager to learn more about her, but her father appeared to be a touchy subject. Uncertain of how to proceed, he decided *carefully* was his best option.

"You've never mentioned him," he said.

"Why would I? He was barely a part of my life. When I was seven, he walked out the door and never looked back."

"I'm sorry."

"Why? *He's* the asshole, not you."

Well, at least she didn't consider him an asshole; Mike supposed that was a bonus.

"He was thoughtful enough to send us a card after our mom died. Though, he did spell my name with a y instead of an ie." Bitterness laced her voice as she ducked her head. "But I guess you forget how to spell your daughter's name when the last card you sent her was for her eleventh birthday. For years, I waited for another card with its five-dollar bill to show up. And then, on the day I turned seventeen, I realized it was never going to happen, and I stopped waiting."

Mike couldn't tell if she was angrier at herself or her father for those years of waiting, but he suspected it was more her.

"Aida doesn't remember him. She didn't realize who the condolence card was from until I told her, but I remember him, and I especially remember him leaving. I believed everything was perfect before that day; I was wrong."

CHAPTER EIGHTEEN

When Mollie grew silent, Mike hoped if he remained quiet, she would continue speaking, and after a few minutes, it worked.

"The man is the biggest cliché there is," she muttered. "He hit forty, had a midlife crisis, banged his twenty-something-year-old secretary, left his family for her, and moved to California. As far as I know, they're still together. I may have other siblings, but I never intend to find out how his life is going. He did put his number on the card and wrote he hoped we could talk, but I think it's better if I leave that door on my life closed."

Mollie saw Mike's gaze fall on her Rolex. "My grandpop's watch," she said. "He died ten years ago. After my father left, he assumed a more fatherly role in our lives."

Mollie's fingers brushed lovingly over the watch face as she recalled her grandpop's warm smile, the way he called her his Mollie-bug, taught her to fish, and would regale her with the stories of the fantasy worlds he created. Every one of his hugs was a bearhug where he lifted her off the ground and spun her around.

He'd helped with her homework; grocery shopped for her mom when she started working two jobs, cleaned their house, cooked them dinner, and loved them all until the day he died of a heart attack when she was thirteen.

She'd felt so out of control, lost, and broken after his passing. Back then, she'd still been foolish enough to believe her dad might want something to do with her again. She could never harbor such secret hopes about her grandpop coming back.

"His son is an asshole, but my grandpop was a good man who loved all of us very much. My father didn't bother to come back for his funeral."

Mike decided not to question her further about her father, but he did wonder if she'd kept the card or his number. "What do you do in Rhode Island?"

"What do you mean?"

"Do you go to college? Do you work?"

"I waitress during the day at a local diner and take a couple of online courses at night. I plan to take more classes online and maybe attend community college once Aida leaves for school, but I'll see how it goes. I put off going to college while my mom was sick so I could help with her care. After she died, I took over raising Aida. Aida's a *good* kid who has her head on straighter than most kids her age who have gone through far less than her, but after losing our mom, I vowed to give her as much of my time as I could. Now, I'm going to pursue a career."

"And what career is that?"

"I'm going get my masters and then my graduate degree in psychology. I plan to work with people who have eating disorders with a focus on teens."

The defiant way she held his gaze made him realize there was more to her revelation than helping people. "That's a pretty specific field," he said, unsure if he was wading into another minefield as he had with her father.

Mollie sipped her water as she contemplated how to respond, but something about Mike made it easier to open up to him than any of her therapists. "They say to do what you know, and I have some experience with eating disorders."

Mike's gaze raked her slender frame; she was lean, but a healthy weight for her height. Then he recalled her words from when they sheltered beside the river. *"It's okay; I'm used to going without eating."* At the time, he hadn't known what to make of those words, but he did now.

"Personal experience?" he asked.

"Yes."

"Do you still…?" Mike tried to think about how to ask the question.

"No. It's something I got a handle on before my mom's cancer diagnosis."

She stared at him for a minute before deciding to continue. She'd told him this much already.

Taking a deep breath, she told him about those years between thirteen and sixteen—the calorie counting, the hunger, the never being thin enough or good enough feeling that followed her everywhere. To her amazement, she revealed more to him than any of her therapists or the friends she made in her group sessions. She even admitted she'd occasionally purged too, though she hated doing it.

"At my lowest, I couldn't sleep because my hips or spine would dig into the mattress, and I couldn't walk upstairs without getting winded. Between my mother's constant worry and pushing me into counseling, and the knowledge that at fifteen, I couldn't climb a flight of stairs without feeling like my heart would explode, I finally agreed to get help.

"It took another year for me to understand my anorexia better and gain control of something I was certain *I* controlled. And in the end, that's what a lot of my disorder was about, having control over *something*. I couldn't control so many things in my life—my dad leaving, my grandpop dying, things with school and friends—but I could control what I ate."

When she finished, Mollie dreaded looking into his eyes and

seeing revulsion or pity there; she'd seen it so often in the gazes of her friends when they realized what she was doing to herself. However, in Mike's eyes, she saw no revulsion or pity; instead, there was only compassion.

"But you're healthy now?" he asked. Listening to her tale of fearing a heart attack while climbing stairs had caused his fangs to extend again.

"Very healthy. It's something I live with every day and probably will for the rest of my life, but I have a grip on it. I eat healthy; I do a lot of yoga as it helps to clear my mind, and I go for walks without tracking miles and calories burned. I stopped counting calories when I eat, I avoid the scale, and if I want a donut, I have it without punishing myself afterward.

"When my mom died, one of my first thoughts was that I couldn't eat, but I took a step back, regained control, and didn't slip into old patterns to handle a stressful situation and bury my grief. I never believed I'd ever get this far with it, and I'm proud of my accomplishments."

Mollie braced herself for the question nearly everyone asked: *why didn't you just eat?* As if it were that simple, as if she hadn't considered eating when she'd been so hungry it hurt, or drooling over a bagel with cream cheese before setting it aside?

She could easily recall the pride that reared its head when she restrained herself from eating something. That twisted pride in herself and how, in one small way, she was better than everyone else who ate whenever they were hungry while she didn't have to give in.

Mollie waited for the question, but it didn't come.

"Those kids will be lucky to have you on their side," he said.

Unexpected tears burned her eyes. He was so different than anyone else she knew, and with those words, he hammered down more of the defenses surrounding her heart.

"What about you? What do you do?" she asked to distract him from more questions about her.

Mike shrugged before rising and wiping his hands on his jeans.

He'd fed while cooking Mollie's food, but one glance at her neck made him hungry again. Typically, he could go a couple of days between feedings, but being around her pushed his restraint.

"For the past thirty years, I've helped raise my nieces and nephews, built houses, and lived life like I was retired, but it's been an interesting thirty years." He gave her a brief rundown of what happened with Liam, his wife Sera, their ten children, and the children of those children. He told her about Jack, David, and Doug and what they'd all been through over the years. "It's been a crazy time."

"Sounds like it," Mollie replied. "What did you do before you became a vampire?"

"I did the normal human things. Played with my friends, visited my grandparent's farm, went to high school, then to college. I was a linebacker on my high school and college football teams." He didn't tell her he'd been the star of those teams. It was so long ago, to brag about it now would put him in line with Al Bundy. Besides, Mollie wasn't the type to be impressed by sports achievements.

"What did you go to college for?" she asked.

"The parties," he answered with a rueful smile. "I even did the frat thing."

"Of course you did," she said with a chuckle.

"I think, if Beth hadn't come along and changed all our lives, I would have gone on to be a coach or gym teacher. I really would have enjoyed coaching."

"I could see you as a coach."

Mike pondered what his life would have been like if Beth hadn't entered it before shutting his imagination down. He didn't like the boredom and thirst that came with being a vampire, and recently he'd felt more adrift and lonely, but he loved his family and his life.

And he wouldn't have met Mollie if he'd remained human.

Watching her as she licked the last of the rabbit juice from her fingers, he knew he wouldn't have changed anything.

"I did buy a house recently," he said. "I plan to fix it up and flip it. I thought it would be a fun project to undertake by myself. Over the years, we've built several homes together and learned how to do every aspect of it, but I'm going to do this one on my own."

"How come?"

"Something to keep me occupied. Lately, I've been feeling a little… I guess you could say bored... or maybe lost."

Mollie's eyebrows rose at this admission. She never would have expected him to say he felt lost. He carried himself with a confidence few others did, but more than that, when he talked about his family and how close they were, love radiated in his voice.

"But you have such close friends and a large family," she said.

"Yes, and they mean the world to me, but many of them are settling down and starting their own families."

"Are you on the lookout for Mrs. Right, Mike?" she teased, yet she found herself breathlessly waiting for his answer.

Staring into her striking green eyes, Mike was becoming increasingly convinced he'd already found her, but he couldn't say that. "I'm keeping my eyes open," he replied with a smile.

Mollie ducked her head when an unexpected blush crept up her neck and into her cheeks. She hadn't blushed this much in her entire life, but she couldn't seem to stop around him. "Wouldn't you eventually grow bored with only one woman?"

"No."

The emphatic answer drew Mollie's attention back to him. "How can you be so sure?"

"When vampires find their mate, they stay with them for life."

"Their mate?"

"Yes. Some vampires have mates, and when they discover that human or vampire, they forge an eternal bond with them through an exchange of blood and sex."

Despite her apprehension about the entire vampire thing, his words piqued her curiosity. "A human can be the mate of a vampire?"

"Yes, but if they are, they cannot remain human. The vampire will be driven by the need to make them immortal to complete the bond and ensure the safety of their mate. I've seen what an incomplete bond can do to a vampire and how unstable it can make them, but once it is complete, they calm again. The bond also makes both vampires stronger. A vampire never strays from their mate, and if one dies, the other dies or goes insane. A vampire will also destroy anyone who threatens their mate."

"And you're hoping to find your mate?"

"Yes."

She couldn't form words to reply as they stared at each other until the seconds ticked away a minute.

"What is your full name, Mollie?" Mike asked to break the tension after his revelation.

He'd considered not telling her anything about vampires and their mates, but if she was his mate, then she should be prepared for what could happen in the future. However, he'd barely delved into the realms of how insane a vampire could go when the bond was incomplete or they were forcibly separated from their mate.

"Would you like my middle name too?" she inquired, trying to sound teasing, but it came out strained.

"Sure."

"Mollie Jean McConnell. And yours?"

"Michael Paul Wright."

Mollie nodded, finished off her water, and wiped her hands on her jeans before digging into her pocket for the pack of gum. She slipped a piece into her mouth and offered one to Mike; he took it. Mollie almost laughed at a vampire chewing gum, but she was too tired to laugh. She returned the dwindling pack to her pocket and examined the woods.

A sad thought occurred to her as the trees swayed in the breeze and tendrils of sun slipped through to dance across the forest floor. "The other humans who escaped with us, they're probably starving, aren't they?"

"I'm sure they've found some way to eat. The survival instinct can make us do things we never believed possible."

"True," she agreed. "But I doubt they have a vampire catching food for them, and I don't think they had any weapons."

"They could have teamed up to work with a vampire."

"Hmm," she murmured. "I wish we could find some of them."

Mike preferred to be on their own unless they located Jack and Doug. He'd set the others free, but he didn't trust any of them, not even the humans. "We should go."

CHAPTER NINETEEN

A FEW HOURS LATER, a crashing sound ahead of them halted Mike. Grasping Mollie's elbow, he drew her behind the trunk of a large maple. The cliffs were only fifty feet away on their right. The woods continued to go to the edge of the cliffs in this area of the forest, but he did not want to retreat toward them. He would survive if he were forced over the edge; Mollie would not.

Mollie swung the rifle from her back and lifted it to her shoulder. They stood at the top of a small hill, and the sound came from the thick underbrush below.

"Don't fire unless necessary," Mike whispered in her ear.

Mollie nodded and kept the barrel aimed at where the noise was coming from. Then a man burst from the underbrush. With his hair in tousled disarray, his chest heaving, and his eyes rolling in his head, he looked as if the end of the world was nipping at his heels.

Mike rested his hand on the barrel of Mollie's gun and pushed it down while he studied the man. "Human," he told her.

The man looked left and right before turning to his left and running in that direction. He only made it ten feet before something leapt from the underbrush and pounced on his back. Mollie's breath sucked in, and she tried to jerk the rifle back up, but Mike kept it down as the man started screaming.

The vampire, perched on his back like a vulture on carrion, had eyes the color of rubies, and blood trickled from its mouth. Mollie didn't know if the blood was from some other unsuspecting victim or because the vamp's fangs had sliced open its bottom lip.

"We have to help him!" Mollie whispered as the man howled.

Mike had been preparing to lift her and run from here. The man's screams would only attract more Savages, and he couldn't have Mollie anywhere near them. If Mollie weren't involved, he would intervene, but he wasn't about to put her life at risk for some stranger.

The sun hadn't set yet, but the shadows of the woods offered some protection from its rays, and he suspected this was a newer Savage, one more tolerant of the sun. It might even be one of the vampires they turned loose, which meant there could be other, newer Savages out there too.

"No, please!" the man pleaded.

Mollie tried to jerk the rifle away from Mike, but he wouldn't release it. Giving up on trying to get it free, she shoved the gun at him and released it. Then she ran toward the man. Mollie only made it five feet before Mike's arm slid around her waist and he jerked her back against his chest. Before she could voice her protest, another vampire burst from the woods and raced toward the man.

Mike clapped his hand over Mollie's mouth when she gasped. The second Savage fell on the human and tore into his wrist. The man wailed as the first Savage bashed his fist into the cheek of the other and knocked vampire off.

"Mine," the first snarled in a voice more animal than human.

The second one launched at the first, and they tumbled onto the man's legs. Sensing a chance to get away, the man clawed at the dirt. He tried to pull himself free of the creatures scrambling to kill each other over which one of them got to eat him.

Mike held Mollie tight as she struggled to get free. He eased his hand away from her mouth, and she turned her head to glower at him. "We have to help."

She lifted her chin defiantly as her striking eyes blazed with fury. And in those eyes, he saw the truth; if he carried her away from here, she would never look at him the same again. She would forever see him as a monster.

"Stay here!" Mike hissed in her ear.

Mollie relaxed against him when he set her down. Mike pushed the rifle back into her hands and strode away. Her relief over his willingness to help the man vanished when she realized he'd be going down there with *two* of those things. She'd witnessed his strength numerous times, but two on one wasn't good odds.

The increasing violence between the Savages covered any noise Mike might have made while descending the hill. He adjusted his grip on the stick he'd honed to cook Mollie's food as the Savages rolled off the man's feet.

The man gawked at the Savages as if he couldn't believe his luck and squealed when he spotted Mike approaching. The man scrambled to his feet, but though they were determined to kill each other, the Savages remained aware of their prey as both vamps seized his ankles and yanked him back. With a broken scream, the man slammed into the ground.

Giving up on destroying each other, the Savages pounced on him again. One sank its fangs into the man's throat while the other claimed his arm. Mike stopped behind them, but they were too focused on their meal to realize he was there. Shaking his head over the obliviousness to their impending deaths, Mike lifted the stick over his head and plunged it into the back and through the heart of the Savage feasting on the man's throat.

The Savage reeled back; its fingers clawed at the wood piercing its body before Mike yanked the stick free. He ignored the dying creature as he turned to the other one, who was no longer oblivious to his presence.

Blood streaked the Savage's chin and teeth as its red-stained lips curved into a sneer. Then it leapt at him with fangs extended and fingers hooked to gouge out his eyes. Mike swung the stick around and battered it against the side of the Savage's face. The blow shattered the creature's cheekbone, knocked it off course, and sent it tumbling across the ground.

Spitting, the vampire righted itself and turned to face Mike before glancing over its shoulder toward the woods. Mike read its intention to flee in the subtle shifting of its body. He could *not* let it escape.

Racing forward, Mike was almost on it when the Savage leapt up and spun toward the woods. He grasped the vamp's neck and jerked it off its feet. Turning in his grasp, the creature lashed out with a fist and spat blood in Mike's face as it screeched. Mike dodged the punch and swung his fist into the creature's chest. Flesh and bone gave way beneath the force of the blow.

The Savage's heart beat against Mike's hand before he enclosed it around the organ and tore it free. The creature's fingers ripped the skin from his forearms before the Savage toppled away from him. Mike gazed at the heart in disgust before releasing it and stomping it into the debris littering the forest floor.

He inhaled a ragged breath as he strained to rein in his baser instincts. The demon in him relished a good fight and blood, and he craved *more* of it. He could *not* let Mollie see that part of him.

Feeling in control of himself enough to face Mollie, he turned to discover she'd descended the hill and was kneeling at the man's side.

"I told you to stay where you were!" Mike snarled.

The bloodlust roused from his kills, his concern for her, and the fact she was *touching* the man's shoulder caused his newly regained control to unravel.

Mollie's eyes widened when Mike stalked toward her. Red started to bleed through the blue of his eyes as his gaze latched onto her hand on the man. The man released a gurgled cry and tried to scramble away, but Mollie held him in place.

"It's okay!" she assured him. "We're here to help you!"

Even as she said the words, she wasn't sure they were true; Mike looked ready to level everything in his way.

"Mike?" she croaked.

The distress in her voice stopped Mike in his tracks; not only had the man recoiled, but so had she. The last thing he wanted was to scare Mollie, but she looked more afraid of *him* than any of the Savages. *Get yourself together!*

Closing his eyes, he distracted himself from the jealousy shredding his insides by kneeling to wipe his bloody hand on the dirt. Lifting a handful of leaves, he also scrubbed the blood from the gashes the Savage left on his arms. He'd already stopped bleeding, and his skin was knitting itself back together.

He didn't look at the others as he worked; he was afraid the sight of Mollie might set something off in him again. For the first time in years, he recalled the night in their friend Kathleen's cabin when vampires attacked Sera. When Liam saw what happened, he'd been more Savage than man and nearly turned Sera right then. It took hours before Liam was stable enough to go anywhere near Sera again.

Mike recalled how helpless he felt while watching the incident unfold. He'd wanted to intervene and pull Sera away, but he couldn't risk setting Liam off further. Liam had already reached a point where anyone touching Sera made him half-crazed. If Mike had tried to pull Sera away, Liam wouldn't have hesitated to kill him, and with the way Liam was that night, he would have succeeded.

It was the only time in his life Mike feared his best friend and what Liam would do if Sera didn't become a vampire. Mike walked on eggshells around Liam until Sera successfully made the transition.

At the time, and over the years, Mike convinced himself nothing like that could ever happen to him. Even if he did find his mate, he would never lose control like Liam. He'd *never* unravel in such a way, but the reminder of Mollie's hands on that man caused his fangs to lengthen with the need to tear the man's throat out.

He ground his teeth together as he scrubbed more vigorously at his arms. He hadn't done anything more than kiss her. Even if Mollie was his mate, he shouldn't feel this out of control already. Their bond hadn't progressed enough for this level of possessive and irrational behavior to take hold.

Mike lifted his head and glanced around the woods. Maybe their bond hadn't progressed, but he already suspected what she was to him, and her life had been in danger since the second they met. The knowledge monsters hunted his possible mate had most likely accelerated his need to keep her safe and make her immortal.

A rustling behind him snapped his head around. He clamped his lips together to keep from sneering as Mollie helped the man into a seated position against the trunk of a tree. The man was deathly pale, blood trickled from the gash in his neck, and his arm looked like someone tried to flay it.

"You're going to be okay," Mollie said as she turned the man's arm over. She tried not to wince as she inspected the injuries. "We'll get you bandaged, and you'll be fine."

She had no idea what they would use to bandage him, and then her eyes went to the quilt she released when she first lifted her rifle. They could use pieces of the blanket to bind the gashes. Reluctantly, she looked at Mike. After the barely leashed brutality she saw in his eyes earlier, she was frightened of what she would see there now, but when he met her gaze, the red vanished from his irises.

"We can use the quilt to bandage him," she said. "I dropped it at the top of the hill."

Rising, Mike kept one eye on them as he raced to retrieve the blanket. When he returned, he strode over to the man's side and knelt there.

The man recoiled from him, but Mike ignored him. "I'll do it," he said when Mollie reached for the blanket.

"If you tear the strips, I can bandage him," she offered.

He could be around the man's blood, but he couldn't watch her touching him again. "*I* will do it."

"Mike—"

Mollie's protest died off when he lifted his head to meet her gaze. She didn't understand the turbulence in his eyes, but she suspected pushing him on this might send him over the edge. His gaze latched onto her fingers when she rested her hand in a comforting gesture on the man's arm.

When a muscle twitched in Mike's cheek, Mollie released the man's arm and Mike visibly relaxed. She had no idea what was going on with him, but she wasn't going to aggravate a vampire, her only ally, and a man she was beginning to consider a friend with some additional kissing benefits.

Mike tore two small pieces of cloth from the quilt and set the blanket aside.

"You're a vampire," the man stated.

Mike would have to change the man's memories before this was over, but there was no point in doing it now. It would only weaken him, and he was sure something else would happen to reveal his vampiric nature again to the man before they were out of this mess.

"You're observant," Mike replied as he reached for the man's arm.

The man recoiled from him. "You'll drink from me!"

Mike tried to keep his patience as he met the man's troubled, hazel eyes. He understood the man's apprehension, and he had every right to be scared as Mike *had* contemplated killing him, but they didn't have time for this.

"No, I won't," Mike said. "Now give me your arm so we can get out of here before more of them come." When the man kept his arm away from him, Mike continued. "Or you can sit here and ring the dinner bell by continuing to bleed all over the place, and we'll leave."

The man paled further and glanced at Mollie. "It's okay," she assured him. "We really are just trying to help, but you have to let us."

The man's eyes bounced between the two of them before he held his arm out to Mike. "Are you a vampire?" he demanded of Mollie.

"No. I'm human, and Mike has helped keep me alive through this. You can trust him."

Can he? Mike wondered as their conversation with each other grated on his already irritated nerves. If she were his mate, his need to protect her and his jealousy would escalate until she became a vampire.

If she agreed to become one. She barely knew him, and what she'd seen of vampires so far wasn't promising. Plus, her sister was in the hands of Savages and probably dead. Before all this was over, Mollie might grow to despise him and his kind.

"What's your name?" Mollie asked the man.

The guy didn't tear his attention away from Mike while he replied, "Holden."

"I'm Mollie."

Holden grunted and blew a strand of his shoulder-length, brown hair from his eye. He had a brown goatee, lean build, and the look of a guy who spent more time on a skateboard than his feet. Mollie guessed him to be in his early thirties.

Mike finished tying the bandage on Holden's wrist. "We have to cover your neck too, or they'll track the scent of your blood."

Holden nodded, and Mike set to work wrapping the cloth around his neck.

"How did you come to be here?" Mollie asked Holden.

"Some buddies and I were at the skate park the other night. One second I was on my board, and the next I was in a cage," Holden replied. "I'm not sure how it all happened or where my friends are now. We ran in different directions when we were freed from the cages. How did you end up here?"

"I pulled over because my car had a flat tire. Someone stopped to help us, but they wanted more than to change our tire," Mollie replied.

"And you?" Holden asked Mike.

"I was in a bar with some friends. The bar was attacked, and we were taken."

"Why are they attacking their own kind?" Holden asked.

"I don't know," Mike replied gruffly. He wasn't about to get into the intricacies of vampire life with a man who would never remember any of this.

Finished tying the bandage, Mike sat back on his heels before rising. He held his hand out to Mollie; he needed to get her away from Holden. His breath caught in his chest when Mollie hesitated before taking it. He inhaled a ragged breath when her hand enclosed around his, and she rose to her feet.

"We have to leave here, now," Mike said crisply as Mollie bent to retrieve the quilt.

Holden glanced between the two of them before rising unsteadily to his feet.

CHAPTER TWENTY

THE CLIFFS HAD STARTED to dwindle in size, and the sun was nearly gone by the time they stopped again an hour later. The same eerie howls reverberating through last night had already started, but this time, they were closer.

Mollie's skin crawled as she scanned the growing shadows. She would give anything to be sheltered somewhere, but there was nowhere to hide. Holden looked about ready to collapse, and the incessant rumbling of his stomach sounded louder than a car engine.

Mike walked over to the edge of the cliffs and gazed down; they were only a forty-foot drop now. Instead of crashing against the rocks, the waves rolled onto a ten-foot strip of sand lining the cliff walls. The fall was still lethal to humans, but he could land on the beach without harm.

However, he had to find shelter soon. The only problem was, he'd been searching for somewhere ever since they acquired Holden and discovered nothing. If he went down there, he might be able to find a way to get Mollie down there and, hopefully, locate a cave or someplace they could hide for the night, but he didn't want to leave Mollie with Holden. His instincts when it came to her, and other men, were skewed right now, but something about the guy bugged Mike; probably the fact he was still breathing.

Stepping away from the cliffs, Mike glanced at Mollie as she surveyed the woods with the rifle against her shoulder. Holden stood far too close to her for Mike's liking. Striding forward, he clasped Mollie's elbow and drew her close against his side when someone screamed just as the sun was vanishing behind the horizon. Mike's gaze lifted to the upper limbs of the trees; if they didn't find something soon, their only hope might be to climb one and try to remain hidden for the night.

"Hurry," he urged, leading Mollie onward.

Lowering the rifle, she practically jogged alongside him to keep up with his long legs. She glanced back to discover Holden struggling to follow them. "We have to slow down," she whispered.

"We can't," Mike said.

His callous attitude irritated her, and she scowled at him. "We're *all* getting to safety."

Mike stopped himself from scowling back at her. When it came to making sure she stayed alive, he didn't care what happened to Holden, but she didn't want to hear that, and he had no time to argue with her.

He was about to turn back for Holden when his attention was drawn to the nearly full moon rising over the sea. The white light shimmering across the gentle waves created a pathway toward the shore. The same thing probably happened every night, but tonight he could *see* the moon rising, whereas the other nights the height of the cliffs blocked his view of the ocean.

That's when he realized the cliffs were almost gone. Mike kept hold of Mollie as he veered to the right and stopped at the edge of the cliffs; it was only a ten-foot jump now. The humans could climb down without a problem, but what if they got down there and there was nowhere to hide? They would be visible to anyone who looked over the cliffs.

Another howl sounded, but this one was practically breathing down their necks. "We have to climb down," he said.

Mollie leaned over the edge to peer at the sand below. A few rocks jutted up here and there along the beach, but the space beneath her was smooth from years of the ocean rolling over it.

She pulled her arm away from Mike and, bending her knees, jumped off the edge. Air rushed around her as she fell; for a second, she felt like she had as a kid when she would jump off the swings to fly through the air.

Then she was hitting the ground. Her knees bent to take the brunt of the impact, and the sand gave way beneath her feet, making the landing easier than she'd anticipated. The man in the moon looked close enough to touch. She'd never seen the phenomenon so clearly before, and it caused hope to fill her as the breeze speckled her cheeks with sea spray. They would find Aida, and they would get out of this somehow.

Then Holden landed beside her and Mike fell on the other side of her.

"What now?" Holden asked.

"Now we stay to the wall and hope we find shelter," Mike replied.

MOLLIE CREPT toward the back of the cave Mike had discovered. Her shoes slipped in the sand beneath her feet, and she kept her hands in front of her, so she didn't walk into a wall. She only made it twenty feet before her palms smacked against a stone wall at the end of the cave.

"You okay?" Mike whispered from behind her.

"Yes," she replied as she turned away from the wall.

The moon's rays dimly illuminated the front of the cave, but Mollie couldn't see anything in the oppressive dark surrounding her. She tried not to think about the spiders and other critters watching her from the shadows as she slid down the wall to sit against it. Beneath her ass, the sand was dry, but the crash of the waves outside chilled her. Unfolding the quilt, she draped it around her shoulders. The rocks may be cold, but the thick walls helped mute the howls and screams piercing the air with increasing frequency.

Holden released a breath, slumped against a wall, and slid to the ground. It had taken them almost two miles of traversing the beach before discovering this cave, and by then Holden was barely standing. His head bent forward, and less than a minute later, his rhythmic breathing filled the air.

"The water comes in here sometimes," she murmured.

"Probably only during storms," Mike assured her. "And the ocean will help mask our scent."

Settling onto the sand beside her, he took the piece of quilt she offered him, draped his arm around her shoulders, and drew her against his side. The warmth of her pliant body against his helped ease some of his remaining tension. He wouldn't mind a cigarette, but he buried the craving.

"I have to find Aida," she murmured before yawning.

"We will."

"Tomorrow, we should head toward the chimney you saw from the lighthouse. Maybe Aida's in that building."

"We'll decide tomorrow." He didn't want to take Mollie where the Savages might be centered, but her sister probably was somewhere near there. Jack and Doug might also still be in that area. "You have to rest."

Before she knew what he intended, Mike lifted her and settled her in his lap. Shock caused her to stiffen, but when he wrapped his powerful arms around her, she relaxed against him. Nestling closer, she lowered her head to his chest. The beat of his heart beneath her ear and the warmth of his body lulled her to sleep.

Mike buried his face in her hair as he cradled her against him, savoring the feel of her in his arms. When she drifted off to sleep, his heart slowed until the two of them fell into rhythm with each other.

CHAPTER TWENTY-ONE

WHEN MOLLIE WOKE the next morning, she discovered Mike kneeling at the front of the cave with Holden at his side. Pink lit the morning sky and glittered across the water as the waves crashed against the shore. The ocean rolled in closer to the cave than it had the night before, but at least five feet of beach remained between the cave and the sea.

Mike's head turned toward her, but no smile curved his lips when their eyes met.

"What's wrong?" Mollie asked as she tossed the quilt aside and rose to approach them.

"I'm going out to find you both water and something to eat," he said. "I don't know how long I'll be."

Red shimmered in his eyes when his gaze flicked to Holden. That was when Mollie understood the idea of going back out there wasn't what bothered him; he was reluctant to leave her here with Holden.

"We'll be fine," she assured him.

"Hmm," he grunted, but his shoulders remained tensed, and his nostrils flared.

Holden eased away from Mike and back toward her, which wasn't the best idea as Mike's hostility ratcheted up until it practically vibrated the walls of the cave. A vein throbbed to life in the center of his forehead as he pinned Holden with a stare that would make the angriest poltergeist flee.

With the way he was acting, Mollie almost suspected Mike was jealous, but though they'd shared some intimacies, she didn't think they'd gotten close enough for that emotion.

Then she recalled how safe she'd felt in his arms as the beat of his heart lulled her to sleep. Maybe they *had* grown close enough for jealousy to become an issue. The idea of anyone else touching *him* made her fingers curl until her nails bit into her palm. Rational or not, short amount of time knowing each other or not, she would hit anyone who tried anything with him.

Rising, Mike strolled over and clasped Mollie's arm; he led her toward the back of the cave. When they reached the back wall, he glanced toward Holden to make sure the human couldn't hear what he had to say to her.

He grasped both her arms before speaking. "You keep that rifle at the ready and don't hesitate to use it, against anyone, if it becomes necessary. I'll hear the shot and get back here as soon as I can," he told her.

"We'll be fine," she said again, but his hands only tightened on her. "There's nothing to worry about."

"Don't trust him because he's human, Mollie. Humans can be as vicious as any vampire."

She wanted to deny his words, but she'd seen enough awful stories on the news to know it was true. "I understand."

Mike released her arm to clasp her chin. "Be ready for anything."

"I will."

He remained unmoving, torn between leaving and knowing the only way to keep her alive was to make sure she had water and food. Lifting her chin, he bent to kiss her. She gasped in a breath before melting against him and grasping his forearms.

Mike only meant it to be a goodbye kiss, but the second their tongues entwined, he found himself seeking to brand himself onto her as the kiss deepened. When he started growing aroused, he broke the kiss before it became impossible to walk out of this cave. Mollie's eyes were dazed as she blinked at him before a smile curved her mouth.

"Shoot to kill if it becomes necessary," Mike said.

Her smile vanished, and her eyes darted to Holden. "It won't be necessary, but I'll protect myself."

Mike hoped Holden deserved her optimism. He reluctantly released her, kissed her forehead, and stalked to the front of the cave. Mike stopped beside Holden, who was leaning against the wall, staring with far too much intensity at the ocean. Mike suspected Holden had seen their kiss, and he'd intended for the human to see it so Holden would know who she belonged to.

"If something happens to her, or if you try anything, I'll kill you," Mike vowed.

Holden's head shot toward him, and his mouth dropped. "I… I'd nev-never do anything inappropriate," Holden sputtered.

Mike scowled at him before turning and leaving the cave.

MOLLIE SAT against the wall five feet inside the cave and across from Holden. The man had barely spoken to her since Mike left, probably because Mike petrified him. Not that she blamed him, after the way Mike was with him, and after everything Holden had endured at the hands of vampires.

The loud rumble of his stomach caught her attention, and she glanced at her watch. Mike left an hour ago. He could be back any minute now, or it could be at least another hour.

"Hopefully he'll be back soon with something to eat," she said to Holden.

He grunted in response. Mollie rolled her eyes and turned back to the waves. The tide had retreated again to expose more beach. Unfortunately, the waves didn't bring any mollusks or seaweed that could be boiled and eaten. There might be crabs in the sand, but she didn't dare expose herself by leaving the cave to search for them.

"Do you really trust him?" Holden asked.

"Hmm?" Mollie had been so absorbed in the sea his question didn't quite register.

"The vampire, do you really trust him?"

"Yes. Mike saved my life, and he's helped keep me alive. I trust him completely."

Something like disgust flickered over Holden's face before he covered it up and looked away.

"You can trust him too," she said.

"I think he's far more likely to kill me than *you* if he gets hungry."

Mollie detected bitterness in his tone. "Mike's not going to use either of us for food. He's been feeding on animals."

"And what if he grows bored with them? I mean, I'm no expert, but I'm guessing human blood probably tastes better than animal to them."

He was probably right, but Mollie wasn't in the mood to debate which blood was better than which. "You can trust him," she said again.

He gave her a look that made her realize he didn't particularly trust *her* either. *Fine, be an ass.*

Mollie focused on the sea again as a shadow fell across the front of the cave. The unexpected lurch of excitement jarring her heart made her realize how much she'd missed Mike. Rising, she held the rifle loosely in front of her as someone entered the cave.

She couldn't see the face, but she knew the slender build wasn't Mike's. Holden scrambled to his feet and staggered back as another man stepped inside. Mollie heard something like sniffing, but with the sun at the backs of the men, she couldn't make out much about the details of their faces.

She edged back as the first man sauntered further into the cave before stopping a few feet away from her. When he moved into the shadows, she got a better view of his lean face, brown hair, and red eyes. He didn't seem as insane as the vamps who attacked Holden, but he wasn't as in control as Mike either.

When the other man stepped next to him, Mollie saw the second vampire had blond hair and red eyes. Their hunger beating against her made her stomach turn.

"Stay back!" she commanded, lifting the rifle to her shoulder. Holden scrambled behind her as she crept further back into the cave. "This rifle has wooden bullets, and I *will* kill you."

"Easy," the first vamp said, holding up his hands. "We're not here to hurt you."

"Then why are you here?" she demanded.

The vamps exchanged a glance before focusing on her again. The blond's eyes traveled to her neck, and she caught the faint gleam of a fang when his lips pulled back.

"Stay away!" Mollie pointed the barrel at the first vamp's heart.

"We're only asking for a little taste," the brunet said.

Mollie steadied her hand when it shook on the gun. She cursed the increasing sweatiness of her palms as her heart jackhammered. She'd told Mike she would shoot to kill if it was necessary, but the sound of a gunshot might only bring more of them, and it would be deafening in this confined space.

If she could get them to go away without shooting them, she was going to try. These men had been out in the sun; they couldn't be as Savage as the vamps who'd held them captive. Maybe they did only want a little taste, but she would *not* be the blood supply for some vampire.

Unless it's Mike. Mollie buried her surprise over the sudden thought and focused on the menace before her.

"Get out of here," Mollie ordered.

"Only a little taste," the blond purred in a tone that made Mollie's blood run cold.

Maybe they weren't as out of control as the other vamps, but one taste would not be enough for them. These creatures wouldn't be able to stop themselves once they started feasting. Behind her, Holden released a strangled cry as he seemed to reach the same conclusion as her. He sounded half on the verge of tears and half on the edge of screaming.

Keep it together, she silently commanded him as she took another step back.

"Get. Out." Mollie bit the words out from between her clenched teeth.

She'd just finished speaking when the blond shoved the brunet at her. Thrown off by the unexpected move, Mollie's hand jerked and she fired the rifle, but the shot was off the mark. Instead of striking his chest, the brown-haired vamp took a bullet to the gut. Mollie's ears rang as the shot boomed throughout the cave.

The blond was nearly on top of her by the time she readjusted her aim, and the brunet was already recovering, though he looked far more pissed. If he got his hands on her, he would have no problem dining on every ounce of her blood. She was about to shoot again when Holden placed his palms on her shoulder blades and shoved her forward.

"Take her!" Holden shouted.

Mollie didn't have time to register her disbelief over his betrayal before the vamps clasped her arms and dragged her forward.

"No!" she screamed when the rifle was wrenched from her hands, and a malicious face filled her vision.

CHAPTER TWENTY-TWO

MOLLIE KICKED out and twisted her head to the side when a hot breath expelled against her cheek. Fingers dug into her flesh until she was sure they were going to shred her skin from her bones.

I'm going to die. She despised the thought the second it crossed her mind, but every thud of her heart was filled with the certainty these were the last seconds of her life.

Then a roar rose to replace the ringing in her ears, and someone squealed. The vampire holding her suddenly jerked forward, as if he'd been struck by a blow. A gurgled, wet sound resonated out of his throat and blood trickled from his mouth.

When Mollie's eyes flew open, her gaze locked on Mike standing behind the vampire. Mike's eyes blazed such a vibrant shade of red that, for a second, she didn't recognize him and believed he was another monster who'd come to drain her dry.

But he wasn't another monster. He was Mike, and he looked *exactly* like one of those Savages.

Fear that Mike had become one of those things and she would die at his hands filled her. "No," she moaned.

The vamp grunted as his body jerked backward a couple of inches. Then Mike grasped his shoulder and snatched the vamp away from her. He tossed the vamp into the wall on her right. Bones crunched sickeningly, but the already dead vampire didn't feel any pain.

Mollie's gaze fell on the heart in Mike's fist. Blood coated him up to his wrist and plopped onto the floor of the cave as his malevolent eyes focused on her. His shoulders heaved with each of his harsh breaths as his eyes burned into her.

Behind Mike, the body of the blond vampire lay on the ground, though she couldn't tell he was blond anymore as she had no idea where his head was.

A hysterical laugh bubbled up inside her. The headless guy didn't bother her; no, it was the knowledge that Mike, the one man she'd come to trust, was about to make her as headless as the blond. After he drained her dry, of course.

The compulsion to laugh abruptly passed and tears burned her eyes. She would not cry. She would *not* leave this world a blubbering mess.

Straightening her shoulders, she held Mike's gaze until it flashed behind her. She'd forgotten about Holden until she heard him whimper. She listened as his fingers scoured rock while he scrambled into the back of the cave, but she didn't tear her attention away from Mike to look at the asshole who'd been more than happy to sacrifice her.

"I saw what you did," Mike hissed.

The hair on Mollie's arms rose. She barely recognized his voice as the fangs he revealed when he spoke distorted it. He stalked toward her before passing her and snatching up Holden.

Mollie blinked when she realized it wasn't *her* he was so enraged with—it was Holden. Panic flooded her when his words from earlier blazed back across her mind. *"Each death pushes them more toward becoming a Savage while it strengthens and weakens them."*

"Mike, no!" she cried when he grabbed Holden's throat. As much as she'd like to pummel the piece of shit herself, she couldn't let

Mike take this step that would only lead toward his darker side. "Please don't!"

Mike's hands froze on Holden's head and throat. He'd been about to break the man's neck when Mollie's pleas and the frantic tone of her voice cut through the haze of fury enshrouding him. Never in his life had he wanted to destroy someone as badly as he did Holden, but he found himself hesitating for *her*.

"He *threw* you to them!" Mike spat.

"I know." Mollie kept her tone as calm as possible. She couldn't let Mike see how irate the knowledge made her or how unsettled she was by the incident. Instinctively, she knew both of those things would send him over the edge. "But you told me the killing of humans and innocents is what turns a vampire Savage. I don't want that for you. You can't kill him."

A fraction of Mike's rage eased when he realized she was telling him to stop because she was concerned about *him* and not the human filth in his hands.

"He's not innocent," Mike snarled.

"No, he's not," Mollie agreed. "But he *is* human, and his death will affect you."

Mike wouldn't experience any guilt over destroying Holden; however, her safety was his primary concern. He knew vampires who had killed humans and maintained their humanity, but they'd all experienced discomfort from the sun afterward, and he couldn't be hindered in such a way while they were caught up in this mess.

Besides, he didn't have to kill Holden to protect her, but they might encounter other humans who would pose a more significant threat to her and who would have to be eradicated. If he killed those people too, he would be walking a treacherous line between retaining his humanity and losing it. Gazing at Holden, another idea for the bastard occurred to him.

He eased his grip on Holden's head, lowered him to the ground, and released him. Bloody streaks from his hands marred Holden's pale face. Shifting his hold, Mike kept his hand on Holden's neck.

He resisted squeezing until Holden's head popped from his shoulders. Holden wheezed as he leaned forward and rested his hands on his knees.

"Gather your things, Mollie; we have to go," Mike said.

When his hand started constricting on Holden's nape, Mike focused on Mollie as she lifted the rifle and inspected it. Seemingly satisfied with it, she slid it over her shoulder before gathering the quilt, folding it, and tucking it under her arm.

Holden's toes scraped the ground when Mike hauled him to the front of the cave and outside. "What… what… are you going to do to me?" he panted while Mike dragged him across the sand.

"Nothing you don't deserve," Mike replied as turned toward Holden. The man was easily a good five inches shorter and seventy-five pounds lighter than him, but Mike felt no sympathy for the weaker human. "Since you like sacrificing those weaker than you, I see no reason not to do the same to you."

Seizing Holden's arm, he pulled it forward and ripped the makeshift bandage from it. Holden squealed when Mike grasped his healing flesh and pulled it apart until blood spilled free. Next, he tore the bandage from Holden's neck.

"The gunshot will draw others here, and they'll find only you," Mike said as Holden's blood spilled down his arm and dripped onto the sand.

"Wait! No!" Holden cried, his eyes rolling in his head. "You can't leave me here! I'll follow you! I'll tell them where you went, and I'll—"

Holden stopped speaking when Mike lifted his head to look at him. "Are you threatening me?" Mike growled.

Mollie didn't breathe as she waited to see what Mike would do. She'd felt a snapping in him with Holden's threats, and she didn't think her interference would stop Mike from killing him this time. When Holden's eyes rolled toward her, Mike stepped in between them and blocked Holden from her view.

"Are. You. Threatening. Me?" Mike bit out each word.

"No… I… you… you can't leave me here!" Holden cried. "You have to keep me safe! I'll follow you!"

Mollie winced; even without seeing Mike's face, she knew it was the wrong thing to say. "Mike—"

But he was already speaking. "Remember, the louder you scream, the faster they'll find you."

"What?" Holden sputtered.

A cruel smile curved Mike's mouth before he stepped back and rammed his foot into Holden's knee. He watched impassively as the joint gave way and Holden crumpled to the ground like the sack of shit he was.

The quilt fell from Mollie's hands when she clapped them over her ears to block the sounds of Holden's tortured screams, but it did little good.

Mike crouched before Holden and rested his hands on his knees. "Keep screaming," he murmured as Holden's tear-filled eyes met his. "They're on their way."

Rising, Mike ignored Holden's cries as he snatched the quilt up along with the discarded cup and pot that had contained Mollie's water. Next to the pot and cup lay two dead rabbits covered in sand. He'd dropped everything on the beach when he heard the gunshot. He slid the cup and pot onto his belt and made sure they couldn't bang together.

Mollie didn't resist Mike's arms when they wrapped around her, but she couldn't stop herself from cringing when she recalled the ease with which he'd unleashed such brutality. Holden's screams had died down, and his hands were grasping at his ruined leg. She briefly met his gaze before closing her eyes. She couldn't see anymore, and she didn't want to be here when the others came for him.

Clasping the quilt against Mollie's back, Mike slid his hand around her head and tucked it into his neck. Then he ran.

CHAPTER TWENTY-THREE

MIKE RAN until the cliffs gave way and the land turned to flat beach stretching toward the woods before he veered back into the thick forest. Mollie hadn't spoken since they left Holden behind. Her hands dug into his back, and her face remained in his neck as her shallow breaths tickled his skin. At first, she trembled against him, but that ceased when they entered the woods.

Mike cursed himself and his lack of control. She never should have seen that brutal side of him. He should have kept it hidden from her, especially after those two fuckers attacked her, but after witnessing what Holden did and hearing his *threats*, all sense of control vanished.

He'd only managed to keep himself from killing Holden because of her, but he hadn't controlled himself enough. He was not naturally a violent man, it was always a last resort, but he hadn't hesitated to kill when he saw those vampires clawing at her. And no matter how much he wished she hadn't witnessed it, he would not hesitate to kill or maim for her again.

Judging by the position of the sun, he'd been running for a couple of hours. When they first entered the forest again, he'd eased his speed but continued to lope across the ground. The reminder he could have lost her caused him to cradle Mollie closer.

Mollie's rumbling stomach, and his need to speak with her and hopefully repair any damage he may have caused between them, slowed him to a walk before he stopped. Mollie clung to him for a minute longer before her legs unlocked against his sides and she slid to the ground. She kept a hand on his shoulder when her legs wobbled, but once she was steadier, she released him.

She kept her head bowed while he gazed at her. Mike's heart twisted. He ached to clasp her chin and kiss her; instead, he stepped away.

"I lost your food and water, but I'll get you more," he said as he examined the section of woods they'd stopped in. To his right, he heard the flow of the waves against the shore, but they were at least a quarter mile away from the ocean.

"Thank you," Mollie murmured as she stretched her cramped legs.

Though what he could do, and how remorseless he could be, unnerved her, she couldn't deny she missed being held against him. Once her revulsion and alarm over what happened faded, she'd found herself comforted by the effortless way he moved across the land and the flow of his muscles against her. While he ran, the trees were a blur and the wind tugged at her hair, but no branches touched them as he dashed around any obstacles in his way.

Lifting her foot to her ass, Mollie bent forward to stretch; resting her fingertips on the ground, she examined Mike while he patrolled the area. He looked as lethal as he had while standing before Holden. The echo of Holden's screams in her ears and the strain radiating from Mike caused her to drop her foot to the ground.

She saw nothing out of the ordinary in the trees as the birds chirped and a squirrel raced through the branches of a pine, but he saw far more of this world than she did.

"Is anything out there?" She was not in the mood to be attacked by vampires again, and she wasn't fond of humans right now either.

"No," Mike said, but he continued to prowl like a guard dog protecting its property.

"Those vampires in the cave, they weren't Savages, were they?"

"No."

"But they would have killed me; I felt that from them. They were unraveling…"

Her voice trailed off when she recalled the unraveling she'd sensed in Mike too. He would have killed Holden if she hadn't intervened. And though Holden was probably dead by now, and that death was, in a way, because of Mike, even if he hadn't been the one to end Holden's life.

What he'd done to Holden was one of the cruelest things she'd ever seen, but he'd done it to protect her and because of what Holden had done to her. He wouldn't have sacrificed Holden if Holden hadn't tried to sacrifice her first. She felt confident Mike wouldn't turn his brutality on her.

"They were starving," Mike said. "They probably would have killed you. Maybe not on purpose, but they were losing control of themselves."

"Thank you for stopping them."

Mollie's breath caught when his head turned toward her. As his striking blue eyes met hers, the vulnerability in his gaze confused her and tore at her heart.

"They never should have gotten so close to you. I should have gotten there sooner," he said.

"Mike—"

Mollie gasped as, before she could finish her sentence, he closed the distance between them. His hands on her shoulders were tender when he pulled her closer to him.

"It will never happen again," he vowed and bent his head to hers.

His breath caressed her lips as his mouth hovered above hers. Tingles of anticipation raced over Mollie's skin. The hair on her arms and nape stood on end as his nearness caused all her nerve endings to come alive. After what she saw him do today, she should step away and put some distance between them. She didn't move.

When Mollie didn't shove him away or tell him to get lost, Mike closed the distance between them and claimed her mouth. He should get away from her, he should make sure their bond never progressed beyond the small steps they'd already taken, but walking away from her would take far more control than he possessed.

His arm snaked around her waist, and he lifted her against him until the enticing evidence of his erection pressed between her legs. Unable to stop herself, Mollie whimpered and squirmed against him in a desperate attempt to get closer.

Suddenly, she hated the clothes between them as her fingers tugged at his shirt and her heart hammered in anticipation. This man could break her in two, and they were caught in a nightmare, but in his arms, she'd never felt more protected or cherished.

Mike's fingers threaded through her hair, and he deepened the kiss until her apple scent burned into his nostrils. Her tongue and lean body were all he could feel as the taste of her ingrained itself on him. She was everything he'd ever wanted, everything he'd been missing over the years, and he couldn't get enough of her.

The cracking of a stick pierced through the fog of ecstasy Mollie weaved around him. He tore his mouth away from hers when he recalled they were standing in the woods, where anyone or any*thing* could find them. A low growl reverberated in his chest as his grip on her tightened.

"We have to keep moving," he whispered.

A rush of fear buried Mollie's disappointment as she recalled where they were. "Yes."

"Oh God." Mollie bent over and rested her hands on her knees. Breathing shallowly, she fought the nausea rolling through her, but her head still spun like she'd taken ten trips on the tilt-a-whirl at a carnival. "Oh God, no."

Mike rested his hand on her shoulder while he gazed in disbelief at the sight before him. Out of everything he'd expected to encounter, *this* had never crossed his mind. And he had no idea what to do about it.

"Gives credence to that whole *Island of Doctor Moreau* theory, doesn't it?" Mollie asked, unable to contain a bitter laugh.

Mike had to agree with her.

"We're so screwed," she whispered.

"No matter what, I *am* getting us out of this. Come on."

Mollie took another deep breath. *Get it together. You have to be strong for Aida. And at least this discovery will make it easier to find her.*

Mollie focused on that hopeful realization as she tried to pull herself from the bleak pit of despair sucking at her soul.

Rising, she met Mike's gaze before turning her attention to the lighthouse they'd left behind yesterday. In the rays of the setting sun, the rotting building appeared more ominous as she realized their journey had taken them in a complete circle of what she now realized was an island.

CHAPTER TWENTY-FOUR

STANDING at the top of the lighthouse again, Mike surveyed the land that he now knew was an island with a more critical eye. They were stuck on an island, but where was it located? Were they off the coast of Canada, or maybe Maine... or somewhere else entirely? And how far were they from the mainland?

Most importantly, how could they get off this berg of land?

He hadn't seen any boats in their travel, but they'd stayed away from the cliffs throughout sections of the island. He'd missed many areas of the shoreline to remain hidden in the forest, and the boats may be located there. There had to be boats somewhere, but he had a feeling they were heavily guarded.

"It will be easier to find Aida now," Mollie said as she gazed over the treetops to where Mike had said there was a building beyond the barn. "If she's still alive, she's in that house or building or whatever it is out there."

Mike rested his hand on her shoulder to give her some comfort as he sensed her sorrow beneath the words *"if she's still alive."*

"And if Jack and Doug are still alive, we'll have an easier time locating them than I anticipated," Mike said. "Plus, we can't be far from the mainland. I'm not sure which direction land is in, but the water separating us from it can't be too big; the Savages wouldn't be able to traverse it otherwise."

"Three bright sides, what about the bad?"

"It's not a large island. I suspect the reason we haven't encountered many others is they've stayed more to the woods while we've been sticking to the cliffs for a while. I'm sure some have gone down the cliffs in search of a hiding place, and others are probably dead, but a fair amount of vampires escaped with us."

A hollow pit formed in Mollie's stomach when she realized what he was saying. "And all those vampires are going to be hungry."

"Many will feed on the animals."

"Why weren't the ones who attacked me today doing that?"

"Because animal blood isn't as good as human blood, and some, even if they're not killers, will refuse to drink it until it's too late for them. They also probably didn't realize we were on an island and might have believed they had a chance to get somewhere with a higher human population soon, so they decided to hold off on feeding. Or they could have been further gone than anyone realized when they were set free, and animal blood no longer satisfied them."

"So that means there may be others who were further gone, feel the same way, and we're trapped with them."

"Yes."

"Great," she muttered.

"There's more," he said reluctantly. He hated to deliver more bad news to her, but she had to know everything.

"What?"

"I covered a lot of ground earlier, but this island isn't very big. With this many vamps and humans running around here, the animal population is going to dwindle. It will take a while, and not all the vamps will kill the animals they feed on, I don't, but others will. However, we have no idea how long we're going to be here, so we need to prepare for the worst."

"Hope for the best; expect the worst."

"Yes."

"Okay. So, we need a plan to get off this island as soon as we find Aida and your friends. We also need a boat, which should be easy to find," Mollie said sarcastically.

"And those boats are probably well guarded."

"Beautiful. Can we build a raft and shove our asses off this rock?"

The idea of being adrift at sea on a makeshift raft while baking under the sun until she croaked, was near the top of her list of ways she did *not* want to die, but it was better than being breakfast for some starved vampire in this hellhole.

"We have no rope or cut wood we can tie together," Mike said.

"Stop being practical," she muttered.

Mike chuckled, but he didn't find anything amusing about their situation. On the horizon, the sky turned a vivid shade of red when the sun dipped out of view. "We have to leave now if we're going to make it to the rock shelter before nightfall."

Mollie followed him from the lighthouse and back outside. She didn't say a word when he lifted her and held her against him. The only way they would reach the shelter before night descended was if he ran there with her. Besides, after what they discovered about this place, she craved being in his arms again.

She buried her face in the hollow of his neck and inhaled his tantalizing scent of cedar and the fresh water they recently washed in. They'd located another stream before arriving at the lighthouse, or maybe it was the same one as yesterday, and stopped to clean themselves with the water. Mike had left her hidden in a pine tree while he went to boil water for her and hunt some food. He'd come back in less than an hour with another squirrel and a pot of water.

She'd eaten while he kept a lookout, and it had eased the hunger in her belly, but she felt another hunger waking as he ran and his thickly muscled body flowed effortlessly against hers. Mollie pressed closer until as much of her body touched his as possible.

It still wasn't enough.

The scent of Mollie's growing arousal tantalized his nose when

Mike stopped before the small shelter they stayed in before. She slid down him, but instead of shying away from his growing erection, her hips leaned into his, and she rubbed against him.

Mike gritted his teeth to keep from groaning when he released her and stepped away. He had to make sure it was still safe inside the small enclosure. Walking was difficult as he made his way to the hollow of rocks, pulled aside the sticks he'd left covering the entrance, and poked his head inside. He scented the air before slipping inside to discover their hiding place still empty.

When he returned, he held his hand out to Mollie, and she took it. Mike stayed near the front to rebuild the cover over the entrance while she slipped inside and settled at the back. He was almost done replacing the sticks when the first howls punctured the air. Mike crawled over to join her and drew Mollie into his arms as the tortured scream of impending death pierced the air.

MOLLIE SAT on Mike's lap as she curled against his chest. Outside, thunder rolled, and the distant flash of lightning illuminated the branches, rocks, and dirt blockading the entrance. She'd woken a few minutes ago, but though her neck ached, she stayed where she was so as not to wake him; he'd slept little over the past few days.

Shifting against her, Mike murmured something that sounded like her name. His fingers twitched against her ass as, sometime in his sleep, his hand had fallen to her butt. She wasn't going to complain about the intimate hold. Then he jerked against her and released a muffled noise.

Fearing something was nearby, and that was why he was so unsettled, Mollie lifted her head to examine the dark crevice. When nothing moved, and Mike's breath tickled her ear, she realized he still slept and must be having a bad dream.

Mollie chanced hitting the light button on the side of her watch. The dim glow under Mike's chin lit his face but didn't penetrate far beyond the shadows surrounding them. His expression was not relaxed in sleep but tensed, and lines etched his forehead. His legs jerked beneath her; his mouth flattened into a firm line as his grip on her became almost bruising.

Under normal circumstances, he would never harm her, but in his sleep, he might do something without realizing it. But how did she wake a sleeping vampire having a nightmare without winding up snapped like a toothpick?

There was a reason they said let sleeping dogs lie. What if she startled him and he reacted by breaking her neck?

Mollie gulped, but when he jerked again and kicked out, she realized she had to wake him. If he didn't kill her in his sleep, he might attract attention if this kept up. She hadn't heard any howls since waking, but that didn't mean things weren't out there, hunting them.

Resting her hand on his cheek, Mollie slid it over until it covered his mouth. *Please don't kill me.*

She gripped his shoulder and gave him a rough shake. His mouth pursed against her hand and a line formed between his brows, but he still didn't open his eyes. When Mollie gave him another shake, his eyes flew open to reveal their ruby color. His lips skimmed back against her palm, and his fangs touched her skin.

Mollie's heart leapt into her throat; she threw herself back to jerk free of his arms, but they cinched around her, drawing her closer.

"Wait! No!" she gasped.

"Easy, shh, it's okay," Mike soothed as the glow from her watch went out, and he realized he'd scared the shit out of her. The rush of her pulse sounded like drums in his ears. "Easy, Mollie."

Ever so slowly, she relaxed in his arms. But she placed her hands against his shoulders and kept her arms ramrod straight in a useless attempt to hold him back should he try to sink his fangs into her.

"I won't hurt you," he whispered, but her anxiety didn't ease.

In the dim light filtering through the branches, her face remained pinched, and her eyes narrowed though he doubted she could see much of him now that her watch was off.

"You... you were having a nightmare, I think," she croaked.

He frowned as he recalled the dream that had gripped him in its bleak depths. In the nightmare, they were attacked, and he was unable to save her. She'd died in his arms after countless vampires fed on her. He'd been helpless to protect her, and even in his sleep, the loss of her tore his heart from his chest.

"Your eyes were red when you opened them," she said.

"It was the worst nightmare I've ever had," he admitted, closing his eyes; she couldn't see them, but he knew they were still red.

"I didn't want to wake you, but you were making noise, and I was scared you might hurt me in your sleep."

"Never. I would never..." His voice trailed off as a hideous possibility occurred to him and self-hatred unlike anything he'd ever experienced swamped him. "*Did* I hurt you?"

"No. You were holding me tight, but you didn't hurt me."

Mike's shoulders slumped. "Good. I swear to you, Mollie, I will defend your life with mine."

Mollie eased against him, but she didn't remove her hands from his shoulders. "I believe you, Mike, but you scared me."

"I'm sorry," he murmured, and his head fell forward.

Mollie finally relaxed her arms and leaned toward him. She couldn't see him, but she heard the distress in his voice. When her arms slid up to his shoulders, his head bowed until it rested against her chest, and he inhaled a deep breath. Sensing he'd been more upset by what happened than she was, she threaded her fingers through his hair and held him against her as she sought to comfort him.

Mike's arms locked around her waist, and he held her close, savoring her warmth. His dream was so real that the bloody image of her haunted him as he clasped the very much alive version closer.

Lifting his head, he gazed into her green eyes, which were vivid in the shadows hugging the contours of her face. He cupped one of her cheeks and ran his thumb over her silken skin before drawing her closer.

Mollie didn't resist when he pulled her to him, and his lips unerringly found hers in the dark. *He can probably see me better than I can see him.*

Mike's hands flattened against the small of her back as her mouth opened to his invasion. He tasted the heated depths of her in long, leisurely strokes. He'd never felt this in sync with a woman before; there was no hesitancy or uncertainty with Mollie as she countered each of his thrusts with ease.

Because she belongs to me. He did not doubt it anymore, not after that nightmare. The woman in his arms was his mate, and he didn't know how he would get them both out of this mess alive. But no matter what it took, he would make sure she survived.

When Mike's hands dipped down to the bottom of her shirt, Mollie didn't stiffen against him as she had last time. She knew this might be the only chance they would have to be together. They had no idea what tomorrow held on this island and, vampire or not, she wanted this man.

When his hands slid under her shirt, Mollie gave herself over to the exquisite sensation of his large palms moving against her flesh. Tomorrow they would go back to fighting for survival, but tonight, she would lose herself in him.

CHAPTER TWENTY-FIVE

MIKE SENSED a giving in Mollie as she leaned in to him with a sigh. His cock strained against the zipper of his jeans as the overwhelming urge to possess her consumed him.

Easy, he cautioned himself. *Take your time and enjoy her.*

He wanted to savor her for hours, but the knowledge he was about to take his mate for the first time had his vampire nature trying to take over. His fangs pricked and lengthened with the impulse to sink in to her delicate throat.

She's in so much danger on this island, and I can make her stronger.

But the transition from human to vampire could take hours, it was excruciating, and she would have to feed soon after. She could drink only from him, but he would have to consume lots of blood beforehand to sustain her. He'd only had animal blood since arriving here, and he hadn't fed today.

He couldn't change her until he was better prepared and they were somewhere secure. Then…

His thoughts trailed off when she rested her hand on his cheek, instinctively calming him with her touch though she couldn't know how close he was to unraveling.

This deep connection to someone that went beyond blood, sex, and family was what he'd been seeking in his life. He'd never experienced it with anyone before. He loved his family, but Mollie was the piece he'd been missing.

Mollie broke the kiss to lift her arms when he tugged her shirt up until it rested beneath her breasts. Mike pulled it over her head and tossed it aside. When lightning flashed outside, it illuminated him enough that she could watch as he feasted on the sight of her. Her black bra was simple and didn't push up her small breasts, but he gazed at her as if she were wearing the sexiest piece of lingerie in the catalog.

After the light faded, she still felt his eyes on her. At one time, anyone else gazing at her in such a way would have made her cover herself up and flared her feelings of inadequacy. But over the years, she'd grown more comfortable with her body, and she didn't feel any shame, especially while Mike was looking at her as if she was the most beautiful woman in the world.

Mike's eyes ran over Mollie again when her arms lowered to her sides. She was long, lean, and delectable. Sliding his hands around her, he unclasped her bra and tossed it aside. His breath sucked in, and his erection jumped against his jeans when he bared her breasts to him.

Bending his head, he kissed her collarbone while he clasped her breasts. Mollie's back bowed as she arced into his touch and her fingers threaded through his hair. She held him closer while his tongue flickered over the nipple his thumb had brought to life.

A couple of years ago, after her mother's death, Mollie had sought something—she still wasn't sure what—from one of the mousy men she'd dated. Alvin was her first, and his touch had lacked something she could never explain.

Mollie remembered doubting what she was doing with him as she was doing it, but lost and lonely, she stayed with him for a couple of months before his job moved him to Arizona. She wasn't upset when he said he was leaving. He hadn't suggested she go with him, and she happily helped him pack. After him, she decided not to date again until she was over her grief, and she hadn't.

However, she had no doubts now as Mike's touch lit her blood on fire and turned her body into something she didn't quite recognize as she shifted to wrap her legs around his hips. She moaned when the movement brought her into intimate contact with the obvious evidence of his arousal.

Lifting herself, she eased back down the rigid length of his erection and shuddered when little jolts of pleasure ran down her spine. Desperate to feel more of him, she gripped the edge of his shirt and tugged it up. Cold air rushed over the wet nipple he'd been sucking when he released it to help her pull his shirt off.

Mike encircled his arm around her waist and, lifting her, reclaimed the quilt that had fallen free of them. He dropped the blanket over the ground before laying her on top of it.

Another flash of lightning illuminated the night, and thunder shook the ground. In the burst of light, Mike's eyes were the most vibrant blue she'd ever seen as he stared at her with a look of reverence she didn't understand, but she thrilled at it. He gazed at her like she was the last lifeboat on a sinking ship, and she longed to be the one who saved him. She had no idea what she was saving him from, but she sensed he needed it.

Then she was left in the dark again. Her breath caught when his hands fell to her waist and he slid the button of her jeans free. Mollie lifted her hips when the zipper slid down before he tugged her jeans and underwear down to her calves. His touch was tender when he pulled her sneakers and socks off before slipping the rest of her clothes free.

Another strike of lightning revealed him kneeling over her with his hand on the button of his jeans. She marveled at the expanse of his shoulders and the thick muscles cording his chest and shoulders before the illumination faded.

Uneasiness slid through her; he was an immortal, powerful being, and she was so very mortal.

Shifting, Mike untied and kicked off his boots before tugging his jeans down and tossing everything aside. He turned his attention back to Mollie, and when the lightning flashed again, he saw the desire as well as uneasiness in her gaze.

"Human and vampires can do this?" she whispered.

Mike smiled as he rested his hand on her chest. The beat of her heart thudded against his palm as the tantalizing scent of her teased his nostrils. "Yes," he assured her.

"What about diseases? I doubt you have a condom." She didn't want to be asking these things, not when her body was screaming for him, but the practical part of her brain was rearing its ugly head.

"Vampires can't carry diseases."

"But you can get me pregnant?" She'd stopped taking the pill when she gave up dating.

"I won't spill in you."

Not foolproof, but neither were condoms.

He knew she was satisfied with his answer when her back arched into his touch as he ran his hand down the center of her body, over her flat stomach, and down to the trimmed patch of black hair shielding her sex from him. When he dipped his hand between her legs, Mollie squirmed toward him as he slid his fingers over her enticing wetness before rubbing her clit.

"Oh," she breathed as her fingers curled into the quilt and pulled it toward her.

Mike slid a finger into her and groaned when her muscles gripped his finger while he moved deeper into her. He teased her as her breath came more rapidly and her body thrust against his palm. He wanted to pull his hand away from her and replace it with his cock, but he found he couldn't stop his exploration of her body or tear his attention away from her reaction to him.

Running his other hand over her breast, he rolled her nipple between his thumb and forefinger. He grew harder when her head fell back to expose the delicate column of her slender throat. While he explored her body, he stretched her sheath further by slipping another finger inside her.

His dick throbbed with need as he watched her breasts sway and her delicious moans filled his ears. She was all he could see, smell, hear, and feel as every one of his heightened senses attuned to her.

Saliva filled his mouth, and his fangs lengthened as he stroked her faster. Her muscles clenched around his fingers, her body bowed, and she came with a cry. Mike slid his hand over her mouth to muffle the sound of her ecstasy, though he longed to hear her screaming his name.

Panting, Mollie collapsed on the ground as another flash lit Mike's face. The ravenous look on his face as he gazed down at where his fingers still idly moved within her caused her haze of euphoria to dwindle. This powerful vampire would consume her in every way possible, but instead of the realization scaring her, she found herself longing for it.

Then his hand slid away, and his eyes met hers before darkness descended. When Mollie lifted her arms to him, he came into them, and she embraced him against her. She'd never experienced anything more sensual than his unyielding body moving against hers as his skin slid over her aching nipples while he settled himself between her thighs.

Grasping his shaft, Mike guided it to her entrance and rubbed against her as he bent his head to claim her mouth. Slick with longing, she parted for him as his head stretched her while he slid further into her. The tightness of her sheath enveloping him nearly caused him to spill as excitement hammered through his body, and a sense of rightness stole through him.

Mine, she's all mine.

Mollie's fingers dug into his back; she wiggled her hips as the size of him caused her some discomfort, but gradually she adjusted to the feel of him as he settled himself deep inside her. She expected him to start thrusting until he finished, but he remained unmoving as his hands caressed her face.

"Mollie," he breathed before kissing her again.

Unprepared for him not to finish himself off and roll away, it took her a second to respond to his questing tongue while he remained unmoving within her. Then he pulled slowly out before sliding back into her. The delicious friction of the movement stoked her already hypersensitive body to higher levels of passion.

Her fingers entangled in his hair as she drew him closer and deepened the kiss. His canines extended against her lips, but they didn't stir anxiety within her; instead, she found herself licking the tip of one fang.

When she wrapped her legs around his waist, the movement drew him deeper into her. She licked his fang again before nipping at his bottom lip and lifting her hips to meet his when he plunged into her.

Mike slammed his palms onto the ground to keep from embracing her, lifting her off the ground, and fucking her until she was too exhausted to move. *Human! Human! Human!* Never had he needed to remind himself he was with a mortal before, but all his restraint was spiraling away.

When her tongue grazed his fang, his restraint crumbled, and slipping his arms around her waist, he broke their kiss and lifted her off the ground. Mollie's eyes flew open to meet his as lightning split the sky and a deluge of rain pounded the rocks over their heads.

Bracing his knees apart, Mike glanced at the ceiling to make sure her head wouldn't hit it before guiding her body against his. Staring into her eyes, some of his control returned as she found and matched the demanding rhythm he set for her.

When her lids started to droop and her breaths came in pants, he knew he was pushing her toward climax again. Bending his head, he caught her nipple between his teeth and nipped at the bud.

Mollie's fingers dug into his sweat-slickened back when his fangs scraped her flesh. She'd believed she would hate the sensation, there was nothing worse than a cat scratch or one from thorns, but she found herself craving more.

If you offer me your blood, I will gladly accept. His words from days ago returned to her. He was inside her, a part of her, yet she yearned for *more*. She didn't understand it and thought maybe she'd lost her mind, but suddenly she had to know what it would feel like to have Mike taking her in more than one way.

She dropped her head to his and nuzzled his ear as she whispered, "I'm offering you my blood."

For a second, he showed no reaction to her words, but then his hands dug into her flesh, and he lifted his head. His thick muscles vibrated beneath her palms, his breathing stopped, and his body stilled.

"What?" he asked, uncertain he'd heard her right.

"I'm offering you my blood. I want to know what it feels like to have you feed on me."

Saliva rushed into his mouth at the idea of it, but he held back. "You're weakened from not eating and drinking—"

"I'm fine, and you don't have to take much, right?"

Right, but once he started, he might not be able to stop until he turned her. Mike was also afraid that tasting her would accelerate the mating bond and he'd become as crazed as Liam before his friend changed Sera.

When his gaze fell to her throat and the pulse of her vein, he realized it was already too late for him. Taking her tonight had pushed him closer to the edge, and the constant threat to her life would only unravel him further. Tasting her blood wouldn't make him anymore crazed for her than he already was.

Mollie tilted her head to the side as Mike's finger glided down the side of her neck. Her heart skipped a beat when he bent forward until his breath warmed her throat.

"If you don't fight it, it will only hurt for a second," he murmured. Mollie nodded as he cinched her hair in his hand and turned her head for better access.

She waited for him to strike, but his tongue traced over her skin as his body started moving again. Closing her eyes, Mollie lost herself to the pleasure he so easily stoked within her. She clasped his nape and clung to him as another orgasm built within her.

"Mike," she whispered.

And then he struck. Mollie bit back a startled cry when his fangs pierced her flesh. She almost reeled back, but as swift as the pain came, it went. One second, it was there, and the next, happiness rose to fill her as she felt the first pull of her blood.

She should scream and fight against him, he was draining *her* blood, yet she became more lost to him. She'd never been so connected to someone before—Mike was in every one of her cells as he became a part of her. Tears of joy burned her eyes as she gave herself over to him completely.

Mike knew she'd surrendered to him when her body slumped against his and her joy radiated through her blood. He'd been right, she tasted better than she smelled, and the second her blood hit his tongue, it flooded him with power.

Her body quickened against his as the muscles of her sheath gripped his dick more firmly. Turning her head into his neck, her small teeth bit down on his flesh to stifle the cry she released when she came apart in his arms. Unable to take it anymore, Mike withdrew from her and held her close as he found his release against her belly.

The heat of his semen branded her flesh as he cradled her to him and retracted his fangs. He'd said he wouldn't spill in her, it was what she'd asked for, but she couldn't help feeling oddly disappointed he didn't finish inside her.

She pressed closer to him as lingering contractions from her orgasm rocked her body. She'd never experienced anything like it before and knew, without a doubt, Mike had ruined her for all other men. How could anyone ever compete with him?

But then, she didn't want them to. She was probably the biggest idiot in the world for allowing herself to fall so fast for a vampire, but it was too late to stop herself; she was a goner.

CHAPTER TWENTY-SIX

"Mollie. Mollie, wake up."

Mollie's eyes fluttered open when the hand on her shoulder gave her a gentle shake. She frowned as she gazed at the sticks in front of her. She'd been dreaming of home and Aida, but with a start, she realized she was far from home.

Bolting upright, she recalled she was naked only when the quilt fell away from her.

"Easy," Mike murmured, stroking his hand over her shoulder.

The events of last night rushed back to her. She cursed the blush flushing her cheeks as she turned her head to look at him. Her breath caught when she found his gaze hungrily drinking in her exposed body. So, it wasn't just a "we're in the dark and fighting for our lives" type of thing last night; he desired her in the daytime too.

When her gaze fell to his crotch and the cock straining against his jeans, her nipples puckered in response. A pleasant soreness remained between her legs, but fresh wetness also spread there as she stared at him.

Tearing his gaze from the slender curve of her back and hips, Mike focused on the far wall. If he didn't look away, he'd take her again, and he had to get her food and water before they left here.

"I'm going to find some supplies for you," he said.

Mollie's gaze returned to the sun poking around their barrier. Gathering the quilt against her chest, she adjusted her position as she searched for her clothes. "Now that we know it's an island, we have to go to the building you saw beyond the barn. Aida *must* be there," she said.

Mike tensed; he'd promised to find her sister, and he would, but he didn't want her anywhere near the bastards who brought them here. But what else could he do with her? He could get her off the island, no matter what it took or how much she resisted, then come back for her sister. He'd bring a lot of help and destroy every prick on this piece of land.

However, if he forced her to go, she would hate him for the rest of their lives. He did not doubt that. Could he hide her somewhere? That would be a better option, and maybe once they got closer to the house and barn, he would be able to find a safe place to keep her, but for now, she would stay by his side.

"There could be other properties here we haven't seen yet," he said.

"It's a place to start," she replied as she gathered her clothes.

"Yes," he reluctantly agreed. "I have to go."

Clasping her chin, he turned her head toward him. Mollie gazed into his eyes before he kissed her. She was starting to lose herself to him when he pulled away and handed her the rifle.

"Shoot to kill," he said.

"I will," she promised.

He pulled the sticks away from the opening and carefully replaced them after he left. Mollie finished dressing, folded the quilt, and settled against the wall to wait for him. The events of last night played through her head on a loop that left her smiling as well as questioning what it all meant. Not like the trajectory of their relationship mattered while death and water surrounded them, but she couldn't help wondering if there could be any future for them.

Ugh, you're acting like an idiotic teen. Any future for you? He's a vampire who has probably had dozens of women, and you're as human as it gets; besides, vampires have mates.

Mollie shifted uncomfortably at the reminder. The woman Mike was destined to be with forever could be out there somewhere. Unexpected jealousy clawed at her chest. She didn't want to give him up, especially not to another woman, but she wouldn't have any choice if he discovered his mate or simply walked away for someone else.

No matter what transpired between them, she would *not* ask him where this was going or what it meant. All that mattered now was finding Aida and surviving. A relationship between them, past relationships, and the future didn't matter when none of it was of any use to them. The present was all they had.

He was only gone half an hour before he returned. Mollie's stomach rumbled when he handed her two rabbits and some water.

Mike carefully restacked the branches while Mollie dug into her meal. He hadn't bothered to hunt for himself today; her blood still coursed through his veins, and though he'd only taken a small amount, he felt stronger than if he'd fed from three deer.

Turning to her, he settled against the rocks to watch as she ate. *His* mate. And he'd gotten lucky with her; she was strong, giving, sensual, and loving. He hadn't waited as long as many other vamps to find his mate, but more than others, and he would have waited more years if it meant he still found Mollie.

Licking her fingers, Mollie tossed the second rabbit aside and drank the last of her water before handing the pot and cup to Mike. He gathered the animal remains in case they ended up having to return here—he didn't want to attract any animals—and left the den.

Mollie followed him into the open and accepted his hand when he offered it to help her rise. She smiled at him when he squeezed her hand, drew her close, and briefly kissed her forehead. "Let's go," he said.

MIKE'S TENSION ratcheted up once they left the coastline behind and cut back into the middle of the island. Through here, the trees were thicker, the shadows deeper, and the hiding places more abundant. He *never* should have chanced bringing her through here. Let her hate him for trying to get her off the island before finding her sister, at least she would be alive to hate him.

Mollie frowned at Mike's back as the anger he exuded increased with every step. She didn't know what had him so worked up, but when she tried to tug her hand free of his, he gripped it tighter.

"What is wrong?" she whispered.

Mike didn't sense anyone nearby, but that didn't mean something wasn't hunting them. "We should have stayed closer to the shore."

"We have to look for Aida."

"We should go back to the shore. I'll find a way to get you off this island, and then I'll come back for her."

"No."

"Mollie—"

"I'm not leaving until I know what happened to my sister. You can run, but I won't."

Mike strove to restrain his temper as he surveyed the woods again. "I'm not running. But you must understand there is a good chance your sister is dead and risking your life to find her is pointless. I *will* come back for her, Jack, and Doug after I get you somewhere safe. There is no safe place on this island."

Fury coiled through her. She realized there was a good chance Aida was dead, but she wasn't giving up until she knew for sure. She didn't need Mike treating her like some idiotic, fragile person who didn't understand reality and would break easily until then. She'd withstood more than most in her short life, and she would *not* break.

"Yeah, right," she retorted. "We leave this island, and you'll never come back."

Mike's eyes were red when they returned to her. She'd seen that color come over them before, but she'd *never* seen it directed at her. She almost backed away from him, but when it came to her sister, she wouldn't back away from anyone—not even a pissed-off, easily two-hundred-fifty-pound vampire.

"I gave you my word I would help find your sister, and I'm going to keep it," he growled through gritted teeth.

The idea she thought so little of him didn't sit well with him, but he had told her that her sister was most likely dead. She probably wasn't in the mood to think much of him right now.

"I have friends on this island too," he reminded her. "I would never leave them behind."

"Then why don't you go search for your friends, and I'll find Aida."

"What?" he demanded, sure he'd heard her wrong.

"I absolve you of your word. I don't know why you've been looking after me, but you don't have to anymore. You don't owe me anything." She didn't want to separate from him, but Aida came first. "Go, find your friends, and I'll find my sister."

Mike stared at her like she'd just told him to put on fairy wings and prance around naked. Mollie crossed her arms over her chest and gazed around the woods. She didn't kid herself into thinking her chances of surviving alone were good, but she'd rather be alone than leave Aida behind.

"That's *never* going to happen," Mike vowed.

"And why not? You've more than paid any debt you think you might have for me getting you out of your cage, and you don't owe me anything because we had sex. I'm sure you've had sex with other women and walked away from them; it's fine, I understand."

"I am *not* leaving you alone or walking away from you."

"Mike—"

"No!" he interjected. "Get that idea out of your head, *right now*! Your father left you; I won't."

She recoiled as if he'd slapped her. He despised the wounded expression on her face and that he was the one to cause it, but her words had pushed him into a state of pissed off he'd never experienced before. Not only did she think so little of him, but even after last night, she would still walk away from him.

She's not a vampire; she doesn't feel the pull of the mating bond. The reminder did little to ease the turmoil churning inside him like lava in a volcano about to erupt.

Mollie didn't know how to reply to him. She'd opened up to him, and now he was using her revelations against her. How *dare* he bring her father into this? "My father has nothing to do with this!" she spat.

"Doesn't he?"

"No," she hissed through her teeth, but she couldn't help wondering if, perhaps, he did. Mike could break her heart, so was she trying to walk away from him before he walked away from her? She'd believed herself over what happened with her father, but she realized now, she wasn't.

"I'm *never* walking away from you, Mollie. Don't suggest it again."

"What do you mean you're never walking away from me?"

Mike hadn't planned to tell her she was his mate until they were off this island. She had enough to deal with without him heaping that on her too, but maybe she should know. As a mortal, she couldn't possibly understand how intense the bond was, but perhaps it would help her to deal with his rising uneasiness and anger better. Or at least he hoped it would.

He opened his mouth to explain to her, but before he could, a branch cracking behind him caused him to spin around. Lifting one of his arms, he pressed it into Mollie's chest and pushed her back as the cracking became footsteps.

CHAPTER TWENTY-SEVEN

MIKE TURNED and plucked her off the ground. Slipping into the shadows of a large maple, he knelt with her behind a cluster of boulders. Two vampires emerged from the woods—a man and a woman. The woman held a crossbow at her side while the man carried a rifle at the ready.

Their reddened eyes, the weapons they carried, and the patch on their black shirts marked them as two of the Savages who'd imprisoned them. They strode through the shadows of the forest, in a place where the sun didn't penetrate the thick conifers, before stopping near a small boulder.

At his side, Mollie eased the rifle from her shoulder and clasped it before her. The two vamps glanced at each other before studying the trees above them. To the left, the conifers were thicker while to the right, oaks and maples were more prevalent and allowed more sunlight to filter through.

The Savages nodded to the left before heading in that direction. Mike watched them walk away with their weapons. Mollie might be able to shoot and kill them both, or at least impair them, but the gunfire would draw more Savages.

If he was going to take them, and their weapons, it would have to be hand-to-hand. "Stay here and don't shoot unless it's necessary," he hissed to Mollie before slipping into the trees.

Mollie didn't have a chance to respond before Mike glided away from her and vanished behind a large tree. He reappeared before fading in and out of view like a ghost floating through walls. Mollie's heart hammered as her attention drifted between him and the vamps he stalked.

What if something happened to him? Just minutes ago, she'd been willing to walk away from him, but she couldn't stand the idea of him being hurt or killed by one of these bastards. She didn't want to lose him; she *wouldn't* lose him!

Lifting the rifle to her shoulder, she aimed it at the backs of the vampires as they moved further away from her. She was a decent shot, but she was no sniper. At this distance, she could only hope to wound them.

Then Mike suddenly emerged next to the man. Mollie flinched but didn't look away when Mike enclosed his hand on the man's throat, lifted him off his feet, and swung him toward the woman. The woman took a startled step back, raised her crossbow, and fired. The bolt slammed into the center of the man's chest.

Mike crushed the Savage's windpipe before he could scream and threw the vampire at the woman. The woman's shot hadn't been a killing one, but it injured the man, and his inability to breathe slowed him. When the Savage fell into the woman, she was shoved backward and almost knocked off her feet.

The man hit the ground as the woman staggered into a tree. Before she could recover, Mike pounced on her. When she swung the crossbow up, Mike seized the end of it and shoved it back at her. It caught her under the chin and snapped her head back. Mike drove his fist into her chest, gripped her heart, and yanked it from her before tossing it aside.

The other Savage was rising when Mike lifted the crossbow, pulled a bolt free and plunged it into the man's heart. The man's mouth parted on an O of surprise, and his fingers scrabbled at the arrow before Mike pulled it free. The vamp staggered toward him but collapsed on top of the woman.

Lifting the woman, Mike removed the pouch of bolts hanging from her side and attached it to his belt before sliding the crossbow onto his back. The scent of apples alerted him to Mollie's approach. Turning his head, he spotted her slipping through the woods as he pulled the rifle from the man.

Adjusting the man, Mike searched him for more supplies. He found a handful of bullets in the man's front pockets along with a butterfly knife. He slid the knife into his pocket. Stepping out from behind an oak tree, Mollie approached him.

"Which rifle would you prefer?" Mike asked as he hefted the gun he'd taken from the Savage. "I'm good with an arrow, not so much with a gun."

"This one," Mollie said, touching the strap across her shoulder. "I already know how it shoots, and they're both the same caliber. Are there any more bullets?"

Mike handed her the ones he'd removed from the vamp. Then she took the rifle from him and emptied the ammo into her hand. Feeling better prepared to continue, Mike rested his hand against her cheek as he sought to reconnect with her. He wasn't sure she wouldn't turn away from him or slap his hand aside, but he hoped she'd gotten over their disagreement.

She couldn't hide her uncertainty, but she still turned her head into his touch and closed her eyes as her lips brushed his palm. Unable to resist, he brushed back a strand of black hair and caressed her cheek with his other hand.

"Let's find Aida," he said, even as the vampire within him screamed to take her from here, but he couldn't tolerate having her hate him.

Her eyes flew open, and she smiled at him. "Yes."

He lowered his hands and was about to turn away when a shadow slid from the trees behind her. Mike pulled her back and stepped in front of her as he lifted the crossbow and aimed at the chest of the vampire who emerged.

"Whoa!" Doug blurted, throwing his hands up.

Unable to believe what he was seeing, Mike blinked before he lowered the bow and grinned at his friend. Doug cautiously studied the two of them before approaching.

"I thought you were going to shoot me," Doug muttered.

"I almost did," Mike admitted as he swung the bow onto his back and strode toward his friend.

Embracing, they clapped each other on the back and held on for longer than usual, but Mike was reluctant to let Doug go. He hadn't let himself consider the possibility they might be dead, but the fear had niggled at the back of his mind.

He also hadn't realized how much he missed Doug and Jack until he saw Doug again. They bickered and occasionally fought, but they'd been friends since he was a kid. Rarely had a day passed in the last forty-some-odd years when he hadn't seen or spoken with the two of them, David, and Liam.

Mollie lowered her rifle as the rest of her annoyance with Mike faded. She couldn't be mad at him when he had that look of love and relief on his face. He'd missed Jack and Doug as much as she missed Aida.

"Jack?" Mike asked Doug when they separated.

"I haven't seen him since we escaped the barn. I don't know where he is or if he's alive."

"He's alive," Mike said confidently. "If anyone's going to kill him, it will be one of us."

Doug chuckled and ran a hand through his blond hair. "True enough. Or a woman."

"More likely," Mike agreed.

Doug's curious gaze turned to Mollie, and his eyes fell to the mark on her throat. The puncture of one fang was barely visible above the collar of her shirt; her clothing hid the other one. When

Mike stiffened, Doug tore his eyes away from her and looked warily back at Mike.

"Just a friend, or more?" Doug said so quietly Mike barely heard him.

"More," Mike answered.

Doug's eyebrows shot up. "Mate?"

"Yes, but she doesn't know."

"Wonderful," Doug murmured. "And the bond isn't complete."

They all knew how volatile a vampire could be when their mate was threatened, and how unstable they were when the bond between mates wasn't sealed. The fact their bond remained incomplete was evident in Mollie's still human nature.

"Have you run into anyone else we set free?" Mike asked.

"A couple of humans and two vamps, but I didn't get close," Doug said. "Come on, let's discuss this somewhere safer."

"You have a safe place?" Mollie asked as she stepped toward them.

"Not exactly safe but safer," Doug replied.

Mike held his hand out to Mollie, and she took it. "Mollie, this is Doug; Doug, this is Mollie."

"You already made these introductions in the barn," Doug told Mike and laughed. Mollie couldn't help but smile at the man's jovial laugh. "But it's nice to meet you again," Doug said to her.

"You also," Mollie replied.

She went to extend her hand toward him to shake his, but Doug was already turning away from her. She frowned when she realized he must've seen the gesture, yet he pretended like she never made a move toward him. Glancing at Mike, she noticed he'd focused his attention away from her and her interaction with Doug.

They were talking about something she couldn't hear earlier, and she had the sinking suspicion it was about her.

CHAPTER TWENTY-EIGHT

Doug pulled back the branches on a spruce tree to reveal what lay beyond. The tree was one of a cluster of spruces fighting for survival amid the oaks and maples surrounding them. The spruce's branches were thick and heavy on the outside, but the sun didn't pierce inside the cluster, and many of the needles had fallen off the dying branches within. The result was a small alcove in the center.

Mike gestured for Mollie to go ahead of him and studied the forest as she crouched to slip inside. Mike followed, and Doug entered last. Mollie gazed around the small space, perfectly situated between the five spruce trees. Needles lined the forest floor, and though a couple of them poked through her jeans when she sat, the ground was soft and dry.

For a moment, as she gazed at the surrounding trees, a sense of security slid over her. She could almost pretend she'd been transported to some magical land—a magical land where all the creatures were looking to kill and eat them.

That thought tore her attention away from the trees and back to Mike and Doug. When Mike settled in beside her, his knee rested against hers while Doug sat across from them. She noticed Doug was careful not to touch her in the cramped area though he jostled Mike when he crossed his legs.

The space was about the size of the small pop-up tent her grandpop set up in her backyard when she was a kid. She and her best friend, Donna, spent an entire week in that tent one summer. They only left it to shower, use the bathroom, gather food, and cool off in the sprinkler when it got too hot.

She didn't know what ever happened to Donna; she moved away before the start of the school year. They kept in touch for a time through phone calls, but when her grandpop died the following spring, Mollie stopped taking her calls and eventually lost touch with her.

"What do you know about this place?" Mike asked Doug in a whisper.

Pulled from the past, Mollie focused on the conversation between the two vampires.

"Not much," Doug said. "I've spent my days searching for you and Jack in a grid pattern. I haven't covered much land, but I mapped the land I trekked."

"Do you have that map?" Mollie asked.

Doug tapped the side of his head. "Right here. If I can answer it for you, I will."

"We know there is the barn and another building beyond it. Are there any more buildings where they could be keeping prisoners on this island?"

Doug visibly paled. "Island?" he croaked.

"Yes," Mike said. "We're on an island."

Doug sat back and closed his eyes. "Well, shit," he muttered. "I've come across the ocean on both sides, but I assumed it was a peninsula or a skinny piece of land. I hoped for it anyway." Opening his eyes, he focused on Mollie. "To answer your question, those are the only two buildings I know about. I've been close to the mansion beyond the barn, which is probably the other building you know about, but I didn't explore much of it."

"Why not?" Mike asked.

"Because it was near sunset, and it's where the Savages are staying."

Mollie gulped. "Are all of them there?" How would they be able to get Aida out if there were a bunch of killer vamps holed up inside the place where she was?

"Not all of them, but I think the majority are. Some Savages, mostly the ones with the security patches, are out all day searching for fugitives. They're not killing all the ones they recapture," Doug said to Mike. "I've seen security dragging some captives back to the barn."

"So Jack could be back in there?" Mike asked.

"He could be, but I doubt it. He wouldn't let them take him alive again."

"No, he wouldn't," Mike agreed.

"But we've heard them killing people at night," Mollie said.

"Those are the Savages from the mansion. When they come out at night, all bets are off, and they don't take survivors."

A tingle of dread ran down Mollie's spine, but at least those monsters left the mansion at night. That meant they might be able to get in and see if they could find Aida.

"Some of the security members are staying in the barn all day too," Doug said.

"That's a new development," Mollie said. "They didn't stay at the barn before."

"Our escape probably changed the way they run things here," Mike said. "They're making sure they keep their prisoners on lockdown."

"Okay, so they're at this mansion and the barn—"

"And some are in the woods," Doug reminded her.

"And they're in the woods," Mollie said. "Aida wasn't in the barn when we broke out, so if she's still alive, she's in the mansion. I have to get closer to it."

"We will," Mike said. Taking her hand, he threaded his fingers through hers and squeezed it.

Doug's gaze went to their hands; a small smile quirked his mouth before he glanced away and tugged at the collar of his shirt as if he were suddenly uncomfortable.

"Who's Aida?" Doug inquired.

"My sister," Mollie said. "Those things came in and took her from the barn before they brought all of you inside. I'm going to find her."

"Do you think she's still alive?" he asked Mike.

Mollie bristled as she glowered at the two of them. "It doesn't matter what *he* thinks."

Doug held his hands up in a pacifying gesture. "Believe me, I've been saying the same thing for *years*, but a few dozen Savages are crawling over the mansion and barn. Not to mention the Savages lurking in the woods, which I estimate to be eight judging by the ones I've seen. You killed two of them," he said to Mike. "By the way, thanks for saving me the effort that would have taken."

"You were stalking them?" Mike asked.

"Yeah. I wanted the crossbow. There's a grouping of boulders about a hundred feet beyond where you jumped them. I was waiting for them to get there so I could corner them and they wouldn't be able to run from me."

Mike loaded the crossbow and held it out to Doug who waved it away. "You killed them, it's yours fair and square," Doug said.

"You're better with it. Besides"—he hefted the quiver of bolts —"they make good stakes."

"You're right; I am better with it." Doug took the crossbow and settled it in his lap.

"The other problem we have is that some of the vamps we let out are hungry," Mike said before telling Doug about the vampires who attacked Mollie in the cave. "They're dead now."

"I had no doubt," Doug murmured, and his gaze flicked to

Mollie. "If the escaped vamps are starting to turn Savage too, we have a *big* problem."

"We do," Mike agreed. "And I bet if there are boats, which I'm assuming there are given we're on an island, I'm betting they're also heavily guarded by security and will be difficult to reach."

"Bastards," Doug muttered.

"Judging by the screams every night, I think a fair amount of the escapees might be dead," Mollie said.

"True," Doug agreed. "And a good amount have been recaptured. It's possible other vamps may have taken out some of the six remaining Savages patrolling the woods during the day too."

"One can hope," Mollie said, and Doug smiled.

"One can also hope that some of the Savages hanging out around the barn and mansion have also been killed. They all hunt at night," Doug said. "I haven't been close to the barn or the mansion since day two, so I don't know if their numbers have dwindled, but I imagine a few of them have been taken out by some escapees."

"Most likely," Mike murmured.

Mollie glanced at her watch; it was after one o'clock. "We still have time before the sun sets. I'd like to see this mansion."

CHAPTER TWENTY-NINE

MOLLIE STUDIED Mike as they traveled through the woods. Ever since they'd left the shelter of the spruces, he'd grown angrier and increasingly distant. His steps became more measured, his shoulders tenser, and she was sure she heard his teeth grinding together. The outline of his fangs against his upper lip was visible.

Doug shot him wary glances, and the further they went the more convinced she became the two of them were keeping something from her. The knowledge irritated her, but she wasn't going to confront them about it, not out here, and not when they were heading to where Aida might be located.

They could keep their secrets as long as they didn't interfere with trying to save Aida.

Doug held his hand up to halt them. *"It's only about half a mile that way,"* he mouthed and pointed ahead.

They fell into a single line with Doug in front and her in the middle as they continued through the trees until they arrived at the edge of the woods. Mollie crouched behind a small tree to study the building across from them. About fifty feet of green grass separated them from a massive, gray stone structure. Mollie gawked at the mansion, and her head tipped back as she tried to take it all in, but that was impossible.

The primary structure was three stories tall, with at least a dozen dormer windows. The length of it was easily the size of two football fields as two-story wings spread out from each side. The mansion looked like something out of a romance movie. It was too beautiful for the evil it housed behind the arched, covered windows and intricately carved wood front door.

For the first time, Mollie considered the possibility they might never locate her sister. How would they ever get in there? And if they did get inside, how would they find Aida? And if they did discover her, how would they get her out again and then off this island?

When her head started spinning, she lowered it into her hands and rubbed her temples. No, she *would* find Aida, she had to. She didn't know if she could take another loss in her life.

But even as she thought it, doubts swirled in her head. *What if Aida is already dead and I'm risking my life and theirs for nothing? But what if she's still alive and I leave her here to die a miserable death?*

Tears clogged her throat, but she refused to shed them. If it were just her, she wouldn't hesitate to go inside; she could never live with the not knowing if she didn't at least try to find Aida. But Mike would go with her, and from what she'd seen of their friendship, she believed Doug would too. Could she risk their lives if her sister was dead?

If something happened to Doug or Mike while they were helping her, she would never forgive herself, but she'd hate herself until the day she died if she abandoned Aida. She was damned no matter what she did, but she couldn't leave here without trying for Aida.

Mike rested his hand on Mollie's shoulder as her rising distress beat against him. "It's okay."

When she lifted her head to look at him, tears shimmered in her eyes. Those tears tore at him. She was his mate; he was supposed to make sure she experienced only happiness and security, but she'd known only melancholy and death since coming to this island.

Mike drew her into his arms, and when she lowered her head to the hollow of his throat, he buried his head in her silken hair. Her sweet scent assailed him as he ran his hands over her hair to soothe her. Her hands slid under his arms and dug into his shoulders.

"I'm going to find out what happened to her," he vowed.

He'd sensed a cracking in her. If he pushed, he might be able to convince her to leave the island, but it would destroy her if she did. She would survive this place if he found a way to take her from here, but she would never be the same, and he'd lose her anyway. He'd rather have her torn from him while she was fighting than watch her rot away until nothing remained of her.

Lifting his head, he met Doug's gaze over her shoulder. His friend stared back at him before turning away.

"I HEAR them leave the mansion and barn around eight every night," Doug said when they were settled in the cluster of spruces again. "They howl like wolves on the hunt when they leave, or at least I assume it's when they leave, as I haven't been close to either of the buildings near sunset. I don't have a death wish."

"So, you don't know if they all go out to hunt at night?" Mike asked.

"No, I don't."

Mike slid Mollie's hair through his fingers while he contemplated Doug's words. When they returned, he'd spread the quilt across the small space for her to lay on as she looked exhausted, but she'd nestled against his side instead and rested her head on his chest. She hadn't said much since they left the mansion and returned to the forest.

"When they go out tomorrow night, we'll attempt to get into the mansion," Mike said to Doug. "Tomorrow during the day, we'll search for Jack and try to get our hands on some more weapons. We'll both have to feed before going in there."

Mollie lifted her head and turned to look at him. "I'm going into the mansion too."

"No, you're not."

"Yes, I am," she insisted. "You'll need more than the two of you in there, and Aida doesn't know you. If you manage to find her, she might be too scared to leave with you."

"Then I'll carry her out of there."

His stubborn refusal grated on her nerves, but she forced herself to remain rational. It didn't matter what he said; she was going in there. However, she preferred not to fight him every step of the way. "You can't carry her; you'll need both your hands free to fight anyone who tries to stop you, and you don't know what she looks like."

"Does she look like you?"

"Yeah, kind of, but there are differences." With her heart-shaped face, golden-brown eyes, and smaller, more curvaceous figure, Aida was prettier, but Mollie wasn't going to share that info with him. She'd lose part of her argument if she told him what Aida looked like. "I'm also not going to let you risk your life for my sister while I sit idly by."

"If you're in there, you'll be a distraction to me," Mike said.

"Then don't let me be one."

Doug twirled his thumbs together as he looked from one spruce to another like they were the most fascinating trees in the world. She felt his discomfort as clearly as Mike's growing ire.

"That would be impossible," Mike grated.

"I think," Doug said, "I'm going to hunt for some dinner."

"It's almost sunset and not safe out there," Mollie protested. "There's no reason for you to leave."

"I'll be fine. I have another location I've camped in before; I'll spend the night there and meet you two here in the morning."

"Wait—"

"Thank you," Mike cut off her protest as he clasped Doug's hand.

"No reason to thank me, I'm happy to be out of here," Doug replied with a grin.

Mollie scowled at Mike when he chuckled. "It's not safe out there now," she insisted.

"It's less safe to stay here," Doug muttered. He swung the crossbow onto his back, and before she could respond, he slid through the trees.

Mollie glowered at Mike. "Are you happy now? You put your friend in danger because you're a stubborn ass."

"He'll be fine," Mike assured her.

And besides, it probably was safer for Doug out there than in here with the two of them. Mike wouldn't hurt her, he had enough control over himself to know that much, but if pushed to the edge, there was no telling what he would do. And no one could push him to the edge like Mollie.

"He's made it this far, and Doug isn't stupid," he said when she glanced anxiously at where Doug had exited. "Besides, if he's hungry, then he shouldn't be around you."

"And you've never been hungry around me before?"

"You make me ravenous in every way," he murmured as his eyes ran over her.

Mollie tried to hold on to her indignation but found it impossible when he looked at her like that. Everywhere his eyes touched, her body heated until her clothes became stifling. If she weren't so determined to go with him tomorrow night, she'd start stripping, but they had to sort this out.

"I'm going with you to the mansion tomorrow," she said.

Mike tore his gaze away from her breasts when she spoke. His fangs lengthened as his fingers dug into the earth; she had him as aroused as she did infuriated. His hand encircled her neck before he pulled her toward him.

"And if I refuse to take you with me?" he asked when their faces were only inches apart.

"I'll follow you."

He was so close that Mollie saw the glint of a fang behind his parted lips. Those same words caused him to snap Holden's leg; with his hand where it was, he could easily break her neck, yet she felt no alarm.

She tried to pull away from him, but he held on to her, refusing to let her go. He admired her will, but she had to know he was the one in charge here. "You'll follow me?" he growled.

"Yes." Not even the red seeping through his royal blue eyes could deter her from her course of action. "You need me in there, and you can't tie me up; you don't have any rope."

"Oh, I can find a way to tie you up, Mollie."

The words were a bit of a threat, but the way he purred them had her nipples pressing against her bra and her sex aching for his touch.

"Try it, and you'll regret it," she said.

"I don't think I would, and I *know* you wouldn't."

CHAPTER THIRTY

He looked like a wild creature with those eyes and his fangs visible. Every part of her should be screaming to run as fast as possible, but her fight-or-flight instinct had abandoned her. Instead, she found herself entranced by him.

"Perhaps I wouldn't," she murmured. Leaning forward, she ran her tongue over his bottom lip before nipping it. "But if you tie me up and leave me behind, I can guarantee it would be the last time you *ever* touched me."

"Would it?" he murmured and slid his hand up to cup her breast. He ran his thumb over her nipple and watched as her lids drooped to half cover her exquisite eyes. "Your body tells a different story, and I bet if I slid my hand between your legs, I'd find you already wet for me."

Mollie buried the resentment his knowledge of her body caused as she cupped his erection. Mike's breath caught when she rubbed the rigid length of him through the denim. "Maybe you would, but I already *know* you're hard for me."

"You're playing with fire, Mollie."

"Good thing I know how to put out the flames."

Before she knew what he intended, he lifted her and laid her on her back. His mouth smothered the startled cry she released over the abrupt movement. The breath she'd been struggling to catch left her when his tongue slid into her mouth. He'd been demanding with her before, but now she sensed something savage beneath his kiss, and an unraveling she didn't understand.

Somehow, she instinctively knew she could ease this unraveling from him if she didn't fear him. She met every remorseless thrust of his tongue and opened her thighs to him. When he settled between her legs, her fingers dug into his back as a part of her she never knew existed rose to the forefront. She suddenly felt as unrestrained in her need for him as he was in his need for her.

Without thinking, she bit his bottom lip. When he growled and pushed more demandingly against her, she bit harder and tasted the coppery tang of his blood when it landed on her tongue. Pulling back, she broke their kiss as horror engulfed her.

"I'm sorry!"

"Don't be," he said, and with his hand still around her neck, he guided her back toward his mouth. "Do it again."

"Mike—"

He crushed his mouth against hers, and when he found her tongue, he tasted his blood on her. His erection throbbed so painfully, he had to undo the button and zipper of his jeans. When Mollie nibbled on his bottom lip again, his heart hammered in anticipation of feeling her small teeth piercing his flesh once more.

Then she gave a sharp tug that spilled more of his blood. Her tongue slid over his skin, licking away the beads of blood as he fumbled with the button on her jeans. He craved her with an intensity bordering on obsession, and if he didn't possess her soon, he would go mad.

Pulling away from her, he sat back to remove her sneakers, socks, underwear, and jeans. Mollie watched as he traced the curve of her calves and then her thighs with his hands. For the first time, she was glad Aida had convinced her to start going with her to have her legs and bikini line waxed. The pain and annoyance had been worth it as she'd probably be a wooly mammoth by now, but then, she didn't think Mike would care as his gaze devoured every inch of her. His hands were gentle as he slid her shirt up and tossed it aside before undoing her bra.

Mike groaned when her breasts spilled free and her nipples stood starkly up from her pink areola. All he wanted was to taste every inch of her ivory flesh before sinking his fangs into her.

Mollie watched each of his graceful movements with fascination as he undressed. She'd felt him last night, and seen him in flashes, but those brief glimpses hadn't done him justice. In the fading light of the day, he was even more magnificent.

Blond hair sprinkled his upper chest and traveled down the line carving through the center of his eight-pack abs. The trail of hair led to the edge of his jeans, and as he tugged them down his hips, Mollie got her first good look at his erection. She gulped as she took in the length of him. Like the man, his cock was more intimidating and enticing in the daylight, and she ached to feel him inside her again.

Mike tossed his jeans aside and focused on Mollie as she lay panting and vulnerable beneath him. He ran his knuckles down her flat stomach, savoring the silken flesh beneath his hand, as touching her helped to appease the demon within him clamoring to claim its mate.

"I'm going with you tomorrow," she whispered.

Mollie bit back a gasp when his hand stilled on her and his eyes flared like rubies glinting in the sun. The muscles she'd been admiring vibrated with tension as he battled for control. Her words had turned him from a man to a monster in a split second; she didn't fear him, but she didn't understand what had happened.

"Michael?"

"You're human." The words were so guttural he barely recognized his voice.

"Yes, but you knew that about me." Her attempt at humor did nothing to ease the stress he emitted.

His gaze fastened on her neck. "You could die."

Mollie resisted the urge to squirm beneath him when his eyes remained on the marks he'd left on her. The only problem was, she didn't know if she wanted to get away from him or closer to him, as monster or man, she still wanted him.

"And so could you," she said.

Then his eyes were on hers again. "You're mine."

He snarled the words, but she sensed a softening behind them, or maybe confusion as he bowed his head.

"Mine," he murmured again.

"Mike?"

His hand slipped between her legs, and her wetness slid enticingly over his fingers. Her hips rose as he stroked her clit before dipping his finger inside her. The look of determined resolve on her face faded as her breath quickened.

Then he withdrew his hand and, gripping her hips, turned her over until she lay on her stomach. He lifted her into a kneeling position and ran his palms over her taut ass before rising to his knees behind her. The heady scent of her arousal intoxicated and unraveled him.

She smells like this for me, and she has to know who is in control.

But even as he thought that, he knew there was no control for him, not anymore. He wanted to dominate her into submission, to make her understand she had to listen to him, but he wanted, even more, to make Mollie his and to shelter her from *every* horror in this world, including himself.

Mike gripped his shaft and guided it to her entrance. When he rubbed the head teasingly over her clit, Mollie pushed her hips back toward him, and Mike smiled. He couldn't control her anywhere else, but he had complete control over her body. The only problem was, she had as much control over him, maybe more, as he couldn't get enough of her and never would.

When he thrust forward and buried himself inside her, a sense of calm descended over him as her body embraced his. He'd found where he belonged, and he wouldn't lose her.

Gripping her hip with one hand, he ran the other one up her back. He followed the delicate curve of her spine up to her nape as he pulled back before sinking deep again. He brushed the bite he'd left on her last night before bending over her to run his tongue across the punctures.

Releasing her hip, he clasped one of her breasts as it swayed with his increasingly demanding thrusts. He nipped at her ear before grasping her hair and pulling her head back. His eyes fastened on the pulse in her neck, and bending his head, he felt the beats of her heart as he licked the vein.

Mollie had never experienced anything like this. It wasn't just that she'd never tried this position, but it was also the closer they grew, the more Mike worked his way into her heart and soul. She'd never been so possessed by a man before that she couldn't tell where he ended and she began.

When he licked her vein again, Mollie tilted her head to give him better access to her throat. A rumble of satisfaction vibrated his chest against her back, and she knew he recognized what she offered him.

His fangs slid into her flesh, piercing her vein above where he'd marked her last night. But as soon as he broke her skin, he retracted his fangs and Mollie moaned in disappointment.

"Would you like to taste my blood?" His warm breath tickled her ear when he asked this. "More of it than you did earlier?"

Mollie's heart jackhammered at the question. Did she want to drink *blood*? The few drops she'd already tasted were sweeter than she'd expected, but the idea of drinking blood was repulsive. But if it was so repulsive, then why did it sound so enticing? She knew what it felt like when he was feeding on her, but what would it feel like to also drink from *him*? It was a question she had to have the answer to.

"Ye-yes," she stammered. If she didn't like it, she could always stop.

Mike froze, uncertain he'd heard her right. Before she could change her mind, he released her hair, lifted his wrist to his mouth, and bit deep. His blood spilled free, and he held his arm before her.

Mollie gazed at the streaks of red sliding down his skin before taking his wrist and drawing it toward her. She'd never pictured herself doing anything like this, but then she'd never expected to be having sex with a vampire either.

Mollie brought his wrist to her mouth and licked the trails of blood from his skin. The second his coppery, yet sweet and potent blood hit her tongue again, Mollie's eyes rolled back, and a wave of ecstasy crashed over her.

When her hand gripped his wrist tighter and her small teeth bit down, Mike nearly lost control and ejaculated inside her. Somehow, willpower kept him from doing so, but he couldn't stop his vampiric nature from taking over. His eyes fell to the new marks he'd created on her, and he sank his fangs into them.

With Mollie's blood filling his mouth and her pleasure cascading over him, Mike lost the last tenuous thread of control he'd maintained. Giving himself over to the ecstasy of her, he pounded into her, and she eagerly met the unrelenting rhythm he set. When his hand dipped between her legs to caress her clit, she screamed against his wrist as she came apart. Mike plunged into her once more before pulling free and spilling his seed against her back.

CHAPTER THIRTY-ONE

MIKE CRADLED Mollie against his chest as her breathing gradually returned to normal. She stretched like a contented cat before rolling over to face him. A smile lit her eyes, and they twinkled in the twilight. He traced the contours of her cheek before sliding his thumb over her swollen, red lips.

"You're my mate, Mollie."

He hadn't planned to tell her, but he was walking a thin line, especially now that they'd exchanged blood. He'd just found his release and tasted her, yet his body clamored to be inside her again and to turn her. She had to be prepared and understand that he would destroy anyone who tried to take her from him.

Her smile vanished. "What?"

"Do you remember what I told you about vampires and their mates?"

The haze of euphoria slid away as she recalled their conversation. "You said when a vampire finds their mate, they mate for life, and their mate can be a human."

"Yes."

"But you also said they could not remain human, and the vampire would be driven to make them immortal."

"Yes."

She didn't know how to respond to him or what to say. She'd been jealous of the possibility of another woman out there that he would spend his life with, but she *never* expected that woman to be *her*. And she'd never considered becoming a vampire.

She couldn't deny she was falling for Mike, and she would have considered dating him if they made it out of this alive, but not binding herself to him for *eternity*.

"You don't have to say or decide anything now," he said. "I couldn't change you until we were off the island."

"Change me?" she squeaked.

His hand stilled on her face as he sought to control his emotions over the terror etching her face. He had dumped this on her while she was dealing with so many other things; she had every right to be freaked, but her response roused his demon instincts.

"If you agree to it. I'm not telling you this because it's set in stone that I will change you. You will decide that, Mollie."

"Then why *are* you telling me this?"

"Because you have to understand why Doug felt the need to leave and why I'll be more volatile if you're in danger. The mate bond is forged through an exchange of blood and sex between vampires, but what happened between us has accelerated my need to complete the bond. I *won't* hurt you"—he prayed he could keep his word and not snap and force the change on her—"but I can become a threat to others. Doug understands that as we've seen it happen before."

Mollie's brain felt like it had joined the circus and was swinging from one trapeze to the other while she tried to sort through his revelation. "How do you *know* I'm your mate?"

"How do you know the sky is blue?"

"Because I can *see* it, and sometimes it's gray or red or pink. You can't *see* the mate bond."

"No, but I can see spending an eternity with you by my side. However, more than that, I can *feel* the rightness of us." He clasped her hand and held it over his heart. "I feel you all the way to the center of my soul. I've never given my blood to another, but I would give you every last drop to keep you alive."

"Mike—"

"I'm not asking for a commitment from you. I'm only asking you to understand why I might change and become angrier, more distant, and unpredictable around you. Seeing you with another man or knowing you're at risk might push me over the edge. I'm asking you not to fear or distrust me if those things happen."

"*That's* why you were so hostile and acted so weird around Holden!" she breathed as understanding dawned.

"Yes, plus the guy was an asshole who got everything he deserved."

Mollie disliked Holden for what he did to her, but she still cringed when she recalled his screams and the brutality of Mike's actions. "Would you have been so vicious to him if I wasn't your mate?"

"No," Mike admitted.

Mollie gulped. "You say I'm your mate, but I barely know you."

He ran his fingers across her cheek and back into her hair to draw her close. He kissed her tenderly before resting his lips against her forehead. "You know me, Mollie. Deep inside, you do. Maybe you're not ready to completely trust me, or yourself when it comes to that truth, and I understand why, but you *know* me."

Is he right? She pondered as her hands curled around his forearms. From the beginning, he'd been protective and caring, and she'd felt a connection to him. She'd trusted him when she had little to base that trust on. And now he was telling her he might become something completely different than the man she was falling for; the possibility terrified her.

"Why couldn't you change me until we're off this island?" she asked as she pulled away.

"Because a newly turned vampire has to feed soon after their change."

Mollie couldn't stop herself from grimacing at his words. She didn't mind his blood, but she did *not* want to be hunting people or animals to feed on.

Mike smiled as he ran his hand over her hair. "I could be the only one you fed on if you turn, but when you first transition, I have to feed well and on humans to supply you with the nourishment you'll require to get through the change."

"I see," Mollie murmured. "But I can't become a vampire; I have Aida to care for, a job, school, my dreams. I can't abandon all those things."

"I'd never ask you to abandon any of them."

"Aida—"

"Will be cared for, as will you. Listen to me; I'm *not* asking you for a decision now. This is bigger than a lifetime commitment, and if you choose to be my mate, your life will forever be linked to mine. If I die, you would either die or go insane, and vice versa. It's scary to think about, but I promise I will do everything in my power to make our life together amazing, and I will make all your dreams come true."

Mollie couldn't breathe as he whispered those words and kissed her knuckles. What would it be like to live forever, with Mike, who was everything she could have imagined in a partner and more? And who was also warning her that he might become an extremely cranky vampire soon? She'd already seen how vicious he could be, and the idea of it getting worse unnerved her.

"What if we get off this island and I decide I don't want to change, what becomes of you if we don't complete the bond?" she asked. Mike shrugged, but she noted the tensing of his muscles and a glimmer of red in his eyes.

"Then I will respect your decision."

"But what will happen to *you*? Tell me the truth."

"A vampire who loses their mate eventually goes insane, and we've had enough interaction that it would most likely happen to me."

"Could you be saved?"

Mike's lips clamped together. She would only accept the truth, but if he gave it to her, she might feel as if he were pushing her into a corner or trying to guilt her into joining him, and he didn't want that for her. She had to make this decision on her own, and she had to stay with him because she wanted to be with him as badly as he did her.

"Mike?"

"Probably not." He believed it was more of a no than a probably, but he wasn't entirely sure. No one knew the future for sure, and there was always a chance he could continue without her.

"I see," she whispered as she studied his deep blue eyes.

This man was so powerful and confident, yet he was telling her that his life was in *her* hands. For years, she'd considered herself nothing special, and many times during those years, she'd despised everything about herself.

It had taken time, but she'd learned to stop hating herself for things that weren't true. She wasn't fat and ugly; she never had been, no matter how skewed her vision of herself was for far too long. Maybe she didn't brim with self-confidence like Aida, but she knew who she was, accepted it, and most importantly, she'd grown to love herself.

But now Mike was telling her that she was uniquely special… to *him*. Resting her hand on his cheek, she ran it across the blond stubble forming a scruffier beard on his square jaw. In the brief time they'd spent together, Mollie had come to care for him more than she ever thought she could care for a man, but was she willing to bind her life to his for eternity?

And not to mention, their relationship hadn't gotten the most normal start. What if outside this life-and-death existence they found each other boring? She didn't think Mike could ever be boring, but it could happen.

Mike gripped her fingers and kissed the back of her knuckles before drawing her toward him. "You have plenty of time to decide,

Mollie," he murmured against her mouth before rolling onto his back and dragging her across his chest.

"Mate or not, I'm still going with you tomorrow."

Mike groaned as her eyes held his. This was a battle he couldn't win without causing irreparable damage to their relationship. "You have to stay with me."

"I will," she promised as she bit her bottom lip.

Unwilling to give either of them more time to think and worry, he slid his lengthening cock between her thighs and smiled when she trembled against him.

CHAPTER THIRTY-TWO

THE SUN WAS CREEPING over the horizon when Doug returned and stayed with her while Mike went out to hunt for them. Mollie was acutely aware of his scrutiny, and she felt like a leper as the vampire with the warm smile went out of his way to avoid her.

"Mike told me what he thinks I am to him," she said.

"He doesn't think it," Doug replied. "He *knows* what you are to him."

"Is that why you avoid me, or do you not like me?"

He gave her a sad smile. "From what I know of you, you seem like a very likable and resourceful person; you're a little stubborn, but I like stubborn. However, I've been around enough mated vamps to know to steer clear of their mates when the bond isn't complete. Mike's been my best friend for over forty years, and he'd kill me for you."

Mollie gawked at him. "No, he wouldn't! He said he'd be more volatile, but he'd *never* hurt you."

"Normally he wouldn't; the way things are between you now, he would. And since I enjoy my life, I'd prefer not to take any chances with him or you."

"I see," she murmured.

She contemplated his words until Mike returned and she devoured the food he brought. Afterward, they went out in search of Jack and more weapons. When afternoon arrived, they returned to the spruces with nothing to show for their efforts.

The sun was starting to descend when they reemerged from the trees and made their way through the woods toward the barn. Nearing the barn, Doug stopped in front of her, and Mike settled his hand on her shoulder.

To avoid the hill, they'd approached the barn from a different direction than the one they'd fled it from. Coming up around the side of the hill put them in a position to face the large front doors. The entire barn was red with white trim, but the two sliding doors were white and had two crossed beams on the front of them that formed an X. That X was painted bright red.

X marks the spot, she thought, and for some reason, a shiver of foreboding raced down her spine.

Mike edged closer to her as, behind the closed doors, a clattering bang sounded. He glanced at Doug when he realized the sound was one of the cages being thrown open.

"What the fuck?" Mike whispered.

"I don't know," Doug replied.

Mike's eyes swung back to the barn when one of the large doors rumbled open. No one emerged from the space the open door provided before a shot rang out. Mollie jumped and instinctively leaned toward him.

Thirty seconds later, a man staggered out of the doorway. Throwing his hand up, the man blinked against the sun while he stumbled around the cleared land. Another cage clanged open, and then a woman fled out the doorway. She recoiled when the sun hit her but lurched forward with her hands in front of her to keep from running into anything.

The man's frame had hollowed out until he was a scarecrow on two legs, but the woman had a healthy build, and Mike suspected she'd spent far less time in the cage than the man. She fled past the man and across the clearing until she came to the fence Mike leapt the night they escaped. Unaware it was there, the woman collided with the fence and stumbled back before falling forward. Gripping the upper rail, she pulled herself over and vanished.

Another cage clattered open, and a man bolted out the doorway. The first man was still reeling around the field when the man ran by him.

"Are they letting them *out*?" Doug inquired in disbelief.

"It seems that way," Mike murmured when another woman exited. "Or at least they're letting the humans out."

"Why?"

"Maybe they're going to let the vamps out next in the hopes the vampires will catch and kill them."

"But there's no guarantee that will happen. If they're trying to turn the vamps into Savages, wouldn't they do it in a more controlled environment where they could be certain the vamps killed the humans?" Mollie asked.

"You would think so," Doug muttered. "But none of this has made any sense to me."

The next woman who raced out the doorway didn't run toward the hill but went straight across the field toward them. Mike's hand tightened on her shoulder until the woman vanished into the woods a hundred feet to their left. She crashed through the trees like a deer fleeing a coyote.

"Let's go," Mike said.

"No, wait." Mollie rested her hand on his arm. "There's a chance they might have brought Aida back to the barn after we left, or even Jack."

Mike opened his mouth to argue with her before closing it. She wouldn't leave here if there was the slightest chance her sister might come out those doors. And it would make their lives so much easier if Aida *did* emerge from the barn. However, he doubted Jack was in there.

Settling back in to wait, Mike watched over thirty humans fleeing the barn. Some came close to them, while others ran for the hill, and others fled in the direction of the mansion. Then the humans stopped coming.

Glancing at her watch, Mollie counted the seconds and then the minutes until ten of them passed. She was about to give up when she heard the distant clank of metal and realized another cage had opened.

Mike's fangs pricked as he waited to see what would emerge from the barn next. After a couple of gunshots, a vampire appeared. Blood trickled from a wound in the vamp's shoulder as he staggered away from the barn.

A shadow hovered at the edge of the doorway before the muzzle of a gun poked out. A flash exploded, and the ground behind the vamp kicked up. The vampire raced faster across the field, lunged over the fence, and plunged down the hill.

"We have to go," Mike said.

"But—"

"He was a vampire, Mollie," he interjected as another vampire sprinted out of the barn. "They're turning the vamps loose now. We can't be here."

"What if Jack's in there?" she asked.

"He's not," Doug said. "And if he is, then they're setting them all free, so we'll find him."

"We have to *go*," Mike insisted.

"Yes," Doug agreed. Rising, he started through the woods once more.

Mollie followed him with Mike close on her heels. Her mind spun as she tried to figure out what they'd seen and what the Savages were doing with their captives. "They gave the humans a ten-minute head start," she murmured.

"If those vampires are starving, that was nowhere near enough time for those people to get away," Doug said.

"And some of them were definitely starved," Mike stated. "A few of the vamps we left behind hadn't been caged long, but we didn't have time to free them. We left the others because they were bordering on starvation and couldn't be trusted around humans. Because of that, we freed more humans from their cages than vamps."

"Which means, if they're letting *everyone* out, then there's soon to be a much larger vampire population roaming this island," Doug said.

"Oh shit," Mollie breathed. She glanced nervously over her shoulder when more gunshots sounded. "How many vampires were left in the barn after we escaped?"

"I don't know. At least twenty-five," Mike said.

Mollie swallowed the lump working its way up her throat as she realized things on this island were going to get a lot more lethal.

"And don't forget they were recapturing some of the escapees," Doug said. "Plus, I'd bet they've brought in more prisoners since we escaped."

"Which means we have no idea how many vampires and humans could soon be roaming this island," Mike growled.

Adrenaline flooded Mike's body as his blood rushed through his ears and pounded in his temples. Dealing with the knowledge of Savages, other freed vamps, and humans running around this island was bad enough, but now they had to deal with an unknown number of *more* threats.

His gaze fell on Mollie's back as she ran behind Doug through the woods. His fangs had extended when they left the shelter of the spruces—he'd given up on getting them to retract—but now they throbbed with his need to tear the throat out of anything that came near her.

He'd level this island if necessary. For the first time, he was glad he hadn't convinced Mollie to stay behind. It was better to have her where he could see her. Knowing she was safe would help keep him calm.

When a branch cracked on their left, Mike grabbed Mollie's waist, and lifting her, he planted her firmly behind him.

Mollie swayed, uncertain what happened. One second, she was following Doug, the next she was staring at Mike's back, and she'd never given her feet the command to move. A blur of movement caught her attention before Doug flew backward and crashed into a tree. Doug's head cracked off the trunk with an audible thud, and he slid to the ground.

Mollie blinked at the man now standing where Doug had been. His shoulders heaved as strange, guttural noises issued from his throat. His collarbone stood out starkly, and his cheekbones dug into his gaunt, ashen skin. When his eyes latched on to her, the saliva dripping from the tips of his fangs plopped onto his chin and slid to the ground.

Mike released a sound that made Mollie's bladder clench. The starving vamp didn't have a chance to react before Mike raced forward, seized the vamp by his throat, and smashed him into the dirt.

The small squeal the vamp released abruptly cut off when Mike crushed his windpipe. The vamp's hands and feet kicked at the air, but he made no sound when Mike twisted his head to the side.

Mollie looked away when she realized Mike was going to tear the man's head from his shoulders. She almost threw her hands over her ears to block the crunching of bone and sinew as they gave way, but it was over before she could.

Mike stalked back toward her, and though she didn't want to see, she got a glimpse of the vamp's unmoving feet before Mike clasped her arm. His eyes were a vivid shade of red when she met them, and his body exuded aggression, but his touch was gentle on her.

"One down," Doug murmured, and Mollie turned to find him rising to his feet. He swayed as he rubbed the back of his head.

"You okay?" Mollie asked him.

"Few brain cells scrambled, my skull's a little dented, and I have one hell of a headache, but I'll be okay." He winced when he rotated his head on his shoulders. "Let's go."

Mollie stared at Doug's retreating back as he made his way

through the woods. Mike nudged her forward, and she fell in behind Doug again. He couldn't hide his pain as he held his head stiffly and kept his shoulders hunched up protectively, but his step didn't falter. Mike stayed close by her side as they navigated the trees and underbrush.

CHAPTER THIRTY-THREE

THEY SETTLED behind some dense foliage on the side of the mansion. Mike made sure Mollie was hidden from view before turning his attention to the building. From here, he could only see the tops of the chimneys. He'd have to get closer to see anything more of it.

And it would have to be him as Doug was still moving like a robot. "How do you feel?" he asked Doug.

"Better. Give me another hour, and I'll be good as new."

And that was about all the time they had left before the sun set. Doug wasn't up for a trek through the woods without being detected, but was he capable of protecting Mollie?

"I'll protect her with my life," Doug said, as if he'd read Mike's mind.

He meant it, but Mike still loathed leaving her. However, he was the only one capable of getting closer without being detected.

"I can go," Doug offered.

Even if Doug could make the trek unnoticed, he needed time to recover before they attempted to enter the mansion. The chances of someone discovering the two of them were slim, and if they were found, they had weapons, and he could return to them in less than a minute.

"No, you can't go," Mike said.

"I won't touch her," Doug vowed.

Mike squeezed his eyes closed as the idea of another man touching her amped up his already elevated bloodlust. Ever since killing that vamp, he'd been walking a fine line between remaining in control and snapping completely, but he stayed composed, for Mollie.

"I know you won't," Mike murmured. "I have to go."

"You're leaving?" Mollie asked.

The apprehension in her voice caused him to kneel before her and cup her cheek. "Only for a little bit, but I'm not going far, and I'll be back here in seconds if you need me. I have to get closer, to see what happens at the mansion after sunset, and to make sure enough of them leave so we can try to enter."

"We'll come with you."

"No," Mike said, stroking his thumb over her silken skin. "One of us will be less noticeable, and this is different than the last time we were here. Then, we left before they exited the mansion and it was still daytime. Now, we're going to be here after they come out."

"But—"

"I'll be fine, and Doug will keep you safe."

Mollie bit back any further protests. They were here because of her, and Doug couldn't be the one to go as he could barely open his eyes beyond slits.

"Be safe," she whispered before leaning forward to kiss Mike.

"If anything happens, fire the gun and I'll come back," he said.

"I will, and I'll shoot to kill," she promised.

He kissed her and pulled away before he changed his mind about leaving. He nodded to Doug and slipped into the woods. Gliding from tree to tree, he stayed out of sight until he neared the mansion. Once closer, he stopped and bent to scoop up handfuls of dirt. He rubbed the soil over his face and into his hair to help him blend in with the woods before continuing.

When patches of the gray, brick building started appearing

through the trees, he settled into a spot where he could see the side and part of the front of the mansion. Dropping, he wiggled forward on his belly before settling in behind a rotting log. Most of his body remained hidden behind the log, but he poked his head around the edge of it to study the mansion.

A vampire's vision was better than an eagle's, but heavy drapes covered the windows, and if someone looked out, he doubted they'd search the ground for any enemies. He should be well-hidden here.

In the distance, to his right, sporadic gunshots continued from the barn, but Mollie's gun remained silent behind him. He tried not to think of her with Doug, but the scent of her lingered on his skin and in his blood. The constant pull to return to her almost launched him to his feet and back through the woods, but through sheer will, he remained behind the log.

Then the sun touched the horizon and streaks of pink and yellow illuminated the sky. A flash of movement drew his eyes to one of the drapes as it swayed back and forth. No one pulled it back to peer out, but someone walked close enough that their passing moved it. It was the first sign of life in this place.

Mike tensed when the sun dipped lower, but nothing else moved until dusk descended and the first star twinkled to life in the sky. The creak of the front door broke into the start of the cricket's song, and even the insects went quiet when Savages poured out the door. Nearly two dozen of the creatures spilled down the stairs and spread out in different directions as they loped across the lawn toward the woods. The inhuman howls and grunts of excitement they emitted chilled his skin.

There was no denying these things were on the hunt.

Most of them ran in the direction of the barn, but some split off and rushed toward the sides. Mike held his breath as two of them raced toward him. One plunged into the woods a couple of hundred feet to his left while the other entered on his right, only seventy feet away.

Mollie! Mike glanced at where the other one had disappeared, but it was too far away to be much of a threat to Mollie and Doug. The one closest to him wasn't though. Rolling away from the log, he slipped into the woods after his enemy.

When the Savage veered to the right, heading away from Mollie and Doug, Mike decided not to pursue it. He'd spent too much time away from her already, and he couldn't risk something going wrong.

"Do we just go in there?" Mollie whispered. Through the trees, she stared at the back door of the mansion, one she assumed led into a kitchen or perhaps the servant's quarters judging by the size of this place.

"I think that's our only option," Doug murmured.

Mollie fiddled with the edges of her sleeves as she gazed at the door. She wished she could see through walls, so she could learn if Aida was in there. But unless she miraculously became Superman between this second and the next, her wishing would get her nowhere.

"I'll approach the door," Doug said. "I'm healed now."

"I don't think that's the best way of going about it," Mike said. "I watched this place for a while, and no one looked out the windows. Granted, it was daytime, but we've been standing here for a good ten minutes, and we still haven't seen anyone. The Savages think they're safe in this place. So safe, I bet they didn't leave anyone behind to guard it, and I don't see any cameras monitoring the outside."

"What do you suggest we do?" Doug inquired.

"Walk right on up there," Mike replied.

Mollie gulped.

CHAPTER THIRTY-FOUR

MIKE SLIPPED from the trees with Mollie close on his heels and Doug following as they approached the mansion. He couldn't watch all the windows on the back side of the house, but his eyes scanned them for movement; he saw none.

He didn't sense anyone nearby in the woods before leaving them, but he remained alert for the slightest shift in smell or the smallest step that would alert him to the approach of an enemy. The constriction in his chest didn't ease when they made it to the back steps.

He had no idea what they might find inside, and he was leading Mollie straight into it. For years, he'd waited for her to enter his life, and he could lose her before he ever experienced life with her.

Easy, he cautioned when his hands flexed, and he had to fight the impulse to sink his fangs into her, change her, and screw the consequences.

But those consequences were far too significant for him to ignore; without enough blood to get her through the transition, she would become some*thing* caught between a human and a vampire and have to be destroyed. He would not allow that to happen, and he would *not* be the one who caused it.

Mollie held her breath when Mike's dirt-streaked hand gripped the knob. There was no way the door would be unlocked. Maybe the Savages didn't have the best security around this place, because what was the point if you lived on an island full of vamps? But they would lock their doors, right? But then what would be the point of that?

She got her answer when the knob turned beneath his hand, and he held the door as it swung inward. Mollie couldn't hear anything over the blood rushing through her ears as she gazed into the kitchen. It couldn't really be this easy; it just couldn't.

The skin on her neck crawled, and she glanced behind her toward the woods line, but she saw nothing there. Doug was also watching the trees and could see far more than she did, but if he wasn't raising the alarm, then they had to be alone, for now.

When Mike stepped away from her, Mollie snatched his hand before he made it more than two steps inside. Something was wrong here; it had to be. They were walking into a trap or the dragon's lair or *something* awful. And Aida might be dead center in the middle of it.

Mike's eyebrows drew together while he gazed questioningly at her. His hand turned over to grip hers, and he squeezed it. The look of panic didn't lessen from her face, and her grip didn't ease on him. She feared for *him*, he realized, both pleased and saddened by it. It was good to know she cared for him too, but he hated that she was constantly in fear.

Then Mollie threw back her shoulders and gave him a decisive nod. She may be afraid, but she would not back down from this. Wrapping his other hand around the back of her head, Mike pulled her close and kissed her before releasing her.

Mollie let go of Mike's hand as she followed him into a kitchen that would have made Martha Stewart jealous. A single recessed light over the double, stainless steel sink illuminated the room. The kitchen was a little too much for a houseful of vampires, especially when she recalled the meals tossed into their cages. Those meals consisted of little more than bread and water with some sandwich meat tossed in. None of it warranted a kitchen this size or with this much modern equipment.

"Why do they have this?" she whispered.

"Many vampires like to have the best, even if it's unnecessary," Mike said.

Apparently, Mollie thought as he led her around the island with two stoves and a basin sink set into the black marble counter. The copper pots hanging from a rack over the island were polished to a shine. She doubted any of it was ever used, but she didn't see a speck of dust anywhere.

Mike led the way out of the kitchen and into a dark hallway that seemed to stretch on endlessly in both directions. On either end of the hall, light shone from under closed doors, but he didn't sense anyone else nearby. His gaze traveled to the ceiling as he strained to hear anything above, but the house didn't even creak.

Turning to the right, he led Mollie down the hall until they encountered a spacious living room on their left. The arched beams of the vaulted ceiling reminded him of the skeleton of a boat as the mahogany wood stretched all the way across the room.

A multi-hued, stained-glass lamp situated next to a tan, overstuffed armchair was turned on in the corner. Its muted glow cast shards of color and shadows across the thick, black drapes drawn over the window beside it. Three more, eight-foot-tall and four-foot-wide, arched windows spanned the front of the house. If the curtains were thrown open, sunlight would illuminate this room for hours every day, but Mike doubted the room ever saw the light of day.

The rest of the room contained furniture matching the armchair, three glass coffee tables, and a white throw rug in the middle of the dark, hardwood floor. Mike glanced at the floor-to-ceiling, gray stone fireplace before turning away from the room and continuing down the hall. Mollie stayed close on his heels, and Doug followed her.

Stopping outside the next closed door, he pressed his ear against it to listen but heard nothing within. Cautiously, he turned the knob and swung the door open to reveal a game room with a chessboard on a tree trunk table, a pool table, and three card tables.

He closed the door and moved on. The next three doors opened to reveal luxurious bedrooms with king-sized beds and bathrooms that looked like mini-spas with their hot tubs and steam showers. One of the rooms had a tray within and on it sat a crystal decanter of blood. The next two doors along the hall concealed a bathroom and linen closet.

At the end of the hall, Mike paused outside the final room, the one with light filtering around the edges of the door and spilling onto the hardwood floors from the crack underneath. He heard nothing moving inside and no voices, but he scented smoke and liquor as well as something more pungent.

Unease churned in his gut as the caustic aroma caused a memory to niggle at the back of his mind, but he couldn't bring it forth. Something was off about this room. Glancing back at Mollie, he discovered she'd removed the rifle from her back and held it before her. The look on her face was one of steely determination as she eyed the door.

Mike looked to Doug who had his attention focused on the hall to make sure no one tried to sneak up behind them. Turning away, Mike rested his hand on the knob. He had no choice but to see what the room held; they couldn't leave here without exploring as much of the place as possible.

When the door opened enough to reveal the room, he tried to jerk it closed again, but Mollie's gasp told him she'd already seen the horror within.

CHAPTER THIRTY-FIVE

MOLLIE HADN'T KNOWN what to make of the mansion while they wandered through it; everything seemed so normal for a vampire residence, and much of it was beautiful. Though she didn't know what normal was for a mansion, or a vampire residence, as she'd never been in either before.

But now she knew normal and beautiful was only a cover for the atrocities the residents of this place committed.

She thrust her hand out when Mike started to close the door. The rest of this place had given them no answers so far, and as much as she yearned to shut the door and try to forget what she'd seen in the hideous room, it might be their only chance to figure out what was going on here. Plus, she only caught a glimpse of what lay beyond, but there would be no forgetting what she'd seen.

When Mollie held her hand out to stop him, Mike hesitated before pushing the door open again to reveal a room the size of a small house. He met Doug's eyes over her head, and when he saw the questioning look in his friend's gaze, Mike realized Doug hadn't seen what lay beyond. Taking a deep breath, Mike stepped into the room, and Mollie and Doug followed.

Doug inhaled sharply and froze in the doorway before continuing into the room with the wooden step of a marionette. Mike edged around Mollie and Doug to grab the door. He searched the hallway for anyone hiding in the shadows, before quietly closing the door.

Mollie tried to absorb everything she saw as she ambled around the room; her eyes took it all in, but her brain screamed denials at the gruesome scene. However, she couldn't hide behind those denials and forced herself to examine the heads mounted on the back wall.

The top three feet of the red wall remained open, but the bottom ten feet were crammed so full that there was only a sliver of space between each of the heads. The eyes of the dead, which looked far too real but *had* to be glass, followed her every step.

The faces were all forever pulled into different, frozen expressions. Some had their mouths shaped into O's, as if they were screaming in terror; others had their lips pulled back to reveal glistening fangs, while some revealed no fangs. Some of them had their lips sewn together and their eyes downcast as if they were cringing from something.

The worst were the ones grinning as broadly as the Joker would after he killed Batman. Their broad smiles were completely out of place with the fact their heads had been severed from their bodies, stuffed with something, and nailed to a wall.

"Are they all vampires?" she whispered to Mike when he came to stand beside her.

"No, but most of them are."

Goose bumps broke out on her arms as her thoughts turned to Aida. Was she being prepared to become one of these *things*? No, Mollie would *never* allow that to happen. Even if Aida were dead, Mollie would make sure she didn't end up here.

Then her frazzled brain took in the gold plaques mounted beneath each of the heads. The newest plaque was dated 2017, and as she started to follow them back, she noted each was from a different year. Kneeling, she discovered the first one in the bottom right corner. Beneath the grimacing man with shaggy brown hair and faded brown eyes was the year 1945.

"There are seventy-two heads here. One for every year since 1945." Mollie gazed at the twisted collection again as realization settled over her. "I'd bet that's also the year the family in the lighthouse died. Their heads might not be here, but those people were some of the first victims of these sick bastards. These Savages wanted this island, and they took it from that family and whoever else might have lived here at the time," she said as she recalled the burnt-out farmhouse behind the barn.

"I think you're right," Mike said.

"And there are two trophies for every year over here," Doug said.

Mollie turned to find him standing in front of a glass trophy case on the other side of the room. The trophy case was so massive it took up the entire wall, but not even half of the easily fifty-foot-long display was full of trophies.

There's room for plenty more. With care, Mollie made her way around the half a dozen, mahogany tables situated in the middle of the room. The room was so big that the four-foot-long and three-foot-wide tables placed against each other didn't take up an eighth of the space.

She tried not to look at the contents of the jars on the tables, but her gaze kept returning to the floating hands and feet. Writing etched the front of the jars, but she didn't get close enough to read what it said.

Seeing the jars, Mike recalled what the familiar, yet evasive odor was: formaldehyde. He hadn't smelled it since his ninth-grade biology class when he and Liam partnered up to dissect a frog. They'd poked at the splayed-out frog and made jokes about it until Mike finally picked up a scalpel and started cutting.

Jack and Doug were also in the class and partnered together. Doug had gotten an A for his work while Jack failed when he decided to remove the frog from its board and dance around the room with it. The boys all laughed; most of the girls giggled and screamed while they hid from Waltzing Walter, as Jack named the frog.

Their teacher had looked like he was about to have a stroke when he stalked toward Jack, snatched the frog away, and escorted Jack out of the class to the principal's office. When they were out of the room, Doug shrugged, picked the frog up from where the teacher slammed it onto a lab table, pinned it back down, and started dissecting it. He'd ignored everyone else who'd forgotten their frogs in favor of gossiping about the fate Jack would meet, which was a two-day suspension, or a vacation, as Jack declared.

Mike had forgotten about that incident until now; he'd also forgotten Jack was voted their class clown throughout all of high school. At one time, Jack had been far less serious about life. When Beth turned him into a vampire, she'd done more than change Jack from mortal to immortal; she'd also sucked away much of his carefree demeanor. Now, Jack was probably the most serious and the grumpiest of his friends.

Grumpy or not, Mike missed him. He wished he knew where Jack was, but at least his head wasn't on the wall, yet. Mike didn't know why those unlucky bastards had been chosen to be mounted like animals, but he would do everything he could to make sure none of them met the same fate.

Stopping next to Doug, Mollie examined the trophies in the case. The glow of the recessed bulbs in the case illuminated the polished collection within. Those bulbs were the only source of light in the room, and she suspected they were never turned off.

Mike stood close by her side, but she didn't look at him as she studied the foot-high trophies displayed behind the glass. The base of the first trophy was white marble; rising from it was a piece of gold, six-inches high and at least three inches thick. A silver man, with one fist raised in the air and his other hand at his side, stood on top of the gold. From its lowered hand, a silver head dangled by its hair. The inscription etched onto the plaque on the marble read:

Final Kill.
Alicio Petit.
2017.

Mollie frowned as she reread the words, but she had no idea what they meant. She turned her attention to the trophy beside it. This trophy was much the same, except the base was red marble and the silver figure on top was a woman. She had one hand raised and three heads dangling from her lowered hand. The plaque read:

Lacey Gordon.
Most Kills; 3.
2017.

When Mollie moved on to the next set of trophies, she realized they'd each been awarded for the same things, but the number on the most kills trophy differed. The heads clutched in the hands of the figures on the most kills trophies also varied to match the number of their kills.

From her cursory search, she discovered the name "Raul Mrack" on half a dozen of the most kills trophies, and he also held the record at ten. For the ten trophy, five heads dangled from his raised hand and five from his lowered one. Raul's name also appeared on three of the final kill trophies. Some other names also popped up a few times, but most were one and done.

Mollie glanced between the heads on the wall and the trophies. "I bet the heads belong to the victims of the final kill. They were the vampires and humans who proved to be the most elusive every year but were eventually killed."

"Most likely," Mike said as he examined the room.

There were no windows in the room. Brown leather chairs were set into the corners of the room and clustered around small tables. Each table held an ashtray, and more than a few ashtrays had the remains of cigars in them. There were five tables in the room with four chairs around each one.

To the right of the heads, the entire wall was made up of a bar with at least twenty stools set up before it. The mirror behind the bar reflected not only the expensive liquor lined up against the glass, but also all the trophies in the room and the heads.

Disgust churned in Mike's stomach when he realized this was where most of the demented pricks spent their time.

"I was wrong," Mollie murmured. "We haven't stumbled onto *The Island of Doctor Moreau*, they've turned this island into *The Most Dangerous Game*."

"Holy shit," Doug whispered as his eyes darted around the room.

Mike vaguely recalled the story from high school English, but he knew it involved a man hunting humans because he'd grown bored with killing animals.

"This is nothing but a game to them, a *yearly* game, and we're the prey," Mollie breathed, her lower lip quivering.

Mike draped his arm around her shoulders and drew her against his side. "They will *not* get you."

Mollie wanted to believe his words, but they'd been plunged into a nightmare, and she had no idea how they were going to get out of it.

"Our escape threw a wrench in their plans," Doug said. "But not much of one."

"But why do they starve some of their victims before turning them loose?" Mollie asked. "There's no challenge in hunting someone who can barely get out of their own way."

"I bet the vamps who participate in this little game pay *big* money to do so, but not all of them are as good at hunting as some of the others," Mike said. "They may not be as skilled, but they're still here to kill, and if they don't get their kill—"

"They'll demand their money back and spread the word that this hunt isn't all it's cracked up to be," Doug said.

"Yes," Mike agreed, and Mollie paled.

"The more skilled hunters probably leave at least some of the weakened vamps and humans for the novices, while they chase the bigger thrill of the more lethal game," Mollie said.

"Most likely," Mike replied.

"But why, if they're Savages and already killing, would they pay big money to come here to do what they already do?" Mollie asked.

"Because they can really unleash their viciousness on this island. Humans can never know of our existence, and the Savages don't want to draw attention to themselves, so they have to cover their tracks when they kill," Mike answered. "But here, the Savages don't have to cover their tracks, can do whatever they want, and be as brutal as they wish with whoever they catch."

Mollie held her hand over her mouth as she fought the wave of vomit rolling up her throat. "We have to get off this island," she choked out.

"We will," Mike said.

Mollie's gaze fell on the jars again, but she didn't go any closer. After everything she'd learned, she suspected the writing on them would match the years of the heads on the walls, and the contents were more trophies from the elusive kills mounted to the wall.

"And there's a memorial wall," Doug said.

Mollie hadn't realized it, but he'd roamed over to stand by the wall closest to the door. Mike and Mollie walked over to join him. Staring over his shoulder, Mollie read the bronze plaque. At the top of the memorial were the words, *"In honor of those brave souls lost in the hunt."*

Below the inscription were names, and after every name was some little saying like, he fought hard, or she was a brave soul, and a hunter until the end.

The disbelief and anger coiling through Mollie threatened to choke her. How hard could he have fought while hunting the starved? And how brave could she have been to pay money to destroy captives? How much of a hunter could he have been, if he lost?

She almost laughed at the ridiculousness of it all, but she couldn't find any humor in this vile room.

"Why would they put this here?" she asked. "Wouldn't they be afraid that broadcasting those they'd lost would scare off potential clients?"

"It might scare off some, but it will entice those looking for a bigger thrill. This is proof the game is *real*," Mike said.

Mollie hugged herself. "It's time to get out of this room."

Doug had already walked over to the door and had his hand resting on the knob. When Mike nodded to him, Doug cracked the door open and poked his head out before exiting the room.

CHAPTER THIRTY-SIX

THEY SEARCHED the rest of the downstairs before making their way upstairs. With the length of the wings, it could take them over an hour to search the upstairs, but they agreed not to split up and to hold off on exploring the third floor.

Halfway through searching the right wing, Mike was closing the door on another bedroom when the door to a room three doors away opened and a human stepped out. The man had a set of white sheets draped over his arm, and his head down as he maneuvered a cart out the door before closing it.

Lifting his head, the human jumped when he spotted them, but then a broad smile lit his face. Bite marks marred his throat and wrists, but healthy color stained his cheeks, and he didn't move as if he'd been fed on too much. The man's butler uniform was crisply ironed and well-tailored to fit his lean frame.

"Back from the hunt so soon my lords and lady?" the man inquired in a formal tone better suited to a queen's parlor than their current surroundings.

The man's smile faded when they didn't reply, and he stared expectantly at them.

"I left something behind," Mike said.

The man's smile blazed back to life. "I will be happy to retrieve it for you, my lord, if you'll let me know which suite you're in."

"No need," Mike replied as he strode toward the man. The wheels on the cart rattled down the maroon carpet when Mike shoved it out of his way. The man didn't have a chance to react before Mike clasped his throat and pulled him close. "I've retrieved it myself."

"Pardon me, my lord," the man squeaked as he squirmed in Mike's grasp.

"We're not part of the hunt," Mike informed him with a smile that revealed his fangs.

The man went still, and the color drained from his face so fast Mike assumed he might faint. When the beginnings of a scream started to erupt from him, Mike dug his fingers in and squelched the sound. The man sputtered as the sheets fell from his grasp and his arms and legs flailed.

"Easy," Mike said. "We're not here to hurt you. We're here for answers."

The man calmed a little, but his breath whistled in and out as his face turned redder.

"I'm going to ease my grip, but if you try to scream again, I'll snap your spine and take away your ability to walk. Do you understand?"

"Ehh," the man squeaked out and nodded the best he could.

Mike eased his grip and maneuvered the man to pin him against the wall. "What's your name?"

"Sc-Sc-Scott," he choked out before greedily gulping in air.

"Tell me, Scott, are there any other vampires in this house right now?" Mike inquired. "And tell me the truth, because if I find out you're lying, I will make you regret it for the rest of the very short life I'll grant you. But if you tell me the truth, we can part as friends, and you can continue on your merry, bed-changing way."

"I… I don't think there are any other vampires here," Scott stammered. "As far as I know, they're all out for the hunt."

"When will they come back?"

Scott's Adam's apple bobbed beneath his hand. "Most won't return until just before sunrise, but others will come sooner, and some will find places to hide so they can stay out all day."

"So it *is* a hunt," Mollie whispered as she gazed at the handsome man with his reddish-brown hair and green eyes. She'd already believed it was a hunt, but to hear Scott confirm it made it all the more real.

"Yes," Scott said.

"Did our escape throw it off?" Mollie asked.

"You're part of the escapees?" Scott croaked.

"Yes," Mike answered.

Scott's pulse skyrocketed against his palm. "They… they were *pissed* when that happened. I thought they were going to call the hunt off, but instead, they spun it to the others as a special pre-hunt to reward their clients. It's worked so well that I've heard whispers it might become an annual thing."

The more Mollie learned about the monsters behind all this, the more she despised them.

"They had to go out and catch more for the big hunt, and they recaptured some of the escapees, but they were able to get the number of captives back up in time to start the hunt tonight," Scott continued.

"And what number is that?" Doug asked.

"There has to be a minimum of seventy-five captives for the hunt, but they prefer at least a hundred. I don't know how many they gathered this year."

"Bastards," Mollie muttered.

"And how many hunters do they have in the competition?" Mike inquired.

"This year there are twenty-five, but that number varies from year to year," Scott said.

"And how many security guards are on the island?"

"I don't know. Ten work the house and barn, but there are others on the island that I've never seen; I only know they exist because I've overheard the others talking about them."

Mike believed him when he said he didn't know. Scott was scared, and his pulse was racing, but he held Mike's eyes and didn't appear to be trying to think of lies before answering. For a human, he knew a lot about the workings of this house, but the Savages probably paid little attention to him and spoke about things when they didn't realize he was listening.

"And where are the guards now?" Doug asked.

"They went out with the hunters who requested to have security with them," Scott said.

Mollie released a bitter laugh. "So not only are they so cowardly they hunt the weak, but they also have guards with them? This place is horrific."

Doug reached out to rest a hand on her shoulder before glancing at Mike and jerking his hand away. Mike hadn't realized he'd tensed at Doug's motion until Scott squeaked. *It's only Doug. He would never hurt her.*

But it didn't matter; he'd been unable to stop the rage boiling within him at the idea of *any* other man touching her. Mollie's eyebrows rose as she gazed at him before she clasped his free hand and gave it a brief squeeze before releasing it. Taking a steadying breath, Mike eased his grip on Scott's throat.

"Are there any other humans in this house?" Mike inquired.

"Yes," Scott said.

Mollie's breath sucked in, and Scott's eyes flickered to her. Hope burst so forcefully through her that for a minute she couldn't speak. "Are they alive?" she finally demanded.

"Yes," Scott replied.

"Where are they?" Doug asked.

"The basement."

"Take us to them," Mike commanded.

Scott gulped again. "Yes. Okay, follow me."

Mike eased his grip on him enough to slide his hand around to

Scott's nape. It didn't matter if he was telling the truth or not; the fact Scott had been wandering the house on his own didn't win him any trust points with Mike.

"Why didn't you run from here when they went out to hunt?" Mollie asked as they strode down the hall toward the stairs.

"And become one of the hunted?" Scott retorted.

"What are you then, a servant?"

"I am whatever they need me to be," Scott murmured.

"They'll kill you one day," Mike assured him.

"Perhaps, but I've already lived longer than the rest of the humans who come through here."

"Don't you want to leave?" Mollie asked.

"Of course," Scott replied. "But I'd never get far before they chased me down and killed me like so many others. Except, to punish me, they'd play with me for a lot longer than they do the others."

Mollie didn't want to think about what that kind of play would entail; the heads were answer enough to that. "So this is all just a game to them?" Mollie asked as they descended the stairs to the massive living room.

Scott shrugged as he led them back to the hallway they'd already searched. "To some, it's a game; to others, it's a lifestyle."

"How does it all work? Do they only hunt people and vampires once a year?"

"No," Scott answered. "The big event, what is happening now, is the only time of the year when vampires outside the club come in to hunt too."

"There's a *club*?" Doug asked in disbelief.

"Yes. The ten members of the club reside here year-round, though they often return to the mainland for weeks at a time. Sometimes, they bring back sport to hunt during the year, but they usually wait for the big event."

"And by sport, you mean humans and vampires?" Mollie asked, sickened by his choice of word.

"Yes," Scott said, seeming not to realize he was talking about living beings.

"Let me guess, the president of this *club*"—Mollie fairly spat the word—"is Raul Mrack?"

"How did you know?" Scott inquired.

"Lucky guess," she muttered.

"And why does the club bring other vamps in for this big hunt?" Mike asked.

"Why else? Money and competition," Scott replied.

"How long does the hunt last?" Doug asked.

"It depends," Scott said. "One year it was only three days before they caught everyone, but last year it went for twelve days. The game's not over until everyone is dead."

"It's *not* a game!" Mollie couldn't stop herself from retorting. When Mike glanced back at her, she took a deep breath to calm herself. Losing control now and getting angry wouldn't do any of them any good.

"How long have you been taking care of the vampires who stay here year-round?" Doug asked.

"Five years," Scott replied.

They'd kept him alive for five years! Did that mean Aida *was* alive? Mollie felt like a kid waking up on Christmas morning, and she barely contained herself from grabbing Scott and forcing him to run to wherever this basement was.

"How old are you?" Mike asked.

"Twenty-three."

They'd turned him into a servant when he was eighteen; Aida was only eighteen! Mollie tried not to get too far ahead of herself. She couldn't handle it if she got her hopes high just to have them crushed, but for the first time, she *truly* believed her sister was alive.

"If you could leave, would you?" Mollie asked.

"Of course!" Scott blurted.

Despite his enthusiastic reply, Mike didn't buy Scott's answer.

He'd been with these vamps for five years, they fed off him and allowed him to live. There was loyalty here.

"You could come with us when we leave," Mollie offered, and Mike shot her a look she decided to ignore. She didn't want to leave anyone behind in this hellhole.

"I would love that!" Scott gushed.

Scott stopped outside the door to what Mike recalled was a small library. Earlier, he hadn't gone inside to explore further, but he'd seen nothing out of the ordinary with it. Scott opened the door and entered the room with Mike on his heels. The scent of old books filled his nose before Scott turned on a switch.

Mike hissed in a breath when light flooded the room. "Turn it off."

"It's fine," Scott replied. "They expect me to move about the house while they're away."

Mike's eyes narrowed at him before he glanced at Doug as he crept over to study a map hanging in a frame on the wall.

"I'll be damned," Doug muttered and pulled it down. Flipping the frame over, he undid the latches and removed the parchment from the glass casing. He set the frame against the wall, rolled up the map, and slid it into the waistband of his jeans. "It's a map of the island," he said to Mike. "And there's a boat ramp marked on it."

"Thank God," Mollie muttered.

"Do you know where the ramp is?" Mike asked Scott.

"No," he said. "I've seen the map before, but I haven't left this house since the day after they captured me."

Sympathy tugged at Mollie's heart, and she almost squeezed Scott's arm before recalling Mike's reaction to Doug nearly touching her earlier.

"How sad," Mollie murmured.

"Where is this basement?" Mike demanded.

"It's hidden." Scott stopped in front of one of the floor-to-ceiling bookcases lining three walls of the room. He ran his hand over the shelves, some of the books, and assorted antiques, before settling on a crystal cat perched in front of a book on taxidermy.

A piercing scream from somewhere nearby drew Mike's attention to the thick, black curtains covering the windows. Doug pushed back a corner of one of the drapes and peered out as the scream rose in pitch.

"What do you see?" Mike asked.

"Just the woods," Doug murmured. "They're torturing someone."

Mike was turning back toward Scott when he glimpsed the arc of an arm swinging at him. He twisted to avoid the blow, but he couldn't avoid the stake entirely. It pierced through the flesh of his shoulder and tore through muscle before coming to a stop against his bone.

"No!" Mollie cried.

From her angle, it looked as if the stake had gone straight into Mike's heart. Something inside her broke at the idea of losing him. Tears of fury and agony burned her eyes as she leapt forward, swung the rifle around, and bashed the butt of it into Scott's chest.

A rib audibly cracked before he staggered into the bookcase. Artifacts clicked together as they teetered back and forth; some settled into place while others toppled and shattered on the mahogany floor. She spun the rifle back around and aimed it at Scott's chest.

"You so much as *twitch*, and I'll kill you," she snarled. "Mike, are you okay?"

She didn't dare take her eyes off Scott. The bastard had made her feel sorry for him and then attacked Mike; she trusted him less than a rattlesnake.

"Mike?" She couldn't keep the note of hysteria from her voice when he didn't respond to her. *He can't be dying! I can't lose him! I won't lose him!*

Her finger twitched on the trigger as a killer instinct she hadn't known she possessed surged to the forefront. If she did lose him, she would make sure Scott paid for what he'd done.

"I'm fine," Mike assured her, though his pride had taken a bit of a kicking.

He pulled the stake from his shoulder and dropped it on the floor before resting his hand on the barrel of her gun. The look on Mollie's face was one of retribution, and he feared she'd kill the prick before they learned if there really were humans here.

Mollie lowered the gun and glanced anxiously at him. "Oh," she breathed when she spotted the blood seeping through the hole in his shirt and the bloody stake lying at his feet.

"Doug, can you get Scott?" Mike asked as the scream outside abruptly cut off.

"No problem." Doug strode forward, and seizing Scott by the throat, he pinned him against the bookcase. The look on his face was nearly as murderous as the one on Mollie's.

"What did he do to you?" Mollie swung the rifle onto her back and stepped closer to inspect the bloody wound.

"It's fine," Mike assured her when she reached for the hole in his shirt. "Really, Mollie." Clasping her hand, he brought her fingers to his lips and kissed them. "It will be healed before we leave this place."

Mollie swallowed the lump in her throat and enclosed her hand around his. Careful of his injury, she slid her arm around his neck and rose on her toes to hug him. "I thought I lost you."

"It will take a lot more than that to take me away from you," he assured her as he slipped his good arm around her waist.

Mollie turned her head into his throat and kissed him before reluctantly stepping away. She yearned to stay in his arms, but they had far too much to deal with here. She glanced at Doug to find him staring at them with a grin that was oddly out of place, considering what just happened.

Mike kept his temper tightly leashed as he stalked toward the human and stopped before him. Scott didn't shrink away from him, but Mike hadn't expected it. Mike couldn't do anything worse to him than anything else he'd endured these past five years. Those years had warped him into nothing more than a puppet for the vamps who controlled him. Mike suspected Scott had also been promised immortality in return for his service, but that promise would never be fulfilled.

Mike shredded the sleeves of Scott's jacket and shirt to reveal two holsters strapped to his wrists. One of them still contained a stake, but the other was empty. He found two more stakes tied to Scott's calves, a knife at his ankle, and a handgun and keys attached to his waist. Mike divided the stakes with Doug before pocketing the knife.

He cursed himself for not checking Scott earlier, but he never thought a group of vampires would allow a human to remain so well armed in their midst. He never could have guessed how thoroughly they'd corrupted this human.

"Are all these weapons in case the clients get out of line with you?" Mike inquired as he handed Mollie the gun.

"They're in case filth like *you* gets in," Scott replied with a sneer.

"They've warped you," Doug murmured.

"These are real bullets," Mollie said as she closed the cylinder on the revolver.

"To keep the humans in line," Mike said. "Or I suppose they qualify as filth too."

"They do," Scott confirmed.

CHAPTER THIRTY-SEVEN

"So, if you're keeping the humans in line, then that means there *are* other humans here?" Mollie asked.

When Scott clamped his lips together, Mollie almost lifted the gun and fired a round into his temple. He wouldn't tell them any more, and he didn't deserve to live, but she couldn't bring herself to kill him in cold blood.

"He was reaching for the cat," Mollie said. "I don't think he planned to try anything against us until we were distracted, and the scream provided that distraction. Try tugging or moving or doing something with the cat."

Mike returned to the bookcase and gripped the cat, but when he lifted it off the shelf, nothing happened. "Is there a basement in this room?" he asked Scott. "I can make you tell me."

Scott snorted and rolled his eyes. "You don't think my masters haven't protected me from the likes of you. Go ahead, try messing with my mind; it won't do you any good."

Mike resisted the impulse to bash the smug smile off the arrogant prick's face, but though the Savages had most likely made it impossible for him to gain control of Scott's mind, he still might need the human. Gritting his teeth, he forced his attention back to the bookcases lining the room.

"You're right," he said to Mollie. "I don't think he planned to try anything until we were distracted. Which means, he would have been as honest as possible so we didn't become suspicious of his true nature. I think there's something hidden in this room."

"Then let's find it," Mollie said.

Doug led Scott away from the bookcase while Mollie and Mike went to work examining the shelves. He focused on the higher shelves while she concentrated on the bottom ones. Mollie didn't care what anything might be worth, or its history, as she started tossing artifacts and books from the shelves in the hopes of locating something to help them.

She tried not to think about the fact Scott might have been leading them into a trap, but the possibility niggled at the back of her mind. Even with the niggling, she didn't stop; they had little else to go on, and she had to find Aida, or at least learn what had become of her.

She grasped a book and went to heave it aside, but it slipped from her grasp when it remained stuck in the bookcase but tipped forward. Mollie jumped back when something clicked, and the bookcase swung toward her. At her side in an instant, Mike lifted her up and spun her away from the opening door.

Mollie held her breath as she waited for something awful to come charging out at them, but nothing emerged when the door stopped moving. She glanced over at where Scott sat in the armchair Doug had shoved him into. Scott's face remained impassive, but he couldn't hide the beads of sweat dotting his brow.

Mike released Mollie and stepped around her to examine what the open bookcase revealed. A steel door with a single silver lock was tucked behind the shelf. Gazing at the thick steel, Mike knew there was no way he could break through it. Then, he recalled Scott's keys.

Stalking over to the human, he bent and ripped the keys from where they were secured to his waist. "Tie him up," he said to Doug, "and gag him."

Doug went to work tearing Scott's clothes off him to use for binds. Mike returned with the keys and sorted through them until he found a larger key that looked like it would fit the lock. Mollie hovered at his side as he slid the key into the lock and turned it. The bolt slid free with a click.

Stepping protectively in front of Mollie, Mike rested his hand on the door and nudged it open. The well-oiled hinges didn't make a sound as the door swung open to reveal what lay beyond. The light from the library illuminated the top of a set of wooden stairs, but the bottom half of the steps remained in shadow.

"Aida," Mollie breathed.

He glanced over his shoulder at Doug as he shoved Scott's sock into his mouth. Doug twisted another piece of cloth around Scott's head and cinched the gag in place. Doug smiled smugly when Scott grunted.

"Mollie, stay up here with Doug," Mike said.

"No, if Aida is down there—"

"We have no idea what is down there, and until I do, I *need* you to stay here. I'll let you know if it's safe to come down."

He couldn't have her storming down there to discover her sister's body, or numerous bodies, piled below. Mike saw her starting to gear up for an argument as Doug approached.

"Please, stay here," Mike said.

The please made her shoulders slump. She didn't care what lay below; she wanted to plunge down those stairs and discover whatever it was, but the look on Mike's face froze her words. He seemed in control now, but anguish etched his features, and his eyes had grown more red than blue.

"Okay," Mollie relented. "But take Doug with you. Scott is secure, and there's no one else in the house. You may need help down there."

"No, he'll stay here with you, and no arguments." He glanced at

Doug who looked about to protest his decision too, but Doug closed his mouth. "I'll be back soon." Drawing Mollie close, he kissed her forehead before releasing her.

Pulling the steel door further open, he discovered a switch on the wall. When he flicked the switch, a bulb at the bottom blazed to life and revealed all the steps. He kept hold of a stake and slid Scott's keys into his pocket before descending.

Mollie's shadow fell over the stairs, and he glanced back to find her standing at the top, anxiously watching his every move. When he reached the bottom, he turned to discover another steel door on his right.

He pulled Scott's keys from his pocket and searched for the one that opened the door above. Hoping it would work for this door too, he slid the key into the lock and smiled grimly when it clicked. Cautiously, he pushed the door open.

Scurrying sounds followed when light from the hall spilled into the room beyond. Whimpers filled the air, and the reek of terror drifted to him. In the back of the room, people huddled together and held each other while they gazed at him.

Beside the door was another switch; he turned it on. The humans cowered further away as they turned their heads away from the single, glass-encaged bulb hanging from the ceiling in the center of the room. The light stung his eyes as it reflected off the white walls, floor, and ceiling.

All the mattresses spread across the floor had a blanket and pillow on them. A tray sat beside each mattress, and judging by the remains on some of the plates, the prisoners had last dined on steak and potatoes. In two corners of the room, open doors revealed the bathrooms beyond.

None of the people looked at him again, and of the sixteen humans, all the women wore black, flowing gowns and were barefoot. All the men wore black shirts and pants and were also shoeless. They also all had bite marks covering their exposed flesh.

Suddenly, he understood what these people were for. The

Savages had come for the hunt, but they had to feed while here, and they couldn't drink from the captives in the barn as they would weaken their game more than the orchestrators of this hunt wanted them weakened.

To deal with the food problem, they selected certain humans and removed them from their cages. From what he could see of their faces and figures, only the best-looking humans were chosen.

These people were meant to keep those above satisfied and fed. The Savages could inflict suffering on these victims by tormenting them and forcefully draining their blood until the other captives were freed and the vamps could hunt. But the club would have to keep the humans here well-fed and clean to make their clients happy, which also explained the kitchen.

"I'm going to get you out of here," he told them. They only whimpered and clustered closer together. "Is Aida here?"

A ripple of movement came from the group in the back corner, but no one responded. Noise from above drew his attention to where he'd left Mollie. Doug went to grab her when she started down the stairs, but she'd already fled beyond his grasp as she ran.

He stepped in front of her before she could see into the room. "Mollie, wait."

Whispered words sounded from within, and then a single head popped over the group. Wide eyes, more gold than brown, met his before the girl ducked again. *Aida.* Lowering his arm, he allowed Mollie to slip past him. She hesitated on the threshold, and her hand flew to her mouth as she gazed at those within.

"Aida," Mollie breathed.

From the back of the group of people, her sister's head emerged. Mollie gasped and struggled to accept that what she was seeing was real. After everything they'd discovered, it was almost too good to be true to find Aida *alive*.

Aida blinked at her, seeming to feel the same way as Mollie as she didn't separate herself from the people who were turning their heads to gaze at Mollie and Mike.

"Mollie?" Aida asked.

The sound of her small, much-loved voice broke Mollie's paralysis. With a cry, she ran toward Aida as her sister separated from the group. Aida staggered toward her with her arms open before they reached each other. Tears streaked Mollie's cheeks as she embraced her sister and they fell to the ground together.

CHAPTER THIRTY-EIGHT

WITH HER HEAD buried in Mollie's chest, Mike only caught some of Aida's rushed words, but it was enough to confirm what he suspected. These people were the food supply until the hunt was over. They'd been forced to shower and change daily as well as eat the meals brought to them. Their blood was taken against their will, which made the experience excruciating for them.

While the sisters spoke, the rest of the people started separating from each other and creeping toward the door.

"Are you really going to get us out of here?" a man asked Mike.

It would be more difficult to reach the boat ramp with a bunch of shoeless humans in tow, but he couldn't leave them here. "Yes."

The man, whose neck was covered in bites, released a small sound and looked to the ceiling as he blinked back tears.

Grasping Aida's cheeks, Mollie pulled her sister away to gaze at Aida's beloved, beautiful face. Her ivory skin was paler than normal, but that only made the gold in her eyes stand out more. Her waist-length, curly black hair shone in the light.

The sight of the bites on Aida's neck and wrists caused red-hot rage to boil within Mollie; it was so intense she thought she might choke on it. Her sister's gushed words revealed much of what was done to her, but seeing the evidence on her hammered home how badly Aida had been abused. Mollie went to touch one of the bites before snatching her fingers back. They looked sore enough without her prodding at them.

"What did they do to you?" she whispered.

"The same thing that was done to you," Aida said as she touched Mollie's neck just above Mike's bite.

"No," Mollie whispered. "I think it was completely different; I gave willingly."

Aida's eyes darted to where Mollie had last seen Mike. "To *him*?"

"Mollie, we have to go," Mike said.

Mollie took Aida's hand and helped her rise. "We have a lot to discuss, but it will have to wait."

"If he's a vampire, we can't trust him," Aida whispered.

"Yes, we can," Mollie insisted.

"No," Aida said, digging her heels in. "You don't understand, Mollie. They can make you see and do things—"

"I understand, but Mike's not like that, and neither are his friends. He's saved my life more times than I can count, and he helped me find you. They're not all the same. You *have* to believe me, Aida, because we can't stay here. The *things* that kept you here are going to come back."

Aida paled further when Mollie mentioned the return of the Savages. Having overheard their conversation, the other people were glancing distrustfully between her and Mike.

"Please, Aida, trust me," Mollie pleaded.

Her sister relaxed a little before bowing her head and nodding her agreement. Keeping hold of Aida's arm, Mollie hurried to join Mike where he waited in the doorway. He gestured them toward the stairs, and Mollie looked up to find Doug standing there.

"You okay?" Mike asked her.

"Yes," Mollie replied, and the smile she gave him lit her beautiful eyes. "I can never thank you enough for this."

Mike cupped her cheek in his hand before bending to kiss her. "Don't ever thank me for it, Mollie. I will do anything for you."

Mollie clasped his hand and rested it against her cheek as love swelled in her chest. So sweet, those words were spoken from his heart, and he meant them.

"Go on," Mike urged.

Mollie nudged Aida, who was gawking at Mike like he was a talking dinosaur. He watched as they started up the stairs before turning back to the room.

The rest of the prisoners stood uncertainly within. "You can trust me, you can stay here, or you can take your chances on your own in the woods once we're free of this place, but we're leaving. Fair warning, the hunt is in full swing."

"The hunt?" a woman asked.

"We'll discuss it later," Mike said. "You're also going to have to travel through the woods barefoot, and if you choose to stay with us, you *will* have to keep up."

He couldn't leave them here, but he wouldn't risk Mollie's life for them either. They all exchanged looks before one of the women broke free and crept toward him. Two of the men followed her, and when Mike stepped back to let them climb the stairs, the rest of the group rushed forward.

When Mollie vanished from view, Mike's chest felt as if a panther was stuck inside trying to get free. He kept himself restrained from shoving people out of his way and bolting up the stairs to get to her as he followed the last of the group up.

At the top of the stairs, he discovered the group had come to a halt ten feet away from Scott. Some of them gazed at the man as if he were the lowest form of life while the others radiated hatred.

"You!" one of the women screeched as she ran at him.

The slap she delivered to Scott's face snapped his head to the side and echoed through the room. When she started kicking and punching him, Doug walked over, wrapped his arm around her waist, and pulled her away. The woman's arms and legs continued to flail as she strove to break free of Doug. Scott's head turned back, and he glared at all of them from a right eye already beginning to swell shut.

"What did he do to you?" Mollie whispered to Aida.

Mollie embraced Aida against her chest when her sister shuddered. Aida was five inches shorter than her and seemed far more fragile than she had before being brought to this island.

"He's the worst of them," Aida said, "and more of a monster than the vampires. Scott took a lot of pleasure in coming to see us when they were done feeding on us and enjoyed watching us cry. He's also the one who made sure we were ready when they came for us and would watch us shower."

Mollie met Mike's eyes over the top of her sister's head. Unlike Mike, killing Scott wouldn't put limitations on her, and she would love to rip the bastard's heart out. When her hand went to the handgun she'd tucked into her back pocket, Mike grasped her wrist.

"You will regret it if you do," he said.

Mollie fought back her resentment and disappointment as she tried to regain control of her temper. He was right, but she still wanted Scott dead. "What do we do with him?"

"We leave him," Mike said. "What they'll do to him when they realize their food supply is gone, and he's the one who brought us to it, will be far worse than anything we could ever do. We have to go."

He clasped her elbow and led her toward the door. She kept hold of Aida as they walked. They were almost to the exit when Mike heard the distant click of another door shutting somewhere in the mansion. He drew Mollie back as he strained to hear anything more.

"Don't make a sound," Mike whispered to the others.

He released Mollie and strode over to press his ear against the wooden door, he listened to the footsteps coming toward them. Whoever it was wasn't trying to be secretive as their boots rang against the wood floor.

Mike edged back and twisted the lock on the knob. It would do little to stop a vampire from entering, but it was a small barrier. He pointed to Doug and then one of the windows. Doug strode across the room and grasped a corner of a drape. When he edged the curtain aside, his shoulders became rigid.

"Fuck," Doug hissed.

Doug glanced at Mike before throwing the drape open. Two leering faces stood on the other side of the glass, their red eyes gleamed malevolently, and their fangs glistened in the light. On the other side of the door, the footsteps stopped, and the knob rattled.

"How did they know we were here?" Mollie asked.

Mike's gaze fell on Scott, who gave as much of a grin as he could with a sock in his mouth. Mike didn't know how he'd done it, but somehow, Scott alerted the club and its followers to their presence in this place. Mike glanced back at the light switch Scott first turned on, but he didn't think that was what had given them away. The Savages expected Scott to move around the house and to tend to their victims.

Then he recalled Scott's hand running across the shelf before settling on the cat that did nothing. Somewhere on that shelf was something used to alert the vamps to any threat in the mansion.

"You prick!" he snarled.

Scott's smile spread around his gag. Behind Mike, something crashed into the door, and it rattled in its frame. Some of the humans cried out and huddled together when the wood shuddered.

"Be quiet," Mike commanded them, and they whimpered before settling down.

Striding across the room, Mike pulled back another drape to reveal two more Savages on the other side. Doug yanked aside another to reveal one vamp, and when Mike pulled back the curtain on the fourth window, he discovered three more Savages.

Eight vampires had already gathered outside, an unknown number of them could be in the house, and possibly more were on the way. If they left through the mansion, they could be trapped in the corridors and would have a difficult time moving so many through the halls.

"You," Mike said, pointing at some of the humans. "Grab those chairs and throw them in front of the door. We're going out the windows."

"They're out there; we can't," someone whined.

"Then don't," Mike replied. He didn't much care what they did as long as they didn't get in his way.

Some of the humans scampered away to obey his command while others remained cowering in the center of the room. He turned back to Mollie as she handed the revolver to Aida.

"They're not wooden bullets," she said to her sister.

"They'll still hurt anything you hit with them," Mike told Aida.

She gazed up at him with round eyes that were amazingly bright in her pale face before setting her chin firmly and nodding.

"No matter what happens, you stay close to me," he said to Mollie. "Unless I tell you to run, and then run faster than you've ever run before."

"I'm not leaving you behind," Mollie protested.

"If I tell you to leave me, then do it. Head for our hiding spot by the lighthouse, and I'll find you there if we're separated." He would do everything in his power to avoid separating from her, but he might not have a choice.

"Mike—"

"Take care of yourself and Aida first." He wanted to tell her to take care of herself first, but she wouldn't.

When her mouth parted on another protest, he gripped her shoulders and drew her close to silence her words with a kiss. "I will always come for you, Mollie," he vowed against her lips. "I love you."

Those last three words robbed the breath from Mollie's lungs. He *loved* her? He'd spoken of the mating bond and how he believed she was his mate, but he'd never mentioned love. Mollie didn't know how to respond as her head spun with the knowledge, and overwhelming emotion clogged her throat.

Then he started to turn away from her.

"Mike!" Mollie cried and captured his hand. She hadn't known what she meant to say to him, but when his blue eyes met hers, the words blurted out before she realized they were on her tongue. "I love you too."

She'd never said those words to anyone outside her family. But she *did* love him.

They hadn't known each other long, but she'd shared and experienced so much with him. He'd risked his life for her, protected her above himself, wanted to share an eternity with her, and he loved her. She had no idea what would become of them, but no matter what happened, he had to know how she felt too.

"I love you too," she said again.

A small smile curved his mouth, but it vanished when the library door splintered with a crack. The people stacking furniture against it staggered away as the door pushed inward a couple of inches.

With Mollie's hand in his, Mike led her across the room toward the windows. Keeping hold of Aida's arm, Mollie pulled her sister with them.

"We'll break the windows out," Mike stated as he approached Doug. He squeezed Mollie's hand before releasing it. "All four at the same time. It will push the Savages back and give us an opportunity to get out before they can try to get in. You two"—he pointed at two of the larger men—"tear down those drapes and use the rod to smash out the glass when we do. Keep the rod as a weapon."

The men nodded and tore the rods from where they hung over the window.

"You ready?" Mike asked Doug.

"As I'll ever be," Doug said and yanked the drape down.

Mike ripped the drape in front of him away, but he didn't bother with the rod as another bang rocked the door and some of the humans started crying. The furniture stacked against the door scraped the floor as it was pushed inward. The three vamps outside the window grinned at him as they eagerly awaited his exit.

Mike turned and lifted the chair Scott was tied to. The human scowled at him, but apprehension glinted in his eyes when Mike smiled at him before speaking. "You're going to be of some use to us after all."

Mike turned the chair around so that Scott faced the glass and looked to make sure everyone else was ready to break out their windows. Scott's useless struggles rocked the chair in his hands, but Mike held it steady.

"Stay in here until I tell you it's okay to come outside," Mike said to Mollie. She nodded as she released her sister and removed the rifle from her back.

"Now!" he commanded and bashed Scott face-first into the glass. He didn't care if the bastard died, but he hoped he survived as his blood would be an attractant for the Savages.

CHAPTER THIRTY-NINE

THE SCENT of Scott's blood and his wails of pain filled the room as the glass gave way and Mike thrust the chair out the window. The three vampires outside scrambled to get out of the way as the chair toppled to the ground. Jumping out the window, Mike withdrew one of the stakes he'd tucked into his waistband. When the first Savage lunged at him, he slammed the stake into the creature's heart before yanking it free.

Mollie aimed at the next vamp running toward Mike and pulled the trigger. Blood bloomed across the center of the vamp's chest, it howled as it fell back, but she hadn't delivered a killing shot.

"Mollie, they're getting in!" Aida cried.

Mollie glanced over her shoulder as the door shoved further inward. To her right, a man screamed and stumbled back as one of the vampires succeeded in crawling through the window. When the vamp pounced on him, the man fell beneath the weight of the monster and toppled to the ground.

Perched on his chest, the vamp reared back and drove its fangs into the man's jugular. It didn't feed but instead pulled back to rip the man's vein out. The man beat at the creature as gurgled cries issued from him.

Turning the rifle on the vamp, she aimed and pulled the trigger, but the thing leapt out of the way, and wood sprayed out from the bookcase when the bullet embedded in one of the shelves. Mollie tracked the vamp's movements as it raced around the room. Her finger tightened on the trigger, but she didn't dare waste another bullet until it stopped moving.

When it landed on another human, she fired. The bullet hit the vamp in the forehead and flung it back. The vamp squealed, its legs kicked against the ground, and it slapped its forehead as if that could knock the bullet free.

Screams erupted around the room as more Savages crawled through the windows. Mollie's knees trembled, and her heart thundered as the door opened another couple of inches. A hand with nails filed into three-inch long, blood-red, razor-sharp points wrapped around the door before a head emerged. The man belonging to those nails grinned at her and Aida before he slipped into the room with the grace of a phantom.

"Mollie, come on!" Mike yelled from outside.

She didn't dare take her eyes off the vamp stalking them as she nudged Aida toward the window. "Go," she said to her sister.

Aida squeezed her arm before vanishing from Mollie's side. The vamp's red eyes never left hers as he bobbed back and forth like a cobra under the spell of a snake charmer. Mollie gulped down the lump in her throat as she edged closer to the window. She may not be a powerful, immortal being, but her entirely mortal instincts were screaming *danger!*

Her heel connected with the wall under the windowsill. Cold air caressed her back, but she couldn't tear her eyes away from the vamp long enough to jump out the window. She knew if she looked away for a fraction of a second, this *thing* would be on her.

Hands gripped her waist and pulled her backward. Unprepared for the abrupt movement, her finger squeezed the trigger and a wild shot embedded in the ceiling. Plaster rained down, coating the vamp's thin shoulders and dark hair as he lunged at her.

Lethal talons and bloodthirsty eyes filled her vision as she fell out the window with the vamp following her. That thing was going to slice her open and gut her in midair, she realized as the vamp's lips twisted into a leering grin. She waited to hit the ground, waited to die, but she was yanked up and plopped onto her feet so forcefully she staggered back.

Mike set Mollie down and launched a fist into the vampire's face that smashed his nose almost entirely flat and indented his face. Bloodlust thrummed through him as the Savage who'd been so confident of his kill on *Mollie* was flung ten feet back into the wall of the house. He crashed into the house with enough force to shake the stone wall; some of the remaining glass fell free of the windows and onto the ground.

Mike's gaze fell on the Savage's red nails, and a memory from the bar flashed through his mind. This prick was there the night they were *taken*!

Mike stepped toward him, intending to finish it, but screams from the library drew his attention. More Savages were spilling inside and going after the humans who remained there. Some of the people rushed forward and tumbled out the windows; the others weren't so lucky.

"There's more coming from the woods!" Doug shouted.

Mike glanced at the vamp slumped against the wall with his chin on his chest. No matter how badly he wanted to kill the Savage, Mollie came first. Taking Mollie's arm, he ran with her and Aida toward where Doug was fending off two Savages.

Mollie tried not to look at the bodies littering the ground as they weaved their way through the Savages and humans scattered there, but she had to as she didn't want to step on them. Seven of the humans were dead already, four stood in the shadows at the corner of the house, apparently waiting for them, and the other four were bolting toward the woods. Two of the waiting people held curtain rods with blood dripping from the ends. The third and fourth clutched broken pieces of furniture in their hands.

Another Savage knelt at Scott's side, feasting on him while Scott's fingers twitched against the armrest of the chair. Mike plunged a stake through the Savage's heart, not to save the human, it was too late for that, but to destroy the monster. The fewer enemies they had on this island, the better, especially since they had no idea how many they faced.

Releasing Mollie, he sank his stake into the chest of one of the vamps battling Doug while Doug tore the head from the other. Doug lobbed the head aside as another Savage slid out the library window.

"Doug, keep Aida with you," Mike commanded.

Doug stepped toward her but hesitated when the girl cringed away from him.

"He'll take care of you," Mollie promised.

Aida's shoulders slumped a little as she glanced distrustfully at Doug, but she allowed him to take her arm and run with her across the lawn toward the woods. Mike followed with Mollie, and the four humans trailed them. If it became necessary, he and Doug would carry the sisters, but for now, it was better to have their hands free, and he wasn't ready to leave the remaining humans behind to fend for themselves.

Howls echoed over the land as they charged into the woods, and some of them sounded far too close. Mollie twisted to see behind her and spotted a small red beacon on top of the mansion. The beacon hadn't been on before, and she realized that whatever Scott hit to alert the vamps to their presence turned the light on.

Aida cried out, drawing Mollie's attention back to her as she stumbled and nearly went down. Doug didn't miss a step as he pulled her back up. Mollie's lungs and her legs ached from exertion as she sprinted to keep up with Mike.

Some of the people were starting to lag as their legs grew tired and the debris littering the ground battered their feet. One of the women released a muffled yelp when her ankle gave out, and she fell to the ground. A man stopped to help her up.

"Wait!" Mollie wheezed at Mike.

"We can't wait," Mike said as another howl pierced the air, this one closer than the last.

The woman staggered to her feet and ran after them again. Then, from out of the night, a shadow raced forward and pounced on the man who had helped the woman. The man didn't make a sound before he slammed face-first into the ground and the vampire sank his fangs into the man's neck.

The woman screamed and darted to her right before disappearing into the forest. Another man battered the vampire's back with a rod, but the slurping sounds only grew louder. Mollie yanked her arm free of Mike's hold and planted her feet. She pulled the rifle from her shoulder and took aim, but as she was about to pull the trigger, another creature emerged from the woods and leapt onto the back of the man beating the vampire.

"Don't shoot." Mike pushed the barrel of her gun down. "Stay with them!" he called to Doug.

Mike ran forward, ripped the first vampire off the man's back, and rammed it into a tree. The other woman with them sprinted over and fell beside the wounded man. Tears streamed down her face as she searched for a pulse.

Mike tore the heart out of the Savage before spinning to find the second vampire launching itself at the woman. The woman didn't have a chance to react before the vamp snapped her neck. Mike staked the vamp through the back and gazed down at the prone form of the man. With a sinking heart, he realized it was too late for the humans, but not for them.

Sprinting back to Mollie's side, he lifted her while she fumbled to secure the rifle on her back again. "Carry Aida," he said to Doug as Mollie's legs locked around his waist.

Mollie clung to him while he sprinted through the trees with Doug and Aida following. All around them, more howls and screams filled the night.

CHAPTER FORTY

It was four in the morning before Mike slowed enough to set Mollie down again. Her cramped legs wobbled so bad she nearly fell over, but she remained standing by leaning against a tree. Aida crumpled to the ground and lowered her head into her hands.

Mollie staggered to her side and collapsed next to her. "Are you okay?" she whispered as she draped her arm around her sister's shoulders and pulled her close.

"Ye-yes," Aida murmured. "He ran so fast I got dizzy."

Mollie pulled Aida closer as she studied the thick pines surrounding them, then Aida's battered feet. Her bleeding had stopped, but dry blood crusted the soles of her feet, and a nasty scratch ran from her ankle to her calf. Releasing her, Mollie sat forward and scooped up some pine needles and earth.

"Probably not the best way to clean cuts, but we have to get the blood off you," she said to Aida.

Aida unfolded her legs and plopped her feet before Mollie. Mollie winced at how battered they were, but using pine needles and dirt, she cleaned the blood off the best she could. While she worked, Doug and Mike scrubbed the blood from them too. Most of it was from others, but they'd both sustained injuries. Mollie had somehow managed to avoid any cuts and blood splatter.

"They were my friends," Aida whispered. Her lower lip trembled, and tears shimmered in her eyes before she wiped them away. "The people in the basement with me; they were my friends. We were all each other had in there, you know?"

Mollie squeezed her sister's calf as anger and sorrow swelled within her. She'd give anything to take away what Aida had endured and make her captors suffer, but she couldn't do either of those things. She hadn't felt this helpless since her mother was dying.

"I know. I'm sorry," Mollie said. "We tried to save them."

"Maybe some of them got away."

"Maybe," Mollie agreed, but looking in her sister's eyes, she realized Aida also knew the truth; they probably would not survive.

She finished cleaning Aida and tossed the debris away. Another howl was followed by a shrieking scream that went on for what felt like hours but was at most only a minute. The eerie silence following the agony was even more unnerving.

Her gaze traveled to Mike when he stepped closer to them. His nostrils flared as his eyes turned red. Mollie held her breath and slipped the rifle off her shoulder while she waited for some monster to launch out of the shadows at them. Overhead, the small breeze caused the trees to creak as their limbs clicked together. Beneath the rays of the full moon hanging heavily in the sky, every shifting shadow felt ominous.

When her finger twitched on the trigger, she pulled it away. The last thing she needed was to fire a shot because she was so wound up. A snapping branch had her rising to her feet as she lifted the rifle to her shoulder.

She steadied her shaking hands but kept her finger away from the trigger; she didn't trust herself not to fire on a squirrel right now. Doug edged closer to them, and Aida pushed herself to her feet.

Through the trees, Mike spotted a shadow slinking toward a target he couldn't see, but he recognized the predatory gait of a vampire. He stepped closer to Mollie and, cupping her elbow, drew her against his side.

The shadow paused behind a large oak. If he could see it, then all the vamp had to do was look this way to see them. Then the vampire dashed forward and vanished. Mike expected a scream to follow, but none did.

Mike didn't speak as he lifted Mollie and clasped her before him again. Her eyes were rimmed with dark circles when they met his, but her grip was strong on his shoulders, and her face was set in grim resolve as she slid her legs around his waist. Aida didn't complain when Doug lifted her, and they started through the woods again.

Mike kept his senses attuned to the world around them as he slipped from one tree to another. They were almost to the lighthouse when the hairs on Mike's nape rose; something was stalking them. Unwilling to let their enemy know it had been detected, Mike didn't change his pace or react in any way. He glanced at the sky, noting the hint of gray on the far horizon, but full daybreak was nearly an hour away; there was still plenty of time for a Savage to hunt.

A subtle rise in Doug's shoulders alerted him that his friend was also aware of their stalker. Mollie lifted her head from his shoulder when the lighthouse came into view.

Nothing will happen to you, he vowed.

When her eyes met his, a small smile curved the edge of her mouth. Gripping her nape, he drew her to him and kissed her deeply before bringing her ear to his lips.

"We're being stalked," he whispered. "Don't let them know you're aware of it."

She stiffened against him but didn't try to search for their enemy. If he said someone was out there, then someone was after them. Her fingers curled into his shoulders, and she held him closer.

"Hold on," he murmured.

Her arms clamped around his neck as he took one more step before bursting into a run that whipped her hair around her face. Between the blur of the world and the hair battering her eyes and cheeks, she couldn't see anything beyond Doug sprinting behind them with Aida in his arms.

Mike leapt over something and skidded to the side before thudding up a set of stairs. She realized they were in the lighthouse only when she saw the overturned chairs surrounding the kitchen table. Then they were rushing through the rest of the house. She glimpsed the slaughtered family before Mike took the stairs three at a time to the tower.

At the top of the stairs, Mike set her on her feet so abruptly she staggered back and almost crashed into the inner wall. Doug clambered through the doorway behind them and all but dropped Aida. Mollie caught her sister before she fell as something monstrous charged out of the stairwell.

The first creature crashed into Mike's chest and knocked him into the half wall in the middle. Mollie gasped when the boards behind Mike groaned ominously. If they gave way, Mike would topple all the way to the first floor again, but they held steady beneath the weight of the two vampires. The second creature to come out of the stairwell went low at Doug's legs and took him out at the knees.

Mollie couldn't see the face of the vampire Mike battled, but a glint of red nails in the fading light of the moon told her exactly who stalked them this far. The vampire from the library healed far faster than she expected after the damage Mike inflicted on him, but though his nose remained crunched, his face had pushed out again.

Mollie shoved Aida behind her as fists pummeled flesh and the vampires grunted while they brawled. She dodged a flailing leg when Mike succeeded in pulling himself away from the boards. Lifting her rifle, she tried to aim at the Savage, but she couldn't get an accurate shot off while he was battling Mike. With his hand on the Savage's throat, Mike spun him around and smashed him off the boards.

More wood groaned, but Mike ignored it as he sank his fingers into the vampire's throat. He should have destroyed this bastard earlier when the creature was weakened. The power of the Savage radiated over his skin. This vampire was older than him, a killer, and stronger, but Mollie's blood in his veins fueled Mike to levels of strength he'd never achieved before.

The vamp's lips pulled back in a sneer and his vicious, red nails sliced down Mike's side. Mike grunted when his flesh splayed open, and his blood spilled free, but he didn't dare ease his grip on the Savage. He'd felt this thing's desire to get at Mollie. She'd escaped him once, and if he got the chance, this bastard wouldn't let it happen again.

Mike would bet money he held Raul Mrack, club president and proud owner of more trophies than any other Savage in the club.

"Raul?" Mike growled, and the vampire smiled smugly.

Somehow Raul managed to get his hands up between them. They came down on Mike's arms, knocking his grip free. Mike grunted and dodged in time to avoid a kick to his chest, but he wasn't fast enough to avoid it altogether. Raul's foot caught him on his shoulder.

The strength of the kick knocked him into the outer half walls. Rotten wood cracked beneath his weight before the wall started to give way. His arms pinwheeled as he tried to stop himself from going over, but it was too late. Already off-balance, there was no defying gravity when the boards splintered apart, and air rushed up to meet him.

A loud cracking caused Mollie's heart to plummet as the railing gave way and Mike vanished. "No!" she cried and lunged forward before stopping herself from getting any closer to the vamp standing between her and the broken boards.

Mike! No! No! NO! Not dead! He can't be dead! But her heart felt as if it were tearing in two, and her hand trembled on the rifle as tears filled her eyes. She pointed the gun at the vamp's back, and in her fury and sorrow, almost pulled the trigger, but the beams supporting the roof blocked her from a kill shot. As much as she wanted to murder this bastard, she couldn't waste her bullets or risk attracting more Savages.

Mollie scrambled back when the vampire with the lethal talons turned toward her. His grin revealed the glistening points of his fangs as he prowled toward her, bobbing and weaving again to avoid giving her a good shot at him. Cruelty emanated from every inch of him as he stalked her with the casual ease of someone who knew their prey was already theirs.

Raul, she recalled as she'd heard Mike call him Raul and seen the vamp's smug smile. She loathed him even more now that she knew who he was.

A crashing bang jerked her head toward Doug and the vampire he battled before they fell backward and disappeared into the stairwell. She winced when their bodies thudded off the steps as they tumbled down. Aida remained at Mollie's back while they edged toward the stairs.

When her sister turned to slip down the stairs, Mollie tried to follow. She didn't make it two steps before a hand entangled in her hair and yanked her back.

CHAPTER FORTY-ONE

AIR TORE at Mike's clothes and hair as the earth rushed up to meet him. Except, he didn't slam into the ground. Instead, he landed on the corner of the roof below. His teeth clacked together when the impact jarred his entire body and his back cracked. Agony exploded across his brutalized spine, and his legs went numb before the pitch of the roof caused him to roll down it.

He got his hands under him and braced himself as he fell the remaining ten feet to the ground. When he crashed onto the earth, his breath wheezed out of his lungs, but he tried to jump to his feet. His numb legs didn't follow the commands of his brain and only his chest came off the ground.

"Mollie," he breathed as he fell back again.

Determined to get to her, his fingers dug into the earth as he started dragging himself toward the door of the lighthouse. He didn't know if his back was broken, if his spine was severely bruised, or if he'd pinched a nerve. His spine would heal faster if it weren't broken, but he didn't think it would be fast enough to get to her in time.

No. He would *not* lose her! And he would not allow Mollie to endure what Raul would do to her.

Drawing on the strength of her blood flowing in his veins and his intense love for her, Mike pulled himself faster across the ground. He didn't care what it took; he *would* save her.

A SCREAM LODGED in Mollie's throat, she kicked backward at the creature when his hands twisted in her hair and tore strands of it free. Tears sprang to her eyes, but she refused to shed them.

When the nails scouring her skull drew blood, she almost released her rifle to beat at them, but he'd probably only laugh at her attempts to get him off her, and she refused to be his entertainment. Plus, she also couldn't bring herself to release the only weapon she had.

Reemerging from the stairwell, Aida flung herself against Mollie and started hitting the creature. Raul gave a mirthless laugh and caught one of Aida's wrists with his free hand. Lifting her off the ground, he held her away from him. Aida twisted in his grasp as he let her dangle in front of Mollie. Aida's face was a mixture of pain and fury as her feet kicked in the air.

"Let her go!" Mollie yelled.

She tried to lurch forward, but Raul bent her head back until he nearly drove her to her knees. Gritting her teeth, Mollie struggled to remain on her feet; she would *not* be subservient to this *thing*.

"Pretty little toys all for Raul," the twisted bastard holding Mollie said and made a clicking sound that sent chills down her back. "But I already tasted this toy." He drew Aida closer until her feet brushed against Mollie's knees. "And she was delicious."

"You prick!" Mollie spat, and Raul laughed.

With a flick of his wrist, he flung Aida away as if she weighed no more than a rag doll. Aida soared a few feet through the air before crashing to the floor and skidding across it until she slammed into another section of rotting wall. The wall shuddered, and Mollie held her breath as she waited for it to give way beneath her sister's weight, but the wood remained intact. Aida's head thudded off the boards before she rolled to the side. Getting her hands under her, Aida pushed herself halfway up before collapsing and going still.

"But first, I want to play with this pretty," Raul murmured and yanked Mollie upright.

Mollie nearly screamed when he skimmed one of his claws down her throat and pushed her shirt lower to reveal Mike's marks on her flesh. Mollie kept the rifle against her chest and her finger curled around the trigger; she'd kill herself before she ever allowed this bastard to destroy her, but that would be a last resort.

"Someone's already dirtied my pretty," he murmured.

"Fuck you!" she spat.

Cruel laughter sounded in her ear before he spun her around and she found herself gazing into the reddest, most sadistic eyes she'd ever seen.

"Fuck me?" Raul drawled as he gripped her upper arms.

"Yes," she said with far more bravado than she felt, considering she was the mouse in the path of the cobra, but this mouse wouldn't go down without a fight. "*Fuck you!*"

She jammed the rifle under his chin and pulled the trigger. The force of the shot and her awkward grip on the gun knocked the gun from her hands and caused them to go numb. The top of Raul's head exploded outward in a shower of gore. Mollie almost threw up when bits and pieces of him rained down over the two of them.

Despite the shocked expression in his rolling eyes and the spasmodic twitching of his body, Raul didn't release her. His jaw clicked as the bullet had torn away a good portion of the muscles in his chin and throat.

"Bi... bi... bi... bi..."

Mollie realized he was trying to get the word bitch out, but like a buffering video, he couldn't move on from where he was stuck. Then his eyes fastened on her neck, and she knew that though he couldn't speak, he could still drain her dry. And her blood would help him heal faster.

"No!" she yelled.

Mollie battered at him with her numbed hands, but they slapped uselessly against his chest as his jaw continued making that ghastly clicking sound. Lifting her foot, she attempted to drive her knee into his groin, but he evaded her blow and yanked her forward. She'd blasted a good portion of his brains out, yet she was helpless to stop him from sinking his fangs into her neck.

Her scream caught in her throat and strangled there as his first slurp of her blood made it feel like someone was taking a razor to her flesh and slicing away her skin piece by piece. She no longer had any concerns over her hands being numb as fire licked over the tips of her fingers, spread through her hands, and coursed up her arms.

What had been so magnificent with Mike was excruciating with this monster. The more Mollie tried to resist, the more she became certain the pain would drive her insane. She swore cracks erupted to race over her bones before they started to shatter, yet somehow her skeleton kept her upright in his grasp. The blood rushing through her ears became a bellow she couldn't drown out.

THE FOUL-TASTING BLOOD from the Savage Doug was fighting flooded his system. Typically, he would have gone out of his way to avoid feeding on one of them, but when he'd crawled inside to discover Doug and the Savage battling each other at the bottom of the stairs, he hadn't hesitated before sinking his fangs into the vamp's ankle.

Surprised by the unexpected attack, the Savage reeled back and punched Mike's cheek, but the blow didn't knock him aside. Each swallow of blood made his stomach turn, but it also filled his body with strength and returned feeling to his feet. His back wasn't broken, since even with the Savage's blood, it wouldn't heal this fast if it were.

Doug plunged his fist into the Savage's chest to tear out his heart when Mike released his bite on the creature. A gunshot reverberated from above as Mike climbed to his feet.

"Mollie," he breathed.

She wouldn't be able to hold out long against Raul, but she was putting up a fight. He didn't look at Doug before racing up the stairs to the lighthouse tower. Leaping off the top step, he almost skidded to a stop when he saw the thing clinging to Mollie. The top of its head was gone, leaving only broken bits of gore behind, yet it was still moving…

Still *feeding* on *Mollie*!

Mike roared as he ran at them. Snaking his arm around Raul's back, he smashed the vamp's chin up with his hand to knock Raul's fangs free of Mollie's neck. Raul sputtered as he stumbled back into Mike's chest. Gripping his shirt, Mike lifted Raul before hammering him into the ground.

Mike caught only a glimpse of the full damage Mollie had inflicted on Raul before he drove his fist into Raul's face. Raul's eyes rolled in different directions as bone gave way beneath the blow, and Mike pulled back his fist to batter him again.

Even when his knuckles broke and nothing but pulverized flesh and bone lay beneath him, Mike didn't cease pummeling him. He couldn't stop because he couldn't get the image of this bastard feeding on *his* mate out of his head. He'd touched her, and he would pay for it.

Red filled Mike's vision until everything he saw became shaded in the color. Adrenaline and something more coursed through his system as his fangs extended. Death and blood became all he could taste and smell and *feel*; it was all he craved until it pulsed through his body with each beat of his heart.

"Mike. Stop." The soft voice barely penetrated the rage driving him as he battered Raul's face into what could only be considered mush. "Mike, stop. Please."

His knuckles hit wood with the next blow, and a hand fell on his shoulder. Recoiling from the touch, he spun on whoever dared to touch him. Mollie released a small squeak as she threw her hands up and stumbled away from him. The pallor of her face, her quivering lower lip, and the terror in her eyes finally pierced through the all-consuming bloodlust.

Mollie didn't dare move as Mike's red eyes remained pinned on her. She'd seen enough wildlife videos to know movement only triggered an attack from hunters, but her heart beat so fast, she was sure it bruised her ribcage. She didn't think he'd attack her, but the man facing her was not the Mike she'd come to know so well.

She saw little of the man she loved in the vampire gazing at her like he wanted to devour her.

Mike struggled to leash the part of him clamoring to drag her beneath him and turn her. *Make her immortal!* Saliva filled his mouth as he recalled how amazing she tasted and how powerful her blood was.

"Mike," she whispered. She was frightened of him, but she was more afraid that what faced her was what he'd remain.

The look of fear on her face caused self-hatred to drown out his more destructive impulses. Not afraid of him; she *couldn't* be afraid of him. What had he done?

"Mollie," he breathed. She stopped backing away, but she didn't stop looking at him like he was a Savage about to strike. And he couldn't deny a part of him had been as Savage as any of the monsters hunting them, maybe more so. "I won't hurt you, Mollie."

She nodded, but distrust lingered in her eyes; unable to stand seeing it there, he turned his attention away from her. Over Mollie's shoulder, he spotted Doug helping Aida to her feet before he gazed at the mess beneath him. He'd beaten Raul so severely that nothing remained of his head except fragments of pulverized bone, flesh, and blood. He'd effectively decapitated the man with his fists.

He *never* should have done this in front of her; he should have retained enough control to keep this side of him hidden from her. He'd cautioned her this could happen, and he'd *known* it could, but he hadn't anticipated the complete mindlessness that would overtake him when he saw his mate suffering.

If she ran screaming from him, he wouldn't blame her, but unfortunately, she didn't have that option. The other Savages would have heard the gunshot, and there was still enough night left for them to come.

Turning away from her, he used Raul's clothes to wipe the blood from his hands and face before rising. "We have to go," he said, barely able to meet Mollie's troubled gaze.

When he strode toward her, he expected her to cringe away from him, but she didn't. "Are you okay?" she whispered.

His self-hatred only grew. She'd just been viciously attacked, yet she was concerned about him.

"Are *you* okay?" he asked instead of answering her.

He went to cup her cheek with his palm but lowered his hand before he touched her. Blood had caked in the lines of his knuckles, and he didn't want Raul's blood anywhere near her.

"I'm fine," she said. "I'm worried about you."

"Don't worry about me, Mollie. We have to go; more of them will be coming."

She paled further.

Stalking around the walls of the lighthouse, Doug peered over the side as he went. "I don't see anyone out there," he said. "We should make a run for it now."

"And go where?" Aida asked.

"We have a place," Mike said and then felt a warm hand sliding into his.

He glanced down when Mollie's fingers gripped his. For a second, he couldn't look at her as his chest constricted and emotion swamped him. He didn't deserve her understanding, but he had it. Slowly, he lifted his head to find her beautiful green eyes filled with love while she gazed at him.

CHAPTER FORTY-TWO

THE SUN HAD RISEN an hour ago, but Mike wanted to make sure it was high in the sky before they left their small alcove. He also wanted to give Mollie and Aida more time to sleep while he and Doug plotted their next move.

Normally, he would go out to hunt, but if their plan worked, they would make it off this island today, and he couldn't risk something going wrong while he was hunting and cooking for Aida and Mollie. He'd gone out to get them water shortly after sunrise, and it waited for when the sisters woke.

"The boat ramp is about two miles from here," Doug whispered as he pointed at the map. "If we carry them, we can cover the distance in no time."

"What about Jack?" Mike asked. "We can't leave him behind."

"I'll go with you and make sure you get to a boat safely, but I'm staying on the island." Doug lifted the map, rolled it up, and put it away again.

"Not alone," Mike said, but his eyes involuntarily traveled to where Mollie sat with her sister in the back of the cave. Her arms were draped around Aida's shoulders as Aida slept with her head on Mollie's chest. Mollie's chin rested on top of Aida's head.

"You have to get them out of here," Doug said. "I'll stay and look for Jack while you find land, contact the others, and bring back help. Actually, bring back an army so we can nuke every last one of these bastards off the face of the earth."

Mike would like nothing more than to do exactly that. If he had his way, he would torch this place until nothing but smoldering rock remained. "Jack might not be alive anymore. You can't stay here alone," Mike said.

"Yes, I can. I survived alone before I found you; I'll do it again. And no, you can't send them for help and stay with me," Doug said as he guessed at Mike's next words. "You'd never allow Mollie to leave this island, return to the mainland, and fend for herself even if you think you can let her go. Besides, you have something more to live for now, Mike, some*one* to live for. That's more than either Jack or I have, and you can't risk losing it; I won't let you.

"Take care of her, get her to safety, and come back with help for us. Besides, I do *not* want to be stuck on an island with you if the bond isn't complete and you have no idea where she is, or if she's safe. That would make you a bigger risk to Jack and me than every Savage here."

Mike ran his hand through his hair; Doug was right, but the idea of leaving his friends behind tore at his insides. Before Mollie, he never would have left this island without them, but he had to get her away from here. He couldn't force Doug to come with them, and he couldn't leave Jack completely alone here.

Doug rested his hand on his shoulder and squeezed it. "I understand why you have to go, and Jack will too."

"I *will* come back for the two of you," Mike vowed.

"I have no doubt."

Tears pricked Mollie's eyes as she watched the two friends; she despised the anguish Mike exuded. "You should come with us," Mollie whispered.

Mike and Doug turned to her. "I can't. If Jack is still alive, I'm not leaving him behind," Doug said.

Mollie knew he didn't want to consider the possibility, she certainly hadn't with Aida, but she gulped and made herself ask, "And if he's dead?"

"Then I'll find his body and get it off this island, but I'm not leaving him to these sick bastards."

Mollie's hands clenched on Aida when Mike closed his eyes. She feared he might change his mind and decide to put them on a boat while he stayed to find his friend. She'd refused to leave without Aida, so she wouldn't blame him if he decided not to go without Doug and Jack, but she couldn't leave this island without him.

Aida released a small snort, and love swelled in Mollie's chest. If she stayed here, then Aida wouldn't leave without *her*. No matter how much she loved Mike, Mollie couldn't let Aida stay here. She had to go now that she'd found her sister. Aida had suffered enough at the hands of these monsters; she wouldn't let her endure any more abuse.

Mike glanced at Mollie and Doug, feeling torn between his best friends and his mate, but in the end, there was no competition. The life of his mate came first.

"I'll bring back an army," Mike promised.

Doug smiled. He'd been around enough mated vamps to understand the way things went. Mike would never forgive himself for leaving his friends behind, especially if something happened to one of them, but Doug had already forgiven him.

When the time came to leave their hiding spot, Mike carried Mollie and Doug piggybacked Aida as they followed the map to the pathway leading to the boat ramp. He and Mollie passed by the area a few days ago, but the path was in an area where the woods were fifty feet away from the cliffs. He hadn't ventured into the open to look at what lay below.

Setting Mollie on the ground, Mike examined the map over Doug's shoulder before gazing across the open land separating them from the cliffs.

"The path should be right out there," Doug said.

"Where?" Aida asked with her eyes squinted against the sun.

"We probably won't be able to see it until we're closer," Doug said. "It appears to be carved into the cliffs."

"The only thing we can do is go out there and find it," Mike said.

"And if something is waiting to attack us?" Mollie asked.

Mike glanced at the sun blazing down from above. "If there is anything out there, then they're not strong Savages. We'll be able to take them out."

He spoke with such confidence, but Mollie couldn't shake the unease churning in her gut. "Security *will* be guarding the boat ramp," Mollie said. "They have to expect someone might accidentally stumble across it at some point."

"I'm sure there are guards nearby," Mike replied. "We'll get by them."

Mollie gulped, but what else could she say or do? She despised the idea of going out there and exposing themselves, but they couldn't wait here until night descended again, and without a boat, they would never get free of this island.

"I'll go first," Mike said.

"No," Doug said. "I'll go. Stay with them."

Before Mike could reply, Doug slipped from the trees and strode across the open expanse of land as if he didn't have a care in the world. Mike rose to go after him but froze when Mollie's scent drifted to him; he couldn't leave her alone. He didn't breathe when Doug stopped at the edge of the cliffs and peered over before strolling further along.

Doug didn't glance at the woods while he continued his examination of the cliffs. Mike tore his attention away from his friend to study the trees around them. The birds and squirrels scrambled and flitted from branch to branch. Fifty feet away, a rabbit poked its head from its hole before hopping out.

They'd stood here long enough that the animals had grown accustomed to their presence, but if something else were stalking Doug through the woods, the animals wouldn't be so open in their movements. When he turned his attention back to Doug, he found his friend partway down what must be the path as only Doug's top half remained above the edge of the cliffs.

Climbing back to the top, Doug turned and waved to them.

"Let's go," Mike grated.

Taking Mollie's arm, he moved her in front of him to keep her protected in case something was waiting for them to emerge before attacking. Holding on to Aida's elbow, Mollie held her close to her side while they walked.

The second they stepped from the woods, Mike almost snatched Mollie back against his chest and retreated into the woods with her. *Just keep walking. This is the only way.*

Mollie didn't breathe as they crossed toward the edge of the cliffs. With every step she took, she waited for something to rush out of the woods at them or to fire a shot. Her anxiety didn't lessen the closer they got to the cliffs either; instead, it increased. They couldn't make it to the pathway this easily.

Yet, somehow, they did.

Mollie stopped at the edge of the cliffs when the twisting pathway carved into the rocks came into view. It was more of a death trap than any real path as it was only two feet wide, lacked a handrail, and looked like an ant's weight could crumple it, but it was the only way down to the three boats bobbing on the waves below.

And those boats! They were some of the most beautiful things she'd ever seen as they were their chance at freedom. Two speedboats were tied to the metal dock jutting a hundred feet into the water. The third boat, a yacht, was bigger than her house and moored about two hundred feet away from the sandy shoreline.

A boathouse, about the size of her house, was tucked against the cliffs and away from the shoreline. The sun glinting off the windows made it impossible to see if anyone was inside the building, but it looked empty, and she saw no one on the beach.

Gathering her courage, Mollie stepped onto the trail behind Aida as Doug led the way. Usually, heights didn't bother her, but she was not a fan of possibly unstable paths that could give way at any second.

She focused on Aida's back while she counted each of their steps in the hopes of keeping herself distracted from the imminent death facing them if the path gave out, or if they made one wrong step. Mike's tension vibrated against her skin, but she didn't dare turn to look at him.

So fixed on Aida, Mollie didn't realize they'd come to the end of the path until her next step was onto the sand. Her head lifted, a smile curved her mouth, and she beamed at Mike. Her smile slid away when she saw the lethal look on his face.

When she reached for his hand, he shook his head, and Mollie pulled the rifle from her back. She'd attempted to wipe the gun clean with the bottom of her shirt, but in the daylight, she saw some of Raul's blood still staining the barrel.

She tried not to recall what happened last night—the viciousness of Raul's attack, and the brutality Mike unleashed on him afterward —but the blood brought it all back. The pain of Raul's bite was something she would never forget, nor would she forget how out of control Mike had been. He'd warned her what he could become if she were in danger, but she still hadn't expected it.

Now she sensed that same potential for violence simmering beneath his surface.

"I won't hurt you," he'd said. *"But I can become a threat to others."*

And right now, he looked as if he'd kill anyone who came near them. Mollie glanced anxiously at her sister, but Mike had to know if he did anything to Aida, she would *never* forgive him, and there would never be any future between them.

"What if the boats don't have keys in them?" Aida asked, drawing Mollie's attention back to her.

"What?" she asked.

"The keys, what if they're not in the boats?"

"Then we'll look in the boathouse," Doug said.

But Mollie's heart had already sunk. Of course, they wouldn't leave the keys in the boats, and of course, the damn things required *keys* to run! Why hadn't she thought of it sooner? Probably because her knowledge of boats didn't go beyond the fact they floated, but still, she should have known they would require keys.

What would they do if there were no keys for them? She could pick a lock, but hotwiring a boat went far beyond her area of expertise. Her gaze traveled to the yacht. Maybe the Savages wouldn't expect anyone to swim out there and would have left the keys in it. They could swim out there; they would be more exposed, but they could make it.

You're getting ahead of yourself. The keys are most likely in the boathouse. Yes, that was what made the most sense, but this had been too easy so far, and she didn't dare let herself hope it could continue.

Shells and seaweed crunched beneath her feet as she followed Doug and Aida toward the dock. The tide had rolled out, and the briny scent of the ocean was stronger as small waves lapped against the shore. The sun glinted off the water as seagulls circled and cawed overhead. After the screams, howls, and carnage of last night, the serene scene was almost surreal.

Doug was the first to step onto the metal dock.

"Stay here," Mike said to her and glanced at the cliffs before following Doug onto the dock. He saw no one above, but if anyone happened by, they'd be less likely to see Mollie and Aida than him and Doug.

Mollie held her breath while the dock jingled and clanked as it bounced beneath their weight. Mike and Doug seemed not to notice as they strode forward like they were enjoying a day at the beach instead of trying to flee the Island of Death.

Doug climbed into the red speedboat on the right side of the dock while Mike stepped into the yellow one on the left. Mollie held Aida's shoulders as her eyes darted over the shore and cliffs. She didn't see anyone out there, but she couldn't shake the sensation of eyes burning into her back.

"No keys," Doug said.

"Same here," Mike replied.

They climbed out of the boats and strode back to the shoreline together. Mike still didn't see anyone on the beach or cliffs, but he couldn't shake the feeling of being watched by more than just Aida and Mollie.

"Mike," Mollie whispered when he stepped off the dock. "I don't like this."

"Neither do I," he admitted, but what choice did they have?

He had no idea what they would do if the keys weren't in the boathouse. He might be able to figure out how to hotwire a boat if he had to, but David was the one who knew the most about boats. Mike could operate one, but hotwiring one was an entirely different ballgame. It didn't matter, he *would* figure it out if it were possible.

He kept Mollie and Aida in front of him as Doug led the way across the wet sand to the boathouse. Reaching the door, Doug glanced back at him before turning the knob. The door creaked open, and Doug poked his head inside before entering. Mollie and Aida stepped into the doorway, but only walked a few feet inside before stopping.

Sliding in behind them, Mike closed the door as he examined the boathouse. White tiling made up the flooring, and at the far end of the building, a spiral staircase led to a loft with a bed and a white comforter. The tiki bar under the loft faced the sliding glass doors overlooking the beach.

"Wow," Aida breathed while Doug made his way around the white, wicker furniture with its blue cushions.

Mike glanced out the windows facing the beach they'd left behind, but the sand remained deserted.

"I think someone lives here," Mollie whispered.

Mike frowned as he took in the boathouse again. "What makes you say that?"

"It's too… too homey," she murmured. "You don't make a place you're only shuttling guests through this *nice*."

"There's a lot of money tied up in this operation, and the vampires who arrive here expect the best. Presentation is key," Doug said as he searched the white bookshelves closest to the kitchen.

"Do they expect food too?" Mollie asked. "The kitchen in the mansion was explained by Scott cooking for the prisoners, but why would they have a kitchen *here*? This building looks newer than the others; it's more modern."

Mike glanced at the small kitchen with its white cabinets, blue countertops, and island with an oven. The refrigerator hummed, and a towel sat neatly folded next to the sink. The building smelled of the sea and lavender; he didn't detect another presence inside, but then, he couldn't see all of the loft.

If there was another door or balcony up there, someone could be hiding outside and could enter again. The club had humans like Scott working for them; they moved freely through the day and would happily slaughter anyone if it would help and increase their chances of becoming immortal.

"No, they wouldn't expect food too," he murmured. "Doug, we have to go."

Mike's hand fell on the knob again as a step sounded from above, and a shadow fell across the wall of the loft. Someone was up there.

"I've got the keys!" Doug cried and hefted a key ring into the air.

The keys jingled at the same time a shot rang out and an alarm blared.

CHAPTER FORTY-THREE

MOLLIE CRIED out when the bullet slicing across her arm tore away a chunk of her skin. Instinctively, she closed her hand over the wound to staunch the flow of blood. It was only a flesh wound, but it burned like someone had taken a hot poker to her arm.

"Mollie!" Mike roared when the scent of her blood hit the air.

Leaping forward, he threw himself on top of her and shoved her to the ground as the next bullet burrowed into the back of his thigh. "Son of a bitch!" he snarled as fire lanced up his leg.

"Are you okay?" Mollie demanded.

"Yes." Mike positioned himself more firmly over the top of her to make sure little of her remained exposed.

"Where's Aida?"

She struggled to find her sister, but all she saw was Mike's solid body covering hers, and the white, front door only inches away from her fingertips. They were so close to freedom, but the way they were lying blocked the entrance and the easiest escape route for Aida and Doug.

Mike lifted his head as Doug ran for Aida and, grabbing her arm, raced with her toward the sliding doors at the back of the house as bullets slammed into the floor. Shards of tile burst into the air around them, but none of the rounds hit their target before Doug and Aida ran under the loft and out of the shooter's range.

While the shooter was distracted trying to take out Aida and Doug, Mike dragged Mollie to her feet. He kept her in front of him, offering his back as a target while he stepped back and flung the door open.

Lifting Mollie against him, Mike staggered into the day. Bullets followed them out the door, but no more struck him or Mollie as they fled the shooter.

And then he saw they were no longer alone on the beach.

Mike pressed his back against the boathouse. He kept Mollie in front of him to protect her from any bullets that might come through the wall as he surveyed the ten vampires gliding across the sand toward them. Dressed all in black, Mike recognized the golden, triangle patch on their coats as the same ones the security in the barn wore.

Judging by their thick glasses and heavy clothing, he suspected these security guards were on their way to becoming full blown Savages, but their employers made sure they didn't go over the edge. These creatures would be of no use to those in the club if they couldn't at least tolerate some sun.

Barely visible in the light of day, a red light flashed over the sand from the boathouse, and Mike recognized it as a beacon used to alert security they had people or vamps trying to escape. There were probably caves nearby that these security members hid in during the day in case someone went for the boats.

The blaring siren of the alarm sounded for a few more seconds before abruptly ending. There was no need for it now that the human inside had done their job and notified their masters they had escapees on the beach.

"Shit," he hissed.

"Aida!" Mollie breathed when Doug and Aida skidded around the corner of the house.

"There's more behind us!" Doug said and nudged Aida toward them.

"We have to get to the boats." Mike lifted Mollie and ran toward the dock.

The second he started sprinting, the security guards broke into a run too. They'd been more than content to prowl forward before, but now they had a chase, and like their masters, they also loved to hunt.

His feet skidded to the side when they landed on the metal dock, and he almost went down but managed to keep his balance. His wounded leg throbbed like a son of a bitch as the bullet worked its way free of his flesh. Gritting his teeth, he pushed himself onward as an excited shout erupted from the security guards. Doug's feet pounded behind him, and the first thud of the Savages' feet hitting the dock reverberated it.

He didn't dare glance back as he slid to a halt next to the yellow boat simply because it was the closest one. He placed Mollie on the bow and turned back for Aida when Doug stopped beside him. He set Aida next to Mollie as Doug leapt over the side, and fumbling through the keys, slid the first one into the ignition.

Mollie scooted across the front of the boat and slid over the side to where the seats were before turning back to help her sister climb down. She searched for Mike, but he was not behind Aida as she'd expected.

"Mike!" Mollie shouted while he untied the first line connecting the boat to the dock and then the second. He didn't jump into the boat but put his foot on the front of it and shoved it away from the dock. "Mike!"

Mollie scrambled to the front of the boat as he remained standing on the dock with those *things* charging at him. The creatures desire to slaughter anything in their way emanated from them as inhuman sounds issued from them and the dock bounced beneath the weight of the approaching stampede.

"Mike!" she screamed as the creatures closed in on him.

"Get in the boat, Mike!" Doug yelled as he tried another key.

Mollie swung her rifle free and barely aimed before she started firing at the vampires. Bullets bounced off the decking, one caught a vamp in the shin, and another in the shoulder, but they did nothing to deter the monsters bearing down on Mike.

Mike didn't dare jump into the boat; if he did, the Savages would only follow him straight to Mollie. By staying on the dock, he provided a distraction to the vampires and would be able to take out some of them while Doug worked on finding the key.

Mollie steadied the trembling of her hand as adrenaline coursed through her. They were only feet away from Mike, and he showed no sign of getting out of their way. Aida fell at her side and started firing her weapon as the first one crashed into Mike's chest and knocked him back.

"No!" Mollie screamed.

Tossing the rifle onto her back again, she scrambled off the seat and onto the front of the boat. Her feet slid on the smooth yellow surface as the rocking boat and the swaying dock caused water to splash over the sides of both.

She remained crouched to keep her balance as she scurried across the front toward Mike. They'd only floated a few feet away from the dock, and she could still reach it. She was about to leap off the boat and back onto the dock when Doug snagged her leg and snatched her back. Pain lanced through her knees when they smacked off the boat's surface, but she bit back a cry.

"Here!" Doug thrust the key ring into her hand. "Don't try the silver ones."

Before she could reply, he darted across the front of the boat and leapt onto the dock. Running forward, Doug crashed into the vamp Mike was fighting. The vampire was knocked to the side, but he dragged Mike with him until they almost toppled into the water. Mike caught his balance at the last second, and palming the creature's face, he pried the vamp off him and tossed it in the water.

Mollie reluctantly turned away from the fight as two more of the guards reached Mike and Doug. Scrambling back to the driver's seat,

Mollie set her rifle on the ground next to her where it would be within easy reach. She fumbled through the keys, ignoring the silver ones in favor of the gold. She settled on one and slid it into the ignition and tried to turn it; nothing happened. The next one was the same.

Grunts and cries filled the air as the thuds of fists hitting flesh and bone shattered the stillness of the once tranquil day. Aida stopped firing her weapon once the battle ensued and they were all so close together. Mollie didn't dare look up; she knew she'd only panic if she saw what was happening.

He's fine, she told herself. *Stay focused.*

Sweat coated her as she fumbled for another gold key. There were at least a dozen keys on the chain, six of them were silver and the rest gold; she was running out of options.

What if the ring doesn't possess the key to this boat? Don't think it, don't think it. But it was already too late; the thought had embedded deeper than a hungry tick.

The boat bounced on the sea and water splashed over the sides when something slammed into it. She looked up in time to see a vampire crouched on the front of the boat with its fangs extended while it leered at Aida.

Mollie fumbled for the rifle, but Aida lifted her gun and shot the creature point-blank in the face. It squealed as it fell over backward. Mollie turned her attention back to the keys.

She slid the next key into the ignition, turned, and got nothing. Cursing, she slapped her palm off the steering wheel. She selected another key as a loud crash sounded and the front of the boat nosedived. Mollie's head shot up to find two vampires creeping closer to Aida.

Aida lifted her weapon and fired at the first one, but it dashed to the side, and when she turned the gun on the second one, nothing happened. Aida looked helplessly at her empty gun before rushing back toward Mollie.

Mollie slid the next key into the ignition but didn't have time to turn it as the vamps bounded after her sister. Snatching up her rifle, she aimed at the one closest to Aida. When she pulled the trigger, blood exploded over the seats, and she realized she'd shot the thing in the stomach. Which only served to piss it off more as it howled and focused on her with a lethal glare.

Mollie pulled the trigger again, but nothing happened.

Stay calm. Stay calm.

She had more bullets in her pocket, but she'd be dead before she could reload the gun. Lifting the rifle, she prepared to batter the creature with it as the vampire leapt toward her on all fours like some demented, bloodsucking monkey.

Mike launched another one of the guards off him and into the water as Aida's shout drew his attention to the boat and the Savage jumping at Mollie. She swung the rifle at the vamp and caught it in the cheek, throwing it off its murderous intent. The attention of the remaining guards shifted from him and Doug to the easier prey in the boat.

"Go!" Doug shouted at him when another Savage pounced on the boat.

Mike leaned back on his heel before bolting across the deck and leaping across the six feet of distance separating the boat from the dock. When he landed, his feet skidded on the slippery surface of the fiberglass hull, but he threw out his arms to keep his balance.

He didn't have time to slaughter the first Savage. Lifting it by the collar of its shirt, Mike picked it up and heaved it overboard as Mollie again swung the butt of the rifle at the vamp hunting her. The creature dodged the gun while the other one narrowed in on Aida who was backing away toward Mike.

Jumping off the bow, Mike smashed into the monster stalking Aida. Thrown off balance, the Savage staggered back but didn't go overboard. More gunshots filled the air and pinged off the metal dock. Mike assumed whoever had been in the boathouse was now coming for them, but he didn't look at the beach.

When the Savage charged her, Mollie threw herself down with so much force she knocked the air from her lungs when she hit the floor. But the move threw the creature off, and it didn't succeed in getting its hands on her, yet. Struggling to breathe, she rolled toward the bench seat at the back of the boat.

Her back connected with the seat, halting her escape attempt as Mike pounced on the Savage stalking her. She didn't see what followed, but the Savage's headless body fell beside her seconds later. Mollie scrambled away from the blood flowing across the white floor and pulled herself up onto the bench seat. Behind Mike, Doug jumped onto the boat and tossed the one who'd been stalking Aida overboard.

More gunshots peppered the dock, running straight up the middle of it. Mollie searched the beach for the shooter but saw no one there. When she tipped her head back, she spotted a man standing at the top of the cliffs with a rifle against his shoulder and a woman at his side.

"It's Jack!" Doug blurted as Mike slid into the driver's seat and turned the key.

CHAPTER FORTY-FOUR

RELIEF FILLED Mike as he gazed at his friend on the cliffs. Jack was alive! Mike had tried not to think about the possibility his friend could be dead, but it had been a nagging worry at the back of his mind. Somehow, they would get Jack off this island now too, if he could get the boat started.

Mollie's heart lurched when the boat engine chugged but didn't turn over. They had the key! More shots peppered the dock, denting the metal and causing sparks to fly up as the vampires on the dock jumped into the water.

"Please start," she whispered as some of the monsters started swimming toward the boat while others disappeared under the dock.

The boat lurched when fingers curled over the side of it and a head popped up. Water poured down the face of the vamp as he leered at Aida. Mollie jumped to her feet, and Aida grabbed the fire extinguisher from where it hung near the steering wheel. Lifting the extinguisher, Aida bashed the fingers of the vamp trying to climb inside. The creature howled, and its broken fingers couldn't retain their grip on the boat.

The engine chugged again, caught, then died. Mollie snatched up her rifle and hammered the butt of it into the face of the next vampire whose head popped over the side of the boat. Blood spurted from his broken nose, but he didn't lose his hold.

"Son of a bitch!" she spat.

Mollie smashed him in the face again and again. When she knocked some of his teeth out, he finally released the boat. The rifle fell to her side, and her shoulders heaved as she searched for another threat, but she didn't see any more of the bastards trying to climb aboard.

Then, like a shark slipping beneath the surface of the water, something thudded against the bottom of the boat. Another thump followed by a silence more unnerving than the noise. Mollie stared at the floor as if she could see through it as their predators sought some new way to get at their prey.

A screeching sound shattered the silence and set her teeth on edge. It took her a second to realize the noise was being created by fingers scrabbling over the bottom of the boat, seeking purchase, or something... worse.

"I think they're trying to disable the boat!" she yelled to Mike.

Gunshots continued to ring over the dock though no vampires remained there that Mike could see. Jack wouldn't swing the gun in their direction to take out the Savages in the water for fear of accidentally hitting one of them or disabling the boat. His friend was only trying to keep the Savages on alert for those bullets.

Mike ignored the sounds from under the boat that reminded him of mice scratching at walls as he turned the key. The boat didn't have an outboard engine, so the Savages couldn't dismantle that, but he didn't know if they could do something else while under there.

"Fucking start," he muttered.

The engine chugged, sputtered, and died again. What if the damn thing didn't have any gas? They couldn't jump into the ocean with the Savages swirling through there, or what if they had somehow managed to disable the boat already?

When he glanced up, he saw the shoreline getting closer as they drifted toward it. If the boat didn't start soon, they would end up beached, and the vessel would be useless to them.

More gunshots rang out, but these weren't as metallic sounding. Mike lurched back when a bullet racing past his nose kissed the tip of it. His head rose as he realized these shots weren't coming from Jack.

Glancing at the shoreline, he spotted a woman standing there with her legs spread and a two-handed grip on a gun. He suspected she'd been the one firing at them from the loft in the beach house. Sand sprayed up in front of the woman as bullets rained down from above, but Jack's rounds were a good ten feet in front of her as his angle on the cliff made it impossible to get a good shot at her.

"Get down!" Mike roared as more bullets peppered the side of the boat.

Mollie lunged for Aida as a Savage who had managed to climb into the boat tore the extinguisher from her sister's hands. A bullet pierced the boat at her feet as she grasped Aida's shoulders and shoved her down.

Releasing Aida, Mollie bashed the butt of the rifle into the Savage's face as a bullet whizzed past her ear. For a second, Mollie almost pissed herself as the whistle of the bullet replayed in her mind, and the Savage staggered backward but didn't topple out. It wouldn't do her any good to hit the ground with this thing still in the boat; she may not get shot, but she would get eaten, and she'd rather take a bullet than be vampire steak tartare.

Grabbing the Savage by the collar of his shirt, Doug yanked it backward and tossed it overboard as a fresh wave of gunfire rang out. Doug spun away from the railing and leapt in front of Mollie when more bullets riddled the boat.

Mollie screamed and lunged for Doug when his body jerked from the impact of the bullets piercing it. Blood trickled from his mouth and bloomed across his chest as he seized her arms and pushed her down next to Aida before falling on top of them.

"Son of a bitch!" Mike spat as the shield in front of the steering wheel spiderwebbed and a wooden bullet embedded in the center of it. "Mollie! Doug!" Mike shouted. He'd seen the blood on Doug's shirt before he pulled Mollie beneath him. Mollie hadn't been hit, but Doug was. "Doug, are you okay? Mollie? Someone answer me!"

No one responded though as the engine chugged, caught again, and purred for a few seconds before bogging down. Mike's heart sank, but then the motor roared back to life, and the boat lurched forward. Mike clutched the handle beside him and threw the vessel into reverse before it crashed into the dock. Water sprayed up around him; the side of the boat dipped down as he twisted the wheel to steer the vessel away from the dock.

On top of the cliff, the woman with Jack grabbed his arm and pointed to something on their right. Jack swung the rifle onto his back, clasped the woman's hand, and fled toward the woods. With a heavy heart, Mike watched them go; he wouldn't be able to get to them and get them off the island now that he didn't know where they'd gone. He'd have to come back for Jack after he got Mollie to safety and made sure Doug was okay.

Mollie remained still beneath Doug's heavy weight as the boat lurched backward. She couldn't see anything beyond his body, but water sprayed the fingers she'd dug into his shoulder. Tears burned her eyes as his blood soaked through her shirt to coat her skin. *He's a vampire; he'll be okay.* She tried to convince herself of this, but she couldn't shake the feeling of dread creeping over her skin.

"Doug?" she whispered, but he didn't respond.

Beside her, Aida's arm rested against hers, yet her sister remained abnormally still. Had Aida also been shot before Mollie pushed her out of the way?

"Aida?"

"I'm okay," Aida said in a choked voice.

Mollie realized Doug's weight and the way he'd landed on her sister was making it difficult for Aida to speak. When the boat suddenly shifted into forward, and the engine roared, the three of them slid back a few feet before coming to a stop. Something smashed off the bottom of the boat, but she felt no sympathy for the Savage who probably just had their skull bashed in.

"Doug?" she asked again. *Please be alive. Please be alive.*

If he replied, she didn't hear it over the hum of the engine and the waves slapping the sides of the boat as it skimmed the surface of the ocean. Mollie closed her eyes to hold back her tears, but some slid free. There was no rise and fall in Doug's chest against hers, and no breath tickled her cheek though his mouth was next to her face.

"Doug," she choked out as she hugged him closer. She feared he was already gone, but if not, he needed to know she was here for him.

The boat continued across the ocean for what was probably only another minute or two, but it felt like an eternity before their speed eased. Mollie couldn't bring herself to release Doug as the boat came to a halt and the engine purred while they bobbed on the waves.

Then Doug's body was eased off hers. Mollie's fingers remained curved into cramped hooks when she released him. She blinked against the influx of light as the sea breeze cooled her flesh. Getting her elbows under her, she pushed herself up a little as Mike carefully lifted his friend and placed him on the bench seat.

"Doug?" Mike croaked.

The broken sound of Mike's voice and the suffering on his face as he knelt at Doug's side tore at her heart. Mike pressed his fingers against Doug's neck to check for a pulse and then frantically moved them to another location and then another.

"No," Mike moaned.

Tears slid down her face when Mike bit into his wrist and placed it against Doug's partially open mouth.

"Come on, Doug, drink," he commanded in a hoarse voice.

He willed his friend to swallow the blood filling his mouth. There had been no pulse, one of the bullet holes in his shirt was dead center through his heart, but that didn't mean anything. Doug was a vampire, *he* was a vampire, and anything could happen. If Mike succeeded in getting some of his blood into his friend, he could still save him; he was sure of it.

"It will heal you, drink!" he ordered.

Mike waited for Doug's throat to make the motion of swallowing and for the healing effects of the blood to take hold, but Doug didn't move.

"This will help you," Mike insisted.

Mike knew he was lying to himself; he could see the truth in the stillness of Doug's body, the ashen hue of his cheeks, the blood spreading across his chest, and the missing beat of his heart, but he refused to believe it.

"Drink, Doug!" Mike gave his friend a shake that caused Doug's head to turn toward him. Doug's once lively blue eyes were unseeing beneath his half-closed lids.

No! Mike screamed inwardly as memories of their life together flashed through his mind.

They'd been friends since they were kids running their neighborhood, riding their bikes uptown to get penny candy, discussing girls, stealing Playboys from Doug's dad, and building forts. They'd played on the same teams together, had many of the same classes in high school, and gone to college together. When Liam and David initially chose different colleges, he, Doug, and Jack went to the same one and joined the same frat. The three of them were turned into vampires only hours apart from each other.

Never had he imagined life without his friends in it, without his *family* in it, but one of his brothers was gone. A bellow swelled in his chest and lodged in his throat as tears burned his eyes, and he swayed between rage and choking grief. Doug, the gentlest soul, the one with the smile that melted women's hearts and brightened everyone's day, was dead.

The bellow erupted from him, and he smashed his fist into the bench seat. The hole he tore through it caused yellow stuffing to explode and rain down on Doug's body. Horror filled him, and he brushed the offending debris away.

"I'm sorry," he murmured. "I'm so sorry."

Mike knew he wasn't apologizing for the stuffing; he was apologizing for his failure to save Doug's life and his inability to get them all off the island alive. He gripped Doug's still warm wrist and squeezed it.

Lifting his head, he glowered at the island on the horizon. One of his friends remained in that hellhole, and no matter what it took, he would get Jack out of there. He would *not* let another one of his friends down.

A sob sounded behind him, and he glanced back to find Aida with her hand against her mouth to stifle her sounds. Mollie sat beside her with an arm around Aida's waist and tears streaming down her face.

Aida pulled her hand away from her mouth. "He died to protect us," she whispered and sobbed again.

Mollie kissed her sister's temple when Aida turned her head into her shoulder. Mike's glistening red eyes briefly met hers before he focused on Doug again. His shoulders remained hunched as if he expected someone to hit him, but no one could deliver him a worse blow than this.

Still kneeling, Mike turned to another set of seats and lifted the top of one to peer at the contents stashed inside. He discovered a white boat covering tucked within and pulled it out before turning back to Doug.

Rising, he unfolded the covering and carefully draped it over Doug's body, but he couldn't bring himself to cover his friend's face yet. Falling back on his knees beside Doug, he rested his hand on Doug's chest and willed his friend to live again. He had a better chance of seeing a unicorn, but he couldn't bring himself to give up on him yet.

Doug's words from earlier played through his mind. *"Besides, you have something more to live for now, Mike, someone to live for. That's more than either Jack or I have, and you can't risk losing it; I won't let you."*

Doug died to protect Mollie, and he did it for *him*. *"I'll protect her with my life,"* Doug had promised, and he'd upheld that promise.

Mike had only one thing to give Doug in return. "I'll make them pay for this," he vowed as he settled the covering over Doug's face.

A hand on his shoulder drew Mike's attention away from Doug as Mollie knelt at his side. She draped her arms over his shoulders and rested her face against his neck.

"I'm so sorry," she whispered.

She'd give anything to take away his suffering, but it was impossible. Only time would help him cope with the loss of his friend, but no matter how much time passed, the sadness would remain, and the hole would never fill. However, he had to know she was here for him.

Mike hugged her against him and buried his face in her hair. He squeezed her tighter than he probably should have, but she didn't protest or try to pull away.

Mollie turned her head to kiss him on the cheek. "I love you."

"And I love you," he said.

CHAPTER FORTY-FIVE

ONCE HE SPOTTED land less than a mile from the island, Mike searched for a secluded stretch of beach. He waited until nightfall before daring to come ashore with their bullet-riddled boat, bloody clothes, and Doug's body.

Once he beached the boat, he removed Doug's body from it before cutting the gas line and using his Zippo and a rag to set it on fire. He didn't worry the police or someone would somehow locate him through blood and fingerprints, but he needed to hide any evidence of Mollie and Aida.

With the flames rising behind them, and with Mike carrying Doug, they trudged along the shoreline and into a small town where they slipped through the shadows until he discovered a man exiting his car. Placing Doug down, Mike snuck up on the man, knocked him out, and stole the vehicle. They couldn't stay in this town; he wasn't going to take the chance the people here were working with the Savages.

Judging by the kilometer speed limit signs on the side of the dark, two-lane road winding through barren fields and pine trees as he drove south, Mike assumed they were still in Canada.

"I'm so sorry about Doug," Mollie whispered. "He was a good man."

Mike winced as the mention of his friend reminded him that Doug's body was stashed in the trunk. Doug deserved so much better, but Mike couldn't give it to him yet. "He was," Mike agreed.

"Are you okay?"

"Yes."

His clipped answers made it clear he didn't want to talk about it. *Please don't blame me*, she silently pleaded. It was *her* Doug died defending; she wouldn't blame Mike if he resented her for what happened.

Swinging her gaze out the window, she stared at the trees passing by in a blur. She tried not to think about Doug, the island, and this whole mess, but then a disturbing realization settled over her.

"The vampires on the island, they have our info," Mollie murmured. "They took our IDs from us, and I'm sure they went through my car."

Mike didn't have his real ID on him when he left home, he wasn't sure he still *had* an ID for the real him, and he didn't have one with his real info on it.

"None of those fuckers will make it off that island alive," he assured her.

"Some of them may have already left the island if they realized things were going wrong and they had escapees who might want revenge," she whispered. "They may not know exactly who got away yet, but it won't take them long to figure out if they kept all our info, which I'm sure they did."

Mike glanced over at her. In the dim glow of the dashboard lights, her skin was ashen. "I'll get you both new IDs, and I *will* keep you safe. They'll never find you."

"But we can never go home again, can we?" she whispered.

Mike reached over and took her hand when her fingers dug into her thigh. "It would be safer if you didn't," he said.

"My mom's ashes are there and all our things. Aida is supposed to start college in the fall, and..." Mollie broke off and shook her head. She blinked away the tears filling her eyes as she recalled all the things and memories filling her home. She would never see them again, but it could be far worse. "We're alive, that's what matters."

"I will figure out a way to retrieve your mother's ashes and anything else of importance to you. With fake IDs and our ability to change and manipulate memories, we can get Aida into another college. I wouldn't recommend her attending the same one she planned to go to, but we'll figure it out. Most of the Byrne kids are good with computers, but Julian is a computer genius. He'll be able to get it all situated; he can probably get her into Harvard."

"I'd flunk out of there in a month," Aida muttered. "I like school, but I also like to have fun, and I don't think they get much playtime at Harvard. I'll find another college. Besides, I think I might like a little time off from learning after this. I'll start next spring, and maybe I'll take some online classes until then."

Mollie wanted her sister to go to college, it was what their mother had dreamed of, but she couldn't argue with Aida about it after everything she'd endured. Aida needed time to process everything and heal before returning to normal life. However, neither of their lives would ever be normal again given everything they now knew about the world.

"Where will we live? *How* will we live?" Mollie asked. "We have money left over from our mom's life insurance policy, but I don't know how I'll get it without any ID or my bank cards."

"We will figure out a way to get the money, and both of you can stay with my family and me." He glanced at Mollie as she turned in the seat to look at him. "We'll protect you, and I want you with me forever, if you agree to it."

Aida's breath sucked in loudly, and Mike glanced at her in the rearview mirror.

"If not forever, at least until you're safe," Mike said to ease some of Aida's fear, but she still looked as if her eyes were going to pop out of her head.

"And who are the members of your family?" Aida asked.

"My friend Liam and his wife Sera have ten children, and some of them also have children. Liam and Sera's children are my adopted nieces and nephews. They're the Byrne kids, or the Byrne clan is more like it," Mike said. "Liam is like my brother—I've known him since we were kids—and my friends, David, Jack, and… and Doug, all live on the same land together. It's a massive property with multiple houses and plenty of room for more."

"Are they all vampires?"

"They are, but they'd never harm you or Mollie."

"So, they're more like you than those freaks on the island?"

"Yes."

"And you want *us* to live with them?"

A trickle of unease slid through Mike. It was a lot to ask of a young girl who'd been severely abused at the hands of vampires, but if Aida refused to stay with him, then Mollie would too, and he needed her somewhere she would be safe.

"You'll be safest there," he said.

Aida didn't respond as she sat back in her seat and turned to gaze out the window. Mollie squeezed Mike's hand. He didn't seem to resent her for Doug's death, but they still had so many hurdles to leap. One of them being her sister.

Mollie would understand if Aida wanted nothing to do with vampires again and chose not to live with them, but she would have to go with Aida.

She tried not to think about it as she focused on what she could see of the passing scenery. One step at a time, and they had plenty of steps to get through before they decided their living arrangements.

Half an hour later, they arrived in another small town with only one road as the main strip through it.

"Stay out here," Mike said when he pulled into the parking lot of the only motel in town. One other car was parked outside the office, which was the only room with a light on. "I'll get the keys."

Using his power to bend a human to his will, he got three keys from the clerk, instructed the man to give them unlimited access on the phones, and left him with false names and no memory of how they paid for the rooms. If the clerk were ever asked to describe them, he would give descriptions of the cast of Three's Company.

He made sure there was no security system and they were the only guests in the ten-room motel before returning to the car. Because of that, Mike wasn't concerned someone would report him carrying a tarp-enshrouded body to whatever police they had in town.

Mike placed Doug's body in the first room he confiscated, went through the door to the second room, and opened the door in between the second and third room. Mollie and Aida had already settled into the third room and looked up at him when he opened the door.

He nodded to them before closing the door and walking over to sit on the king-sized bed. He didn't like having Mollie out of his sight, but she needed time with her sister, and he had some things to deal with. Lifting the phone from the bed stand, he dialed Liam's number.

Liam answered on the second ring. "Hello."

"Liam," Mike said.

"Mike! Where the *fuck* have you been? We've been trying to call you for days, and your phones aren't given off a location, so we had no idea where to start searching for you!"

"We ran into a lot of trouble up here."

"How bad?"

"Real bad."

"Jack and Doug?"

"Jack's still caught up in it." He'd prefer not to break the news about Doug over the phone, but he didn't have a choice. The problem was, he didn't know how to make it easy, but then there was never an easy way to tell someone a loved one was dead. In the end, he decided just to rip the band-aid off. "Doug's dead."

Dead silence came across the line, and it was almost a full minute before Liam spoke again. "Are you sure?"

"Yes."

Liam's breath exploded out of him, and Mike heard the cushions of a couch sinking. "Oh shit." Grief laced Liam's voice as his breathing became labored over the line. "What happened?"

Mike filled him in on the details in a flat, monotonous tone. If he allowed emotion to get involved, he'd tear this room to shreds. He was almost done with the story when the door opened and Mollie walked over to sit beside him. She rested her hand on his thigh and her head on his shoulder while he spoke.

The warmth of her body helped calm him; he slid his arm around her waist and pulled her against his side. On the other end of the line, he heard someone enter the room as he finished speaking with Liam and then the whispered voices of David and Sera, but Liam didn't respond to them.

"We have to get Jack," Liam finally said after at least another minute of silence.

"We will," Mike said. "We're going to need a lot of help to do it and to eradicate every bastard on that island."

"I'll bring help," Liam said. "Do you think the ones who caught you will flee now that you've escaped?"

"No. I think they believe they're untouchable. It will only be more of a game to them when we return."

"Assholes," Liam breathed. "Where are you?"

Mike told him the name of the town in northern Labrador.

"We'll leave soon."

It would take them over a day, possibly two to drive there, but they would get there as fast as they could.

"Your mate," Liam said. "Are you going to change her before you go back to the island?"

Mike's hands clenched on the phone and Mollie's knee. He longed to take her mortality from her and make her stronger, but he couldn't. "No."

Mollie frowned when Mike's tension ratcheted up, but she hadn't heard what irritated him.

"That's probably not a good move," Liam said.

"It's the one I'm going to make," Mike stated. "I have to go now. We still have a lot to take care of here. I'll call you when I get a new cell phone; if I can find one in this town."

"Be careful."

"I will," Mike said and hung up.

He kissed the top of Mollie's head before rising. He couldn't stand to be apart from her but being too close was also difficult as she was a temptation he had to resist.

"We have to get supplies," he said, and she nodded.

CHAPTER FORTY-SIX

HE TOOK the two of them to the clothing store the clerk told him about earlier. He didn't dare leave the sisters alone in the motel while they were still so close to the island. There could be more possible enemies here, or the Savages could send out humans and security in search of their escapees.

Mollie picked the lock on the back door of the small clothing/grocery store that also sold bait and feed for livestock. They each took some clean clothes from the racks, sneakers, and Mollie stole some bandages for her arm before they returned to the motel to shower.

Hopefully, no one would notice the missing articles of clothing. The last thing they needed was to be seen around town wearing stolen clothes. Staying here would attract the attention of the locals, as he doubted they got many visitors in town, and being labeled as thieves would not be good as he couldn't change the memories of *everyone* here.

When they were showered and changed into their new jeans and long-sleeved shirts, they went in search of food for Mollie and Aida as well as himself. The only restaurant in town, a small diner named Musco's, was still open; two other customers were inside.

Mike's wounds were healing, but he required blood. While Mollie and Aida ate pancakes and sausages, Mike fed on the staff and the customers before erasing their memories of the encounter.

Back at the hotel, he left Mollie and Aida in the third room while he returned to the second and closed the door. Glutted on blood and healing fast, he called Liam back to tell him he hadn't been able to locate a cell phone. Mike doubted there was any cell phone service here as, after capturing them, the Savages took them further north.

MOLLIE SAT on the edge of the bed as she rested her hands on her knees and gazed at the closed door between her room and Mike's. Ever since they arrived in this town, she'd felt Mike pulling away from her, but she didn't know why.

"He's a good man, for a vampire," Aida said as she sat on the edge of her bed and flipped idly through the three TV channels.

"Would you stay with him and his family?"

Aida's hand stilled on the remote as she gazed at the TV. "Do we have any other choice?"

"We could figure out something else."

Aida started flipping through the channels again. "As long as they don't try to eat us, I'll be fine staying with his family."

"They won't."

"That's what they said about the dinosaurs in Jurassic Park too."

Mollie chuckled. "Mike's older than us, but he's not Jurassic old."

A small smile curved the corner of Aida's mouth before it slid away. "He wants you to stay with him forever."

Mollie took a deep breath before plunging in. "I want that too."

Aida's hand froze on the button before her head turned slowly toward Mollie. "As in you *want* to be a vampire?"

"Yes."

"Are you serious?"

"As a heart attack."

Aida tossed the remote aside before scrambling over the bed to sit across from Mollie. "Do you understand what you're saying? What that would make you? What you would have to do, *forever*?"

"I do. I've been thinking about it for a while now."

And, deep down, she'd known this was the path she would take. She loved Mike, and in the end, it was as simple as that.

"I'm not going to leave you. I'll stay close by while you're at college…" Her voice trailed off when Aida winced. "Aida?"

"College seems so silly now, doesn't it?" Aida asked. "After everything we know and everything we've been through, how can we go back to *normal* lives? Or as normal as we'll get once we enter the vampire equivalent of witness protection."

"Because we have to return to as much normal as we possibly can. That's the way life goes. Big things happen, but the world keeps turning, and we have to keep going with it because there is no other choice."

"You're not returning to normal; you're saying you plan to plunge into the insanity."

"Yes, but I'm not giving up my dreams. I'm still going to college, whether online or at a university, it doesn't matter, but I still plan to help people. Besides, an eternity of sitting on my ass without anything else to do would get rather tedious after a while, don't you think?"

"I think you could find plenty to do with tall, blond, and gorgeous over there," Aida teased.

Mollie forced a smile, but Aida's words caused jealousy to twist through her. It was unreasonable, given that Mike was precisely as Aida described, but she didn't want anyone looking at him like that. He was *hers* and hers alone.

"When would you do this?" Aida asked.

"Soon."

Aida's eyebrows drew together as she gazed at Mollie. "But you barely know him. Why don't you wait and see if you can still stomach him a year from now when the lust burns off, you're asking him to wash his hair out of the sink for the thousandth time, and you can't stand each other anymore?"

She knew Aida couldn't possibly understand, *she* barely understood, but she would never grow tired of Mike. He would annoy her, as she would him, but she would never stop loving him. She felt the truth of that in every inch of her body.

"There's a reason why waiting might be impossible," she said.

Mollie filled Aida in on the things Mike had told her about mates and what they meant to a vampire. Her sister's mouth fell further open, and her eyes got bigger as Mollie spoke. When she finished, Aida sat for a few minutes before responding.

"It's almost romantic considering how bloodthirsty some of them are and how vicious they can all be."

"Mike's not like the ones who held you captive," Mollie said.

"I know, but I've seen what he can do, and he's vicious. He beat that one guy's head off with his bare hands."

Mollie inwardly cringed at the reminder. "I was there."

"Will you be violent like that?"

"I'm sure I will be if anyone threatens someone I love."

"And do you love him?"

"More than I believed I could love a man, and I want a future with him. Before Mike, I never saw myself trusting or loving someone enough to settle down with them."

"That's because our sperm donor was an asshole, and you never got over him walking out on us."

"Thank you, Dr. Freud," Mollie retorted.

Aida laughed and held up her hands. "Just calling it as I see it, and I don't have the psych classes you have."

"Hmm," Mollie muttered as her thoughts turned to their father.

For years, she'd refused to admit her father leaving had any effect over her relationships, or lack thereof, with men, but Aida was right. However, she would *not* let her father taint what she had with Mike.

There were lots of good men in the world, and Mike was one of them. Mollie brushed her fingers over her watch as she recalled her grandpop, the only man before Mike who never let her down.

"I don't want to lose you," Aida said.

"You won't," Mollie vowed. "I won't do this unless I have your blessing."

Aida blinked at her. "But you love him and can envision an eternity with him when I can barely see past three months with any of the guys I've dated. And before you try to analyze me, it has nothing to do with our donor; I get bored easily."

It was true, Aida preferred to play the field and didn't stick to a type as Mollie had before Mike. However, none of the guys Aida dated held her attention for long. The same with subjects at school; Aida wanted to learn it all, but she couldn't settle on anything she loved enough to do it for the rest of her life. Her plan with college was to study everything and hopefully decide on something.

"I do love him, very much," Mollie said. "I want to spend an eternity with him, but I love you too, and I won't lose you."

Aida's eyes filled with tears before she flung herself across the space separating them and into Mollie's arms. "You'll never lose me," she sobbed. "No matter what, I'll be here for you."

Mollie lowered her head to Aida's as she ran her hand over her sister's silken hair. "And I'll always be here for you." Mollie braced herself for Aida's reaction to her next words, but she had to tell her all of it. "Mike also said mates can't live without each other, they either go mad or die if something happens to the other."

Aida lifted her head from Mollie's chest and blinked at her. "So, if you become a vampire, if he dies, you die or go bonkers, and vice versa?"

"Yes." When Aida stiffened in her arms, Mollie rushed to get her next words out. "I'm hoping Mike can wait for a little bit. He said it would become more difficult for him not to complete the bond as time progresses, but I have to make sure you're safe and settled before we do anything just in case something does happen to one of us."

"Well, if something happens to you while you're mortal, then I lose you anyway, and becoming a vampire would make you stronger. Plus, I've seen him in action; not much is going to take that guy out, so I don't think you have to worry about that."

"Aida—"

"You love him, Mollie, anyone can see that. You've put your life on hold for me since Mom got sick, and I won't let you do it anymore. I'm eighteen; I have a plan in life, sort of, but I'll figure it out as I go, I always do. However, I'll never forgive myself or *you* if you use me as an excuse to keep putting your life on hold. If this is what you want, do it and do it tonight before he snaps, because that won't be pretty."

Mollie didn't know how to respond, and she was saved from having to do so by Aida's next words.

"It's not fair; I'm going to get old and wrinkled while you stay forever young," Aida muttered.

"Who knows, maybe you'll become a vampire too," Mollie teased, and Aida shuddered. Mollie's amusement vanished when she recalled the agony of Raul's bite. That pain was something Aida experienced for days at the hands of the monsters holding her captive. "Do you want to talk about what happened while we were apart?"

"I don't... don't know if I can," Aida said in a hitching voice.

A knock on the door separating their rooms brought Mollie's head up before Mike cracked it open and peered inside.

"Everything okay?" he asked when he spotted Aida clinging to her.

"Fine," Mollie said, giving him a small smile, which he didn't return.

"I have to step out for a minute; I'll be in shouting distance. So if you need me, for *anything*, scream," he said.

"We will," Mollie assured him as Aida pulled herself from Mollie's arms and sat beside her on the bed.

"I won't be gone long." Mike closed the door behind him when he left the room.

Mollie yearned to go after him and comfort him too, but Aida needed her, and Mike didn't seem ready for that.

Aida lay on the bed and rested her head on the pillow. "I do like him," Aida said. "And I really like that he's not *your* typical wimpy guy. About time you stepped outside the box and found yourself a hottie."

Mollie grabbed the other pillow and playfully hit her sister with it. Aida smiled as she batted the pillow away.

"So, do you want to talk about it?" Mollie asked.

Aida shrugged. "You saw it. They kept us in that room, Scott took pleasure in humiliating us, and they fed on us. It hurt."

"I know." Mollie's hand went to Raul's marks on her neck before she yanked it away. She didn't want any reminder of that guy. "Did they do anything else to you in there?"

"They didn't rape us. That would have made us damaged goods."

Mollie did a double take at her words. "*What?*"

Aida sat up beside her. "Scott informed us we were all going up for auction when the hunt was over, and whoever purchased us would be able to do anything they wanted to us. Until then, only feeding was allowed as the vampires didn't want *damaged* goods. They didn't care if we were virgins or not, but they would not pay for us if any of the other vampires there raped us; that was for our purchaser alone to do. Raul and some of his cronies stood guard to make sure feeding was all that transpired before the auction."

"Monsters," Mollie muttered.

"Definitely," Aida replied and curled up against Mollie's side.

CHAPTER FORTY-SEVEN

MOLLIE WAITED until Aida was asleep before carefully removing her sister's arm from her belly and tiptoeing over to the adjoining room. Mike had poked his head in when he returned a couple of hours ago then retreated to his room. She hadn't seen or heard him since then.

She didn't knock on the door; if he was still awake, he knew she was coming. If he was sleeping, Mollie didn't want to wake him, but she needed to see him.

When she opened the door, she discovered him on the bed with his back against the headboard. His clasped hands rested on his stomach, and the glow of the TV flickered over the planes of his handsome face.

Mollie froze as she took a moment to take him in. He was magnificent, but the strain of the past few days and the loss of Doug had etched lines around his pinched mouth and created a ruthless air about him that wasn't present when they first met.

Mike didn't move as Mollie stepped into the room and closed the door. The stolen blue shirt she wore was baggy on her slender frame, and the jeans rode high on her ankles, but she was still the most enticing woman he'd ever seen. He desired her, but he didn't dare make a move toward her. With the state he was in, he had no idea what he would do to her.

When Mike remained motionless as she crept toward him, Mollie felt her confidence about their relationship wane. Maybe now that they were off the island, he'd changed his mind about being her mate. He certainly wasn't acting like the warm, passionate man who had held her for hours and protected her life above his.

He'd said he would keep her safe on the drive here and wanted her forever, but had he changed his mind? Had he, after some time alone, concluded Doug's death was her fault and hated her for it?

"Are you… are you okay?" she asked tremulously.

Mike was about as far from okay as it got; he'd spent part of his evening hauling ice into the room next door to dump it in the tub and onto his friend's body. He did *not* want to bury Doug here, but he didn't know how they would get his body home before it became necessary to bury it. The ice would only hold off decomposition for so long, and he couldn't stand the idea of Doug rotting in this place.

Not to mention, the scent and sight of Mollie were working the demon inside him into a near frenzy as it clamored in his head. He waged war with what he craved versus what was best for her.

Mine! Claim her. She's yours. Give her immortality; protect her!

Yes, because immortality worked out so well for Doug.

Mike closed his eyes as a fresh wave of grief broke through his incessant, claiming instinct.

"Mike?" Mollie whispered when he grimaced.

When she rested her hand on his arm, he flinched from her. Unable to suppress her dismay over the reaction, Mollie snatched her hand away. Had he been playing with her on the island so he could have her blood?

No, that made no sense. He may have needed to feed, but he wouldn't continually defend her and risk his life just for her blood; she was sure of it. He'd had plenty of other options for a food source with the animals running around. But even if he hadn't been playing with her, he was still pulling away, and she had no idea why or what she could do to stop it.

"I'm sorry; I'll leave you be." Tears burned her eyes as she turned and hurried away from him.

Mike's eyes flew open when he heard her retreat, and though it was probably best for her, he couldn't let her go.

Mollie's hand flew to her mouth, and she staggered back when Mike suddenly appeared in front of her.

"Wait," he said hoarsely. "Don't... don't go."

For a second, she couldn't speak over her thundering heart. She'd never seen him move that fast before. Then she finally formed words. "What is going on, Mike? Why does it feel like you're pulling away from me? Do you blame me for Doug's death?"

"No! Of course not. I blame those bastards on that island, and they *will* pay for it."

Mollie's shoulders slumped in relief.

"But it's best if there's some distance between us now," Mike continued.

Her relief vanished as, with those words, he dug into her chest and tore her heart out before stomping on it. Her father probably uttered something similar to her mother before walking out to be with his secretary.

"I see," she said in an icy tone she didn't recognize. "Fair enough then."

She went to sidestep him, but he threw his arm out to stop her. Mollie glared at the offending arm, refusing to touch him before she turned her glower on him. The anguish etched into his features stole her breath.

"I don't know if I can control myself around you, without changing you, not anymore," he said. "Not after everything that has happened and how far our bond has progressed."

She tilted her head back to study him. Then she realized she hadn't told him about her decision. He remained in limbo, heartbroken by the loss of his friend and uncertain about their future.

"But I want to join you, Mike. I've told Aida, and she's okay with it. We'll have to figure things out with her, and I still want to go to college, but we can do it, together. You said you needed to feed on humans and feed well before the change could take place; you've done both tonight."

Hope flared in Mike's eyes; he reached for her before lowering his hand. "I want... no, I *need* you, but I can't."

"I don't understand, why not?"

Mike ran his hand through his hair as he released a harsh breath. She was offering herself to him, *tonight*!

He would give anything to join with her and make her his forever. If he let himself get lost in her, he might be able to forget, for a little bit, the hole inside him Doug's death had created.

But he couldn't do it. He could not change her tonight or anytime soon. The demon tore at his insides, begging to break free and seize control, but he would control the selfish beast as he wouldn't condemn her.

"I'm going back to the island, Mollie. I have to go back, for Jack."

"I know, but what does that have to do with *us*?"

"I won't bind your life to mine before I go."

She felt as if someone had picked her up and plunged her into the Arctic Sea as understanding dawned; he wasn't sure he'd return to her. "You are *not* going to die on that island."

"It is a possibility, and I won't risk your life because of my selfishness."

"Mike—"

"I will not take you as my mate and condemn you to death if I don't return."

Mollie didn't know what to say or do. She'd never be able to convince him to stay away from the island, but... "Won't you become increasingly unstable if we don't complete the bond?"

"Yes, but I will control myself. I have so far." He knew he was probably lying to her, but then he was also lying to himself. Every second, he felt his control slipping further away. "I *will* control it."

But he couldn't control himself. She could see that truth in the compression of his lips and the hint of red that was now a permanent fixture in his eyes. She saw it in the way he held himself so rigidly while keeping himself restrained from her.

Aida. She had her sister to worry about. If something happened to him and they were mated, what would become of Aida? She couldn't leave her sister all alone in this world.

She recalled Aida's earlier words. *"I'll never forgive myself or you if you use me as an excuse to keep putting your life on hold. If this is what you want, do it and do it tonight before he snaps, because that won't be pretty."*

She could walk out of this room, Mike would understand, and Aida didn't have to know about this conversation, but Mollie would never be able to meet Aida's gaze again without feeling guilty for withholding this from her. And if she walked away, she could be condemning Mike to death if he returned to the island while barely in control of himself.

If she walked out of this room, she'd curse herself as a coward for the rest of her life, even if he did return. And if he didn't return...

She refused to think about the possibility. He *would* return to her.

Stepping closer, Mollie ignored the stiffening of his body when she rested her hands on his chest and ran them over his shirt. "You won't have to control it," she murmured.

"Mollie—"

"This is *my* choice to make, and I made it. Can we do this tonight? Did you feed enough?"

He'd fed more than enough, but he clutched her forearms with the intention of moving her away from him.

"Don't push me away, Mike. I'll never forgive you if you do."

"If I die—"

"You won't die, because not only will you be more in control, but the bond will make you stronger, and you will fight harder to return to me."

"What about Aida?"

"She said I couldn't use her as an excuse to push this off, so you definitely can't use her."

"The change is excruciating, Mollie. You will endure a lot of pain as your body transitions from mortal to immortal."

"Birth is always painful, or so I'm told, but I will get through it."

Mike groaned as her words melted his resolve to keep his distance from her.

"And when you return, we'll have an eternity ahead of us," she whispered as she stepped closer.

"Mollie—"

"But you have to give me the chance to have that eternity with you first."

When his mouth descended on hers, Mollie knew she would get her chance.

CHAPTER FORTY-EIGHT

Pleasure consumed her as Mike filled every part of her. His body had possession of hers while his blood slid down her throat and his fangs pierced her neck. His wrist against her mouth blocked her cries of ecstasy while his joy suffused her.

"We'll be able to mentally communicate with each other when the bond is complete," he'd told her before they started this.

She couldn't read or sense his thoughts yet, but his emotions swirled through her as if they were hers while his sweat-slickened skin moved against hers. They were so wholly together that she couldn't tell where he started and she stopped.

One. They were one, and they would always be one. Mollie's fingers dug deeper into his back when his next thrust pushed her over the edge. Her back bowed beneath the heavy weight of his body as pleasure crashed through her.

Mollie released her bite on his wrist to gasp out her next words. "Come inside me."

Mike was helpless to disobey as her ongoing orgasm caused the tight muscles of her sheath to constrict around his cock.

Tears filled Mollie's eyes when she felt the pulsations of his release within her. She locked her legs around his waist and dug her heels into his ass to keep him inside her though he didn't show any signs of withdrawing while he continued to feed on her.

Weakness spread through her limbs. She should be frightened of it, but she couldn't find any fear in the euphoria surrounding her. Somehow, his wrist was against her mouth again, and his blood was trickling into her; she didn't recall how it had gotten there, and she didn't care as her heartbeat stuttered.

"Mike." She couldn't be sure if she'd spoken the word or not. She didn't know if she were still clinging to him or floating through space as the room and everything else slipped away from her.

And then, she knew pain.

A scream rose and caught in her throat as she arched off the bed. Her entire body was nothing but one giant charley horse, but no matter how much she tried to straighten out and ease the cramp, it would not let up. Whimpering, animalistic sounds came from somewhere; it took her a while to realize they were coming from *her*.

"I'm here, Mollie. I'm here. It won't be much longer. I love you."

The words were whispered in her ear, but when she turned her head, she saw only darkness. "Mike?"

Again, she didn't know if she'd spoken his name or not.

Mike wiped the hair back from Mollie's sweaty forehead and dabbed it with the damp washcloth he'd retrieved from the bathroom. He'd give anything to make her agony his own, but the only thing he could do was hold her as his blood twisted her body into something different.

Self-hatred and hope warred inside him as she whimpered again, and her eyes flew open. Their gazes locked, but her eyes remained unseeing as she whispered his name.

"I'm here, love," he assured her.

Then her eyes closed, her hands eased their grip on the sheets, and she collapsed onto the bed. Leaning over her, Mike anxiously searched for a pulse and found it racing on the side of her neck. But as his fingers pressed against her vein, the rapid beat of her heart eased. The worst of the change had ravaged its way through her body. Now she would rest before waking, and then she would feed, from *him*.

Excitement gripped him as he pictured his mate's fangs sinking into his neck. *My mate.* He'd been waiting to find her, empty without her, and now she'd made him complete.

He tried not to think about Doug and the loss they'd all endured, the unfairness of it all as he slid his arms around Mollie and pulled her close. Tonight was only about the two of them; the coming days would be about revenge, and he *would* get it, but until then, it was just him and his mate.

MOLLIE GROANED AS SHE WOKE. Every one of her muscles felt like she'd run a marathon without any prior training. She had no idea why she hurt so bad as exhaustion clung to her, but the enticing smell of something close by refused to let her slip back into the sleep her body craved.

Snuggling closer, Mollie nuzzled the flesh touching her nose. A familiar cedar aroma wafted to her.

Mike, she thought with a sigh.

When she kissed his neck, an unfamiliar tingling started in her gums and a knot of hunger twisted in her gut. She almost whimpered when her tongue slid over his salty skin. Mike's arms locked her against his chest as she opened her mouth. The tingling in her gums intensified, and then something prodded her bottom lip.

Is that a fang? Even as she wondered it, instinct took over, and she sank her fangs into his neck.

The sensation of piercing flesh caused Mollie to jump, she tried to pull away, but Mike kept her in place.

"It's okay," he murmured. "Take what you need. Take *everything* you need from me."

Mollie remained rigid against him, afraid to move for fear she'd hurt him. She didn't recall thinking about biting him before fangs she hadn't known she possessed connected her to him. She should withdraw, but she had no idea how to get the things to retract enough to do that.

Then the first drop of his blood hit her tongue, and the knot in her stomach twisted tighter.

"Drink, Mollie," he commanded as he ran his hands over her hair.

Mike's dick became rock hard when she drew his blood into her. Gradually, she relaxed against him and whimpered as her hands ran over his chest before digging into his shoulders. She wiggled over him until her body was flush against his while she consumed more of his blood.

He felt her pain easing as his blood filled her, and when she opened her legs and slid herself down the length of him, his cock slipped into her wet heat. Mollie thrust her hips against his, and he felt a wildness rising to take her over.

"Fuck, yes." Gripping her hips, he plunged her more forcefully onto his shaft.

Turning his mouth to her shoulder, he bit deep, and she lost complete control of her body when his mind swirled up to mix with hers. Pleasure and love rolled into one as Mollie felt the bond he'd spoken of enveloping them.

"I love you." It took her a second to realize he hadn't spoken the words floating through her mind.

Tears of joy spilled down her face when they became bound together for eternity.

CHAPTER FORTY-NINE

MOLLIE SAT on the edge of the bed and stared at the phone. She ran her hands nervously over her thighs before gripping her knees. She didn't want to do this, but she had to. Lifting the phone, Mollie dialed the number she'd gotten from information and listened while it rang on the other end.

"Hello," a male voice answered on the fourth ring.

Mollie's mouth went dry; her words froze in her throat as the familiar voice plummeted her into a past she'd done her best to forget.

"Hello," the man said again, this time with more annoyance.

"Da—ah, Nolan McConnell?"

There was a moment's pause and then, "Yes."

Mollie had no idea what to say. She hadn't exactly planned out her words, but then she didn't know how one prepared for this. "My name is—"

"Mollie."

He remembered her; she guessed that was a good start. "Yes."

"Mollie," he said again in a voice that sounded as if he didn't believe it was her. "How are you? Is everything okay? Is Aida okay?"

And he remembered her sister too.

"Yes. We're both good."

Well, good enough, considering everything they'd gone through. Mollie had no idea why she'd been compelled to call this man. She was moving into a new future and a new life; digging up the past was never something she intended to do, but for some reason, this was something she *needed* to do. She wouldn't let her father's memory taint what she had with Mike, and Mollie suspected if she didn't resolve her feelings with him at least a little, it would.

"I've met someone," she said.

"Is it serious?"

"Yes." The stilted awkwardness of this conversation only made it worse, but she couldn't bring herself to hang up.

"Is he a good man?"

Better than you. He won't leave us. Mollie bit the words back. She hadn't made this call to throw things in her father's face.

"Yes. I love him very much, and he loves me. We're married." Or the vampire equivalent of marriage anyway.

There was a long silence, and then her father blew out a breath. "I wish I could have been there."

Mollie had no idea how to respond to that. *He* would have wanted to be there for *her* marriage when he'd been there for so little else of her life?

"I've made mistakes, Mollie, so many of them. I wish—"

"I didn't call for an apology or anything like that!" Mollie interrupted. If he said he regretted the things he'd done, she'd probably start ranting, and she didn't want that.

"Then why did you call?"

"I don't know," she admitted.

"Do you need anything? I can help if you do. I can send money if you need it."

"No. We don't need anything." She'd done quite well on her own with Aida, and she would only do better with Mike at her side. "I guess I called because I'm moving on with my life and I have to let go of my anger at you. Otherwise, it will haunt me for the rest of my days, and I won't have that."

Silence followed again, but this time it extended so long she thought he might have hung up.

"I understand," he finally said.

She didn't see how he possibly could understand, considering his father had been a wonderful man who never would have walked out on his family. Mollie buried her resentment before she crushed the phone. She'd spent most of the day trying to adjust to her newfound vampire senses and strength, but she still had a lot more to learn and control.

"I should probably go," she said.

"Wait!" he cried, and Mollie heard the panic in his voice. "Don't go yet! So many years ago, I messed up, and I never knew how to fix it. I understand if you hate me, but I'd like to know more about you and Aida. If you hang up, I won't blame you, but... but if you can talk for a few more minutes, I'd like to speak with you."

The hitch in his voice and his desperation froze her. He'd walked out of her life and never looked back, but she found she couldn't hang up on him.

"What would you like to know?" she asked.

"Anything. Are you or Aida in college? What do you do for work? Are you both happy? Please tell me you're happy."

Mollie's shoulders slumped. "Yes, I'm happy."

MIKE STEPPED into the hotel room and frowned when he spotted Aida sitting in the dingy brown chair in the corner as she flipped through the TV channels. He'd left her and Mollie in here, but he didn't see Mollie.

"Where's Mollie?" he asked as he set a paper bag of food on the bedside table. He'd gone out to get food for Aida and to feed for him and Mollie.

"In the other room," Aida murmured.

Then he heard Mollie's voice drifting through the door. "Who's she talking to?"

"The sperm donor." At his confused look, she sighed. "Our father."

"Oh," Mike said, not knowing whether to laugh or hug the girl. She tried to sound and act casual, but the undercurrent of tension in her voice belied her flippancy.

Mike glanced toward the door again. He didn't sense any distress coming from his mate, something he would have expected from her while dealing with her father. "Really?"

"Yep." Aida tossed the remote onto the nightstand and drew one leg up. She hugged it against her chest as she lowered her chin to her knee.

"You didn't want to talk to him?"

"Why? He left when I was two. Mollie has memories of him, but I don't have any, and I never missed him in my life."

She couldn't entirely sell her indifference. Walking over, he rested his hand on her shoulder and squeezed it. Aida came with Mollie; they were a package deal he would have accepted even if Aida was a selfish brat. But she was far from selfish, and he admired the young woman's spine of steel.

Aida could have let the unfair circumstances of her life turn her into a person who pitied herself and blamed the world for everything that went wrong. However, like Mollie, she chose to grow stronger instead of weaker by all her losses.

"He lost out on two beautiful, strong, proud women," Mike said.

Aida's mouth parted, and tears formed in her eyes before she glanced away. Mike removed his hand from her shoulder and walked over to the door. He almost entered the room but changed his mind. Mollie needed this time to sort through things with her father, and he would give it to her.

Lifting the bag of food from the table, he handed it over to Aida. "Enjoy, kid."

"Thanks," she said and pulled the bag open to reveal the ice cream, chips, candy, and cooked hot dogs he'd gotten from the gas station down the street. "This is enough to give me a coronary."

"But you'll be happy beforehand."

Aida chuckled as she pulled out a plastic spoon and the pint of ice cream. "Damn right I will be."

Mike settled on the bed. A few minutes later, the door between the rooms opened, and Mollie entered. "You okay?" he asked as she walked over to sit on the bed beside him.

"Yes," she said and lay down next to him.

When Mike pulled her into his arms, she settled her head on his chest and listened to the reassuring beat of his heart while she watched Aida devour her ice cream. She was amazed to realize she really *was* okay.

"What did he have to say?" Aida asked as she licked her spoon clean, tossed it in the bag, and dug inside for more food.

Mollie filled them in on the conversation with her father.

Aida froze in the middle of squeezing a ketchup packet onto the hot dog tucked into a yellow, plastic container on her lap. "Why did you call him?"

"Because it's time to let go of my anger," she said, and her fingers curled into Mike's chest. "It's time to start fresh. I always insisted I wasn't angry at him, but then I realized I never got over him leaving."

"Hmm," Aida grunted as she tossed the empty packet into the bag by her feet. "How's his life going?"

"I didn't ask."

"Really?"

"Really." She didn't want to be angry anymore, but she also didn't want to hear that he was living it up on the west coast, lounging by the pool every day with his possible wife and children. If they spoke again, she'd ask, because she would like to know if she had other siblings. "If we talk again, I'll ask, but I got what I needed out of the conversation."

"And do you think you will talk again?" Mike inquired.

"I think so," Mollie murmured.

"Hmm," Aida grunted again.

"Would you like to talk to him next time?" Mollie asked her.

"Nope."

Aida set her untouched hotdog into the bag by her feet. Mollie knew better than to push the issue; Aida could be as stubborn as a mule when she didn't want to do something.

Aida lifted the bag and dropped her foot to the ground. "I'll let you two lovebirds be."

"Stay," Mike said when she started to rise. He wanted time alone with Mollie, but he sensed Aida's unhappiness, and she was his sister now too. "We'll watch the news together."

Aida hesitated. "Are you sure?"

"Yes."

Aida's smile tugged at Mollie's heart as her sister settled back into the chair and retrieved her hot dog. Maybe she wanted nothing to do with their father, but Aida still craved a family and love. They were close, they counted on each other for everything, but the two of them versus the world got lonely at times, and now they both had the opportunity to expand their family.

Mollie hugged Mike closer. *"Thank you,"* she whispered into his mind.

He kissed the top of her head.

CHAPTER FIFTY

THE SPILL of headlights flooding the room roused Mike from sleep. He glanced down at Mollie nestled securely in his arms and then over at Aida slumped in the chair in a position that would make it difficult for her to move her neck when she woke.

The headlights from multiple vehicles bounced over the walls before stopping in front of his room and illuminating the brown drapes covering the plate glass window. He'd given Liam his room number, but there was no guarantee it was his friend out there now.

Shortly after arriving here, Mike ditched the stolen car, so the only other vehicle in the lot was the clerk's, but that didn't mean the vampires from the island hadn't somehow tracked them here. His fangs pricked as his killer instincts surged to the forefront. If their enemy awaited them, he'd tear every single one of them to shreds.

Carefully, he lifted Mollie's arm and slid out from under her as the cars turned off. Walking over to the window, he pulled back the edge of one curtain to reveal four vehicles in the lot. As he watched, Liam, Stefan, and Isabelle climbed out of one car; Ian, Paige, Willow, and Julian out of another, Ethan, David, and Mia from the third, and Aiden, Maggie, Abby, and Brian from a Jeep.

A soft step alerted him to Mollie and Aida's approach before they both stopped beside him. Ducking under his arm, Mollie positioned herself to peer outside, and Aida slid underneath her. As she stared out, Aida craned her neck back and forth to stretch it out.

"Is that your family?" Mollie whispered.

"Yes, and they're your family now too," he reminded her. "Yours also," he said to Aida, making sure the girl knew she would be protected and accepted by them from here on out.

"There's a lot of them," Aida muttered, but she couldn't hide her smile.

"There's more at home, but mostly the children."

Mike released the curtain and went to the door. Opening it, he stepped back to let everyone inside. The somber air surrounding the clan didn't diminish their smiles as they all embraced and spoke over each other while Mike introduced them to Mollie and Aida. Mollie was a little hesitant at first, and he sensed her becoming overwhelmed, but she slowly relaxed. Aida was more outgoing and welcoming of their hugs while she spoke with everyone.

Mollie kept her smile in place as more and more vampires came forward to embrace her and welcome her to their family. Mollie had always wished they had more relatives to lean on, but she couldn't help feeling dazed by the sheer number of vampires and their easy acceptance of her and Aida.

Mike rested his hand on Mollie's waist when her distress beat against him. "It takes time to learn everyone's names," he said. "I've been with this clan since before most of them were born, and I often call them by the wrong names. If you forget someone just say, 'hey you.' It's easier."

"And those kind of assholey comments are why we call them The Stooges," Isabelle said with a warm smile as she squeezed Mollie's arm. Then her brow furrowed, tears filled her eyes, and Stefan stepped forward to rest his hand on her shoulder. "Or they were The Stooges," she muttered before turning away.

Mike drew Mollie closer against his side when grief stabbed like a knife through his chest. Julian came forward to greet Aida and

Mollie. Mike didn't miss the double take Julian did when he saw Aida or the fact the young vampire stayed close by Aida's side while she spoke with Ian and Paige. Mike had never heard Julian talk about a girl before, but he suspected Julian might have discovered his first crush.

When the introductions ended, and Stefan, Brian, Aiden, and Ethan left to get the keys to more rooms, Liam rested his hand on Mike's arm. "Can we talk alone?" Liam inquired.

"Will you be okay if I go speak with Liam for a bit?" Mike whispered in Mollie's ear.

She still seemed overwhelmed, but she smiled and rested her hand on his cheek before kissing him. "I'll be fine."

When Mike stepped away from her, Abby and Maggie grasped her arms and led her into the third room where Paige, Mia, Willow, Isabelle, and Ian were studying the map Doug stole from the mansion. Aida and Julian followed the others and closed the door behind them.

Mike stood facing David and Liam as, from the other room, the drone of voices continued.

"Where is Doug?" Liam asked.

Mike closed his eyes and took a breath to brace himself for having to see Doug again. He'd seen too many dead bodies over his years as a vampire, but none of them had ever bothered him. Doug's would haunt him for the rest of his life.

"This way," Mike said and led them into the next room. The others would eventually want to see their uncle and friend too, but this time was for them alone.

Mike flicked on the light switch in the bathroom to illuminate the broken blue floor tiles and green tub. It was the last place he wanted Doug to be, and he could have buried Doug already, but he knew the others would want their chance to say goodbye to him.

Mike stayed by the green sink as Liam and David approached the tub. They gazed at Doug with similar expressions of rage and sorrow.

Mike gave them a few minutes to take it in, but he knew that days from now, the loss of Doug still wouldn't have sunk in. They'd all known this day might come for one of them; if they'd remained mortal, they could all be dead by now, but none of them had ever truly expected to lose one of their own.

"There are a lot of Savages on that island," he finally said. "We may need more help than what's here."

"There is none," Liam said without taking his eyes off Doug. "Sera and Emma had to stay with the children. Aiden contacted Ronan to see if he could send some help, but he has his own problems with the Savages and can't help."

Mike's teeth clenched as his thoughts turned to his nieces and nephews going to that island. "They all have young children, and Willow and Julian haven't fully matured yet. They can't put themselves at risk."

Willow turned nineteen in January, and Julian's eighteenth birthday was April first, but neither of them had fully come into their vampire powers yet.

"They all insisted on coming," Liam said. "I tried to talk them out of it, but they refused to be deterred. Jack wouldn't leave one of them behind, and they won't leave him behind. They also believed it was best if both mates came. They didn't want their children to see what would happen to the mate who remained behind if they lost the other during this.

"With Levi still so young, Emma had to stay with her son, and Sera agreed to remain to watch the other children; Kyle and Cassidy will help them. Willow and Julian are going to stay here to protect Aida and Mollie. It was the condition they agreed to upon coming with us."

"I see," Mike said. He still didn't like it, but his nieces and nephews were powerful, immortal adults who could make their own decisions.

"I didn't like it either," Liam said. "I also didn't like leaving Emma and Sera behind as the only two fully matured vampires, but none of us wanted any of the children near this, and we knew this would require as many of us here as possible. The compound is safe, and the two of them are strong, but it still makes me nervous," Liam said.

"Understandable," Mike said. It made him nervous too. "We'll find Jack and end this as soon as we can."

"We *will* make them pay for this," David said.

"Yes," Mike agreed. "What do we do with Doug? We can't keep him in this tub much longer, and I didn't want to bury him so far away from home, but…"

"But there's no other choice," Liam said when Mike's voice trailed off.

MIKE AND MOLLIE spent most of the next morning in bed. By the time everyone arrived the night before, and they buried Doug in a secluded spot overlooking the sea, it was too late for them to set out for the island to rescue Jack. They had to find boats, discuss a plan, and learn as much as they could from Mike, Mollie, and Aida about what to expect and the layout of the land.

Doug's funeral was simple, far simpler than Mike would have preferred, and he vowed that one day, his friend would have better. When they returned to the motel after the burial, everyone went their separate ways with the agreement to meet again at noon. Until then, most of them needed rest and some time alone.

With the funeral over and his family gone to their rooms, Mike had sunk onto the bed, and for the first time given in to the tears he'd kept suppressed since Doug died. Doug was gone, and nothing would ever fill the hole his passing had created. Cradling him in her arms, Mollie held him until his tears subsided and he lost himself to the miracle of their love for each other.

Lying in Mike's arms, Mollie could almost pretend he wasn't going to leave her and walk back into danger, but as the red numbers on the bedside clock climbed steadily toward noon, she stopped pretending.

"I'm a vampire too; take me with you," she whispered.

"No," Mike said as he ran his fingers over her arm and savored the feel of her bare body against his. "You're newly turned and could be more of a danger than a help if you lose control there."

"I've handled the change well so far."

"And how do you think you would handle seeing a lot of blood? Remember how much you saw when we were on the island. If you lose control, you could get yourself killed. I won't be gone long, and Julian and Willow will help you hunt animals to feed on if it becomes necessary, but you can't come, Mollie."

"Mike—"

"Believe me, I'd rather have you with me than leave you behind, but we can't risk it with you being so newly turned."

She knew he was right. Just thought of blood made her fangs tingle; what would happen if she were tossed into the middle of the hunt and surrounded by all that blood again? She shuddered at the thought of losing control and becoming a Savage.

"You'll come back to me," she whispered.

"Nothing could stop me from returning to you. *Nothing*. We're going to get Jack, and then I will be back in your arms."

His mouth found hers as he pushed her onto her back and slid his thigh between hers. When he lifted his head to look at her again, the love in his eyes stole her breath.

"You're mine forever, Mollie."

She smiled as she rested her hand on his cheek. "And you're mine forever."

Bending his head, he reclaimed her mouth. Later, he would go rescue his friend, but for now, it was just the two of them, and she had no doubt he would return to her. Their love and this bond consuming them could never be broken.

The End

Look for Jack's story, *Unforeseen* (Vampire Awakenings, Book 9) coming in 2019!

Stay in touch on updates and other new releases from the author by joining the mailing list.

Mailing list for Brenda K. Davies and Erica Stevens Updates: https://www.brendakdavies.com/ESBKDNews

If you haven't had the chance to start it yet, check out the Vampire Awakenings spinoff, The Alliance Series! *Eternally Bound* is the first book in this series and focuses on Ronan.

WHERE TO FIND THE AUTHOR

Erica Stevens/Brenda K. Davies Mailing List:
https://www.brendakdavies.com/ESBKDNews

Facebook page: https://www.brendakdavies.com/ESauthfb
Facebook friend: https://www.brendakdavies.com/EASfb

Erica Stevens/Brenda K. Davies Book Club:
https://www.brendakdavies.com/ESBKDBookClub

Instagram: https://www.brendakdavies.com/BKDInsta
Twitter: https://www.brendakdavies.com/BKDTweet
Website: https://www.brendakdavies.com
Blog: https://www.brendakdavies.com/ESblog
BookBub: https://www.brendakdavies.com/BKDbkbb

ABOUT THE AUTHOR

Brenda K. Davies is the USA Today Bestselling author of the Vampire Awakening Series, Alliance Series, Road to Hell Series, Hell on Earth Series, and historical romantic fiction. She also writes under the pen name, Erica Stevens. When not out with friends and family, she can be found at home with her husband, dog, and horse.

CPSIA information can be obtained
at www.ICGtesting.com
Printed in the USA
BVHW042146160620
581702BV00009B/293